"From darkness, O E'li," they whispered, "from darkness preserve us. From evil, O E'li, from evil defend us. From darkness, O E'li . . ." Thus did they pray to the very god who had not thought to shield them from darkness, who had not lifted even a hand to defend them from the evil that yet ravaged their city and tormented their land. The chain set, they lit wands of pungent incense and, trailing smoke and prayers, walked around the outside of the circle, sunwise three times. Low and stern, their voices demanded that evil not be allowed to enter into this chamber.

Dalamar watched them, narrow-eyed. They prayed, and yet, here evil was, standing ready to learn its fate, evil in the shape of an elf who was not blinded by the light.

DRAGONLANCE Classics

Murder in Tarsis
John Maddox Roberts

DALAMAR
THE DARK

Nancy Varian Berberick

DALAMAR THE DARK

Cover art by Bradley Williams
Map by Sam Wood
First Printing: January 2000
Library of Congress Catalog Card Number: 99-65589

9 8 7 6 5 4 3 2

ISBN: 0-7869-1565-X
620-T21565

U.S., CANADA,
ASIA, PACIFIC, & LATIN AMERICA
Wizards of the Coast, Inc.
P.O. Box 707
Renton, WA 98057-0707
+1-800-324-6496

EUROPEAN HEADQUARTERS
Wizards of the Coast, Belgium
P.B. 2031
2600 Berchem
Belgium
+32-70-23-32-77

Visit our web site at **www.wizards.com**

For my dear friend Douglas W. Clark,
a boon companion whether the road winds through
sun or shadow.

Acknowledgments:

I'm happy to have this chance to express my appreciation of the editors who worked with me on *Dalamar the Dark*, Patrick McGilligan whose excellent suggestions I've long been in the habit of taking, and Mark Sehestedt who helped me tame the wild wordage.

As well, it is my pleasure to thank Miranda Horner for her cheerful patience while finding herself bestormed in my thousand questions. When you find depth in the setting of this novel and consistency in detail, you see Miranda's fingerprints.

Prologue

～

In the Hall of Mages, in the secret heart of the Tower of High Sorcery at Wayreth, the dark elf stood in perfect stillness. Dalamar Nightson. Dalamar of Tarsis. Dalamar Argent. Once, long ago, he had been Dalamar of Silvanost. He wore dark robes given to him by the head of his order, Ladonna herself, silver-stitched with runes of warding—ancient runes like those upon the outer wall of the Tower, marks whose meaning few knew, but he understood. As had become his habit, whether abroad or indoors, he wore the hood of that robe up, shadowing his face, leaving only his eyes to be seen.

Light shone down pale from the unseen ceiling high above. It made no shadow. It gave no cheer. Though torches stood in brackets upon the walls, none were lit. No sound whispered in the vast chamber, not even the sigh of the breathing of the four gathered in the hall.

Upon his high seat, Par-Salian, the Master of the Tower of High Sorcery and the Head of the Conclave of Wizards, sat, tall and straight. Except for his white hands, those veined, gnarled hands, twitching restlessly to some private thought, he might have been carved from alabaster. To the right of the Master stood Justarius, his red robe the color of poppies, and Ladonna stood at Par-Salian's left. The regard of the three sat upon Dalamar like a weight. He did not move or indicate in any way his discomfort. He simply stood before the heads of the three Orders, breathing the perfumes of magic, musky oils, herbs, and, as always, dried roses.

Outside the Hall of Mages, two corpses lay in state. Even as these four gathered, mages of all the Orders went into the Rear Tower to pay respect to a woman all had known and a dwarf few had. Both had been mages.

Inside the Hall, Ladonna came forward, her beautiful face shining in the eerie light, her silver hair glittering with jewels, her fingers with rings. One step she took, her black velvet robe moving like shadows, and she took it smiling. "You have done well, after all, Dalamar Nightson."

After all. Dalamar allowed her a lean smile. "Did you doubt me, my lady?"

She did not return his smile. "Strength and will. These are always to be questioned in everyone."

Dalamar inclined his head to agree. "And so, I have passed your test."

Justarius raised an eyebrow, the expression clearly speaking his surprise at the temerity of this fledgling mage. "You are bold, young mage. Perhaps over-bold."

"I am bold, my lord, in proportion to my need." Dalamar swept the three with one swift glance. "Is that not what *you* need, a bold mage who is not afraid to risk what he has in order to get what he wants? Or what *you* want?"

Justarius's eyes flashed at the impudence. "What can you possibly know about—?"

Ladonna raised a hand. The rings sparkling on her fingers lit a simple, calming gesture. Justarius subsided, but the color of his anger still showed in his face.

"My lady," Dalamar said, stepping toward Ladonna, "I have done all you asked. A life you valued was lost in the doing, but what is one against many?" He looked around the chamber at the three gathered. "My part in the matter is finished. How else may I serve you?"

Ladonna's smile did not reach her eyes when she said, "We will see what you can do, but first tell me this, Dalamar Nightson: What do you know about the Tower of High Sorcery at Palanthas?"

Dalamar's pulse quickened at seeing what flickered in the eyes of Par-Salian, of Justarius, and even of Ladonna herself, though she strove to hide it. Fear. Fear swiftly hidden, but fear nonetheless.

"I have heard what everyone has," he said softly, "that the Tower has been long shut up and lately opened." He inclined his head to one and all. "And I have heard what only a few know—that he who holds it forbids you or anyone entrance to that Tower."

White robes rustling like the voices of ghosts, Par-Salian leaned forward. Seeing him, Dalamar had the same feeling he always had when looking upon a human whose count of years was not so many as his own and who yet looked like an elf of three hundred years or more. How swiftly their candles burn!

"You have heard rightly in much of what you say," Par-Salian murmured. "He is a powerful mage, this one who took the Tower. His like has not been seen in many long years, perhaps in centuries. But you are wrong, young Dalamar, if you think he forbids the Tower to everyone. He does not."

Par-Salian smiled, a small tugging at the corners of his mouth. That smile did not warm, and Dalamar braced to deny the three mages sight of him shuddering. White as alabaster, so he'd thought Par-Salian. Now he thought the man was white as ice—that cold were his eyes. With a gesture, the Master of the Tower took in the two standing beside him.

"You see here before you three of the most powerful mages in Krynn, but the mage who sits in the Tower of Palanthas is stronger than any one of us, and he will become stronger still." His expression grew hard. His face seemed made of stone. "He calls himself the Master of Past and Present, and we wonder what work he is at there in his Tower. It seems to us all that it would be a good thing to know."

Ladonna lowered her eyes and smiled a secret smile. Justarius scowled. In the smile, Dalamar recognized ambition. He felt at once that the Head of the Order of Black Robes knew she held her place only so long as the upstart in

Palanthas did not want it. In the scowl, he recognized a similar feeling. It was widely known that Justarius would succeed Par-Salian as Head of the Conclave and Master of this Tower when Par-Salian chose to stand down. This station, too, the mage in Palanthas could claim if having it appealed to him. These things ambitious people were wise to consider, but it seemed to Dalamar that the three most powerful mages in Krynn feared something else, something more.

"And so you see," said Par-Salian, "that some things are known about this Master of Past and Present. Here is another. Though he has scorned to take what power he might rightfully gain by challenge, he keeps to himself, perhaps creating power and position outside the Orders and the Rule of High Sorcery."

The shock of such an idea ran like lightning along Dalamar's nerves. Before he could think, he spoke. "This cannot be permitted, my lord!"

Par-Salian nodded, but absently. "That is easy to say. We have said it here time and again. But now we must do something. I have said the mage has not locked the gates of his Tower against all. He will admit an apprentice, a student."

Quiet again, his eyes modestly cast down to hide the spark of his own sudden ambition, Dalamar murmured, "Why would he, my lord?"

Par-Salian did not reply. He nodded to Ladonna, who said, "I do not know why. I only know he will. I have asked it, he has said it. A student of our Order, a dark mage, he says, one who has at least two wits to rub together. If I were to send him a student"—Dalamar's heartbeat quickened, and Ladonna's level gaze told him she sensed the sudden beating—"I would send a spy. I imagine that if he took in a student, he would know that. Perhaps he would seek to turn the spy."

"He would not turn me, my lady." Dalamar stopped, keenly aware that he had not been invited to volunteer.

She smiled, a lean tugging of her lips. "I don't think he

4

would. You are uniquely schooled in the virtues of balance, are you not?" Then, before Dalamar could respond she said, "Indeed, you are."

Justarius nodded, at last in approval. He glanced from Par-Salian to Ladonna, and it seemed to Dalamar that some communication passed among the three. Par-Salian inclined his head, as though in response, perhaps even agreement.

"We will not command you, young mage, to take up this apprenticeship. We cannot, for the one who does this work will put his life and perhaps his very soul at risk the moment he speaks his acceptance. And if he is found out"—Par-Salian shook his head—"he will die. That death will be a terrible thing, and a long, long time coming."

Dalamar took that warning seriously. Yet, hadn't he been risking his life, by some accounts even his soul, for magic's sake since the first moment he felt the sparkle of magic in his blood? To serve as apprentice to the one mage in all of Krynn who could make the Heads of the Three Orders afraid . . . ! He smiled, but secretly, in the shadow of his hood. What wonders of sorcery could he learn from this mage who'd stolen a Tower right out from under the eyes of the three most powerful magic-users in Krynn? Uncounted! What power could he gain, what strength, what insights? They were legion!

Dalamar lifted his hands and put back the hood of his robe, letting those gathered clearly see his face and his eyes. One and all, the Heads of the Orders kept still, allowing him the choice.

"My lords, my lady, I accept the apprenticeship, and I accept your mission."

Justarius nodded grimly. Ladonna said nothing. In the eyes of Par-Salian, Dalamar saw not satisfaction but, strangely, sorrow.

It was as though, knowing what had been, the Master of the Tower could know what might be. The thought a warning, Dalamar looked back. . . .

Chapter 1

"Tell me, then," said Eflid Wingborne, his head tilted slightly back as he looked down the length of his thin nose at the small bundle Dalamar had placed in the exact center of the narrow cot. "Will you be easier to find now, Dalamar Argent, or will I still have to send servants to hunt you down when I need you?"

Dalamar stood still in the shaded corner of the small room. In the shadow, he shaped his expression to one that might lead Lord Ralan's steward to believe he considered a humble answer. In truth, he considered no such thing at all. He concentrated upon the image of two hands holding hard to something—the temper it would do him no good to lose.

"You will find me," he said, eyes low to hide his contempt. "Never worry, Eflid—"

"*Lord* Eflid."

Dalamar held back the sardonic smile that twitched at the corners of his lips. Lord Eflid, indeed, by virtue of the fact that his mother had been briefly wed to a lordling of so minor a family within House Woodshaper that the name of it was not recorded except in small letters at the end of a long, long scroll. Eflid had not been the son of that man, but he still claimed the title, at least among the servitors he ruled.

"Never worry," Dalamar said again. He looked up, leveling a long cool stare at the steward, the kind he knew gave Eflid shivers. "I am here."

Eflid's eyes narrowed, glittering and green. "And here you'll stay, boy—no more wandering for you. Be grateful Lord Ralan hasn't dismissed you entirely. I've heard they are looking for a servitor down by the docks, a boy to haul fish and repair nets. Let me look up and not find you when I want you, and that's where you'll be working."

Boy, he said, *boy*. With nearly ninety years to him, Dalamar was young by elf standards, but he was no boy. Yet Eflid's sneering address said that were Dalamar to attain one hundred years and ninety, still he'd be a boy in the eyes of those he served. Dalamar met Eflid's narrow stare and did not look away, and so Eflid must.

His face flushing with anger, and with shame for having been the first to turn his glance, the steward growled, "Now unpack your gear and get to work. You're expected in the kitchen. There are floor tiles in the oven room needing repair." He pulled his lips back from his teeth in a cruel imitation of a smile. "Don't you have some pretty little spell you can work on them? To keep your hand in, as it were?"

Laughing, Eflid left the room, not closing the door behind. Alone, Dalamar looked around at his new quarters. Motes sparkled, golden bits of dust dancing in the light of the sun shafting in through the east-facing window. The light was not so misty as it had been when it shone on the path away from the Servitor District and the house that had been Dalamar's family home for so many years. His father had inherited the small house from an uncle who had been canny enough to save the steel coin to purchase it from a woman who repaired leather shoes. Until then, his father and mother and Dalamar himself had lived in the halls of those they served, a family who met during the days only in passing and sometimes spent an evening together after the high folk had no more use for them. The little house with its tiny garden had become Dalamar's upon the death of his parents, and he had lived there, with the permission of the Head of House Servitor and of Lord Ralan, ever since. Five years he'd gone out from his home to that of his master, each day in the dawn, and five years he'd returned there in the long purple twilights of summer and the short sharp ending of winter days. No more, and the privacy afforded him in his own home, the sense of being master there where no one could order him about, was all gone. Now he must live in Lord Ralan's house, quartered in this small room in the servant's wing. Here among those too poor to have their own houses, among the untrustworthy, he would stay. Lord Ralan had declared it, and Trevalor, the head of House Servitor, had agreed.

Dalamar turned from the glittering shaft of sunlight to the bed. The room afforded him little by way of furniture, only this bed, a small table upon which stood a thick white candle, and a chest of drawers by the window. He had no chair for himself and none to offer a visitor.

From the bundle on the bed, he took out his clothing. He did not wear the dun clothes of a servant but the white robe of a mage. This was not usual, for among the Silvanesti, who structured their lives to conform to a rigid caste system, no one was lower than servitor, and none deemed less worthy of learning the High Art of Sorcery. Dalamar's talent was strong, though, and when House Mystic learned of it, they did what they must for fear that, unguided, he would go outside the bounds of Solinari's white magic to wild magic or worse, to Lunitari's red or Nuitari's black magic. They made him a mage, dedicated him to god-Solinari, and taught him grudgingly. For the teaching, he was glad but never grateful.

He'd worn the white robe for nearly two years now, but before all, Dalamar was still a servant, his talent and skill at the command of others. So it had been today, his hours claimed and counted. All the while he worked, Dalamar felt himself pulled away, his attention barely on his task, his soul yearning northward to a place no steward or elf-lord knew about. In a cave beyond the river lay the hiding of his secret studies. There he kept dark tomes filled with magic forbidden to all elves. He'd discovered the books by accident, found them tucked in the far reaches of the little cave, a treasure left by some bold dark mage who'd come secretly into the elven kingdom where none such would ever be welcome. Come and gone, he'd left his books behind, and they'd lain there a long count of years. Each bore an inscription that had, upon first sight, struck fear into Dalamar's heart. *To the Dark Son, from a dark son, by night are we bound.* Thus had a mysterious mage dedicated himself to the son of the Dragon Queen, to Nuitari whose obsidian halls lay in mansions of the sky just beneath the secret moon, the black moon. Yet soon Dalamar's fear had eased, and during the months of the summer past, he had taught himself more about magic, spells, incantations, and arcane philosophy than he'd been allowed to learn with House Mystic. The little northern cave was Dalamar's refuge. His secret trips there, time stolen from his master, were the cause of Eflid's anger and, ultimately, the reason for Dalamar's new status among Lord Ralan's servants, housed and untrustworthy.

Dalamar tossed a spare robe of plain white wool and two sets of hose onto the bed. He tucked a pair of boots into the corner, soft dark leather ones he'd only lately purchased and not yet worn. A belt of knitted wool, the color of the sky when the last light is nearly gone, and the small bone-handled knife a mage is allowed for ceremonial use were the only other things he'd brought here from his home.

Outside the window, the morning grew warm. The air sat heavily over the city as it does when a storm is brooding. Though no breeze blew, still Dalamar smelled the herbs in the kitchen garden, the twining scents of mint and basil, of horehound and sage and sweet thyme. Before he'd been caught away from his work, he'd been assigned to assist the old man from House Gardener who tended Ralan's herb beds. Now he was consigned to the hot kitchen and the cross-eyed cook whose best delight was to harry potboys and torment the young girls who stood in the corners to flirt with the bakers' lads. The loss of his privacy, these menial tasks, this fee he paid for a day away was steep indeed. Yet, though he did not like the price, he did not regret it. He had chosen his path this morning, clear-eyed and knowing what he might have to pay.

Dalamar thought about choices as he walked out of the room and down the long airy corridor. No one would think he had any, a servitor whose life's path was ordained by ancient custom. Yet this year, in the summer, Dalamar had made a choice, one no one imagined he would consider. He must learn more of magic than the crumbs House Mystic granted.

Sunlight splashed into the corridor from open doors and wide windows. Shadow barred the tiled floor where sunlight did not reach. Into sun and out to shadow he went, walking. How far would he go for the Art of High Sorcery denied him by House Mystic? All the way to the Dark Son himself? Out in the light of the day, in the thickness of the air, Dalamar looked away north, not to the small place where his secrets were kept, but farther to the land beyond the forest where the armies of Takhisis brooded. She was god-Nuitari's mother, that Dragon Queen, and his father was the god of Vengeance, Sargonnas himself. Their son was a child of magic and secrets, and Dalamar could think of no better god to whom he could dedicate his own secret heart.

Blasphemy! It was blasphemy in the Silvanesti kingdom to think such a thing.

Dalamar shivered, quick excitement running up his spine. He could choose if he wanted to choose. He could make a forbidden god his own in secret and silence, and no one would know. Such power there was in secrets! Smiling, he walked through the garden, a generous place enclosed on three sides by hedges of wisteria, on the fourth by the servants' wing of the hall. Though they waited for him in the kitchens, he took time to enjoy the heady scent of dewy roses and the tang of curly mint underfoot. Water bubbled from a fountain, a marble basin held in the hand of a statue of Quenesti-Pah, the goddess offering comfort. A golden finch settled on the rim of the basin, bright feathers already changing to autumn dress.

Dalamar did not walk alone there. A cleric passed him on the path. The tall young elf nodded greeting to him, a lord by the look of him, high-headed and comfortable. His robe of white samite gleamed in the morning light. Silver thread embroidered the sleeves, and upon his finger a ring shone, a silver dragon whose eye was a bright amethyst. A cleric of E'li, no doubt come on the business of the Temple.

Dalamar returned the absent, silent greeting in kind, in no mood to tug the forelock or wish anyone the blessings of E'li. The cleric went round the north side of the garden and through an arched gate. Beyond lay the private garden of the lord and his family. This one was confident of his welcome.

Dalamar went into the dark kitchen where the cross-eyed cook stood scowling, fair certain what his own welcome would be. Waves of heat greeted him, rippling in the air, the heat of the night's baking still trapped in the cavernous stone room.

"Aye, there he is," growled the cook, a woman so thin it seemed she was but flesh stretched too tightly over bitter bones. "Lord Eflid promised me I'd have you this morning early, Master Mage. Now where have you been, eh? Out running again . . . ?" Her voice became as the voice of an insect buzzing, nothing to pay heed to, and Dalamar walked past her through the kitchen and into the oven room where the scent of years of baking clung to the walls with stubborn, yeasty persistence.

Dalamar knelt on the floor before the first broken tile. He pressed his hands together, feeling the tingling of magic as he gathered up the words of a spell, stone-heal. The smell of the kitchen faded. He dropped into a state of being none but a mage could know, that state of touching power from gods, of taking it and shaping it and using it to his will. The cook's voice receded, words growing thin, like mist rising to sun.

" . . . Who he thinks he is, some ragtag little mageling out of the Servitor District . . . never did teach him his manners

or how to behave among his betters . . . never should have
given him the white robe—never. Too far above himself,
that's what . . . "

The spell words invoked the bright energy of magic, that
energy sparkling in Dalamar's blood, warming his heart,
lending him power only mages and gods knew. This was all
that mattered, magic and nothing more. For it, he would do
everything.

* * * * *

The red dragon drifted in the midday sky, slipping effort-
lessly from updraft to downdraft, one current to another.
Wide wings spread, long tail moving like a ship's rudder,
Blood Gem traversed the sky, the first of the highlord's
dragons to sail out over the aspen forest of the Silvanesti.
He looked down through the canopy of trees and saw the
silver threads of rivers running. Along the great Thon-
Thalas, he saw towns, small and large, their buildings like
smudges on the land. Here, in these little towns, they did
not build so much with stone. Here they built with wood.
He opened his jaws wide to grin.

So much tinder, he said to the rider upon his back, the
long-legged human woman who heard him not with her
ears but in her mind.

No, Phair Caron said, her voice slipping into Blood Gem's
mind like a tendril of black smoke. *Not tinder! We'll burn the
forest if we must, but something must remain. We're to take these
arrogant elves down from their high perches, but we have to leave
something for the army to occupy and a cowed populace ready to
work for the Dark Queen and support her advance. Dead elves do
us no good at all.*

Blood Gem snorted, and a small fireball burst alight in
the sky. *Dead elves offer no resistance, and we can fill up that
aspenwood—or what my kin and I will leave of it—with slaves to
do whatever work will be required.*

Phair reached out to pat the red's shoulder, not a gesture the dragon felt, but one he recognized and appreciated in its intent. *It isn't about working slaves, my friend. Or it's not all about that. What it's all about is reaping souls, eh?*

For the Dark Queen.

Phair Caron nodded, again an unseen gesture, but one felt.

All they did, she and her dragons, was for the Dark Queen, for Takhisis. Dark Lady, you are my light, Phair Caron thought, the thought a prayer. In darkness, yours is the light of balefires, of funeral pyres. In darkness, yours is the hand that reached out to me. She sighed, thinking of the dire glory of Her Dark Majesty. It had been but a mere handful of centuries since Takhisis had re-entered the world and come back from the Abyss after the fall of Istar. Her door into the world was—and Phair Caron thought the irony delicious— the ruin of the very Temple of Istar where the mad King-priest of the city-state had proclaimed himself a god and brought down the ire of all deities upon the world that condoned his madness. During those centuries Takhisis had wandered abroad, laying plans, seeking allies among the ruthless to elevate to commanders in her growing army— Phair Caron grinned, a wide, wolfish grin—and waking dragons to pair with those commanders. Now Takhisis had an army of ogres and goblins, of dragonmen and humans, led by her commanders, her highlords.

And waking dragons, Blood Gem echoed, sighing as though he yet recalled his long sleep and sudden waking. *Now we are here. We are hungry to fight in her cause, Highlord, and we yearn to taste elf blood.*

Phair Caron spoke aloud, her words carried upon the wind of their flight. "Soon enough. Soon enough you'll have what you want." She laughed, suddenly and sharply. "But elf blood is a pale drink, my friend. Watery and weak." She pointed downward to where the Thon-Thalas widened and the lights of Silvanost could be seen in the distance.

"These elves have no use for any god but their puling gods of Good, Paladine—E'li, as they call him—and his weakling lot. They'll all be on their knees to us before the moons go dark."

And it would be, Blood Gem knew, like sweet wine on the Dark Lady's lips to see those Silvanesti elves bow the neck to her highlord, to be forced to tear down their pale temples to weak gods and use their vaunted skills to erect shrines to the dark gods. Morgion of the Black Wind would spread disease through their ranks. Hiddukel would turn all their feeble truths to lies. At last Takhisis herself, Her Dark Majesty, would rule in that land where her followers had for so long been forbidden to enter.

The dragon climbed higher and turned north toward the borders of the Silvanesti. Behind, in the southern foothills of the Khalkist Mountains, the bulk of Her Dark Majesty's army waited, thousands of soldiers, humans, ogres, goblins, and—Blood Gem made a sound of disgust—and draconians, the misbred dragonmen, spawn of an evil magic-making that corrupted the eggs of dragons. These were Takhisis's fiercest fighters. All the army waited impatiently to fall upon this forested land of wealth and beauty that for centuries had been denied to everyone but the Silvanesti themselves. High in the peaks of those foothills, a strong wing of red dragons brooded, impatient to take to the sky and, with their riders, lead that dark army into battle.

It will be a glorious battle, the dragon mused, his thought matching his rider's.

Phair laughed, the sound wind-torn from her throat and flung out to the hard blue sky. "It will be, and we will soak the forest with elf blood!"

Soon?

The highlord said nothing, but Blood Gem knew her, deeply as dragons know their riders. She had laid her plans in the winter, and those plans called for an army so strong that the elf defenders would crumble before it. A blood-lusty soldier, she was also a canny strategist. She would not commit her army until she was certain her numbers would overwhelm the elves. More soldiers were coming down from Goodlund and across the Bay of Balifor. Once these arrived, she would be ready. Until then, she would play as a cat played with a mouse—cruel games to amuse herself. Phair Caron despised elves, and of all elves, she despised Silvanesti most. If anyone needed a picture of that hatred's birth, Blood Gem knew the perfect one.

A near-grown girl shivered in the shabby winter streets of Tarsis, her rags clutched around thin shoulders, the bones of her face too clearly defined by hunger-carved flesh. In glittering gold, a party of Silvanesti walked past, holding the hems of their robes high out of the running gutter. One turned and saw Phair, the child whose face looked more like a skull than not. With one hand the elf drew aside the hem of his robe, the silk and the brocade all glimmering with jewels. With the other he covered his mouth and nose as one of his companions tossed a copper coin at Phair. The coin fell into the gutter, landing in a pool of muck.

Phair scrambled for it, never minding that she had to scrape through mud and worse to find it. Here was a week's worth of food! Enough to keep her sister out of the brothels where most of the gutter-girls went to earn their bread. Phair had served there herself at need, but never would she let her sister do that. Never. When she looked up, a word of thanks on her lips, she saw only the backs of the elves and heard one say, "Filthy gutter wretch. Why did you do that, Dalyn? The creature is no concern of ours."

"None," his companion had agreed. "But that will keep it from following."

But the gutter creature had followed, Blood Gem thought as he soared over the Sylvan Land. She followed those elves right home, didn't she? It took her a while of years, but she did. And now, a highlord in the army of the goddess elves most hate, Phair Caron had a kind of thanks to offer for their treatment of her, that thanks too long deferred.

Blood Gem banked and turned, soaring away north again. When he came within sight of the Khalkists and the northern border of the Sylvan Land where the trees were not so thick, he felt the uplifting currents of hot air. Three villages were afire, the acrid fumes of terror and dying wafted up to the sky. All around the smoking ruins, bodies lay, most looking like they'd been nailed there. Some had been—nailed by spears and ashwood lances. They looked like insects pinned to a display board. An impatient detachment of the dragonarmy had broken through the burning barrier into the stony area beyond where those three villages had lain. The dragonmen weren't going unmet, for even as they ran raging into a fourth village downriver, elves met them with bows and steel.

Phair Caron laughed again, and again the sound of it was torn from her lips. "Look there! Defenders. Now, that won't do, will it?"

It would not. With startling speed, the red dragon dropped down from the sky, bursting out of the bitter blue sky right over the battle. On the ground, the elves looked up, their faces pale ovals. One, a bold fool, lifted his bow and drew to launch an arrow. Blood Gem roared, the sound so loud the air trembled, the earth itself shook. Screams, like the thin whine of gnats, came up from the battleground. The elf who fancied himself a fortunate archer fell to his knees, terrified. His bow, like a little stick of tinder, fell to the ground.

Tinder, Blood Gem thought. *Ah* . . .

He thrust hard with his mighty wings, gaining the heights again, and turned round over the village. Nothing was afire there, not house, not barn, and certainly not the crowding aspenwood. This wasn't good. On the ground, a phalanx of draconians charged into the midst of the defenders, maces whistling, their ghastly voices like the screaming of stones. From so high up, Blood Gem saw the blood gleaming on the terrible points of the maces, though he did not smell it. Just as well, just as well. Had he smelled the blood he'd have been able to smell the misbegotten dragonmen too. He banked and turned. Upon his back, Phair Caron shouted a wild battle cry.

Roaring, Blood Gem dropped low over the aspens as the draconians drove the elves into the darkness of the forest. Behind, a house burst into flames, the fire kindled by a flaring torch in a draconian fist. Inside a woman screamed, a child wailed, their cries damped by the whoosh and roar of the roof catching. The sweet stench of burning flesh drifted upon black smoke.

"A pretty little fire!" Phair Caron shouted. "But we can do better!"

Blood Gem filled up his lungs with air and, as though those lungs were a bellows, he pushed air out past the place in his throat where dragonfire lived. Death's own banner, flames poured from between his fanged jaws. Flames touched the tops of the aspens, and Blood Gem flew past those, firing the trees beyond and to either side. Elf voices shouted in terror. Men, women, and children were herded into a deadly trap, bounded on three sides by fire and on the other by creatures from nightmare, winged draconians whose reptilian eyes held no warmth, whose powerful tails could break the bones of a foe with one swipe. The least of the tribes of dragonmen, these were the Baaz, and they loved nothing better than killing. Some, it was said, did feast on their kills.

"Now take us back," the highlord shouted. "This has been diverting, but I have work yet to do before the night is over."

Reluctantly, Blood Gem turned north toward the Khalkists and the army's camp. Behind them and below, the draconians finished their work, burning every house in the village, killing each man and woman and child they found.

One or two escaped. Phair Caron could see it from the heights, but she did not regret that. Let them run. Let them flee downriver to the other towns, wailing the song of their terror until it reached the ears of the elf-king, Speaker Lorac himself. Let him know she was coming!

Chapter 2

On days of sun, Dalamar labored indoors in his lord's steamy kitchen, in the musty wine cellars where he was set to catching rats, or in the attics under the high eaves, where it was Eflid's pleasure to give him the task of sorting through old clothing during the breathless hours of hot afternoons. On days of rain, Eflid made certain that Dalamar worked outside, sometimes in the gardens to brace slender plants against the downpours, sometimes after the rain, slogging through mud to repair what damage had been done.

"It's not fair," murmured the young woman who served at the lord's breakfast table. "He treats you worse than he treats any of us, Dalamar. How do you stand it?"

"It's our way," Dalamar said. They stood in the doorway to the kitchen garden, looking out into the day hung heavily with mist and leaden clouds. He plucked a wisp of straw from the floor, a stray bit of packing from a crate of wine. "An old pattern. Eflid wants something from me, and I want to be sure he's not going to get it."

The young woman, Leida, the daughter of a mother who had served in Ralan's hall all her life, child of a father who yet served there, looked at him with luminous green eyes. She had once thought she was in love with a Wildrunner, a young man she saw striding about the city, handsome in his leathers and green shirt. No matter that their life-paths would never cross. No matter that a son of House Protector would never have looked her way but to tell her to refill his mug of ale. When war took the charming soldier north, Leida had wept for as long as an hour, and then she turned her attention closer to home and the dark-eyed mage who seemed suddenly more handsome than the Wildrunner for being so much nearer.

"What, then?" she asked Dalamar. "What does Eflid want?"

Using only the agile fingers of his right hand, Dalamar tied a knot in the straw. "A servant humble and biddable."

Leida laughed, her green eyes sparkling. "He'd spend all his days trying to make you into that, and he'd die never seeing it done."

"They're his days to spend." Dalamar shrugged. "And that's how he wastes them."

"And you? You don't mind it?"

He looked at her long, and when he answered, he spoke coolly. "I mind."

Leida shuddered, for she saw something in his eyes to make her think of a wolf lurking beyond the light of a campfire.

That morning, rain had poured down in sheets. Now at noon, the sky was still. Clouds hung leaden, threatening to burst, and the garden was filled with mist and the fragrance of mint and thyme and sweet chamomile. Brown muddy water ran like small rivers round the beds, carving new shapes. Leida's yellow hair loved the mist, springing into little curls around her cheeks. She wore it short, though elf women seldom did, because she liked the feeling of air tickling her neck.

A pretty neck it was, Dalamar thought. A gloss of mist, perhaps of sweat, lent a sheen to the skin of her slender neck. He lifted a finger and caught the droplet. His eyes on hers, feeling her move toward him though she moved not at all, he tasted it. Rain. Lightning flickered fitfully, illuminating the garden. Leida's eyes widened. She lifted her head in the way she had of showing off her charming ears. Sweetly canted, they were like the petals of some lovely flower, white and elegant. Her lips moved in a sudden smile. She glanced over her shoulder to the silent, cavernous kitchen. Potboys had finished their work of scrubbing the pans and plates from breakfast. The cook had gone into the storeroom beyond to take the count of what would be needed to prepare the evening meal. The bakers, who labored in the night, were long asleep in their quarters.

Leida looked into the eyes of the mage. Perilous eyes sometimes, strange eyes at best, she'd never looked there without feeling a quickening of her breath and the excited leap of her heart. *Dangerous*, warned the little chill running down her spine.

"Dalamar, there is a quiet place I know . . ."

A quiet place in the attic, in the little room where the linen was kept. In her own small chamber, perhaps. Or his. Dalamar leaned close to taste the rain on her neck. Eflid forbade any union between the servants in Lord Ralan's hall. He would have no alliances forged, no distractions created. He would lift the minds and hearts from us all if he could, Dalamar thought, and have a small army of automatons.

His lips still on the soft flesh of Leida's neck, Dalamar smiled. She felt it and came into his arms, lifting her face for his kiss.

His kiss was not like fire, as she had often imagined. It was like sudden lightning. The blood in her leaped, and her pulse drummed. "Come to my room," she said, her words felt against his lips rather than heard. She took his hands and stepped away, holding them, pulling him, laughing. "Come with me. . . ."

Outside, the morning's rain still dripped from the eaves, gurgling in gutters and along the channels it cut for itself beside stone paths. Leida laughed again, bright against the gray day.

The shadow fell upon her like a thin grim cloak. Eflid's hand closed hard on her shoulder, and his voice hissed like a snake's in her ear. "Go where, eh? Slut—"

Leida cried out in fear, perhaps in pain. Swift, Dalamar grabbed the steward's wrist. Before he could think yea or nay, he broke Eflid's grip with one sharp twist. Loathing like poison flared in the steward's eyes. He pulled back, trying to free himself. He failed. Color drained from his cheeks. Rage and fear warred in him.

"Let go," he snarled. Dalamar did not. "Boy, I mean it." His voice shook, but only a little, and only he and Dalamar knew it. "You'd better let go—"

Outside, lightning flashed. Thunder rumbled then suddenly roared. In the garden something white moved through the mist, like a ghost on the rain-running paths. Leida gasped, slipping behind Dalamar into the dark safety of the kitchen. Her footfalls sounded in the darkness, swift as she ran past the deep hearth, the long tables, and the shelves of pots and pans. Gone, she did not look back, and no one looked after her.

On a second flash of lightning the ghostly figure in the garden became a man, a cleric running ahead of the storm, the hem of his white robe hitched high out of the mud. Splashing and slipping, he dashed for the kitchen.

Dalamar loosed his grip on Eflid's wrist. "Your master has a guest, *Lord* Eflid," he said, mocking the man with the title he did not own. "You'd best tend him, eh?"

"Aye, and I'll attend to you later, boy."

"Do you think so?" Dalamar nodded once, an ironic bow. "Well, you may try, as ever you do."

The cleric came into the kitchen, the storm on his heels, thunder at his back. Dalamar moved aside, barely hearing the man's reply when Eflid hustled him inside, fawning and bowing, assuring him that a fire would be made for him, wine brought. "Lord Ralan will be pleased to see you, my Lord Tellin. Come with me. Yes, right through here into the study."

Dalamar looked up at the sky, the lightning cutting through the clouds and the rain pouring down, then he turned and left the kitchen. He had countered Eflid's threat with a threat, and he thought he could smell the docks and the fishers' nets.

Idiot, he thought. He tucked his hands into the sleeves of

his robes, clenching fists he wanted no one to see. Neither did anyone see the rage on his face as he went through the kitchen, the dining hall, and along the corridor to the servants' wing and his own tiny chamber. Had any looked into his eyes, though, he would have found rage there. Rage as cold as winter's rage, fury like a storm over Icewall Bay. Idiot! To risk a comfortable enough position for the sake of a girl he'd have enjoyed once, perhaps twice, then never bothered with again. He deserved what fate he'd earned, the reek of fish at the docks, the endless mending of nets, the constant slap and groan of the river outside whatever poor hut he would be given as home.

* * * * *

Firelight glowed on rich polished oak, making Lord Ralan's desk seem to be crafted of gold. It warmed the mahogany of chairs to deep red, and the crystal carafe looked as if it had been cut from one whole ruby, so deeply did the fire's light shine in the wine. Outside, the world hung gray, pouring with rain beneath a sky the color of lead. Inside, ah, inside the study of Lord Ralan, things were far more pleasant.

Lord Tellin Windglimmer had been standing awhile, unattended in Ralan's study, but the wait was not an unpleasant one. Warm by the fire, he passed the time looking around at the high ceiling of his host's study and the tapestries on the walls, each depicting a scene from Silvanesti history.

Upon the grandest of those hangings Silvanos was shown, a king in his kingdom. He stood in the midst of a circle of towers, each tower representing one of the Houses of the people. In that tapestry even an elf child could read the history of his people and know how in ancient days Silvanos gathered together all the tribes of elf-kind and imposed upon them an order, a structure of Houses that survived even to this day. The head of each house, the Householder, became a member of the Silvanos Council, the Sinthal-Elish, and from them the king and all kings who followed sought advice when he wanted it or endured it when his council insisted he hear it.

First, the ancient king anointed House Silvanos, which people now knew as House Royal. He then ordained House Cleric, among whom lived the priests, temple-keepers, and those who maintained the records of the nation. The defenders of Silvanesti were men and women of House Protector. In his wisdom, Silvanos had gathered to himself magic-users, and he created for them House Mystic, giving to them the charge of training mages. He said to them, and they swore to him, that the magic of red Lunitari, which existed for its own sake, and that of Nuitari, which existed in darkness, would be forbidden. No other magic would be done in the kingdom but that of Solinari—white magic, the magic of Good. It had ever been so, and what shoots from that mystic branch that had tried to grow toward the magic of Lunitari's neutrality or Nuitari's darkness were ruthlessly pruned. They were taken to the Temple of E'li, accused and judged in the dread Ceremony of Darkness, then cast out from the kingdom and the company of their kindred to survive as best they might among the outlanders, humans and dwarves and minotaurs. The exiles were named dark elves, for they had fallen from the light. They did not have a long history of survival, those dark elves, for there were few Silvanesti who did not view life among outlanders as life among madmen in lands of chaos. When they died, they most often died by their own hands.

Great Silvanos also created other castes: House Metalline for the miners; House Advocate, where tradition was kept and law was made; House Mason of the stone-wrights; House Gardener, whose folk grew the food that fed a kingdom; and House Woodshaper, whose folk had the magic of wild spirits sparkling gently in their blood. One other house the king made, and that was House Servitor. This creation of his did not turn out to be what he'd hoped, for he had first called to him the elves of the Elderwild, that strange clan of hunters and explorers who seemed, perversely, to thrive in the hinterlands away from others of their kind. Silvanos, seeing no worth in their wild ways, sought to fit them into his caste structure as servants. The leader of that clan, Kaganos the Pathfinder, defied the king's will and took his people out from Silvanesti Forest. He would not condemn them to serve in the halls of others when he could lead them to a place where they could live free as hunters and practitioners of their own strange kind of wild magic. And so, Silvanos, who would not constrain those who wished to leave, no matter how mad-minded their choice seemed to him, created House Servitor from all those left un-housed, those whose menial jobs and skills fit nowhere else.

Every elf child knew this. Tellin had known it from the cradle, for his was a family of record-keepers, and history ran in his veins as blood.

"Good day, my Lord Tellin—good, if you like rain." Lord Ralan came into the study, flushed, a little harried, or perhaps, Tellin thought, somewhat impatient. "Forgive me for keeping you waiting. A matter having to do with a servant."

"Please, do not apologize," Tellin murmured. "I have been enjoying the wait."

Ralan nodded to the tapestry. "My mother's family had it for generations. She brought it to her marriage, and it is said that this is an accurate depiction of Silvanos, for it was made only decades after his death by one who actually knew him." He smiled, the quiet contented expression of one who is certain of his truths.

"It is lovely," Tellin said, though he did not think the tapestry had so grand a history as Ralan or his family imagined. He said no such thing to his host, however. Instead he murmured, "But I wonder why we don't see the Tower of the Stars there, only the towers representing the various Houses."

Ralan pursed his lips and frowned, thinking. History was no favorite study of his. "I think my father once said that's because Silvanos himself was our tower, our tower of strength, our Tower of the Stars." He shrugged. "Or did he say that the tapestry was woven in the time before the Tower was built? Ah, well, I don't recall. Either makes a good story."

Tellin smiled, agreeing that either did. Ralan was a good host, a good friend to the Temple of E'li, generous to a fault, and, if truth were told, devoted to the Dragon's Lord, blessed with a simple faith that never wavered. "We are the best beloved of the gods of Good," he often said, "the first-born, the people who never gave up faith." Ralan, like many elves, took great pride in his faith and comfort in the belief that the gods of Good must love elves better than all other folk. How could they not? After the Cataclysm, out-landers went searching for gods to replace those they believed gone from the world, elevating mortals, praying to who knew what, but the elves had never lost faith.

Ralan filled glasses from the crystal decanter, one for him and one for his guest. Tellin accepted the wine, and when he saw Ralan settled into his good mood, he hitched up his courage. In the pocket of his robe a small gift lay, a prayer-scroll. Somewhere in this house was Lady Lynntha, Ralan's sister. Perhaps she stood watching out a window, her sil-very hair the same color as the rain falling, her eyes gray as the storm-sky. Perhaps even now she lifted a lovely hand to trace an idle pattern upon the windowpane, in the mist her sweet breath laid there. They had known each other as children when Lynntha came to worship in the Temple of E'li and Tellin was a boy wondering how closely his fate would be tied to the same temple. When they had entered adolescence, they had not moved in the same circles. How could they? Tellin lived in his books, and Lynntha was the daughter of a House whose strictest tenet forbade the mingling of Woodshaper blood with that of any other House, even House Royal. It was a magical bloodline, one that carried down through the generations talents of earthheal and woodshaping no other elf shared.

And yet . . . and yet he had not forgotten Lynntha, her smoky eyes, her silvery hair. He had not forgotten how sweet was the curve of her cheek or the sound of her voice. Lynntha yet lived in the family home, an estate beyond the city, and though her parents were five years dead, she remained unwed. The matter, of course, was in her brother's hands now, and Tellin had heard no whisper that a marriage was in the offing. What did he hope? That he would trot out the old formula, the strange and lovely words of another time, and say to Ralan, "I would that I might take your sister to wed, my lord, and I trust you will grant me your weal and your blessing to pursue my suit with her." Did even his wildest dream imagine that Ralan would suddenly look at the traditions of his House and see them as nothing, or that Lynntha herself would do that? Yes, he hoped these things, and he was a fool for hoping, but he didn't know how else to be.

Outside the storm had redoubled its efforts, rain beating down like tiny silver spears. A servant went by the window, head low, dark hair plastered against a pale face. He looked like the fellow Tellin had seen in the kitchen with Ralan's steward, and he didn't look happy.

"All right," Ralan said, smiling. "Tell me what you want from me now, friend Tellin."

They were not old friends, the lord of this house and Tellin Windglimmer, but they were long-time acquaintances. They had developed, over the years, an easy relationship, one that did not run deeply but did depend upon a certain understanding. Ralan liked to burnish his pride with acts of good will, and Tellin liked to accept those on behalf of the Temple of E'li.

"No temple gifts," Tellin said. He cleared his throat. It had gone suddenly dry. When that didn't work, he took another sip of wine.

"Not today? Well, well. But the servants have been bundling up clothing for the poor and setting them aside for you since the last time the moons were full. What am I to do with it all?"

Tellin moved uncomfortably, then said, "Well, of course I'll happily take what you offer, Ralan, but—"

Lord Ralan raised a brow. "But that's not what you've come to ask for?"

Tellin took the little scroll from his pocket. The light of Ralan's fire glinted on the silver knobs of the spindle. "This—I have made this . . . I mean, I have brought this, a gift . . ."

"A gift for me?" Ralan reached for it, then let his hand drop when he saw the look of sudden confusion on his guest's face. "Ah, not for me. For whom, then?"

"Well, for your sister." Tellin took a breath and forged ahead. "I remembered that Lady Lynntha used to like the Dawn Hymn to E'li. When she was a girl, she would sing it and her voice used to rise up above all others in the morning service. And I thought, well, I had heard that she is here, visiting you. I thought—"

Ralan's expression grew cooler by degrees. "You thought you would present this to her." He held out his hand again. Tellin gave him the scroll. "This is your work, yes?" He turned the spindle so that the firelight ran on the silver. He unclasped the roll and let the first few inches of parchment slide to show the text of the prayer framed in a flowing hand, the capitals of each stanza illuminated in green ink. Diamond dust had been carefully sprinkled onto those tall letters before the ink had dried, and the tiny bits of diamond had cut Tellin's fingers to bleeding as he'd worked. Ralan looked up, his eyes still and calm. No sign did Tellin find of displeasure, but none of welcome either. "This is what you do at the Temple when you aren't looking for alms, eh?"

"Well, this is what I do sometimes. Most times I'm but a record-keeper."

Ralan put the scroll aside, setting it carefully on the table beside his chair. "I'll tell Lynntha it's a gift from an old friend." He emphasized the two words with great care. *Old friend*, said his tone, and *not* a potential suitor. They did not marry outside of their own clans, the folk of House Wood-shaper. They had the magic of wild spirits in their blood, and they would not dilute that, no matter whose heart was at stake. "She'll be happy to have it and to know that you remember her."

"I appreciate it," Tellin said. "Thank you."

Ralan drew breath to speak, then stopped and frowned. "Tellin, I find myself in need of a favor."

Tellin nodded. "Indeed. I'll be happy to help. Tell me how."

"There's a servant my steward has lately . . . um, been talking about. The boy's not working out here, and I'd thought to send him on back to Trevalor, but that would mean a letter explaining the trouble, or worse, a visit from Trevalor himself to bow and scrape and apologize."

He smiled wryly, and Tellin returned it. Few who had to deal with the head of House Servitor found their dealings pleasant ones. Trevalor covered himself in obsequiousness as aging women deck themselves in jewels. In the case of the grand dames, the glitter hides fading glory. In the case of Trevalor, the excessive displays of humility hid some-thing more, a sense of resentful entitlement. He was, as a Householder, a member of Speaker Lorac's Sinthal-Elish. And he was, as the highest member of the lowliest caste in elven society, not one accorded a great deal of respect. "The man is just damned unpleasant," Tellin's father had once said. Tellin had never encountered Trevalor and come away feeling otherwise.

"In any case," Ralan sighed, "I'm not at all sure what the trouble is with this servant—not much interested either, come to that. I'm thinking you might spare me the ordeal of listening to the whole story from Eflid, then hearing Trevalor's song and dance about it all. The boy's a mage, and we thought it would be handy to have one of those around. I guess it hasn't been, but maybe he'll do you some good. Take him off my hands, Tellin, will you?"

Tellin glanced out the window again, at the rain driving down and the gray-green blur of the garden. He remembered the servant going by a few moments before, dark-haired, pale of face, his eyes afire with some emotion. That's the one, he thought, that's the one they want to get rid of.

"What's his name, Ralan?"

Ralan shrugged. "I don't know. Dalamar . . . something. You'll take him then?"

Well, why not? Tellin nodded. "I'm not the one who acquires servants for the Temple, but, yes, send him along with the clothing and the bedding, Ralan, and I'll take care of matters with the head of the Temple . . . and with Trevalor."

"Ah, good, then." Ralan looked around at the warm fire, the tapestries hung upon marble walls, and he felt the truth of what he'd always believed. The elves were the best beloved of the gods, and he was, among the best beloved, a fortunate man. Now, it seemed, even his house was falling into better order. After today there would be one fewer complaint from Eflid about the servants. "See how nicely the day worked out? We're all happy now."

Or some of us, Tellin thought, eyes on the scroll Ralan had set aside and did not now seem to remember. He wondered whether Lynntha would receive it, and then he put the wondering aside as unworthy. Of course she would. He was almost certain of that.

Chapter 3

On the first night of Autumn Harvest when the red moon and the silver had but newly risen over the forest, a child looked up from the garden of her family's little home in the Academy District. She was a small girl who had just slipped down from her father's shoulders, their stroll through the garden at an end. In the air the poignant smell of autumn hung, the spicy scent of the year's end. The little girl sighed, for these scents always made her feel sad in a good kind of way. She looked up to see if the pattern of the stars had changed, wondering whether Astarin's Harp had swung up the sky early, as it did in autumn. E'li's Silver Dragon used to hang in the sky, opposite the Five-Headed Dragon of Takhisis, but those constellations were gone, though no one had seen the stars fall from the sky.

"It's why outlanders think the gods are returning to the world," her father had said. "For the Dark Queen is the ruler of evil dragons, and we see those in the world again. E'li is the patron of the good dragons, and those who shine like brass and bronze and copper and gold, even silver, are E'li's."

"But where are the good dragons?" the little girl had asked. She had known only tales of evil dragons in her short life, those who served Takhisis, the red and the black and the white and the blue.

Her father could not say, for he did not know. People asked themselves often where the good dragons were. Never did they find an answer. With E'li, some said. But that begged the other question: As the dragons of Takhisis brought war to the world, where was E'li to counter the evil?

The little girl didn't think long on such complicated subjects. In any case, the Harp was not yet up, but something more interesting was in the sky. A long shape passed across the face of the silver moon, winged and sinuous.

"Look!" she cried. "Father, look! What is it? Oh! Oh! Has E'li come?"

The creature turned, banking wide over the city. The little girl gasped. Her father cried out in dread to recognize the creature as a blood red dragon, dark against the silver moon, its wings wide and streams of fire pouring from between fanged jaws.

"In E'li's name—!" the father cried. His invocation died upon his lips as the dragon swung low. Moonlight glittered on the battle harness of the rider and the wyrm. The light of red Lunitari glinted from one single point, the head of a spear. Blood ran cold in the elf staring up. His daughter's hand clutched his, but he did not feel it.

Throughout the city, bells began to ring, mournful tolling from the docks and the temples, alarmed booming from the Market and Guild Districts. On maps in every hall, in every tower, in the mind of any who had sketched one, it seemed that the distance between the Khalkists and Silvanost had suddenly shrunk, and the prayers of the best beloved of the gods had in them now notes of desperation.

*   *   *   *   *

"What spells do you have, Dalamar Argent?"

When Dalamar didn't answer at once, the cleric Tellin Windglimmer looked up from his pen-work and smiled encouragingly. A friendly smile, Dalamar decided, of the kind a lord is pleased to offer a servant if he's feeling generous.

"I have all the spells allowed to me, my lord," Dalamar said, lying smoothly and keeping any thought of his stolen studies and his hidden spellbooks far from his mind. He had seen, only this morning on his initial tour of the Temple's inner precincts, a cold corridor, a locked room round which only whispers hung. In there, behind sealed portals, lay the place where clerics could prepare the dread Circle of Darkness, that ceremony by which an elf was cast out from his kind and flung into exile. Murderers endured that shame, as did traitors and those caught worshiping other gods than the gods of Good or those mages found out in dark or neutral magic. The cold that crept out from beneath that door was like winter's own chill. Even in high summer a man walking there would shiver. Did Dalamar fear the cleric would guess or see some tell-tale trace of his guilt and find reason to condemn him? No. He kept those thoughts hidden from long practice, a habit he dared not break.

"Some of the spells I have learned, my lord, allow me to deal with animals, to befriend or defend against them. I have spells to charm appropriate to my teaching and some divination skills and skills with elements. I am adept at spells of protection and those having to do with weather, and I have made a special study of herbs as they pertain to the workings of magic. If you ask at House Mystic, you will hear that I am a mage of minor account." Now he did smile, a thin curling of his lips. "But even they will tell you I am one of some skill and talent."

Sunlight poured in through the wide windows of the Temple's scriptorium, great swaths of golden light, glittering on the long, sinewy form of a dragon, wings spread, jaws wide. Fangs of ivory, talons of gold, and scales of beaten platinum, here was an image of E'li, the Dragon's Lord himself. Somewhere in the deeps of the Temple, chants were being sung even now, in deep voices and high, the rhythm of them rolling forth and back.

> *From the might of the Dragon Queen, protect us, O E'li!*
> *From her claws and rage, from her fury, defend us!*
> *From the sway of the Dragon Queen, protect us, O E'li!*
> *From her fire and sword, from her terror, defend us!*

The light splashed across the red-tiled floor, across the broad marble table where Tellin worked, illuminating the mundane lists so they were as lovely as precious manuscripts. The cleric put down his pen, lifted the list he'd been making, and placed it atop a stack of others.

"I have asked in House Mystic," Tellin said, "and they make a good report of your skills."

"But not so good a report otherwise," Dalamar said.

Tellin shook his head. "In House Mystic they have nothing ill to say of you. In your own House, however . . . " He shrugged. "Well, you know as well as I what is being said of you now. You have, all in the space of a month, been confined to your master's hall and then cast out from it." He rose and walked around the long table. The hem of his white robe whispered on the stone floor. He folded his hands inside the sleeves of his robe, leveling a long blue stare at Dalamar.

A judging stare, Dalamar thought, a weighing look. Well, look as long as you like, my Lord Tellin. You will see what I allow you to see. And he made his eyes hard, his smile cool, challenging the cleric to see past those.

"It must be hard," Tellin said at last, his voice low and thoughtful, "it must be painful to feel such talent as you have running in you and not be allowed to use it more creatively than you have."

Dalamar stood still, startled. Without thinking, he hunched his shoulders a little, as though against intrusion. When Tellin smiled, the expression of one who is pleased to have hit a mark, he forced his muscles to relax. He would have to be careful around this one.

"Yes, I imagine it is hard," Tellin said. "But I hope you will be pleased to exercise your skill more freely here, Dalamar. And, I will see if I can convince House Cleric to teach you more."

Dalamar's breath caught in his lungs, a hitch he did not let Tellin see. "More, my lord? More of magic . . . why?"

Tellin shrugged. "Because I require you to have more. Look," he said, turning from the subject and back to the work table.

He swept aside a pile of blank parchment leaves and pulled another, older sheet from under the stack of records. He turned it so each could read it right side up. It was a map. Not all of Krynn did it show. The western lands of Solamnia in the north, Abanasinia in the south, the Isles of Northern and Southern Ergoth, of Cristyne and Sancrist, even the lands beyond Icewall Bay were absent. The maker of this map was interested only in Silvanesti and its near neighbors, and so the Silvanesti Forest looked like the center of the world. The Plains of Dust lay to the west, as did Thorbardin of the Dwarves beneath the Kharolis Mountains. The city of Tarsis lay south from there, and the lands of Estwilde and Nordmaar to the north. Across the Bay of Balifor lay Khur, Balifor, Goodlund, and beyond there the Blood Sea of Istar where, a long time ago, the kingdom of Istar had ruled the world of commerce and culture until the Cataclysm. Now there was only a great whirling maelstrom where that land had once been, a sunken ruin beneath the water and some few isles beyond where minotaurs lived and human pirates lurked.

"What do you know about the war, Dalamar?"

Curious, Dalamar took a closer step, and then another. He pointed to Nordmaar, to Goodlund and then Balifor. "Though everyone in the city seems to think there will be one, my lord, I know there already *is* one. It's been being fought for some time now, since Phair Caron swept into Nordmaar in the summer last year."

Tellin raised a brow, curious. "That's an odd way to put it. There have been treaties holding the Highlord back for some time now. War has not been imminent, and we have certainly not been in it."

"Do you think so?" Dalamar shrugged. "Well, most people do. But isn't it odd to think that we, of all the world, will be invisible to the Highlord, that her Dark Mistress will burn her way across Krynn and leave our land untouched? Yes, I know that we are the best beloved of the gods. One hears that all the time. That doesn't seem to matter as regard the treaties House Advocate made with Phair Caron. Those treaties are already ash, my Lord Tellin. And if treaties are ash, how long before the forest itself is burning?"

He traced a mark in the air above Silvanesti on the map, the mark indicating the Barrier Hedge that had so long withstood in-comers. One word he whispered, and the invisible mark became visible in the air as a ragged orange glow. Fire!

Dalamar glanced at the cleric. He saw neither startlement nor anger, but he did see agreement. "But you have thought that, too, haven't you? And you are laying plans against it."

Tellin's blue eyes glinted sharply. "Yes, I have been putting up stores here in the Temple, and I have been looking north waiting."

Dalamar glanced out the window, away across the gardens and out beyond the open gate to the road he'd taken from Lord Ralan's hall. He had, only this morning, come from there with cartloads of clothing and bedding, the very things Eflid had set him to sorting in the attics on the hottest days of summer.

"Waiting for refugees," he said. "Are all the temples of the city making these plans?"

"Yes, we are. But we won't be housing them here in the city. That would be impossible. We don't have the food or the room for that. It would be a disaster to try. " He shrugged, one who'd thought the matter through, or who had heard others speak their own thinking. "In any case, we've made our plans. Clerics in the various temples will gather clothing and bedding and medicaments and send them out to the cities up-river, to Alinosti and Tarithnesti, to Shalost in the west. The temples there will house and feed those who flee the war.

"Here, we are putting by other kinds of supplies, among them herbs for salves and ointments and infusions. These we'll gather and prepare for both the army and the refugees, sending supplies where they are most needed."

"Very neatly planned," Dalamar murmured.

Tellin flicked him a quick glance, wondering whether the mage mocked. "Yes, we think so. And so you see, I'm glad to know that you have made a special study of herbs, Dalamar. Do you know," he asked, eyes keen, his regard sharp and searching, "where the best herbs are to be found?"

Dalamar answered carefully, not certain he understood the intent of Tellin's question. "In the gardens of the temples, my lord, to be sure."

"Indeed. And if that were so, would I have asked my question?"

Dalamar smiled, this time with some real warmth in spite of himself. The cleric did have a little blood in him after all, enough to rise to a flush of anger. "No, my lord, I don't imagine you would have. I do know places across the river and into the forest where one may find such herbs as lobelia and cohosh and gentian and whatever else you might need that doesn't grow in temple gardens. I have made," he said with not the least note of wryness in his tone, "good use of the time I spent away from my Lord Ralan's hall."

Tellin lifted the map from the table and rolled it carefully. "So it seems. And if I tell you to map these places for others to find, will you do that and return here each day in good and fair time?"

Or will I run away north, to the secret place, the cave and the magic? Will I spend illicit hours at forbidden studies? The questions were like longing to Dalamar, an ache in his soul. He had not been able to study those tomes or practice the darker arts in many long weeks. Had he missed them? Yes—the magic more than the darkness.

Sun on tiles, light glinting off the tiny scales of a platinum dragon, these things shone brightly in Dalamar's eyes. He moved to turn away from the glare, but he didn't, for he was struck by a sudden thought, a swift understanding that he did long for something not necessarily darkness. Only magic, only that, and if Lord Tellin could convince the white-robed mages of House Mystic to offer him the teaching he craved, if they were to acknowledge the talent in him, that talent they could not deny but would not honor, he would take his magic there. Like a man standing upon a threshold, he felt drawn one way and then another, into light, into shadow.

Making no choice, hanging in the moment, Dalamar looked at his new master long and with steady gaze. "I will do what you ask, my lord."

"Have I your word?"

Tellin's narrow-eyed glance stung Dalamar to bristling. "The word of a servitor? Why, what good is that to you, Lord Tellin?"

"As good as you show me it is, and I say this with confidence. You don't look like a liar to me, Dalamar Argent."

Dalamar nodded, the nod a small bow, the only one he'd made to Lord Tellin Windglimmer in all the time he'd stood in the scriptorium. "I will go now, and if it pleases you, my lord, I will return before midday."

Chants rose up and fell, birdsong stitched through the staid rhythm like silver thread through a dark tapestry. Another voice drifted through the temple-song, soft and low, a woman's voice murmuring in the garden. Dalamar and Tellin looked out the window and saw Lady Lynntha. She stood, silvery in the sunlight, her long hair bound high upon her head and held there with gemmed pins so that it seemed she wore a glittering crown.

"I wish to see the Lord Tellin," she said, soft to a gardener walking by. "Will you find someone to announce me?"

Tellin blushed, his face flamed red and he glanced at Lynntha's hands and the small scroll case she held. Dalamar noted this, and he said nothing about it, but he did volunteer to show the lady into the scriptorium.

"Yes," Tellin said, eyes on his papers again. "Please do that."

Dalamar bowed, hiding his curiosity, and walked out into the garden. "My lady," he said, gesturing toward the open window behind. "I have come from Lord Tellin Windglimmer, for I have heard it that you wish to see him."

She glanced at him only briefly, not recognizing him as one who had lately served in her brother's hall. Her hands held the scroll case gently, careful of the delicate embroidery. She hung in a hesitating moment, as though some hard-won resolve were melting. She took a breath, and it did not seem to hearten her.

"Servant," she said, her eyes straying past him to the window and the cleric sitting at his desk. Her cheek flushed, not so brightly red as Tellin's, only the delicate tint of a rosy pink petal. "I have changed my mind. I don't need to see Lord Tellin. Only take this to him." She put the scroll into Dalamar's hands. "Say to him that I appreciate the care he took in crafting this, but I cannot accept it. I cannot . . . "

She turned and left. With no other word she walked out of the garden, her slender back straight, her shoulders a firm line against the pain Dalamar had seen in her long eyes. And what is that? He wondered, walking back into the scriptorium. What is that between a member of House Cleric and one of House Woodshaper? A hopeless dream, and my new master won't be happy to have this gift of his back.

Yet Tellin was not so unhappy as Dalamar had imagined he would be. He took the scroll case and looked at it a long moment, then set it upon a stack of unused parchment, the colorful embroidery bright against the creamy vellum. He looked up, and when he saw Dalamar still standing there he said, "A gift returned, and a gift exchanged."

"How exchanged, my lord?"

Tellin touched the case, an exquisitely embroidered hummingbird under his fingertips. "When I gave her this gift she thought fit to return, the scroll had no case. Now," he said, stroking the silken bird gently, "now it does."

All this Dalamar considered interesting, and he thought about it later in the evening when the sun had set and he was unpacking, yet again, his meager possessions. Was he a fool, Lord Tellin Windglimmer, to set his heart on a woman he had no chance to win? They treated their marriages like gifts from the gods, those of House Woodshaper—gifts not bestowed outside their own clans. A fool, yes, Lord Tellin was that.

And yet, such foolishness Dalamar understood. He, too, had set his heart upon a thing he must struggle to have and might not gain. "I will see," Tellin had said, "if I can convince House Mystic to teach you more . . . because I require you to have more." He'd made his offer almost casually, a man with some power who uses it easily. How would it be, Dalamar thought, to trust this lordling cleric? Well, not difficult, for he would not be forsaking his secrets in hope of gaining what Tellin suggested he might have. He'd keep his secrets and see what happened. Quietly in him, like the first thin tendrils of smoke to signal a fire, an old dream roused. It was seldom granted that servitors be taught magic, never that they learn enough to venture out of the kingdom across the Plains of Dust and into the Forest of Wayreth where stood the Tower of High Sorcery, the only one of the five ancient citadels of learning to have survived the Cataclysm. The Tests of High Sorcery were administered in that tower, grueling exercises in magic devised by the Conclave of Wizards, the heads of the orders of the White, Red, and Black Robes. The mage who survived his Tests was one reckoned worthy of respect anywhere in Krynn.

How, thought Dalamar, how would it be if I could take the Tests . . . ?

He looked around at his new quarters. The room allowed

him in the Temple was no larger than that in Lord Ralan's house, but it was bright, having two windows, one facing east into the garden, the other facing north. As he settled for sleep, the scents of the garden drifting in through the windows, it seemed to him that no matter how things turned out, whether he learned more of white magic or sipped his dark secrets, he'd found better work than he'd had in a while.

Through the east window the light of the two moons shone, the red mingling with the silver. The lights of the Tower of the Stars graced the darkness, the tower itself glittering with gems caressed by that moonlight. Dalamar closed his eyes, sinking into darkness, seeking sleep as chanting from the Temple made a heartbeat for the night.

From the might of the Dragon Queen, protect us, O E'li!
From her claws and rage, from her fury, defend us!
From the sway of the Dragon Queen, protect us, O E'li!
From her fire and sword, from her terror, defend us!

When at last he fell asleep, Dalamar did not dream of magic or the threat from the north or any other thing. His sleep was long and deep, but once he woke, thirsty in the night, and poured water from the green pitcher beside his bed. He had a thought in his mind, waking, and that was of the map he had seen on Lord Tellin's worktable, that one in which the Silvanesti Forest sat as though it were the center of the world.

But we are not, he thought, setting aside the cup and slipping again beneath the red woolen blanket. The blasphemy didn't frighten him, and if he dreamed afterward, those dreams did not disturb his sleep.

* * * * *

A scream tore the silence, ripping the velvet night in the Tower of the Stars. In the bedchamber of the king, the scream sounded again, and this time it was made of words.

"You must not leave me!"

Footsteps ran in the corridor, whispering on marble floors. Voices called one to another. Alhana Starbreeze found her father's steward running out the door of his own chamber.

"What is it?" she cried. "Lelan, my father—"

The steward hushed her, but the pallor of his plump cheeks gave lie to the calmness he pretended to have. "A nightmare, I'm sure, Princess. Your father has had a nightmare. No more than—"

Moaning, the Speaker of the Stars cried, *"Don't leave—!"*

Alhana ran into his suite, through the antechamber, and into her father's bedroom. Her pale night robes and silent footfalls gave her the seeming of a ghost. The king sat in his bed of silk sheets, clutching satin covers. His eyes starting in his head, he stared at her, open-mouthed.

"Father!" She flew to his bedside and took his cold hands in hers. "Father, I'm here. It's Alhana." He did not seem to know her. She cast a swift glance at Lelan and saw the steward had already poured a glass of water. "Take this, Father, drink."

With trembling hands, the Speaker of the Stars took the glass. He drank, the water dribbling. Alhana wiped his chin dry, tenderly as a mother might. "Lelan," she whispered, "light candles, then leave us."

Light sprang up as Lelan kindled one candle after another, fat white pillars and slender green tapers, all the candles in the Speaker's bedchamber to drive out the darkness of night. The faint scent of honey drifted on the air as the beeswax warmed. When he'd done that, Lelan hung at the threshold, wanting to stay. The sharp glance Alhana gave him decided the moment. He turned and ran down the corridor, his footfalls like whispers and rumors of fear. The steward gone, Alhana took her father's hands again, pressing them warmly. It seemed he knew her now.

"Alhana," he whispered, "dearest child."

"A nightmare," she said. "Father, you had a dream. Look, you are here in your own chamber."

He looked around, but only because he followed her gesture, not because he believed he was anywhere outside of nightmare. Thick woolen rugs lay scattered on the cool marble floor, their bright colors muted by night, blue and green and dawn's pink all changed to gray. Upon deep cushioned chairs were brocaded pillows. Tapestries hung on the pale marble walls, and one long mirror bordered in gold graced the wall opposite his bed. A little writing desk stood below an east-facing window, a place for the king to sit and look out at the Garden of Astarin as he tended his correspondence. In the far corner of the room, a niche made by the joining of marble walls, his personal altar stood, whitest marble upon which sat a golden image of Quenesti-Pah and the wing-spread platinum image of the Dragon's Lord, E'li, whom some in the outside named Paladine. None of these familiar trappings stilled Lorac's restless eye.

Alhana chaffed his hands, and softly she said, "Tell me, Father. Tell me what you dreamed." For she believed that to expose the nightmare to the light of the waking world would kill its power.

Shivering, he sighed. "Oh, gods, it was . . . I went wandering down all the roads of place and time. I walked in the world where the dogs of war are running, and I heard—" He groaned, hunching over. "The voice said, 'You must not leave me! I will perish!' "

"Who spoke? Father, who spoke?"

He looked at her, his eyes clearing. She thought he would answer, but he did not. "In my dream I walked through Nordmaar and Balifor and Goodlund, out to the Blood Sea of Istar. And . . . and when I came there, the dream changed. Right under me, all around me. There was no gaping wound in the world. Alhana, I saw the city itself, Istar!"

Storied Istar, in all its glory of gold and delight, as she had been more than three hundred years ago when he'd come there, a young elf seeking the Tower of High Sorcery that he might present himself and take the Tests of Magic. The buildings soared high, painted in jeweled tones, gleaming in sunlight, sighing in moonlight. In his dream his soul had sailed upon the chants wafting out from every temple, the voices of elves so beautiful that the Kingpriest himself wept to hear them, his heart so full that words could not express his joy. These were the chants of eternal peace, songs lifted to E'li, whom they named Paladine in Istar, to Quenesti-Pah, to Majere the Master of the Mind, to Kiri-Jolith whose sword wields only justice. In Istar, the Fisher King, Habbakuk, was revered, and Astarin the Bard, whose name means Song of Life.

"It is," Lorac said to his daughter, "as though I am telling you a dream, and yet telling you a thing that happened in waking life. For it did. It did happen that way when I went to Istar, there to take my Tests."

Then he grew still, his eyes suddenly shuttered. His lips moved to shape two words: *Save me!* It seemed to Alhana that those two words caused the light of the candles to dim and the air in the chamber to grow suddenly cold.

In a low voice, Lorac told how in the sky above Istar the light changed from the lovely golden of sunset to a shivering green. Dreaming, he'd looked around himself, fear quivering in the far and secret chamber of his heart. From where the green light? He followed the light until the Tower of High Sorcery rose up before him. Out from the Tower, like beams lancing out from a lighthouse on a storm-swept night, the light shone. From there, as well, came the voice. *Save me!*

In his dream, Lorac walked past gates that swung open at his word. The guardians of the Tower, creatures of magic set to ward by mages most powerful, stepped back before him. Mages came to greet him, and they led him inside where an old man, a mage whose name no one knew, told him he was expected. *The world will be lost!* The cry echoed throughout the Tower, down all the corridors, in all the chambers, high and low, as Lorac followed the old man. Yet, though the cry echoed, no one in this dream but Lorac seemed to hear it or feel the urgency growing in its tone. Led by the nameless mage, he wended the maze of corridors, passing through one chamber after another, and it seemed to him that the Tower went on forever, wide as the sky and broad as the world itself. At last, they stopped in a small chamber, one no larger than could fit two grown men standing abreast.

"And the nameless mage, he said that I must not touch or take anything. I must leave all as I saw it."

"And did you?" Alhana asked, her face white in the candle's light.

"I told him—I told him I would do as he wished. And the man vanished. When I looked back into the room . . ."

When he looked back into the room, he saw that a table had appeared, a simple trestle of scarred wood. Upon it sat an ivory stand, like two hands cupped, which held a clear glass ball shining in the unlit gloom. *Save me*, the globe whispered. *Disaster is near and you must not leave me here in Istar. If you do, I will perish and the world will be lost!* He reached, and he lifted the globe. It warmed in his hands, and he looked around again, like a thief in the night. Take nothing, the old mage had said, touch nothing. Await me here. But the orb, nestling in his hands, cried out in piteous tones, cried out for the sake, not of itself, but of the world it longed to save. Swiftly, silently, the young mage, who was the old man who dreamed, whispered the words of a spell. The crystal globe became as nothing, not only invisible but without substance. That nothing he put inside his robe, and he walked out of the little chamber, out of the towers, and out of the city that soon would fall and, in falling, change the face of the world.

"Child," said Lorac Caladon, he who was a king, the Speaker of the Stars, "my child, I am ashamed to confess it. I left the city a thief."

Silence settled upon the room. In the corridor beyond Lorac's door, torches whispered to themselves in their brackets on the walls, the hushed voice of tamed fire. Somewhere down that corridor Lelan waited, the chamberlain who obeyed his princess but surely did not sleep for fear his master would call him and not be heard.

"Father," said Alhana, leaning close to kiss his cheek. She took his hand again and pressed it to her own cheek. "You are no thief. You simply had a nightmare, and one cannot be blamed for what deed he does in dream. Now, I beg you, please settle yourself and try to sleep again."

Unspoken between them was the knowledge that the day to come would bring another round of council meetings, and Lord Garan of House Protector would come to give what news his Windriders brought from the borders. Lately his news had been good, or not bad. Phair Caron held her position, brooding in the foothills of the Khalkist Mountains, but no one expected that to be the case for long. Garan would plead again to make an offensive strike, to fall upon the Highlord and take her by surprise. The Speaker and the Head of House Protector did not agree. Lorac demanded patience until more troops could be moved to the borderlands. Garan said patience would be the death of them. "She is building up her own forces, my lord king. I know it! Let me strike now!" This time, perhaps, he would plead his case with sufficient vigor to convince Lorac that what elven troops now stood at the border would be enough to make such a strike effective.

Lorac looked up. The king seemed far older in the eyes of his daughter than he had only this morning. "Child, it was a dream, but . . . it was a dream of truth."

The night fell into utter silence. Alhana did not hear cricket-song, the nightingales in the Garden of Astarin had no voice. "Father, what do you mean? What are you saying? That you, of all people, did steal—?"

"I did not steal it," he said, his face changed, growing oddly cold and still. "I did not steal the globe. I rescued it."

With more energy than Alhana imagined he had, Lorac left his bed. He put on his robe of blue silk, his slippers of soft green leather, and took his daughter by the hand. An urgency was on him now. His fingers grasped hers with enough strength to make her wince.

"Father, what—?" He pulled her toward the door and the corridor beyond. "Where—?"

Once outside his chambers he took her to the railing, the marble ward against the far drop below. Behind them torches flared in silver wall brackets. Somewhere a woman's voice whispered, and a man's murmured in reply. Nearby were the libraries, and a light shone out from under a heavy oaken door—scribes working late.

"Look," the Speaker said, pointing down into the well beyond the railing, down into the audience chamber. His throne stood there, mahogany and emerald, and the Words of Silvanos inlaid with silver. *As lives the land, so live the Elves.* Beside the throne stood a rose glass table. "Do you see those ivory hands, there on the table?"

She did. The sculpture hadn't been there even this morning.

"I had it commissioned in the summer. I thought the time might come . . ." He stopped, then said, "The hands are empty now." Lorac's voice echoed into the well, the echoes like wings rustling round the throne and the ivory sculpture. "But come, come with me."

He pulled her along. She followed, thinking they would take the spiraling staircase down into the audience hall. They did not. He took her far down the corridor past closed doors and curtained alcoves to a smaller, darker staircase. They entered a narrow doorway, and she had to duck her head to pass through.

The air in that lightless place smelled faintly damp. Lorac whispered, *"Shirak!"* and a globe of golden light appeared above his head, moving as he did and lighting the way down narrow stone steps through a passage Alhana had known about but never taken. This way lay a dungeon, not one for keeping prisoners—those were dealt with in other towers.

Cold seeped through the soles of her soft slippers as she ran after her father. Down and around, spiraling into darkness with only that one golden light bobbing above, at last, she saw green light pulsing in the distance below—light like the kind you see when sun shines through aspen leaves in spring. When they reached the floor at last, Lorac led her to the far corner of the dungeon, a place where—had it been meant to hold prisoner—bars would have been erected, chains installed. Upon a small table, not one so lovely as that beside Lorac's throne, sat a crystal globe. It seemed no larger than a child's marble, and yet Alhana knew instinctively that this was not the case. It *felt* larger, no matter what sight told her. She closed her eyes, not wanting to see it. In the utter darkness, an image sprang: The strange sculpture of empty hands beside her father's throne filled at last, filled with this orb that seemed small yet felt large.

"Father, what is it?"

He turned to her, smiling. "It is a Dragon Orb, Alhana."

She frowned, stepping closer, then away. Power pulsed in the globe, throbbing like a heart in the night. The skin on the back of her neck prickled. "This is what you took?"

"Rescued," said the king quickly. "I rescued it. It cried out to me, and I rescued it. This orb has the power to command dragons. It was one of five, crafted by wizards in a far distant time. Two we know are lost. This third is here. The others . . . ?" He shrugged. "I don't know where they are, or if they still exist. But I do know this, for I have studied what small lore is left of them—a mage with the strength of will to control the magic of an orb will be able to control dragons."

A damp breeze drifted through the dungeon, touching Alhana's cheek with cold fingers. "And the mage who tried but could not control the orb? What would happen to him, Father?"

Lorac turned to her, his pale face shining, his eyes alight. Ignoring her question, he said, "How would it be, my Alhana, if suddenly Phair Caron found her dragons answering to my will? How—?" He cocked his head, his eyes gone soft and unfocused, as they had been when first he woke from his nightmare. "Listen. Do you hear it? The world will be lost . . ."

Alhana heard nothing, but she did not say so. Softly, she touched her father's arm, the silk sleeve of his robe cold and damp under her fingertips. "Father, come away. Come away. You frighten me!"

He turned, and though he looked at her, he did not see her. His were the eyes of a young man who stood a long time ago in the Tower of High Sorcery at Istar, the eyes of an old man who not even an hour ago woke screaming from nightmare. He said nothing, though, and he let her lead him away from the dragon orb, back up the narrow cold stairs.

* * * * *

In the morning, when the last rosy fingers of dawn were withdrawing and leaving behind a hard blue autumn sky, Dalamar woke to the tolling of all the bells in the city of Silvanost. Over the tolling, he heard frightened voices and running feet.

"What is it, my lord?" he called to Tellin, hurrying past his window. Lord Tellin didn't know, and Dalamar dressed to find a better answer. Outside, he found the temple-folk, clerics and servants alike, running into the streets already clogged with people, students running from the Academy District, advocates from the Embassy District. From the Market District and the Servitor District in the west, men and women and children came, following their neighbors to the heart of Silvanost, to the Garden of Astarin round which the temples clustered, where the Tower of the Stars stood, tall against the sky. Griffins sailed above the Tower, their wings golden in the new day, their harsh cries, like battle cries, filling the sky.

"What's happened?" Dalamar asked his master again.

Grimly, looking north, Tellin said, "The Barrier Hedge is on fire. Phair Caron's dragons have set it alight!"

A cleric, overhearing, cried out. Others picked up her shout and sent it round and round the gathering until the Wildrunners at the gates of the Tower looked at each other, silently wondering whether they would be called upon to quell a panicky mob.

"Look," Dalamar said, pointing north and then south, east and then west.

Ripples of motion shivered through the crowd, starting at the four corners and making itself into a parting of the sea of people as, one after another, the lords and ladies of the Sinthal-Elish left their homes and went among their clans, speaking words of comfort or offering quieting gestures. They came, one and all, to the Tower of the Stars, for it had been appointed that they meet with the Speaker at this hour. Not one of them, not even Lord Garan of House Protector, looked up to the griffins and the Windriders. They went as though upon any ordinary day. From them, calm emanated, and certainty and a measure of peace.

All would be well said the Householders by gestures and with words. The people heeded, for how could they not? These were their lords. This was the council of the king, and who should know better? In groups and singly, the citizens of Silvanost returned to their homes or the tasks they had left. In the sky the griffins circled, round the top of the Tower of the Stars, and one of all that crowd looked up at them and expressed his unease.

"It doesn't look good, my lord," Dalamar Argent said to

the cleric beside him. "Windriders circling the Tower as if they expect some attack from the sky, the Barrier Hedge on fire . . . " He looked away north. He had never seen the Barrier Hedge. In all his life he had never gone father than his secret cave in the north of the woods, but he could imagine the hedge now, a wall of flame. "Phair Caron has made her move at last."

Chapter 4

They came, old men and women, children and babes in arms. They left footprints in blood on the stony ground. Their tears watered the earth, and their lamentations terrified the birds of the air. On days of pouring rain and on days of sun, they came walking, staggering through the aspenwood in the golden season, in autumn so beloved of elves. They came, an army of misery, disease, injury, and despair, an army of woe. The careful shaping of the forest fell to ruin before them, and the trail they left behind was one of deer carcasses, sodden campfires, worn out boots, and of their own dead. Old men fell, their hearts broken and refusing to beat. Old women collapsed and did not get up. Small children died of exposure. Mourning, they simply covered the dead with brush and moved on.

In the days of Phair Caron's border raids, the refugees had been a trickle, a few fleeing the burning of villages in the northmost part of the land. By the middle of the month of Autumn Harvest, the trickle became a stream, running down to Silvanost. They shivered in the cool nights, sleeping on stony ground. They had only the clothes on their backs. Some fortunate few carried ragged blankets to wrap round their weeping children. They had no young men to protect them. No one who looked strong enough to turn into a soldier ever survived a ravaged village. Those were killed at once. The draconians sweeping through villages sought them out as robbers seek gold. Before the eyes of screaming old men and women, wailing children, the young and healthy were cut down and killed.

The aged, the sick, the children, these were allowed to leave each village, even encouraged to do so. It was the favorite tactic of Phair Caron's mage, Tramd o' the Dark.

"Let them go," he cried over each slaughter. Some said they saw him, a tall human on dragonback. Others said he was a dwarf, still others an ogre. But then others would say, "Who would imagine a dragon letting an ogre ride?" However it was, all agreed that the mage's voice, magic-aided, boomed over the burning villages and towns like the bellowing of a terrible god. "Let them go! Drive them out! Let them spread fear like disease! Let them clog the forest and fill up the cities with need and terror!"

War raged behind this army of woe, little villages aflame, awash in blood. To the east, out by the Bay of Balifor, a great fire burned. The Barrier Hedge was in flames. What then for the elves? What then for the best beloved of the gods?

* * * * *

In the Temple of E'li, the Dawn Prayer lifted upon the winged voices of the old and young, men and women. Day after day, Dalamar woke to it until he could no longer hear it as anything but the sound of desperation. To him, it was the helpless cacophony of people bleating like sheep to a god who—if he had indeed returned to the world as rumor said—had not bothered to stop the hand of Takhisis from ripping apart the kingdom of the Silvanesti. Lords and ladies came to pray, as did merchants and masons and gardeners and servitors. Elves of high station and low trooped in for morning services, for noontide worship, and were often back again for Day's End prayers. The smoke of incense hung in the air, stinging the eyes and making old ladies cough. It did nothing to cover the odor of fear permeating the Temple of E'li and all those others clustered round the Garden of Astarin as reports came to the city of burned villages in the north and west, of battles on the border. Some of those battles between elves and the dragonarmy were victories. Others were not. Troops of Wildrunners practiced war-work on the training grounds around the barracks, their cries and the ringing of steel on steel heard even in the Garden of Astarin. Others moved out of the city, marching north even as flocks of citizens marched to the temples and dark rumor ran like smoke through the city. The Speaker and his council were considering the idea of evacuating the kingdom if Phair Caron broke past Alinosti.

"Why don't they do something?" Dalamar muttered, watching out the window of the scriptorium on one of the last warm days of autumn. One of the last he knew, for each time he went in the forest to hunt for herbs to fill the Temple's storerooms he saw signs that colder weather was coming. Seed dropped fast now. Stalks withered. The plants drew all their life downward to hide it under the ground till spring. Farther north, in the forest where his secret texts lay hidden beneath magical wards, mice and voles had moved inside the cave. He had been obliged to put a warding on each book to protect it from the incursions of nesting creatures.

Lord Tellin looked up from his pages—lists or reports or some small work of his own—past Dalamar to the garden. People stood in small groups, some just come out from service, others waiting to go in. His eye searched for one in particular, Lady Lynntha, who had been each day at the earliest service, lifting her voice in the Dawn Hymn.

"Do what?" he asked Dalamar, but absently. He saw her, tall and slender, standing a little apart from a group of other young women. She looked around idly. This had been going on since the day she'd come to return Tellin's gift. Her voice was now a regular part of the prayer services.

"Anything." Dalamar saw glances meet, Tellin and Lynntha's. Dangerous, he thought, dangerous, my Lord Tellin. "All they do is pray and feed troops up to the border."

"And these things are nothing?" Tellin reached for his pen, found the quill's tip split, and took up another.

"Yes." Dalamar turned his back to the garden and the

people milling there. "Lord Garan, I think, would agree."

Tellin looked up, surprised and perhaps amused to hear so bold an opinion from a servant. He had heard one or two similar opinions in the last weeks. Dalamar had changed since he had returned to the Grove of Learning to take up his studies in magic again. He grew bolder, more confident, and it seemed to Tellin that this was both a good thing and bad. He did want a mage skilled in the healing arts, one who could put his talents to use should that become necessary. Who would not want one near who knew how to imbue a salve with magical properties? And yet . . . and yet there were these bold, striding opinions, which, even if they sometimes matched Tellin's own thoughts, were not seemly in a servitor.

Perhaps this, he thought, is why we don't allow them too much knowledge of art and literature and magic. They overreach. And yet, Tellin didn't think the reach of this careful and cunning servant often exceeded his grasp.

"Do you think Lord Garan would agree with you, Dalamar? Well, perhaps. But hindsight—"

"Yes," Dalamar interrupted, "it's the best sight. Still, seeing backward, I know that a mistake was made to forge treaties with Phair Caron. Another was made when the king delayed Lord Garan's hand for the sake of building up troops. The Highlord, it seems, built a stronger force than we can muster."

The words fell like the ring of steel into the room. Tellin looked away from the garden, his eyes dark and troubled. He heard the truth of what Dalamar said, and he knew that truth was being whispered in other quarters. Still, it was not right to engage in such speculation with a servitor.

"Easy enough to say," Tellin murmured, shuffling his pages to say he'd done with this talk, "now that all deeds are done."

Dalamar took a moment to decide whether he would accept dismissal. Then softly he said, "I suppose you're right, but seeing forward, I know how that mistake can be rectified."

Tellin put aside his quill again, this time not smiling. "Have you been making war plans, Dalamar? Isn't that better left to—"

"—to my betters?" Dalamar shrugged. "I suppose you might think so, my lord, if you thought the heart of a servitor were not as deeply filled with love for his homeland as the hearts of lords and ladies."

Tellin winced. "I'm sorry. I didn't mean—"

Yes, said Dalamar's cool smile, you meant just that. "Look what my betters have wrought. Have you heard it," he said, "that the refugees from this war are not marching neatly to the cities on the river? People with maps thought they would do that, but people in terror simply run. These are trampling their way to Silvanost, hungry and cold and frightened. Come, I suppose, to see what the best of their betters have to say about things."

Tellin's eyes narrowed at this impudence. Dalamar wondered whether he had pushed the cleric too far. He did not back down, though. He had been a long time considering his plan, and most of this morning looking at the maps in this very room when what he should have been doing was sharpening quills, scraping parchment clean, and laying out the lists of stores for Tellin to review and amend.

"My Lord Tellin," he said, striving to keep a tone that wouldn't alienate his master. "I have a lot of time to think out there in the woods where the herbs are. And I have a chance to hear what is being said in the city among the people. Lords and ladies, they don't look to see if a servant is near. We are invisible to them. And so they speak freely, and we listen freely. I know we elves held our hand too long, and now we suffer for it. We let advocates and emissaries steer our defense, as though we were in some court of law and not at war. We put our trust in treaties that Phair Caron had no mind to honor. Now we are too late to the border with too few soldiers." Softly, he said, "You know that as well as I, my lord."

Tellin looked out the window again. Lynntha's voice lifted in sudden laughter. Her brother had come to escort her home from the Temple. He watched her turn and walk away, lovely on Lord Ralan's arm. Her cheeks were sun-gold. Her silver hair, caught back from her face and captured in a glittering jeweled net, hung heavy on her long slender neck. What would happen to her if the Wildrunners could not hold the border? Who would defend her and keep her safe?

Tellin shuddered and looked at Dalamar, his impertinent servant. "Tell me," he said, reluctant to show enthusiasm, and yet curious. "Tell me what plan you have."

And then what? He could not go to the Speaker of the Stars and say, "Beg pardon, my lord king, but my servant has come up with a brilliant plan of defense." Certainly he could not! War plans from the servant of a cleric whose duty it was to keep the records in the Temple of E'li? This was idiocy! And yet, he was curious.

Dalamar sensed that curiosity as if it were something to smell. He crossed the tiled floor and took out a map from the chest of drawers. He spread the map upon the marble table and said, "First, my lord, let us agree that we are not at the center of the world."

Tellin listened, growing by turns astonished, disbelieving, and finally accepting. When Dalamar had finished talking, the sunlight was long gone from the garden, having moved around the back of the Temple. Noontide services had come and gone. Somewhere out by the docks a bell tolled.

"Of course," Dalamar said, and now he smiled a little, "if you think this plan is good, you must take it to whomever you decide needs to hear it and say that it is your own. After all, who would heed the ideas of a servitor?"

Tellin sat back, shaking his head. Who would heed a

servitor, indeed? No one. Yet, who but a mage could explain this idea? No one.

* * * * *

Dalamar stood in the Tower of the Stars. He looked up into the high recesses of the chamber and watched the light of stars and the two risen moons glimmering down the walls, dancing on the gems imbedded in the marble walls. Almost, he thought, you can hear that light laughing, singing the songs of the spheres. All around him he felt the ancient magic that had made this marvelous place, echoes of spellcasting done hundreds of years before. Any who chose to attend could feel the wispy remnants of that ancient magic, but none felt that tingling, that echo of mighty spell-work as a mage did. To stand here now was like hearing music drifting out from a distant window, ancient songs and old, old melodies.

Voices of another kind drifted down into the audience chamber from the gallery, ashy whispers with no tones to let him determine one from the other. Beside him, Lord Tellin tried to keep a calm, respectful stillness in this place of power, but the cleric could not hold quiet for long.

Tellin looked around in the great audience chamber, eyes darting here and there, from the magic-wrought walls to the silk-woven tapestries to the nine steps leading to the broad high dais where King Lorac's throne sat, a magnificent high seat of emerald and mahogany. Upon the mahogany where the king's shoulders rested, words of inlaid silver gleamed in the starlight: *As lives the land, so live the Elves.* Beside the throne a table stood, its surface made of rose glass, and upon that rosy surface an ivory sculpture of cupped hands, empty hands.

Dalamar looked down at the floor and his sandaled feet, and he drew in all his thoughts, gathering them, stilling them, and keeping them safe and private in the quietness

ithin himself. Those empty hands touched him deeply.
he eloquence of their beseeching matched a feeling he'd
ad all his life. Fill me up! Enlighten me! Grant me what I
eed and deserve! He would not look at the empty hands
gain. It was enough that he felt the ache of their yearning.

A footstep sounded on the stairs above. Three shadowy
gures came down the long winding staircase, their way lit
ot by torches but by two glowing spheres of magic-made
ght. The king, Ylle Savath of House Mystic, and Lord
aran of House Protector descended from the gallery to the
udience hall. Their robes rustled, whispering to the stone
eps—Lady Ylle's green robe of damasked silk, the king's
rocaded violet robe, Lord Garan's unadorned robe of rusty
old samite. Dalamar caught his breath, in spite of himself
npressed, for these three wore upon their backs more
realth than any servitor might hope to possess in all his
fe.

When the elf-king's foot touched the floor, the two
oung men, mage and cleric, each dropped to one knee.
ellin lowered his gaze and then his head. His hands, white-
nuckled, were still, but just barely. His face shone whiter
nan the king's, whiter than his robes. His lips moved, per-
aps in prayer. These things Dalamar saw out the corner of
is eye, his head only a little lowered.

Soft like the sigh of wind through the aspens, Ylle Savath
poke a word to dismiss the spheres of light. Now only the
ght of torches shone, and shadows leaping all around the
all as she said, "My lord king, here is a cleric and his ser-
ant who have requested audience of us all. The cleric is
ord Tellin Windglimmer. You might remember his grand-
ather who was head of the Temple of Branchala in the years
vhen I was a child."

The Speaker made a sound of assent.

"And his servant," said Lady Ylle, "is Dalamar Argent,
vhose mother was Ronen Windwalker and whose father
vas Derathos Argent of House Servitor." She lifted her head,

regarding Dalamar from beneath hooded lids. Her voic
was as cool as winter frost. "He is magic-taught."

Lord Garan moved restlessly, reacting to the news tha
the servant kneeling here in the Tower of the Stars was
mage. Steel rang, chiming faintly. Garan wears mail benea
that rich robe! Dalamar thought.

"Him?" Garan whispered to Ylle Savath. "He is traine
in magic? Could they find nothing else to do with him?"

Was there no other way to handle the embarrassment
a servant so inconveniently born with magic singing in h
blood? Dalamar felt his cheeks begin to flush. He closed h
eyes, willing the blood to retreat from his face, willing hir
self to keep still.

In the quiet, a footfall, slow and light on the marble floo
Lorac Caladon walked into the hall. He put a hand on Tellin
shoulder to bid him stand. He put another on Dalamar
and said, "Rise, young mage."

Dalamar lifted his eyes, and when Lorac offered the bare
twitch of a smile, he mirrored it not because he felt it, but
let his king know that he appreciated the courtesy.

"Lord Tellin," said Lorac, his pale eyes growing keen an
cool, "I have heard that you wish to come and speak to m
of the war."

Tellin lifted his chin, and he held his king's gaze. "I d
my lord king. I am not," he said, bowing to Lord Gara
"one who studies war, and I know there are others who—

Dalamar glanced swiftly from the king to his counselo
and to Tellin mouthing courtesies and compliments an
spending his words telling the king how much he did n
know about the matter he'd come to lay before them.
would not do.

"My lord king," Dalamar said, stepping a little forwar

Tellin's words died, the eyes of the august turned towar
the servant who should have kept his place and remaine
silent. Dalamar smiled at each, a small, cool gesture
acknowledgment.

"My lord king," he said, as though the silence had been what he was waiting for. "Lord Tellin has been good enough to use his name to get for me a thing my own name or station would not have availed. But now that I am here, and you are here, I will say this: I know that the war does not go well, and I know that the Highlord is bringing forces in from Goodlund and Balifor to augment her army."

"Silence!" Ylle Savath snapped. The light of the wall torches ran in her silvery hair. Shadows made her chin seem sharp, her patrician nose like the beak of an eagle. "Servitor, you have overstepped your bounds." She looked at the king and Lord Garan. "He should be removed."

Lord Garan stepped forward, his face flushed with the same anger that had made Lady Ylle's cheeks go pale. The impertinence of servants was not to be borne, and the presumption of this one who came prating about things of which he had no understanding—!

"I will remove him, my lord king."

Tellin moved, as though to object, but another was before him. Lorac laid a hand on Lord Garan's arm, a firm grip.

"No." Torches flared and sighed in their brackets, the light of their flames ran laughing in the jewels embedded in the wall. Lorac shook his head. A troubled look passed across his face, like a shadow running. "The boy doesn't lie, does he, Garan? He is having no groundless fantasy?"

The Head of House Protector scowled. Garan glared at Dalamar, but he did not deny what Speaker Lorac said.

"Now," said the king to Dalamar, "you have presumed to tell us what we already know. Tell us why you have come to speak the obvious."

"I do not come to speak the obvious, my lord king. I come to speak of a way to turn the tide of this war in our favor. I have a plan, and I think you will appreciate it when you hear it."

"A plan?" Lady Ylle snorted disbelief. "Now we are taking advice on battle tactics from temple servants?

61

Really, Lorac, how much more of your time do you have to waste?"

As much as I please, said the king's haughty glance. Aloud he said, "Patience, my lady. You and I have lived long enough to know that good news comes out of strange quarters. Lord Tellin is spending fistfuls of the goodwill that his family name earns him. No doubt he feels he spends it in a good cause. That says something in the servant's favor. Let us hear what these two have come to say. And"—he looked at Tellin, white in the face, and at Dalamar, who stood straight and tall and still didn't flinch from his king's scrutiny—"let us do so in a more comfortable place."

Lorac turned, looking at none of them, obliging all to follow as he led them into an alcove off the main chamber, a small room redly lit by hearth and torch.

"Are you mad?" Tellin whispered to Dalamar as they followed the king and his counselors. "Speaking that way to the king himself?"

"No," Dalamar murmured. "Quite sane, my lord. And as you will note"—he smiled—"we are here where we need to be."

All around the private chamber of the Speaker, candles glowed, orange pillars scented with barberry, green scented with pine, and white scented with the oils of winter-blooming jasmine. The colors of the candles and their delicate perfumes acted as heralds to the changing season. Tiny points of light danced in a breeze coming through the slivers of space between windows and sills. Shadows jumped and light leaped, drawing the eye round the little room. A wide, tall hearth dominated the south wall, the mantle filled with candles. Before it ranged large, comfortably cushioned chairs.

Wordlessly, the Speaker gestured his guests to chairs and assumed his own nearest the fire without waiting to see how they sorted themselves out. They did not do so easily,

or no one could quite reckon where in the arrangement a
servant must sit. In the end, and not unhappy with it, Dalamar did not sit at all. He stood behind Lord Tellin's chair
and gained for himself a commanding view of all those
gathered.

"Children," said the king, "tell me now what you have
come to say."

Dalamar glanced at Tellin, as a matter of form, and when
he cleric gestured, he said, "My king, it is plain to even the
humblest member of my House that the courage of Lord
Garan's Wildrunners will not likely stand against the
greater numbers of Phair Caron's army."

In the silence following his words, he heard the
speaker's breath hitch, just a little.

Lord Garan hissed a curse. "How dare you say that,
nageling?"

Dalamar ignored the insulting tone of Garan's voice and
he offensive diminutive. He looked to the king and spoke
only to him. "I dare say it, my king, because what I say is
true. It might not be convenient that this truth is noticed by
servitor, or that a servitor has considered it and reckoned
way around it, but not the less, what I say is true."

"You have a quick tongue, Dalamar Argent." Lorac leaned
forward, looking at Dalamar narrowly over the steeple of his
fingers. "A quick tongue, and you would do well to use it
now to tell me what plan you have made."

Fire snapped in the hearth, and ashes fell slithering into
he fire bed. Dalamar's mouth went suddenly dry, and the
words of an old saying came mocking to mind: *Who leaps,
leaps best when he knows where he will land.* Of course, who
doesn't leap at all, knowing or unknowing, gets to stand at
he edge of the precipice until he must turn back with nothing earned but the failure to act.

Unacceptable.

"I would strike at the Highlord from behind, my king,
and—"

Lord Garan's laughter snapped out, stinging. "You'd d
that, eh? Haven't you heard that all the northern lands from
Khur to Nordmaar are occupied by Phair Caron's army?"

"I've heard," Dalamar murmured, his eyes low, a smal
smile playing around his lips. He looked up again, assum
ing an expression of innocent frankness that fooled th
Head of House Protector not at all. "No doubt you'v
heard, my lord, that there is a mage or two in the kingdom
with skills that might facilitate my idea? Illusions skillfull
cast will make our forces advancing from the south seen
invisible to the eyes of the Highlord's army, while at th
same time other illusions will make it seem they are bein
attacked from the north." He smiled, a chill twitch of hi
lips. "At which time, they'll turn to fight what isn't ther
while the Wildrunners surround and attack them . . . from
behind."

Ylle Savath, until then silent, lifted a hand, with th
simple gesture capturing the attention of all. "My lor
king," she said, "it might be well to remind this servitor tha
illusions are not the province of White magic. They are th
province of Red magic. Here," she said, turning a glanc
upon Dalamar that was cold as winter and as dangerous
"here we practice constructive magic."

"And yet," Dalamar replied in his mildest tone, "it seem
to me that we had better learn to construct some illusions
my lady."

Ylle Savath's eyes glinted sharp as knives. "If you ar
suggesting we practice any magic other than Solinari's, yo
come perilously close to blasphemy, Dalamar Argent."

Blasphemy.

The word hung in the stillness of the room. It seemed th
flames in the hearth whispered it, once and again. At las
Lorac stood, his face expressionless and masked b
shadows.

"Young mage," he said, inclining his head in the onl
bow a king need make, that of courtesy to one of his people

"Young cleric, you have my leave to return to your homes. May E'li bless you on your way."

He lifted a hand and dropped it again. The flames in the hearth fell. The torches dimmed. Thus did the elf-king, the highest of all mages in his land, signal that there would be no more conversation here tonight, on this subject or any other.

* * * * *

Cardinals sang their chipping songs in the hedges of the Garden of Astarin. Late-goers, they were the last songbirds to sleep, the heralds of nightingales. The light of half-moons shone down, red and silver on the path away from the Tower of the Stars. Dalamar's blood sang brave songs, as it did when he was preparing to work magic. He had stood before the king, before Heads of Households, and he had laid out a bold plan, one he knew could work.

"It was a waste," Tellin said, "a waste of time and a waste of—"

Dalamar raised an eyebrow. "And a waste of the good will your family name gets you? Do you really think so, my lord?"

Tellin snorted. "Did you see the way Lady Ylle reacted to your idea? 'Blasphemy,' she called it. I tell you, Dalamar, you won no friends there. You won no favor with Lord Garan either, lecturing him on battleground tactics. What, by the names of all the gods of Good, makes you think either of them will second your plan to the king, even if Lorac is interested in it?"

Dalamar stopped, standing a long moment listening to the night. Wind sighed in the trees. Somewhere in the darkness a child laughed, and a woman's voice lifted in evensong, a lullaby for her baby. Lights glimmered in all the hollows and on all the hills. Towers built of marble rose up white in the starlight, some grand and high with wings of rooms reaching out from the base, others smaller and built in humbler imitation of their wealthy neighbors. A nightingale sang, and another joined in, their sweet liquid notes sounding in his heart like the very song of the nighttime forest.

"My Lord Tellin," he said, "they are talking of leaving here, the king and the Sinthal-Elish. You've heard the rumor. If things keep on as they are . . ." He looked away north to the borderlands. "If things keep on, I don't think it will be long before they make up their minds."

Tellin shuddered, his eyes dark in the night. Elves leave the Sylvan Land? Wasn't that, too, a kind of blasphemy? "How could they even consider it?"

Dalamar looked over his shoulder to the Tower of the Stars rising above the whispering crowns of the aspens. Light shone from windows normally dark at this hour. Yes, the king sat waking. He was thinking, turning over the plan presented him by a minor mage of a lowly House, a scheme that bore the taint of blasphemy. Of this, Dalamar was certain, for a dragonarmy savaged his northern reaches, and Lorac Caladon had no choice but to consider all options. Whether he'd choose this one or not, none could say. But he was considering.

"Desperate people, my lord, do things they might not otherwise consider."

Tellin smiled, but without humor. "So you've solved all the problems, have you, Dalamar?"

"No, my lord, not all."

In silence, he followed Tellin through the Garden of Astarin, past Astarin's temple where chanting prayers were sung, round the fragrant beds of jasmine and late wisteria, of starweed and moonflower and nodding columbine. Men and women of House Gardener worked there by the light of tall torches, watering flower beds, for such work was best done at night while the earth has respite from the thirsty sun. The earthy scent of wet dirt drifted up. Fireflies

lanced in the recesses of each hedge, hungry for the larvae
of slugs.

It had been, indeed, love of his homeland that moved
Dalamar to conceive this plan he'd put before the king—a
real and abiding love such as every elf knows. He had not
thought more than this moved him, not until this moment
in the Garden of Astarin with the fireflies winking and the
scent of jasmine in the air. As he walked, a wild hope rose
again in his breast, one he'd thought banished. When his
plan succeeded—and he knew it would—he would ask Lord
Tellin to present his case to the mages of House Mystic, to
ask that he be instructed as all other mages are, fully in the
magic art. He dared hope now, for he'd stood among lords
and spoken with a king who had heard him out, a king who
might well heed what he heard.

When this plan proved itself, he would tell Lord Tellin
that he wanted to learn all the magic he could and then one
day go to the Tower of High Sorcery at Wayreth, there to
apply to the Conclave of Wizards in hope that they would
grant him permission to take his Tests of Sorcery.

* * * * *

Two days later, in the morning, while Dalamar sat in the
scriptorium with the usual basket of quills to sharpen, a
message came to the Temple, a short missive tersely worded,
saying that the servitor Dalamar Argent must go to the home
of the Head of House Mystic, and he must be there before
the noon hour. Dalamar presented himself long before that
time, where he learned—not from Ylle Savath herself but
from one of her mages—that he would be among those who
would travel north to the borderlands, there to bespell a
dragonarmy.

"Let him live or die by his plan," Lady Ylle said on the
day that Lorac announced he'd follow the advice of a
servitor.

That she'd said as one pronouncing a dark doom. Yet, Dalamar heard her command as the first note of a brave song, one to tell of his dream, long thought impossible, at last waking to reality.

Chapter 5

Phair Caron looked over her army spread out below like a great dark sea, restless and hungry. The long-legged woman in her red dragon armor, the lusty shape of her not hidden by mail and breastplate, stood like a queen overseeing her kingdom. Her hair, normally bundled up under her dragon helm, hung loose now to her shoulders, a golden spill of waving curls to catch the sunlight. It was her beauty that softened, if only a little, a face long ago shaped to hardness by want and rage. Eyes the color of the blue edges of swords, she looked around, satisfied. The tors of the Khalkist Mountains were her stony halls. Rising higher than the towers of any elf-lord, they housed her well. All round their base supply camps ranged, cook tents and food depots, even a small city of smiths with their forges. The smoke rose up like the smoke over a battleground. Anvils rang as brawny human smiths worked at repairing breastplates and greaves, at forging new blades for swords damaged in the fighting. She could have wished for dwarf smiths, but those were hard to come by, locked up in Thorbardin while the Council of Thanes decided whether or not to get involved in the war.

Phair Caron looked west to the land of Abanasinia, whose spine was the Kharolis Mountains. The estranged cousins of the Silvanesti lived there, the wood-dwelling Qualinesti. Humans lived there, and hill dwarves. Already Verminaard, the Highlord of the Blue Wing, had his eye on them, laying cruel plans and ready to swoop down upon those lands like an eagle after its prey. One day, if not sooner then later, all these lands and all the people who lived therein would belong to Her Dark Majesty. The forces of Takhisis would sweep south to Icewall and north to

Solamnia to topple the towers of Vingaard and Solanthus. In her might, the Dark Queen would range even so far as the Ergoths. All of Krynn would be hers, a shrine to her glory built upon the bones of those who defied.

Her blood humming in her, her heart high, Phair Caron looked south, to the dark line of the Silvanesti Forest. The Highlords of Takhisis would be as kings and queens in Krynn. She smiled, a wolfish baring of her teeth. *This* Highlord would rule from Silvanost, and she would have for her slaves the lords and ladies of Lorac Caladon's court.

A roar came up distantly from below, the sound of her army, the restless hordes of humans and goblins, draconians and ogres. It had not been easy, organizing this army of disparate races. Humans refused to camp near ogres, who would not be anywhere near goblins. No one could get within striking distance of any of the three breeds of draconians without small wars erupting, and among them, the Baaz hated the venomous Kapaks, who loathed them in turn and despised the Auraks.

A long dark shadow passed over the hilltop as Blood Gem sailed on the warm currents, drifting on the sky. Terror kept all the factions of the Highlord's army in line, the dread of the dragons sunning themselves upon the tors. Often bored between forays into the forest, the mighty wyrms were happy to snatch a recalcitrant ogre or insubordinate human right out from the crowd of his companions and make a proper example of him. The dragons were Phair Caron's insurance of good order. With that general order insured, she practiced the kind of hard-handed control for which she had become known among the Dark Queen's Highlords. Whichever of her lieutenants failed to keep order among his men failed only once. There were, here and in the lands she'd early conquered, plenty of others willing and able to take the place of the man or woman who could not maintain discipline.

Above, a wing of dragons circled in the sky, long lazy

rounds that took them out over the aspen forest just turning gold with the approach of autumn. Blood Gem abandoned his lazy circling and went to join his kin. Phair Caron felt the joy in him as he looked down upon the destruction he and his kind had wrought, the smoldering, and the wide swaths of land that would not see a tree again for many long years.

It is good! the dragon called, feeling her thought touch his mind.

It is good, she agreed silently, the woman who had once scrambled in gutter-filth for a bent copper tossed her by an elf too disdainful to wait for her thanks. The flames of her ambition, of her long need for revenge, burned in her blood, firing her heart and her soul. It seemed to Phair Caron, as she stood upon the heights, that she could see as far as Silvanost, as far as that day when Lorac Caladon would be led before her in chains, condemned to death, the sentence carried out by stoning in the widest square of his city.

A small figure moved among the army, his step determined, his way clearing easily before him. Goblins moved aside, their ranks rippling as he went. When he crossed the unofficial boundary between their camp and that of the ogres, it was the same. This one went untroubled as soldiers who had only the day before dealt mercilessly with elf villagers scrambled to get out of his way. Thus did the mage Tramd o' the Dark make his way to the high side of the army's encampment, the place where water came down in trickling streams from the tors. Two tents stood there, a small space apart from each other and well apart from all those housing the lieutenants and captains of the dragonarmy. One was of red silk and had a bright red pennon waving from the center pole. Peaked, even chambered, it stood like a splotch of bright blood amidst the dun and black and browns of the army. The second tent was a simpler affair, smaller, with leather sides and no pennon flapping from the pole. To the first Phair Caron looked, for she knew that was where the mage was going, head down and moving quickly.

Blood Gem, she called.

My lady?

Tell him to meet me in my tent.

As you wish, my lady.

The red dragon peeled off from the others, stretching his long neck and bugling to the sky. The army moved, shifting like an uneasy sea before a storm wind. Ogres raised knotted fists to the sky, all bravado. Humans moved restlessly among themselves while goblins scurried. In the far eastern part of the encampment, draconians gave no sign of having heard. They felt about dragons as dragons felt about them. Tramd stopped and looked up, then he turned his steps away from the red tent and toward the leather one.

Phair Caron smiled grimly. He was a good mage, this Tramd, and a good man in the field when it came to leading battles from dragonback. Among the elves he was known and not known, his presence felt in bloody carnage, though no two elves ever seemed to be able to agree on a description of him. Ogre, human, dwarf, even once an elf—all these were reported as being seen leading the attacks on the villages, a mage whose terrible voice boomed out over the burning and the killing. They thought he was a shapeshifter, some terrible creature out of the bloody Abyss. He was not that, though he was terrible.

Phair Caron went bounding down the hill, the horned dragon helm tucked under her arm, her long sword slapping against her mailed thigh. A good man, terrible in battle, but Tramd had an annoying habit of disappearing from time to time. About this, they would now speak.

* * * * *

When Phair Caron entered her tent, Tramd turned from the map pinned to the north wall. He had been studying it, his head thrust a little forward, his shoulders a little hunched. All of Silvanesti lay upon that map, the burned reaches and the forest beyond.

"My lady," said the mage, whom the elves of the northern border feared, whom the members of the dragonarmy itself did fear. "I am here as you asked."

Outside, the sound of the army was the sound of an ocean, ebbing and flowing, five thousand voices mingling with ten thousand more, undercurrents of ringing mail, blades belling on blades as warriors practiced their skills. The song of her army! Phair Caron set her dragon helm on the small table, straps whispering against the rough wood, steel ringing faintly in the musty air. She hooked a stool with one foot, dragged it behind the table, then sat. In silence she looked at the mage, leveled a long blue stare at the handsome face he showed her. Tall as a barbarian Plainsman, he wore a human shape today. His hair matched hers in thickness and in golden color, and the beard he wore grew long to the belt of his black robe.

Phair Caron smiled, but only to herself, only inwardly. Shaped like a man, a woman, an ogre, a draconian, whatever guise he liked, this mage was no shapeshifter. He was a dwarf. His gestures sometimes showed it, his expression and turns of phrase often bespoke it. He wore avatars the way a courtier wore his fabulous wardrobe, each scraped up from the earth itself, by magic shaped of clay and stone, each chosen exactly for the occasion. And so, Tramd did not, in fact, stand here beside her. This avatar was only a lifeless creation enlivened by the mind of a mage who lived in a far place Phair Caron had never seen. Nor had she ever encountered him in his true form. He would never permit it. Those who thought they saw him, saw what the mage wished to be seen, and if his whim decreed that anything of his true physical existence be presented, it was only his voice.

"I looked for you, Tramd. This morning when the captains came to give me their reports of yesterday's battle,

I thought you would be among them."

A voice shouted outside. Nearby someone cursed, but the curse suddenly cut off. The scent of blood hung thick on the air. Phair Caron didn't look around, and into her stony stare Tramd shrugged, a small gesture. "I had other business."

A frisson of anger raced through her. "Indeed. It seems you have had other business often."

Tramd raised an eyebrow. "If you want to ask about my business, ask. You'll get the same reply I always give: Your business is yours, and I will make it mine because you ask. My business is mine, and no one needs to make it their own."

A dark-cased insect crept across the floor—a beetle of some kind and nearly half the size of her palm. Absently, Phair Caron crushed it, smiling to hear the crackle of its shell bursting. She lifted her booted foot to look at the mess, satisfied. "Careful, Tramd. You're not quite right in your statements. You make my business yours because it suits you to go throughout Krynn with my army. Times might change, my friend, and you might find it doesn't suit me to have you here."

The avatar's handsome face remained quietly calm, and his green eyes glittered. "Times always change, my lady. I don't worry about that."

His coolness irritated her. She traced the winding pattern on her dragon helm, a line to suggest the tail of a dragon. Eyes narrowed, she stared at the avatar of a mage whom she had never seen. A pile of rotting flesh with a keen-edged mind, that's what rumor said of Tramd o' the Dark. Sometimes in the night she would recall the tale, and that story made even her shudder. There are tests mages take if they want to be more than hedge-wizards, more than mere peddlers of love potions and salves to banish warts. No one had ever said the tests were easy ones. Still, how many who spoke so blithely of those tests understood how truly terrible they could be? Not many. Tramd, wherever the man himself did stay, knew how terrible. It was said—and he never denied it—that his body was ruined in the tests, so badly ravaged that only magic and the will of a mind so powerful kept him living.

As though idly, Phair Caron said, "Can't you wait till the conquering is done before you begin searching for loot?"

Blood mounted to Tramd's bearded cheeks. That characterization of his quest was an insult. "Lady, you push me—"

On the hilltops, dragons bugled, the mighty reds shouting to one another, preening, strutting, anxious for battle. One flew overhead, and a dark shadow ran on the ground, rippling on the walls of the tent. Phair Caron felt their eagerness as her own.

"Enough!" she snapped. "It is you who push me. From now on, you leave my army when I tell you to. You don't come and go at your own will. The campaign will move faster now. The elves are throwing all they have at the border, and all they have isn't going to be enough. We'll be striking harder and more often. I need you here."

He said nothing for a long moment, yea or nay, as another dragon flew over—and then another, their shadows tangling on the leather tent walls. When he looked up, his eyes gleamed coldly, a man who has weighed matters and decided what to do. "As you will, my lady. Now, there is a small matter to discuss. One," he said smoothly, "that repeatedly comes to my attention as I go among the army."

When she gestured, he stepped around the table to the map pinned to the tent wall, the dragon shadows spinning webs of shade across his back. With one sweeping gesture, he indicated all of Silvanesti. "We've won some battles here, my lady. And yet we hang back, keeping to the tors."

She shrugged. "And?"

"And the army wonders when we will move into the forest."

Phair Caron laughed. "Looking for more loot than can be found in little villages, are they? Heads all filled up with the fabled treasures of elven cities?" She turned her head and spat. "I don't care. We do this as we have always done, as we did in Nordmaar and Goodlund and Balifor—not until the cities are clogged with refugees, until the armies have to fall back to defend the people, will we leave this place. In the meantime, let them come against us. Let them spend men and strength and treasure in getting to us."

"And so . . .?"

Phair Caron shrugged. "So, kill a few of the naysayers—very publicly—and get on with organizing the next raid." She turned from him to the map pinned to the north wall of the tent. "And yes," she said, granting an oft-given boon, "you may keep the heart-blood."

He did not acknowledge that but left in silence. After a while, the long winding wails of a killing that would take some time rent the silence. Phair Caron smiled.

* * * * *

The songs of birds fell silent. In the boxwood bounding the Garden of Astarin, the cardinals were mute. Gray titmice, purple finches, and humble sparrows had nothing to say. Mockingbirds went deep into the hedges, the white chevrons marking their wings hidden, their boisterous cries a thing for another day. No butterflies hovered over the small pots of sand scattered round the garden. Ladybirds did not dot the late roses. It was as though all the creatures of the garden had fled or now stood in awe of the great gathering of elves.

If the garden stood silent, it was perhaps the only quiet place in Silvanost. Not even the sky kept peaceful. Golden griffins circled the city with proud Windriders on their backs. Sun glinted from the harnesses of the riders and the cruel beaks of the beasts. There were two dozen in the sky, an outrider of the six full prides that would converge upon the borderlands. Upon the back of the largest griffin, head high, his jeweled sword belted on, his mail shirt of finest linked steel shining, Lord Garan of House Protector led his pride to the Tower of the Stars where the Speaker stood upon the highest balcony.

Alhana stood beside her father. The king glittered in gold and silks. His daughter, her hand on his arm, shone white as a lily, her dark hair piled high upon her head and dressed in diamonds, her robe purest white samite. As Garan passed them, the lily princess lifted her hand, and Lord Garan removed his helm in salute.

"Lord Garan!" the people cried, the women waving green kerchiefs from their balconies, the men cheering mightily from the windows. "Lord Garan, for E'li! Lord Garan, for Silvanesti!"

On the ground, the voices of the army rose and fell, filling the courtyard and the streets around the Tower of the Stars. To hear the Wildrunners, to see them, any would think they were nothing but an enormous party of hunters out to provide a Feast Day's fare. Laughter skirled high in rough joking and horseplay. The colors of the army, the green and gold of the beloved aspenwood, sailed in the chill autumn breezes. Upon the balconies and in the windows of the towers surrounding the home of the Speaker of the Stars, men and women and children in brightly colored clothing came to stand and watch the Wildrunners, some cheering, others silent. All tried to keep each moment in memory, impress each sight upon the heart. Below them, in the green and the gray, were the sons and daughters of House Protector. The regard in which they were held crossed the threshold of every House, for here was the proud flower of Silvanesti might, men and women sworn to spill their blood, break their hearts, and offer up their lives if must be.

These were but a small part of the army massing. In

Shalost, to the north and west, Wildrunners were coming. This force from Silvanost would join them, for it was in Shalost upon the grounds of Waylorn's Tower that griffins would be gathering, the mighty beasts prepared to carry the archers into battle. The army of Silvanost would have a two-day run to Waylorn's Tower, and once in the forest, the Wildrunners would vanish into silence and shadow, dispersing in groups of no more than a dozen, often less. The army of the Silvanesti did not travel like the armies of any outlander nation. They were elves, the least experienced among them would be indistinguishable from a shadow if he so willed.

Out where the southern edge of Garden of Astarin lay shining in the sun, near the Temple of the Blue Phoenix where those of House Woodshaper lived, the gray and green became edged with white, like a cloud dropped low over a hillside. Mages came, a long line of them, and their scent—spices, dried rose petals, oils, and herbs—granted exotic undertones to the smell of leather and steel and sweat of an army gathering. At their head marched Ylle Savath. She who ruled House Mystic would see to the execution of this magical maneuver—this servant's plan!—and leave nothing to chance. It had not been so hard to find spells of illusion, though such were not the province of white magic. What was forbidden among mages here was also recorded. The mages she had chosen for the job were those she deemed worthy, those who had sterling reputations and would swear to discharge this alien magic and never touch it again. Among these, at the far end of the line, was one of whom she was not so certain, and yet one she felt compelled to include. "Let him live or die by his plan," she had said to the king. She felt deeply that such impudence as Dalamar Argent's should be met with the charge to lay his life where he asked others to lay theirs.

* * * * *

78

The heady scent of magic filled Dalamar's heart. All around him were those who had once counted him as no one among them, and who now knew that he had forged the plan to which they dedicated their strength and their will. In him, the deferred hope flamed. He would come out from this worthy of all House Mystic had denied him. Who would forbid him the knowledge he needed now? Who would say then, "No. You cannot go and take your Tests of High Sorcery"?

A hand gripped his shoulder, and a low voice said, "Good morning to you, Dalamar Argent."

Dalamar turned to find Tellin Windglimmer beside him. "Have you come to wish me luck, my lord?"

Somewhere a trumpet sounded, a bright note soaring above the rumble of the crowd. A ripple of excitement passed through the Wildrunners, and their joking and laughter fell to a muted murmuring. The shape of the crowd began to change as they formed themselves into small groups.

Tellin smiled, a wry grin. "Well, I do wish you luck." He let a fat pack drop at his feet. "But that's not why I'm here."

"Indeed?" Dalamar drew breath to ask the begged question, then held. Tellin's eye had wandered and, wandering, stopped. On the grounds of the Temple of the Blue Phoenix, a woman stood, hands clasped and gray eyes searching the crowd of Wildrunners and mages. Lady Lynntha smiled suddenly, swiftly, then turned when someone spoke to her. Lord Ralan took her arm and led her back from the edge of the crowd.

Again, a trumpet called, its notes like silver floating on the day. From outside the city's gates a war-horn sounded, deep and low. City called to forest, and forest answered. Color drained from Tellin's face, the pulse jumped in his throat, and he said, "I'm here because I'm going north with the army. There are a few other clerics going, too."

"To administer to the souls of soldiers, eh?"

Tellin caught the ironic tone Dalamar didn't try to hard to hide. "Why, yes," he said, "of course."

But his eyes were still on Lady Lynntha, on her slender straight back and her crown of silver hair. When she lifted her hand to brush a straying curl from her cheek, that pulse in his neck beat harder, hammering until Tellin saw her truly gone into the crowd. The cleric hefted his pack and slung it over his shoulder. Out from his pocket, jogged by the sudden motion, a brightly embroidered scroll case fell. Dalamar bent to pick it up. When he dusted it clean with the sleeve of his hem, the scent of the lady's perfume graced the air, lilacs and ferns.

"My lord," he said, handing the case to Tellin.

Lord Tellin put the case back, looking suddenly defensive. "You are not," he said, coolly, "the only man in Silvanost with dreams."

So it seemed, but Dalamar didn't think his dream would be harder to earn than Lord Tellin's. In House Mystic they respected talent or could be brought to do so. In House Woodshaper they didn't care who you were, cleric or war hero—if you were not of their clan, you still weren't going to marry one of their dear daughters.

* * * * *

Red light glowed in the smallest corner of the brazier. Shadows crawled up the silk walls of the red tent and flowed down again from the top. Tramd dipped his fingers into a black earthenware bowl and drew them out tipped with blood. Heart-blood, he sprinkled it upon the stones ringed round his small fire, painting runes on the stone, hunt-runes, treasure-runes, runes to ensure luck. He was, as Phair Caron guessed, a dwarf. Not here, not now in this tall barbarian shape, but in the far place where he dwelt, in the high towers of his citadel, he was a dwarf. He knew about runes, and he knew about luck, for dwarves count on one as heavily as on the other.

The runes writ, Tramd watched as the fire baked the blood black and small cracks appeared in the marks. Into those cracks he looked—past blackened blood, past stone itself, and into a small corner of the Plane of Magic. The darkness swirled under his glance. He drew a breath in, let a breath out, and the fire danced.

"Come," he whispered, the voice of the avatar shaping the will of the mage. "Come out and be ready. Be ready to run."

The darkness deepened, then shifted, taking form on the distant plane that exists outside the world of the five senses. On the red silk walls, shadows swirled and ran together, small children of that darkness, massing at the top where the vent hole drew out the smoke. In one corner of that mass, something bright grew, like an eye opening.

Tramd held his breath, aware of the eye, not daring to take his attention from the cracks in the baked blood. The cracks closed, a little at a time, healing, but were he to look away, even for an instant—such things would flow out as would chill the hearts of dragons and strike such fear into the souls of mortals that they would run mad. The eye glowed, went dark, then glowed again. The cracks in the blood healed, slowly.

On the wall the shadows took one shape, that of a hound with squinting eyes and jaws agape. The hound's howling wound through the soul of the mage, a long, eerie wail like the cry of a wolf separate from his pack. Fire sighed, and the black blood-runes closed their wounds, shutting out darkness. Tramd sat back on his heels, looking up at the red wall, the shadow-hound seeming to breathe as the red silk moved to a vagrant breeze off the tors.

"Hound," said the mage, his eyes on the eye, his will chaining the beast even as the beast heard his voice. "Hound, will you hunt?" The glaring eye blinked, light, no light, light again. The hound would hunt. "Go down into the forest," Tramd commanded. "Go out and search, and come back to tell me what magic you find, book or artifact, scroll or ring or pendant. Go, and then come again."

The shadow-hound slid from the wall, a waking thing, though not a living thing. Through the night it ran, a child of darkness passing through darkness as fishes do the sea. Down into the forest, beneath the light of the three-quarter moons it ran into the burned lands, the place of charred trunks and ash where now and again embers winked, eyes in the ruin watching the shadow-hound run. In villages it ran, and when it passed by houses where people slept, it passed as a nightmare, a chilling of sleep, a groaning. When it passed through ruin, it ran faster, for nothing remained to find there. Some things of magic it discovered, for this was a kingdom where mages were honored. The hound sensed rings of power, swords whose blades had struck down ogres, whose gemmed hilts wore runes of strength to turn back curses. It found these things in the little towns between the burned borderlands and the straight-running King's Road. Swift as a cold wind out of winter, the hound passed the encampment of a horde of elves, ragged folk, bleeding folk, old women and men and little children who sobbed themselves to sleep. Sleepers woke wailing when the hound slipped round the light of their fires and ran swiftly on.

Beneath the eyes of Solinari and Lunitari and the eye no one saw but some felt, Nuitari's dark moon, the beast of magic ran. It passed the perimeters of many camps of Wild-runners, and some magic it found there. This it did not bother to reckon. Its master would pick the bones of these dead when they fell in battle. One more thing of magic it found, some books enspelled by wards. Three were slender, nothing strongly shining. A fourth, thick and old, was a thing worth noting. The hound discovered these in a cave not far from the city of the elf-king, fair Silvanost, the shining jewel upon the breast of the kingdom.

Satisfied at last, the shadow-hound returned to the tent

of its master. All the things that the shadow-hound had discovered and reckoned gained it better than praise from its master.

"For the count of twenty," said Tramd to the fire-eyed darkness, "you may run among the sleeping, out there in the army. Take what you will and do with it as you please."

The hound slipped out from under the tent, red eyes gleaming like embers after a burning. Curious, Tramd stepped outside the tent. In the cool night he watched the shadow run, rippling over the ground, formless now. The cold light of stars shone down. The moons had set. Like red eyes in the night, the army's myriad campfires glowed. He watched the hound course, the shadow running, and he felt his blood stir, the blood of the avatar, the blood of the ruined heap of flesh and bone lying far away in a bed of silks and satin. The hound leaped—he felt it!—and it tore something from a sleeping warrior. Not something to bleed, not something to break. It tore out the soul of the luckless one and four others besides.

Tramd smiled. He sighed and felt the shadow-hound fill up with the essence of its victims, their every thought and wish and dream, each fear, each weakness, the sum of their spirits. He laughed, a low and terrible sound like stones grinding together, as the beast took those souls and dragged them back to the darkness from whence it came.

He watched as the un-souled ran wailing among the army, screaming. He saw them caught, saw them killed, and he heard the ones who did the killing say to each other, "Madness. Just as well they're dead." After all, these were ogres, and sometimes those went mad and had to be killed. In the place where the hound dwelt, though, the wailing and screaming never ended.

In the morning, Tramd noted all the things of magic the shadow-hound had located, reckoned where they were and marked them upon the map he kept in a small silver coffer. He had done this in each land the Highlord's army swept through, a treasure hunter hunting. As he had in Goodlund, in Nordmaar, in Balifor, he would visit all these places once the people had been brought to heel and Phair Caron's governments were set up. He would take these treasures and test them. While he wondered if one of the things found here would be the treasure he had so long quested for, Tramd ate some breakfast, then went out for a walk in the new day. His wondering done for the time, he went to tell his Highlord that a great army of elves was on the move. "And the refugees we sent running into the forest are now only a short journey from Silvanost. They're hungry and ragged and ready to eat the autumn harvest and still look for more from the winter stores.

"My lady," he said as she looked up from her breakfast of wine and cheese, "the beginning of the end of the elves is here."

Chapter 6

In the dawn of the day, with the sky turning to rosy
lavender and the late night mists rising from the little lily
ponds in the Garden of Astarin, Alhana Starbreeze went
through the Tower of the Stars, through high chambers and
low, in search of her father. She went in silence, as was her
way. Her soft leather slippers made no sound upon the
marble floors. The hem of her azure damasked gown did
not whisper against her ankles. She wore upon her arms the
golden bracelets her father had given to her mother upon
the day of her birth, nine circlets, each shaped like twining
vines. These did not ring one against another as she went,
for she walked with her hands clasped before her, tightly
held so that her knuckles shone white where bone pressed
against flesh.

She went from room to room. In his empty bedchamber
a green tunic lay upon the bed, embroidered in silver runes.
Beside lay hose of softest brushed wool. At the foot of the
bed on the cool marble floor stood Lorac's slippers, golden
leather tanned to buttery softness. A small coffer of mahogany chased with silver sat unopened beside the tunic. In it,
she knew, lay the Speaker's jewels, necklaces, pendants, circlets to hold his hair from his brow—all made by the most
skilled dwarf smiths in the days when there had been commerce between Silvanesti and Thorbardin. That was a long
time ago. Now the dwarves kept themselves apart from the
world in their mountain fastness, and the Silvanesti elves
stayed always within the confines of the Barrier Hedge. The
only thing they had in common was their need to keep
themselves removed from the rest of the world and a stubborn disdain for outlanders.

Alhana did not find her father in the library or the music

room. She hastened to the solarium, but he was not there. Neither was he in the arboretum, though she had hoped to find him there, enjoying the rising light in those sweet sunny rooms where flowers grew in riotous profusion. She went out onto the gallery where it rounded the well of the audience chamber, and her heart sank.

A green glow, shimmering and shining, reached up from the floor of the audience hall and stained the white marble rail and balustrades to the unpleasant green of algae scumming on a still pond. A cold sheen of sweat broke out on her face. She had seen this light before, in dark dungeons in the late watches when her father had waked from nightmare.

Her hand on the cold marble rail, Alhana leaned over, looking down into the well, and there she saw Lorac Caladon. He sat upon his throne, hunched over a little. He held something cradled in his hands, a thing from which that dreadful light emanated. The green glow shone upward, giving his face a terrible hue, a corpse's hue.

Alhana shuddered. Her heart pounding, she lifted her skirts and ran swiftly across the floor to the wide, winding staircase.

"Father!" she cried, her voice ringing in echoes around the gallery and into the well of the chamber below.

He looked up, but only slowly, as one who is roused from a deep sleep. His face held no color but that of the orb's green glow. With startling suddenness, his eyes flashed, like lightning leaping out from running clouds.

"Be still!" he called.

And he was her father. He was her king.

Alhana stopped midstep, her hand upon the cold marble banister, her foot poised to take the last step.

"Father?"

His voice an ugly snarl, he said, "Be still."

The light of the orb pulsed, like a malevolent heart beating.

Far away, up in the gallery, she heard the voices of servants talking to each other, a woman's raised in question, a man's enjoining silence. Alhana took a step closer to her father, down from the last stair and onto the floor of the audience hall.

"Father," she whispered, "Father, you frighten me. Are you well?"

He did not move, not even to look at her. Another step, and another, and now, by the last light of day, she saw her father's lips tremble. Why, this is the trembling of an old man, she thought, the thought itself like a whisper of treason.

Lorac old? Lorac trembling? Lorac—oh, dear gods, was he frightened?

The green glow faded, drawing back from the king's face, from the hall, and returning to the orb itself. Emboldened, Alhana took another step and then another. At last, when Lorac made no protest, she ran swiftly across the hard marble floor, her little slippers pattering now, her arm-rings jangling in metal's harshest voice. She ran, and she knelt beside him, the Speaker on his throne.

He sat in perfect stillness. His face, like marble, showed no expression, but his eyes, his eyes . . .

Alhana Starbreeze covered her father's hands with her own, gently. When he did not resist, she lifted the orb and set it upon the stand. In the moment she did, she nearly dropped it. The stand, once white ivory and shaped like two hands lifted in offering, had changed. It was the same stand. She knew it. She could see that, but something had warped it. Something had scraped and clawed it, and now it was not two hands at all, but one large, broad claw with five talons curled. Into those talons, into that claw, the dragon orb of Istar fit as neatly as it had always done.

"My child," whispered the king, her father looking up at her, "my poor Alhana."

His eyes were awash in sadness so deep, so terrible, that

Alhana, seeing them, felt she would fall into them as into a drowning pool.

"Father." She touched his face and held it with both hands. Beneath her hands she felt a trembling, the flesh of his face quivering. It was, she thought in horror, in pity, as though he longed to weep but had lost the ability. "Father, please tell me. What is wrong?"

He looked at her from within the frame of her white hands, and now she saw that his pupils were dilated, grown so wide that they gave his eyes the appearance of being coal black. Alhana shivered, and she withdrew her glance in fear. But she did not withdraw her hands, for she feared that if she let him go, her father, the king of all the Sylvan Land, would fall away, spinning down into a terrible dark place.

"My child," he said, his voice quavering. "My child, the world is lost."

What spell had the orb cast to catch him? What spell out of doomed Istar worked here in Silvanost?

"No," she murmured, stepping back, her hands still on him so that he, too, must rise. "No," she said softly, urgently, her arm around his shoulders. How thin they seemed! How bowed down with care! "Father, the world is *not* lost. Neither is the kingdom. We have the gods on our side. We have E'li himself, and so we *will* prevail."

Lorac said nothing to agree or protest. Breathing shallowly, like a man in sleep, he allowed her to lead him down from the throne and up the long winding staircase to his chambers. They went in haste, or as quickly as Alhana could manage, for though she neither saw nor heard servants in the gallery, she did hear their voices in the various chambers they passed. She must not allow Lorac to be seen in this condition, not under any circumstance.

Once safely inside her father's suite, she found his chamberlain there, old Lelan, and gave the king into his care. Whispering and hushing, Lelan took the king to his bed and settled him there, sweeping all his careful arrangement of clothing to the floor and tossing the mahogany coffer into a corner of the room as though it were all some pile of leaves blown in with the wind.

"What has happened to him, Lady?" he asked, pulling the bedsilk up over the king's shoulders, daring from long affection to smooth the king's hair back from his face as he would a feverish child's.

Alhana shook her head. "I don't know. I found him like this." She said nothing of the Orb. "Tend him as best you can, Lelan, and be certain to say nothing to anyone. My father will come to himself soon, and we will see that he suffers only from lack of sleep and too much care. I don't have to tell you how deeply it would embarrass him to learn that news of this"—she groped for a word—"this discomfiture had reached *anyone's* ears."

Lelan bowed. "It will be as you say, my lady."

It would be, she knew, and that knowledge made up the full sum of her confidence as she walked out into the gallery again. Down in the audience hall where the Emerald Throne sat, where the Dragon Orb crouched upon the transformed stand, green light again pulsed. Very faintly it shone now, as though from a great distance.

By the light of that glow Alhana Starbreeze had the sudden vision of her own hands upon the crystal globe, her own fingers grasping the smoothness of the Orb, light shining through and showing what flesh hid—bones and muscle and even blood pulsing through veins. She saw herself lifting the Orb and carrying it all the way up to the gallery, there to lean out over the rail and fling this artifact of unholy Istar down to smash upon the cold marble of the floor below.

And yet, even as she longed to do that, she knew she would not. In some far part of her soul she knew that she *must* not. The Orb was not only an artifact of Istar, it was an artifact of Lorac Caladon's Test of Magic. The Orb and the King of the Silvanesti were inextricably linked.

The world is lost! So the king had whispered, so her father had groaned as he stared into the light of an orb that had seen the Cataclysm take Istar down into the sea and reshape the face of Krynn.

Alhana turned her back on the light pulsing like a long slow heartbeat, and she went along the gallery to her own quarters. There she sat in the embrasure of the tall window that faced northward. A wisp of fragrance drifted through the open window, the scent of morning in Silvanost, of the dewy herb beds in the Garden of Astarin, the pungent odor of boxwood, the sweetness of breads and cakes as the bakers trundled their wares to the kitchen doors of their customers. It all smelled too normal, so real and safe. And yet, not much was normal these days, and what was real—the war on the border, the refugees on the King's Road, a hungry horde, a shambling host—did not inspire her to feel safe.

* * * * *

Lord Tellin sat in utter stillness, quiet in body, quiet of speech, quiet—Dalamar was certain—in heart and soul. Sitting beneath a tall aspen, beneath leaves gone golden, the cleric was like a statue, something hewn from the raw strong stone of the earth, unmoved and unmoving. He sat but a hand's breadth from a fall that would have killed him if he moved too swiftly or the wrong way, a long stony tumble to the floor of a narrow glen.

Did he breathe? Dalamar looked up from his work of sorting spell components and squinted at Tellin. Faintly, the sweat-stained cloth of his white robe rippled over Tellin's breast. He breathed, but only barely.

The Windriders on griffins had long since flown away north, gone in the night under cover of darkness to take their positions for the battle. Dalamar didn't miss them. The odor of lion's musk and bird mustiness was not a

leasant one. He looked up at the sky where storm clouds
ung low. Beneath them the aspen leaves glowed like a
ing's hoard of gold. All around them, mages and Wild-
unners sorted themselves out into two groups, the sound
f them like the rattle of swords, the rumble of storms soon
o come. Tellin, though, sat at peace beneath the branches
f a lone aspen, and didn't seem to hear them. Upon his
nee lay a scroll containing the Dawn Hymn to E'li, but he
ad a keener eye for the embroidered scroll case than for
he scroll itself. It might be argued that he knew the hymn
y heart, but if it were, Dalamar wouldn't be the one argu-
ng. If Lord Tellin had any prayer in his heart now, it was
hat all the barriers of tradition and law fall before a return-
ng hero, that Lord Ralan would grant a cleric his sister's
and.

Dalamar bent his head over his work, checking to see
hat the oils he had brought—of heliotrope, mimosa, and
andalwood—remained safely stoppered in their earthen
ials. He had sealed these with wax from candles on the
ltars of E'li. So Ylle Savath had commanded all her mages
o do. He lifted each and smelled, scenting nothing on the
wax and so knowing the seals were true. He examined each
mall pouch of herbs, flax seed, rowan bark, and elf dock.
Il these were sound, no pouch had become torn or
ncinched in the northward run.

A damp wind rose up, chill here in the north of the king-
om, smelling of rain and sorrow. Aspen leaves rattled,
ounding like regret, and on the wings of the wind came the
aint trace of smoke. Tellin looked around frowning, then
hook his head, realizing the truth of the smoke. It didn't
ome from this encampment of Wildrunners. Lord Konnal,
;aran's second and the commander of his ground forces,
ad firmly forbidden fires. They were too close to the
order for that. This smoke was old and heavy, the smoke
f a large burning that had happened some time ago.

"A village," Dalamar said.

Tellin nodded. The smoke was the death-flag hun
above one of the villages or towns that had fallen to Phai
Caron's raiding parties. They'd seen too many of those o
the way north, ghost-villages where the land lay black
where trees stood staggering with their bark burned off an
others lay felled by axes for the savage joy of killing whe
there were no more elves to murder. And there had bee
murder done, great murder and terrible killing. The proo
lay in the wolf-picked bones littering the villages, th
empty-eyed skulls gleaming white in the moonlight. B
sign of clothing, it became sickeningly clear that reports o
selective killing—of the murder of men and women o
fighting age only—were true. The dragonarmy was depriv
ing the elves of defenders and leaving the weak and hungr
to drain resources.

Voices rose, then hushed suddenly, the sound of th
Wildrunners getting ready to depart. Lord Garan had mad
his plans so that the city of Sithelnost would not be caugh
between two armies, so that it would not find itself on th
fall-back route if—gods forbid—his army should have t
retreat. So the Wildrunners and the mages now sat at th
stony edge of the forest, west of the Thon-Thalas and we
north of Sithelnost. The Trueheart Mines lay but ten mile
outside the western bounds of the forest itself, the high tor
where Phair Caron had her base camp less than half tha
distance north and east. Most of the soldiers would con
tinue north to the border, there to wait word to begin th
attack on Phair Caron's army. All but a few of the mage
would stay here, hidden below in the glen. Protected by
guard of Wildrunners posted high on the glen's walls, th
mages would be able to work their magic in reasonabl
safety. Those of the mages who went with the bulk of th
army were strong in the skills of mindspeaking so that the
could relay Lord Garan's commands back to Ylle Savath.

Ravens spun out, black over the glen, cawing and raspin
and sailing down low. Something lay dead down there, an

he raucous ravens rejoiced.

Lord Tellin said, "You wish you were going with the Vildrunners, don't you, Dalamar?"

Dalamar shrugged, head low as he replaced the pouches nd vials into his leather scrip. Never looking behind to the rop below, to the ravens calling the feast, Tellin came and at beside Dalamar, his erstwhile servant.

"It doesn't seem fair, does it? That you have to stay here vhen you want to be there."

Again Dalamar shrugged. He hadn't yet become used to ord Tellin's keen eye, quick questions, and the uncomfort- ble insight. Sometimes it seemed the cleric could look right nto a person's heart and see the joys there, the fears, and he sorrows. Others among the army liked that, Wildrun- ers coming to a cleric for comfort and assurance in these ays before the battle. Dalamar didn't like it at all. He was oo used to his privacy and well content to keep to himself. And, were truth to be told—though this truth must never e!—he found little comfort in the idea of E'li's abiding ove. Each time he heard the phrase or listened as some leric spoke of the god as the Dragon's Lord, the Defender f Good, he felt like one hearing the hollowness of a lie.

Where was E'li the Defender while young elves were eing killed by the legions of Takhisis? Where was the Dragon's Lord while warriors on dragonback drove old nen and women and children out onto the road to starve nd die? Not here, certainly not here.

The wind grew damper, cooler still. "It's all right," Dala- nar said, breathing the smoke of a cruel burning. "I'm here, ny lord, and taking my part in the plan."

It was a small part, though perhaps only he thought so, or Dalamar, who had conceived this bold plan Lady Ylle nd Lord Garan had scorned and Speaker Lorac had mbraced, was not chosen to stand in the enspelled chain of nages, bound hand and heart to each other and dedicated, ody and soul, to the weaving of those powerful spells of illusion that would confuse the Highlord's army and give the Silvanesti their chance to rid their borders of the threat that had so long brooded there. No, he was to be a minor part of his own idea's execution, in the web of the magic but standing only to support the working mages with his own strength so theirs would not fail. What, after all, could a mage do in such a strong weaving of magic if he had but simple apprentice skills? Nothing, nothing. And yet, murmured a bitterness in his heart, he was not what they thought him, was he? He had more skill than they might imagine, those skills acquired and nurtured in a darker place than any school Ylle Savath permitted.

"Come on," Dalamar said, cinching his scrip tight and standing to stretch his long legs. "Let's see if we can find ourselves a place in the ravine before every mage around starts crowding in."

"Ah," said Lord Tellin, "I'm not going into the ravine. I'm going north with the Wildrunners." He twisted a wry smile. "They say it's all very nice to have a cleric with the army, but better if he earns his keep. I'm going to be one of the runners between the commanders of the ground troops. But I'll walk down with you. There's a Wildrunner down there who wants me to bless a medallion. Come on, let's go."

In brooding silence Dalamar followed the cleric down the winding narrow path that would take them to the glen's floor. The lower they went the fainter the sounds of the departing Wildrunners became. The breeze that had quickened above, died now between the stony walls of the glen. From below drifted the cries of ravens at their bloody festival. The way was rough and the footing unsteady. As Tellin's sure stride took him down the path, and the white shape of him was seen now only as shimmering in shadows, Dalamar remembered a thing he'd overheard about himself one night in the kitchen of Lord Ralan's hall: "If that one was a dwarf, you'd say he was of all dwarves the most dour. I don't think there's even a word in our tongue to say as much about him."

It had not been a compliment, but Dalamar wouldn't deny it had been a reasonably accurate observation. He was not a man possessed of many friends. If truth were told, there were very few people he liked, even fewer he respected. Smiling grimly, he realized the whole lot of those he respected went walking ahead of him, the cleric Tellin Windglimmer who dared a dream as unreachable as the one he himself held.

He looked down into the shadows of the glen where day had not yet come, down where ravens quarreled at their breakfast. A sudden gust of wind tore at his stained white robes and whipped his dark hair all around his face. Lord Tellin cried out, stumbling, his footing lost. His heart thundering as though those were his own feet staggering, Dalamar grabbed the cleric's arm and pulled back hard. Tellin staggered but held his ground.

Shuddering, Tellin gasped, "Thank you."

Dalamar bent to pick up the pouch Tellin had let fall. His hand shook, but bending and reaching hid that. Out from the top of the pouch peeked Lady Lynntha's embroidered scroll case, a hummingbird in flight above a ruby red rose. He poked it back down and returned the pouch.

"Have a care, my lord," he said, his mouth still dry with the sudden fear. "It would be a shame to lose you before the army gets to use you."

Lord Tellin laughed weakly. They went the rest of the way in silence, down into the glen where they parted ways, each vanishing into the restless crowd of white robes.

* * * * *

In the tent of the Highlord, the scent of leather and steel and sweat mingled with stinging smoke and the remains of Phair Caron's breakfast. Food depots had been moved in the night, and all the stores hauled around the back of the nearest tor. The forges were still, their fires low, the smoke that had hung over the camp dissipating on the morning breeze. On the tors dragons woke, stretching long necks, their red scales shining in the sullen light of a sunless day. One sounded a long bugling cry—Blood Gem, eager for the day and the battle. Outside, the army moved, battalions of ogres forming, squadrons of humans taking up their swords and barbed lances. They sounded like a distant avalanche, stone rolling unstoppable down a mountainside, sweeping all before it into death.

Phair Caron smiled, liking the image. She heard the voices of draconians, their language like cursing, as they belted on their harnesses and took up their swords, but she saw no goblins. That was because two nights before they had ranged out in small troops, her spies and her scouts.

One goblin had come to her in the first hour of the day to tell her he'd sensed a great commotion in the Silvanesti Forest, elves marching north. "But I don't know where the griffins are, lady," the goblin had said, sniveling as all its kind do, scuffling the dirt and looking at her out the corner of its eye as if it were the third hound in a hard pack. "Sky leaves no track, wind tells some things and not others." Goblin-talk, but she took his meaning. Griffins and Windriders were near, but not seen. Well, Garan of the Silvanesti was no fool. He had his griffins secreted somewhere and never mind the stink of them.

Outside, one sharp voice shouted an order, and another responded. Phair Caron looked around at the bare essentials of her camp-life—a small coffer in which she kept her clothing, the table upon which her breakfast lay scattered in grease and bones, the map still pinned to the tent wall. No more did she have but her war-gear, and that lay ready upon the lid of the coffer. With careful, precise motions, she lifted her mail shirt of shining steel and pulled it over her head. It settled comfortably on her shoulders, the weight of it like the hand of an old friend. She drew on her trews of red leather and belted on a long, tooled leather scabbard. She took up her hair and braided it, winding those braids round her head like a golden crown. She lifted her dragon helm and placed it on her head. Last, she reached for her sword. The grip, made of one whole ruby, fitted perfectly into her hand. Sliding the blade into the scabbard, she whispered, "I am yours, Dark Majesty. Lady of Death, Lady of Dread, my soul is yours, my heart is yours."

Her prayer made, she walked out into the young day beneath an iron sky. If the sun rose, it rose far away and behind a gray curtain of storm waiting to be born. Outside the tent, two human soldiers snapped to sudden attention. On the ground before them lay the dragon saddle, a hulk of leather and straps and steel. She gestured to it, and one of the two hefted it onto his shoulder. The other she dismissed with a curt word, sending him into the mass of the army to find his troop, his captain, and his place in the battle. She went to a clear place near the tors and bid the soldier wait. He did, his eye on the Highlord and the dragons on the heights.

"Stand easy," she said, and she didn't blame the man for his unease. She asked a lot of her soldiers, but not the impossible until the impossible was necessary. For some, like this one, it was only barely possible to stand still and not flee the great beasts on the tors.

Phair Caron lifted her head, smelling the damp breeze, the stink of sweat and leather, the musk of dragon, the weary odor of campfires being doused. These things she smelled as one who encounters a favored perfume. On the tors the dragons roused, their cries contentious, the beasts growing restless. Hawks and eagles and the gulls from the sea had abandoned the sky. Even ravens kept low, hiding in the shadows of the tors, waiting.

"It is good," she said to the day and to the soldier beside her.

A scar-faced youngster from Nordmaar by the blond look of him, one of those who'd early seen the wisdom of running with the strongest wolf, he said, "Milady, it is." He looked to the tors again, the red dragons preening. He swallowed hard, but managed a grin. "We'll carve those elf bastards to ribbons."

She slapped his shoulder—he staggered a bit—and said, "Go now, back to your troop—unless you'd like to help me haul the saddle onto the dragon."

Color mounted to his face, a flush of embarrassment because he'd like to have gone away, or one of pride for being asked to help the Highlord at this important task. The youngster held his ground. "I'm at your command, Milady."

Phair Caron's laughter rang out against the tors. He, and thousands other. Nearby, soldiers stopped what they were doing, some curious, others moved to cheer. She raised her arm, circling her fist in the air. Blood Gem lifted up from the stony height, wide wings spread. The soldier went white, but he stood firm as the dragon sailed down to the clear place where Phair Caron waited. At the Highlord's request, Blood Gem bent his knees, bringing his bulk closer to the ground. Together, the guard and his commander hefted the saddle, shifting it onto the dragon's broad back.

"Enough," she said when that was done. "Go now and find a good place for the battle."

He saluted, and then he bowed, his eyes on hers, a little in love with her, but mostly terrified of her. "The Dark Queen go with you, Milady," he said.

"She always does. Now, go!"

Phair Caron completed the task of saddling the dragon herself, and no one in her army had the temerity to offer to help. She had long ago learned that in battle she must harness herself and harness her dragon. No one else could do that so well as she. No one else could be counted on. The dragon lowered a wing for her to climb, lifting her when she was steady and letting her clamber into the saddle.

Her heart found a rhythm unlike any other she knew, thundering on the brink of battle. She looked around at the other dragons spiraling down from the tors, her captains saddling their steeds, her army spreading around her, finding the shape of their battle formations. Her blood ran in her, racing through her veins, slamming through the chambers of her heart, sounding like the drums of war. Somewhere Lord Garan of the Silvanesti waited, his army in place, his Windriders ready to take the griffins into battle.

"It's strange we don't smell the griffins," she said. "I usually smell those things no matter if they are upwind or down."

Blood Gem turned his head, his long neck snaking back so that he and his rider were eye to eye. He opened his mighty jaws wide and the dull light of the gray morning slid lazily along fangs that were as long as Phair Caron's forearm. *Never worry, lady. I have a taste for griffin today. We'll flush them out no matter how deeply they hide.*

She looked back over her shoulder to the dark shadows of the tors. The wind came from the east, and she imagined that she could smell the sea so far away. She looked at her five commanders. Each sat ready upon his own crimson steed with five wily warriors ranged behind, ready to support the legions on the ground. Beside her, Tramd rode upon Doom. The mage's handsome face shone lively with anticipation, cheeks flushed, blue eyes glinting. Seeing him like that, it wasn't easy to remember that here was simply unliving flesh made animate by the will of a mage who resided in a place that he'd not chosen to reveal to Phair Caron.

"All right," she said, her right hand gripping the hold on the saddle, her left filled up with her ruby-gripped sword. "Let's do what we do best, my friend."

With a wild cry, Blood Gem lifted from the ground, and in the moment his roaring began, the sky filled up with a concerted shout like war-horns winding as the rest of the red dragons leaped into the sky. Wide wings outspread, they sailed from the tors, each with a helmed and armored rider, the Highlord and her mage and four of her strongest, most canny commanders.

Screaming his joy, Blood Gem thrust downward with powerful wings, surging ahead of all. Upon his back Phair Caron matched his battle cry, her voice the rough song of all her rage. She pumped her fist in the air, saluting her dragon riders. One after another, the mage and her commanders returned the salute.

Below, her army had found its shape, five legions of ogres and humans and the dark-spawn of Takhisis's heart—the fierce dragonmen who were neither human or dragon-kind, but a hideous combination of each. They went like an arrow, the dragonmen at the fore to make the arrow's point, the other companies spreading out behind so that, from this cold height, they looked like the arrow's shaft.

This glorious arrow she would loose right into the heart of the Silvanesti nation.

The speed of her flight took her out past the foothills, out where her raids had blackened the forest with burning. Nothing grew there now, nothing lived. All the game was dead or had fled, and the vegetation was burned to the root.

Phair Caron laughed, and her laughter echoed in the roaring of her dragons.

"They will starve in winter, those elves, and they will sell their souls to me for food if ever they want to eat again!"

Blood Gem banked and turned, taking her back over the army, the roaring mass of warriors who now longed to loose every horror of war as though setting a feast table for their Dark Queen. Phair Caron lifted the visor of her dragon helm. Sword high, she flung back her head and loosed her wild war cry again. The cold wind of the heights stung tears from her eyes and tried to snatch the breath from her lungs. That no wind could do, for it seemed to Phair Caron of

Tarsis that from the day she'd scrabbled in the gutters of the city for a copper tossed by an elf complaining of his supper, she had been aimed like a weapon in the hand of the Dark Goddess herself, right at this killing moment.

"For Takhisis!" she shouted. And on the ground, the dark tide of her army echoed her roaring charge.

In the very moment the cries reached her, as her heart was rising, her blood running hot with the lust for killing, Phair Caron turned and saw what had become of the griffins.

They were behind her.

Chapter 7

Dalamar stood in the glen, far down in the stony bed where the last shadows of night still clung. All around him the damp air hung with the heady scent of magic. He stood hand in hand with those mages chosen by Ylle Savath to surround the circle of nine spell-crafters who now joined their minds and hearts in order to weave a grand tapestry of illusion. One by one, Dalamar felt the joining, the forging of invisible threads in the building of a web of magic. Strong as steel mesh that web, but Dalamar knew—they all knew—that in only a little time the web would weaken as the makers did, steel changing to gossamer. As if by magic.

Sandalwood oil and mimosa and wisteria oils mingled with burned bloodroot and the bitterness of wormwood, even the scent of dried rose petals. At the surface of consciousness, Dalamar was aware of these sensory messages. Another level down, he heard the chants of mages like himself who worked to support the strength of the illusion-crafters, the dreamweavers.

Earth and bone, bone and earth, my strength your own, there is no dearth. Earth and bone, bone and earth, my strength your own, there is no dearth. Earth and bone, bone and earth . . . Earth and bone . . .

In the deepest part of him, there was only magic, power running like a river spinning in spate, and he, in every part, every cell, every fiber of his heart, felt that power as the sky feels lightning. It belonged in him! It was part of him, the part he was born knowing and feeling and longing to nurture. He embraced the lightning, the power he took into himself and let run out from himself and gathered back in again.

Ah, gods—!

On the lip of the glen, Wildrunners stood, looking outward, arrows nocked to bowstrings, keen eyes moving restlessly. Dalamar felt their presence, their wild hearts, their eagerness for battle. They are killers, he thought, eager for their work.

That thought echoed along the chain of mages, rolling like thunder in the hearts of his fellows. The young woman on his left and the middle-aged man on his right, each clasped his hand tighter, then loosed a little.

Be still, they said in silent gesture. *Don't think.*

Swiftly he banished all thought and gave himself again to the work of reaching out to the small knot of dreamcrafters, standing in the heart of the larger circle.

Earth and bone, bone and earth, my strength your own, there is no dearth. Earth and bone, bone and earth . . .

Strength flowed out from them, and Dalamar, with the eyes of magic, saw that strength, that power, as bright bursts of light that faded the farther it ran from them. This light all the mages in the larger circle called to themselves, embracing and tending and pouring it back out, not to the dreamweavers but into the stony earth itself. From there it would return to the ones who needed it, as ground-lightning leaps up to the sky. It was, not a little, like making love, the giving and the taking and the fiery magic made from each. The young woman on his left pressed his hand again, but not to hush, for that thought of love-making had been hers. She lifted her head, eyes alight, chestnut hair flowing all around her in the winds of magic.

She was, Dalamar thought, like a woman in the throes of passion.

His body responded to the thought, to the power running as though to a woman's fevered touch. The eyes of each woman he'd lain with shone before him, in all layers of his consciousness he felt their touch, smelled their sweet breath, and the sound of their hearts was like the sound of the sea—

Groaning, he shut out all thought of love-making, all consciousness of the woman beside him. He demanded utter stillness of himself, for the magic running in his blood burned now. He no longer felt it as sparkling, but as a thin stream of fire running, little flames leaping like the wild manes of crimson horses. He burned, he burned, and those in the chain burned with him, their faces bathed in sweat, their eyes wide and dark, like the eyes of demons.

* * * * *

The griffins dropped into the sky from nowhere. They came not from the east nor from the west, not from the north nor from the south. They were simply there, screaming their eagle-screams, golden wings beating the sky like thunder. Upon the back of each, an archer, a keen-eyed Windrider, loosed bolt after bolt.

Phair Caron shrieked in rage, shouting to her commanders. "Defend the ground! Defend the ground!"

On the ground, the sound of the army changed from the lusty war cries of soldiers certain of victory to the confused and swirling shouts of panic. Out from the shadows of the hills where once the dragons had found themselves sunny places to warm their cold blood, legions of Wildrunners came pouring. Like a river, they flowed down the slopes, shouting defiance; they poured in from the west, from the east. Thundering prayers to gods whose names fell upon the hearts of the Dark Queen's army like curses and pain, the elves roared up from the shadows of the forest in the south.

"E'li!" they screamed. "Kiri-Jolith! Matheri!"

The red dragons formed a deadly phalanx across the sky, Blood Gem at their head. Gouts of flame burst from their jaws, fire pouring down on the closing armies. The first acrid stench of burning flesh drifted up almost instantly. One dragon roared with glee, then another. Doom and

Slayer banked and turned, soaring high after the griffins and the Windriders, leaving the ground forces to the others. Talon dropped low, Red Death coming in after her, eyes alight, jaws gaping. These two loved the game of grab and snatch, ripping soldiers from the ground and flinging them out over the backs of their companions.

I have a taste for an elf! Red Death roared.

I have a taste for two! Talon bellowed.

Blood Gem said nothing. He only banked and turned again, flying low over the army, the dark hordes of Takhisis turning and turning, trying to fight an army that came at them from all sides. Curses drifted up from the ground, howled in agony, sobbed in terror; the sky filled with the stench of blood and bowels loosed in death. Like a small storm ground-born, great clouds of dust rose beneath trampling feet. Beneath the iron sky, above the dying and the bleeding, the dragon and his Highlord saw the truth of the battle all in the same cold instant of clarity. Talon, snatching for an elf, got instead the ogre she thought was engaged with the Wildrunner.

There were no elves! There was only illusion!

Spitting out ogre bones, gagging on ogre guts, Talon roared in fury. In fury she slashed wide with her tail, shattering the bones of three humans who failed to flee. She took out four more before her rider got her under control.

Over the field the dragons roared, loud in voices mortals could hear: "Magic! Magic! You fight shadows!"

On Blood Gem, Phair Caron shouted to her captains, cursing them, driving them, demanding that they get the dragons off the field and out of the sky so that the ground leaders could control their forces. She ordered in vain. Her army shattered into a confused mass of warriors trying to defend themselves against foes from all sides. Foes who were not there, who were no more substantial than ghosts, no more real than a child's threat.

Doom rose upon the currents, flying near now, almost

level with Blood Gem. Tramd, red in his armor, his golden hair braided in two thick lengths and his beard in one, shouted, "They only know what they see and feel, Milady! This is magic that goes deep into the mind!"

"Then dig it out!" the Highlord shouted. Below, her warriors died of nothing, of imagination, and bled where they fell, so powerful was the image in each mind. "Dig it out!"

He tried, roaring spells, with wrenching strength strapping himself to his saddle and using his hands in the dance of gesture that makes the most powerful magic. On the ground, nothing happened to suggest Tramd's magic was more than the shouting of a child. Ogres and draconians, humans and goblins, they died, each believing himself in hand-to-hand combat with mortal enemies. Some jerked in the death-dance of the arrow-struck. They bled and bled though no arrow pierced them. Others fell with blood pouring from their mouths, streaming as though a dagger had loosed it from their hearts. To change this, the mage would have to ferret the illusion from every mind on the battleground.

And so men died of arrows that were not real, ogres perished beneath the talons of griffins that did not fly, and draconians—dead in their minds—let their bodies do what draconian bodies do upon death. Some turned to stone, while others fell beneath ghostly weapons and changed to hissing pools of acid into which their fellows fell and died screaming.

Again, one dragon broke free from the others. Blood Gem soared high, far above the army and out past the other dragon riders. His shadow ran on the killing ground, black on the bleeding mass, until he reached the very tors beneath which lay the Highlord's tent. From there he showed her the thing she most needed to see: The greatest concentration of the illusory army was in the north and the east and the west. The forces in the south were smallest.

In the south was the real elven army, and those of the

Highlord's army who died there, died of arrows of oak and steel, of fire-forged blades in the hands of flesh-and-bone elves. Blood Gem swore to it, and he proved his belief by swooping low over the battleground and snatching up an elf from the melee. He broke the Wildrunner's back with one blow of a taloned claw, gutted him, and flung him bleeding to the ground.

Illusions don't bleed, but in the Dark Queen's name, how was Phair Caron to convince those fools on the ground who were dying in an illusion the elves had created? Her fist filled with her sword, she turned north and south, west and east, trying to see through magic's fantasy. Her army fought ghosts, and the ghosts came from where?

The sky thundered, wind beneath the wings of another red as Tramd came near. "Mages!" he cried, thrusting his fist southward. "Illusion-makers! I feel the magic coming from there!"

One order she gave, screaming it in rage. *"Find them! Kill them!"*

On the ground, the Wildrunners advanced, tearing into the dragonarmy with the abandoned fury of those sworn to defend their homeland with blood and bone. Out from behind the tors, like sun from behind lowering clouds, came another flight of griffins, pride upon pride, and the largest, the oldest, was a male whose reputation was known among dragonkind. That one was Skylord, and if Phair Caron had never heard of the beast, she knew well the rider.

"Son of a bitch," whispered the Highlord of the Red Wing of the Dark Queen's army. "Son of a *bitch!*"

Lord Garan of the Silvanesti House Protector raised a mailed fist, his war cry ringing out in the cold air, clear as a clarion call as he led his vast flight of archers out from the shadows of the tors. Arrows rained like hail, leaping from the horny scales of dragons as the griffins and their archers flew in close to each of the remaining five, never aiming for the dragon riders or even the heart or belly of the beasts.

Those elf archers had clear and simple targets—the eyes of the dragons.

Up from the ground a spear few, the steel head of it shining dully under the leaden sky. Launched by the brawny arm of an enraged ogre, the spear went high, soaring, and it struck the flank of one of the griffins. Blood blossomed on the golden hide, a bright stain so vivid that the truth of it could not be denied.

This time the Lord of House Protector and his griffins were not illusions, and this time the dragonarmy was well and truly caught between two forces of elves, one on the ground and running from the south, one in the sky and fighting anywhere it damned well pleased. Between, magic yet ran, and ogres and draconians and humans all fought ghosts as the plan of a minor elf-mage, a servitor in the Temple of E'li, bore fine and bloody fruit.

* * * * *

Dalamar closed his eyes, dropping down deeper into the magic, into his own heart, his own soul. He gathered the light running, the strength pouring out from Ylle Savath and her nine mages, filling himself with it, then letting it rush out again, raging into the earth.

A voice lifted up, crying in pain, in joy, the emotions no different now, one from the other. In the magic, in the whirling of light and dark and light again, with the strength pouring into him, pouring out of him, Dalamar couldn't tell whether that was one voice lifting up or the united cry of all the nine illusion-crafters. He searched around him using the eyes of magic, trying to make out figures in the spinning of light and dark. He saw only one person, tall and thin, and seeing her was like seeing the after-image of someone glimpsed in the moment of a bright flashing light. He willed his sight to clear, and saw the figure more sharply now. Ylle Savath, her face scored with lines of strain, running with sweat, lifted her two hands, and those on each side of her lifted theirs.

"*Solinari!*" she cried, her voice ringing round the glen, bounding back in echoes from one wall to another. "Lend us your bright shining light! O Lord of the Silver Magic, lend us your strength!"

Down from the heights came a rumbling, then a roaring, like the sea coming wild to the shore. The Wildrunners lifted their own voices, shouting. Did they join their voices to Ylle Savath's, calling upon the son of Paladine and Quenesti-Pah? Did they shout to Solinari of the Mighty Hand? Dalamar had no way to know. All words were one now, and that one word ran raging like fire in him and in all those to whom he was bound, hand and hand, linked in the chain of enchantment.

All words, the one word, ran through him, racing along the pathways of his veins as if they were his very blood, racing, leaping through him and reveling around him. The energy of the magic, of the voices, of all the hopes given wing and set free to fly to the god, tingled on his skin, raised up the small hairs on the back of his neck, then set the dark hair of his head flying as though he were winged and wind-borne.

Soft like a shiver, like the first cold breath of winter, something rippled along the chain, hand to hand, heart to heart.

Doubt.

Weariness.

The nine mages joined in Ylle Savath's spell-weaving knot shuddered.

Understanding.

Heart thundering, Dalamar tried desperately to make his mind blank, to ignore the feelings pouring through the magic. He gripped the hands of Benen Summergrace to his left, pressing hard, feeling their fingers grind one against another.

Someone cried out, wailing in woe.

"Solinari!" Ylle Savath shouted, her voice like an eagle's piercing the sky, flying to the silver mansions where the god lived, there beneath the moon that bore his name. She threw back her head, her face to the graying sky. "Solinari! Stand by us!"

And yet, though she prayed, her cry resonating in Dalamar's flesh and bones and in the hearts of all those gathered, her prayer came too late. Distracted by the exhaustion of one of her mages, Ylle Savath shuddered and lost control of her spell. Each mage felt the spells of illusion lose strength and coherence. Each mage tried desperately to regain focus, to weave the magic again.

Down from the sky, like ripping, like tearing, the voice of a dragon roared. Fire leaped across Dalamar's vision of magic, flames red as the sun, running like blood. Another dragon roared, a third shouted, and a woman's voice raised up in shrieking. It was a scream of agony and a feral, triumphant war cry. It was as distant and as near as though the one who screamed stood but a reach away. All the magic in Dalamar, in his heart, his bones, all that brightness spiraling around every cell of his body, leaping like lightning from one to another—

All that fell apart, turning to ash and lifelessness in the falling.

When he opened his eyes, staggering in the light of day, a light that seemed like darkest midnight now, Dalamar saw that two mages lay dead upon the ground. One was the woman who had held his hand in the chain. The other was Ylle Savath, and upon her face was writ in death such an expression of horror that Dalamar must look away and hope he would never recall the sight in nightmare.

* * * * *

A half-dozen Wildrunners, youngsters with long legs and swift feet, stood with one white-robed cleric in the shadows of the forest to watch as two armies met like boulders crashing down in avalanche. The elven illusion was gone, melted away, the air over the battle still shimmering as though in the heat of a high summer's day.

"Who could keep it going forever?" said one of the soldiers, striving for an off-handed tone. "They said they couldn't, and so . . . it's all right. All must be going according to plan."

The ground beneath the feet of the Wildrunners and the lone cleric trembled, groaning, as elven army and the warriors of the Dark Queen flung themselves at each other as though blood were their only food and they had come starving out of winter. Swords shining in the dull light of the sunless day, they hacked and they killed. War axes harvested. Daggers drank deeply.

"We'll have one more mission for you," Lord Konnal had said when he'd positioned the exhausted runners along the edges of the forest, in the place between the stonelands and the foothills of the mountains.

One more, and that a mission of mercy, one that might succeed or might well fail.

Brush rustled deep in the shadows—a young man who'd broken the stillness to scratch an insect bite. A soft moaning sounded from the darker shadows behind him. The mages, who had spent themselves in mindspeech as the illusions were being set up and executed to perfection, sat huddled and weak, helpless in the doubtful shelter of the forest's shadows. One, whose name was Leathe, whispered to the cleric, "My Lord Tellin." She said nothing more. He knelt beside her, and their voices joined in the rhythm of prayer. He did not look so lordly, his white cleric's robe stained with dirt, his hair hanging lank with sweat. Leathe, though, looked worse. Her hair hung around her shoulders, and it had been black in the morning. Now it was silver-streaked. So hard had she labored in magic, calling from one mind to another, relaying the commands of Lord Garan to Konnal and of Konnal to the mages back in the glen. When they had gathered their strength, the mages would be escorted by Wildrunners—and one cleric—back behind the lines, back to the glen where surely the dragonarmy would never penetrate.

The prayer done, Tellin left the mage and went to stand among the Wildrunners again. "We'll have to move soon," he said, eyes on the north and the rage of battle, "or be overrun by the two armies."

One and another, the Wildrunners traded glances. They didn't like doubt from a cleric, and yet they didn't think he was wrong to doubt. Lord Garan might well hold the army of the Highlord for a while, but he could not hold it forever. Unless they chased the enemy all the way back to the Khalkists, the elven army would be giving ground soon.

Leathe groaned deeply, and she looked up, pointing to the sky where red dragons sailed, spilling fire out of their maws. Dragonfear, like cold claws, gripped the elves on the ground, twisting their guts with terror.

"Time to go!" shouted a Wildrunner, Reaire Fletch.

Tellin's heart hammered against his ribs. He looked wildly around at the exhausted mages trying to stumble to their feet, at the Wildrunners grabbing onto white-sleeved arms and dragging up those who could not rise.

Someone slapped him hard on the shoulder and shouted, "My lord cleric! Time to go!"

Time to go, time to go. Dragonfear leaking down from the sky, creeping like a fog of poison into his heart, Tellin grabbed Leathe's hand and dragged her to her feet. His legs threatened to give way. All he wanted was to fall to the ground and curl up tight against the terror of the dragons. Who would not be afraid? Who would not?

None, but he dared not give in to terror now. Though it withered his heart and turned his knees to water, though his legs threatened to fail him and spill him onto the hard ground to grovel in terror—he dared not. He clenched the mage's hand in his. Another's life depended on him now, on his heart and on his courage. If he fell screaming, if he gave up his charge to terror, Leathe would die. Still holding on tight, Tellin ran, dragging Leathe with him back into the forest, into the aspenwood where the trees arched golden over the dark paths. All the while he ran, he heard the others stumbling and crashing through the brush, finding paths or forging their own. With Wildrunners behind, the warriors were ready to turn and fight at need. Tellin remained the guide for the mages if none survived but he.

Screaming, Reaire fell. Tellin stumbled and, staggering, flung a look over his shoulder. Reaire lay sprawled upon the ground, neck twisted and hands clenched into fists of pain. In one instant of clear-seeing, the arrow's cock-feather glared brightly, the color of dragonfire. Another Wildrunner leaped the corpse, but she got only a long stride past before she, too, fell, pinned to the ground by a quivering lance. Tellin's blood ran cold in his veins. The dragonarmy was breaking through the ranks of the Wildrunners! Or they were flowing around them like relentless water pouring past stone.

"Leathe, run!" he shouted, glancing over his shoulder in the very moment the mage fell, a bright blossom of blood staining her white, white robes. Her hand fell away from his, her grip broken by death.

High above, the gray sky vanished as the tops of the tall aspens burst into flame, the voice of the sudden fire like the roaring of dragons. By the lurid light Tellin saw that there were no Wildrunners protecting their backs now. All of them were dead. In a short time, there were no mages left alive. Exhausted, some fell with hearts burst and bleeding. Others died of flame-fletched arrows.

None but he lived now, only he, running and gasping, falling and sobbing.

All the others were dead. Dead or changed into ogres and dragonmen, for these were all he saw behind him, fists filled with swords, eyes mad with rage, and running down into the Silvanesti Forest.

* * * * *

Doom dropped low over the burning treetops, lower than he would have if he'd been given his choice. He had no choice. He was driven by an urgency that goaded like bitter spurs in his mind, the commands of the mage whose body lay in ruin upon a bed of silks and satin in distant lands. So powerful was that mage's mind that Doom would not have needed the intercession of the avatar clinging to his back in order to hear and be obliged to obey Tramd's commands.

In rage-filled joy, he sent a burst of flame ahead, glorying in the fire, in the terrified screams of the white-robed elves scrambling and scattering on the ground.

Enough! the mage cried in his mind even as the hard-handed avatar pulled back on the thick leather reins, obliging him to rise above the trees and the fire. *Burn it all later! Now we must find the mages!*

For barely an instant the dragon thought he would roll and turn and send the avatar tumbling to the ground, just to let him know what he thought of this puny creature's imperiousness. The mage felt that thought. In Doom's mind, Tramd showed himself to be stronger, more ruthless, easily capable of destructions and killings far worse than any a red dragon could contemplate.

And if I die, little wyrm, you will die with me. It will be my last act, and so loudly will you scream that Takhisis, all the way in her deepest, most lightless dungeon in the Abyss, will know we're coming.

The dragon didn't doubt it. He shot up to the sky, leaving the burning below and heading south again, ahead of the fire. Tramd knew what he hunted. The smell of it teased his nostrils the way a hound scents a stag in the thicket. Doom felt the knowledge passing along the mental connection between them—what the prey looked like, how it sounded, how it smelled. They hunted elves, white-robes.

Doom sailed over the forest, the stench of burning in his nostrils. He flew in joy, with a speed unrivaled by any of the reds in Phair Caron's wing, for he was older, stronger, and leaner than any of them. Upon his back the avatar sat the saddle with the skill of a long-time dragonrider, moving as the dragon moved, anticipating his rising and dropping by the feel of muscles. So powerful were those muscles that even the thickest leather could not shield the rider from the punching and loosing. In Doom's mind, deep as his most powerful urges, Tramd's will moved, demanding that what he sought be found.

* * * * *

Tellin ran, each beat of his heart like a fist trying to punch out the cage of his ribs. Each breath burned in his lungs, and the sweat pouring down his face stung his eyes to near blindness. He ran, stumbling and righting himself. He ran gasping for the glen, and his thoughts made themselves into curses or prayers as though by their own will.

They did not know! They did not know!

He must warn them, illusion-crafters and the Wildrunners who protected them. He must find them and tell them that the dragonarmy had broken the ranks of the Wildrunners and would soon be raging through the forest.

He ran to warn, and he ran trying to leave behind the blood and the killing. How many of the weary mages and the valiant Wildrunners had died? All died. All, all, and into that dark well of a word no number was admitted, for none seemed great enough to encompass the horror of those deaths, the rending pain he felt when he recalled the screams and the terrible, sudden silences.

He ran, and he had a sword in his hand. How had he come by it? He couldn't recall. They had not all been elves who'd died in that slaughter he left behind, and this sword, covered in blood, bore the garnet-eyed head of a dark dragon engraved on the hilt. Shuddering, he tightened his grip on the sword, the weight of the steel heavy and awkward in his hand. He had never lifted a weapon like this, none of any kind. No matter. He had it, and he didn't know what in the name of all gods he would do with it, but he knew it as well as he knew his own name: He would never let the sword go.

Tellin staggered, then stopped, struggling for breath, trying to listen both ahead and behind. He heard the din of battle behind, the roaring of dragons, the screams of the dying, the exultant cries of those who killed and turned to kill again, elf and foeman. He heard nothing ahead. Would there be Wildrunners on the lip of the glen to greet him—or to see him pounding down the forest paths, deem him an enemy, and kill him? It hardly mattered if they gathered him in or filled him full of arrows. It only mattered that he reach the glen and scream his warning, or give it with his last breath, dying.

Branches whipped his face, and he left his blood on the leaves. Roots reached to trip him, felling him as though he were an axed tree. The third time he fell, the breath blasted out of his lungs, leaving him lying face in the dirt, gasping. He clawed at the ground, shuddering, and when at last he could breathe again, he climbed to his feet.

Behind him the forest was on fire.

Tellin saw no flames. He heard no crackling or even the hushed roar of trees being consumed. He smelled the smoke, that's how he knew.

"Dear gods," he groaned, his voice a harsh croaking. "O E'li who has so long watched over us, shield us now!"

And then, sorry for the breath wasted, Tellin stumbled on.

The ground dropped down now, and the paths looked familiar, recognizable as the ones he'd take from the glen.

Then they'd been rising. Now they fell, and he regretted that, for a lowering path is harder to run than a climbing one. No matter. He must run.

He didn't see the dragon, the red scar against the sky like a smear of blood on an iron shield, until he came within sight of the first Wildrunners standing guard at the head of the trail. The four must have heard him running, for they stood with strung bows, waiting. Tellin flung up his arms, and he saw the sword in his fist too late to remember to drop it.

Four arrows knocked to bowstrings. Four Wildrunners pulled back to let loose the shafts. Breathless, he could not cry out his name or even shout *Friend!*

No need. No arrow flew. No Wildrunner challenged him. A voice shouted from far down in the glen. "Dragon! Dragon!"

The beast dropped down from the sky, darting like a lance in the clear sky-path over the glen. As one, the four Wildrunners loosed their shafts, sending their arrows buzzing into the sky. The steely points bounced harmlessly from the dragon's scaled hide. Upon the beast's back, a red-armored warrior, helmed and bearing a sword in his gloved fist, howled such a scream that the dragon itself must echo.

Chapter 8

The dragon came roaring fire over the treetops, turned, and rose higher. On the turn it dropped again, shooting down the length of the glen like a spear loosed by a furious god. Upon its back the red-armored rider howled, a sentence of death in the ears of each mage, Wildrunner, and in the heart of one cleric. Yet, even as smoke rolled down from the north, great roiling billows black against the sky, upon the edge of the glen the Wildrunners stood their ground, never looking north, never fretting the fire as they swiftly nocked a second flight of arrows and loosed them against the dragon. Bolt after bolt, they bounded from the dragon's hide, and only one came close to the mark, the dragon's only vulnerable place—the eye.

On the floor of the glen Dalamar watched, the dregs of magic like a poison of lethargy in his blood, his muscles trembling with exhaustion, and tried to track the flight of each arrow, knowing that each shaft would fail its target. All around him the voices of mages swirled, weary voices, ragged with strain, shredding under the weight of panic and exhaustion. They sounded like children, querulous and frightened, helpless to affect what must happen, the slaughter sure to come.

And at the top of the glen, there beside the tree where he'd earlier sat to meditate, Lord Tellin Windglimmer stood, a long sword clasped in his two hands.

In the name of all gods, Dalamar thought, where did he come from—and what is he going to do with that sword?

Dalamar could not guess, and yet the sight of the cleric, long sword in hand, jolted him from his lethargy. The dragon came nearer. Dalamar grabbed one mage by the arm, then another, shoving them ahead of him, south along the floor of the ravine.

"Get up into the forest!" he shouted, yanking a woman up from the ground where she'd fallen after the unweaving of the magic. "Get up to the high ground and into the forest!"

She went, scrambling on hands and knees, panting, sobbing, and maybe praying. She left little prints of blood behind, the marks of her hands where the stone scraped them raw. Others followed, the stronger helping those who had not yet recovered their strength. One after another, they found the path and dared the way up. The wind of the dragon's passing buffeted them, rocking Dalamar back on his heels. The beast turned again, and the tip of its wing swept two mages from the perilous path, sending them screaming to the floor of the glen.

Tellin's voice came echoing from above, suddenly sharp and loud as that of any commander on the battle ground. He swung his sword once over his head to get the attention of the mages still on the path, then pointed the blade into the forest.

"Get to the trees! The dragon can't follow there! Hurry!"

They ran. They scrambled and fell and crawled to their feet again, one by one clawing their way up the path to the woods. The dragon made another pass, another long roaring shot through the narrow glen. The red-armored rider leaned out and low, cutting the legs out from another mage, roaring with laughter as the elf fell, bleeding, screaming, and rolling into the glen. Unstoppable, the dragon soared high again, climbing.

Tellin shouted, "Dalamar! Come on! Up here!"

But Dalamar didn't move. He stood in the glen with the two mages who had died in the magic, Ylle Savath with her thick white hair spilled all around her and Benen Summergrace whose face had once reflected such wild joy as to make her look like a woman in grip of passion. Deep in Dalamar a fire burned, and it was a fire of rage.

"Dalamar!" Tellin stood inches from the edge of the drop

into the glen. Behind him a Wildrunner whipped another arrow from her quiver. She fit it swiftly to the string. "Come out of there!"

High in the sky, away north over the trees, the dragon banked and dropped, ready to make the last pass.

Dalamar put his back to the path. He stood braced, legs wide, and reached deep down into himself to see what strength he had left for magic. Some, some.

"Dalamar!" Tellin shouted. "Come out!"

He didn't heed. He refused to let himself hear anything now but the sound of the sky, the sound of the dragon coming for him. He counted his strength and thought it enough. He searched within for all the spells he knew—and counted them worthless, for they were only the small simple spells he'd been grudgingly allowed. There were others, dark, secret spells learned in the summer, but he had been a long time away from those tutors, the books hidden in his cave outside of Silvanost. He hadn't read the words of those spells in too long, and he dared not try to cast them from memory. To mis-speak even a word . . . the spells could fall useless or kill him. And they were small spells, too, no matter if he'd read them only an hour ago and could cast them with perfect accuracy. Against a dragon they would do as much good as spitting.

Yet, perhaps there was one spell, one every mage knew no matter the color of his robe, no matter which of the three gods of magic heard his prayers.

"Dalamar!"

Out the corner of his eye, he saw Tellin on the top of the glen, his robes stained with mud and blood and sweat. The cleric stood braced and ready, the thick, heavy broadsword in his two hands awkwardly gripped. Idiot! Dalamar thought. He'll swing himself off the path if he tries to use it.

Like thunder, the dragon roared. In his ears, in his heart, Dalamar heard the mage's laughter echoing between the walls of the glen like the bellow of a wind-wild sea.

"I see you, mageling. You are mine!"

"No!" Tellin shouted, and the voice of the cleric, used to soft prayers and gentle chanting, ripped through the glen, bounding off the walls like curses. "Dalamar! Get out!"

Dalamar held his ground. He need shout only one word, two little syllables, and shout them with all the force in his lungs and all the strength of magic left in him after this long day's work. How much was that? How much?

Whatever strength he had, whatever meager power exhaustion didn't claim . . . it would have to be enough.

Larger and larger the dragon grew as it came closer, trimming its wide wings for speed. It seemed to Dalamar that he saw nothing now but the maw of the beast and the red-gloved hand of the mage reaching for him. With all the breath in his lungs, with all the strength in his heart, Dalamar shouted, *"Shirak!"* and a great ball of light burst overhead, flaring in the air between him and the dragon.

The beast roared, then screamed high in pain.

On the high side of the glen a Wildrunner cursed, blinded by the light. In the same moment, another cheered, his voice rising up in bloodthirsty caroling. "Again! Let fly those arrows again! Archers!"

Blinded by his own light, Dalamar stumbled and turned, reaching out to find the wall of the glen and tripping over the hem of his robe after the first step. Screaming, the dragon rose up high to the treetops, then shrieked in the sky, blinded not by light but by the green and gold arrows of the Wildrunners. Sightless, it staggered in flight, then fell, dropping hard, and the sound of it hitting the trees was the sound of storm coming down, crashing and cracking and the slow aching scream of trees being split apart and torn up by the roots. One wing broke close to the dragon's shoulder, and the other was pierced through by raw splintered trees, pinning it.

"The dragon's down!" shouted one of the archers. Above the dragon's screams that voice sounded like no more than insect buzzing. Still, Dalamar heard it, and he knew what words the Wildrunner shouted. "It's down! Swords! Swords! Go! Go! Go!"

Howling, they went, Wildrunners tearing into the ruined forest. The sound of them at the killing filled up the forest, echoing to the sky—the shouts of savage glee, and the thunderous roaring of the dragon, the blind beast thrashing and crippled.

Dalamar, sightless as the dragon, stumbled forward, staggering over the stiffening body of Ylle Savath. He was saved from falling when a hand grabbed his arm hard.

Tellin! Tellin, of course.

"You!" Dalamar cried, laughing, his knees gone weak with relief. "You, my lord cleric with your sword! You should run take your part in the kill."

The dazzle still on his eyes, he heard a soft hissing, a sound like snakes.

"That's why I'm here," said a low, heavy voice right beside his ear. "A dark mage come to rid the world of elf-mages."

All the sounds of the dying dragon and the cheering Wildrunners faded, no more distinct now than if a thick wet fog had come to dampen them. A chill slithered down Dalamar's spine. Mind racing, Dalamar tried to remember if he'd heard the sound of the cleric's death-cry in all the fighting. Sight slowly clearing, he saw that the hand on his arm was red-gloved and much larger than Tellin's.

Dalamar's ears rang with the din of the dragon's death. Someone cried out, a long rending shriek that ended in a bubbling sob. One of the Wildrunners had come too close to his prey. Then the cries changed, so suddenly that the elf fighters couldn't have had time to know their luckless companion was dead.

Fire! Fire! Fire in the woods!

All this Dalamar heard as he looked up into the black eyeslits of a dragon helm, and looking in there was like looking into the swirl of a maelstrom—or into the eyes of a madman.

A dagger sang from its sheath, shining dully in the sunless day. "Don't move, my mageling."

Dalamar stood still as stone. The tip of the dagger pressed against his throat pricked sharply to assure the mage's meaning. Move, then die. He barely breathed, but he noted that his captor's voice was slurred now, as though he were a drunkard speaking, or a man who'd taken a terrible blow to the head. The dragon's screams shook the air, even so far down as the floor of the glen. Dalamar felt ground beneath his booted feet vibrating to the thrashing of the beast. The red-armored warrior moaned, a soft sobbing.

Dalamar's stomach tightened with sudden understanding. This mage had been riding the dragon, and some who did that liked to forge a link with the dragon, mind to mind. The slurred speech, the dull, lightless eyes—these told Dalamar the mage had not managed to break the link before the beast went down. He was still somewhere in the mind of the dying dragon, feeling its death, perhaps soon to die with it. Hope sprang in Dalamar, with the adrenaline and blood running hot in his veins. But no matter what ran in him, still the mage stood with the tip of a dagger pressed cold against his throat, and whatever strength he was losing as the dragon died, his hand was still steady on the dagger's grip.

Softly, a step. Dalamar heard and never lifted his eyes. Still, he smelled the sweat of the one who stood there behind the mage and above him on the path. Mingled with the stink of sweat and blood was another, softer scent—temple incense of the kind that drifts always through the trees in Silvanost, the heady fragrance sailing out from the white temples erected to white gods and smelling in all seasons like the forest in autumn. Lord Tellin Windglimmer stood upon the path at the narrow part where earlier that day Dalamar had plucked him back from a fall. He had his sword in hand, gripped tightly, lifted high. In his eyes shone a terror to speak of the choice he must make, that choice and chance taken all in an instant—kill the mage or see Dalamar die.

The red-armored rider straightened suddenly, as thoug
he knew someone was behind him. He turned, his hand sti
on Dalamar, and he screamed, a high and terrible soun
winding up to the sky. His rage and the dragon's in whos
mind he yet partly dwelt, his pain and the dragon's, all thos
unwound in his scream.

"Fire!" they shouted up there in the forest. More voice
than those of the few Wildrunners shouted, many more. So
diers were coming down through the forest, retreatin
before the dragonarmy. "Clear out! Fire!"

The mage lifted his hand, and Dalamar knew the gesture
of magic. No matter which path a mage follows, the danc
of hands is always the same. The moaning voice issuin
from within the helm sounded hollow, and the words
spoke twined one 'round another in a complex pattern c
sound growing darker and darker. As did the sound, so di
the glen, for the air purpled as though a thousand dusk
came to fill the space between the stony walls. It crept u
from the ground, hiding the bodies of Ylle Savath and Bene
Summergrace.

Tellin's face shone white in the gathering gloom. Hi
sword came up, the blade so long and heavy that it nearl
overbalanced him. Paladine's cleric, E'li's acolyte promise
to the temple from his birth, swung down that blade with a
the strength in his young arms, striking to kill. And if E'
lived in that cleric's heart, it was Kiri-Jolïth himself wh
sharpened his eye and made heavy his hand. The blade hi
the armor and rang as it must not have done since it felt th
last stroke of the forgeman's hammer. It bounded back o
Tellin, who swung again, wildly, staggering at the edge c
the path. This time the blade found softer resistance, cuttin
flesh at the elbow joint of the armor.

The red warrior whirled away screaming, high and pierc
ing. He flung back his head, cursing while blood poure
from the wound, darker than the crimson armor.

"You are dead!" he shouted to the sky, to the cleric whos

word had cut him. The link with the dragon was gone, severed by pain. His eyes shone bright and blue as blades. "You are *dead!*"

Out of the dusk a hand reached, ghostly, curse-born, and made of red mist like blood. Cold to his bones, Dalamar saw the hand grow with each moment, until it seemed to blot out the sky above the glen. Behind, Tellin choked and gagged. Dalamar turned swiftly on his heel in time to see the cleric fall to his knees. The sword tumbled from his hand, clattered on the stone, and went end over end into the glen.

"My lord!"

Tellin's face grew red, and his eyes bulged wide—a man strangling. In the sky over the glen, the hand was now a fist showing white knuckles.

"No!" In rage, Dalamar whirled on the red-armored mage. "Let him go!"

The mage laughed—a bitter, groaning sound—and fell over onto the stony floor of the glen in a rattling, clanking heap. Tellin gagged and crashed to his knees. Now his lips were turning blue, his face white.

"Tellin . . ."

Dalamar scrambled up the path and caught the cleric just as he collapsed. In the sky, the hand remained, squeezing. In Dalamar's arms, the cleric choked, a haze of disbelief on his eyes, as though the hand he saw, that red hand hanging over the glen, were the hand of some terrible demon.

"E'li." The name of the god came out from his blue lips like a groan of agony. He lifted his own hand, but not so far. His eyes on Dalamar's, the last of light and life fading, he said again, "E'li . . ."

But the god who had not answered the prayers of all the elves in Silvanesti in many long months did not answer the dying prayer of his cleric now. The light went from the eyes of Lord Tellin Windglimmer, and the soul departed from his body. Only lifeless clay remained, heavy in Dalamar's arms, the burden of it weighing far more than it would have seemed to in life. The magic-made hand faded, drifting away like mist before a breeze. Upon the floor of the glen lay the remains of Ylle Savath and Benen Summergrace, of the cleric felled by the dragon, and the red-armored mage himself.

There was not much of the last. No body lay there—only the helm and armor, and these were empty, a shell. What had been of the mage was gone, fallen to earth. Nothing but dust lay within the armor. Ah, but he wasn't dead, though no flesh lay within the armor. Like a ghost on the night, a wailing ran along Dalamar's nerves, not a sound to hear but a thing to feel, as one feels the first cold wind of winter.

Shivering, Dalamar turned to the dead man in his arms, the lord who had come all the way to the border questing after a dream he would likely never have realized. On the ground, dropped on the stony path, lay something bright. Dalamar reached for it, taking up the embroidered scrollcase Tellin had carried out of Silvanost, the gift returned and the gift granted. He turned it over in his hand, the humming-birds hovered over ruby red roses, their tiny needle-like beaks dipping into pearly dew. He brushed it clean against the sleeve of his robe. The dust did not all come off, much of it ground into the delicate needlework, dulling the rose to brown.

"Is he dead?" asked a woman, a Wildrunner on the path above. She stood bleeding, her arm in a rough sling, her head wrapped in a rag through which her blood seeped. This one had come off a battleground, only recently come from the front lines. "The cleric, is he dead?"

Dalamar nodded, and he tried to hand her the scroll case, for it seemed to him that it weighed as heavily as the dead man did.

She shook her head.

"Didn't you serve him back in Silvanost, at the Temple of E'li?"

Again, Dalamar nodded.

The Wildrunner looked up the hill to where the dragon's corpse lay, to where the bright flames of fire shone not so far away. "Keep it, mage. Maybe you can get it back to his family and get yourself a reward for your trouble. But now"—she jerked her head back toward the forest and the fire—"now, leave the dead and come help me get the living out of here."

Thus do soldiers speak who are often in the company of corpses. Dalamar nodded, and he eased the body of Tellin Windglimmer onto the stone, arranging his limbs in some decent order and bending to close his eyes. That was not easily done, for he had been as well strangled as though he'd been hung with a noose.

"My lord," he said, but he didn't know what else to say. He hadn't known this cleric long, and they had not shared much more than unreasonable dreams and this plan that might see those dreams realized.

Dalamar smiled, a bitter twist of his lips. How fast dreams die!

"My lord, you saved for me my life." It was an old phrase, something out of poetry or prayer—he didn't remember which. The kind of thing Tellin Windglimmer would have liked and written out in lovely script with shining illuminations. Dalamar offered it in gratitude and folded the cleric's hands on his breast. "Go with E'li, for you will find with him your peace."

But if the old phrase fit, it seemed to Dalamar that the traditional blessing was awkward as a lie.

* * * * *

Down through the forest ran the mages and their escort of Wildrunners, though they did not run hard, and they did not run long before stopping often to rest. Too weary, the mages and many of the Wildrunners were weakened by wounds. They crossed the King's Road in two days' time,

and by then no sign of a great burning could be seen in th
north. It had rained there, heavily if the massing clouds wer
to be believed. If the fire was not drowned, it was no longe
strong.

Other things the people had to grieve for, though, fc
upon the King's Road they found the forest in ruin, foule
by the leavings of a horde of refugees—the campfires, th
bones of old kills, boots that had failed, torn clothing, some
times even a kettle or a pot that had grown too heavy t
carry. Among this lay the refugee dead, those who had los
will and strength and could go no farther than where the
fell. Ravens picked over these, cleaning the bones of elve
who ran from the dragonarmy only to find death in th
sweet forest miles away from Silvanost.

Some wept to see the dead, the picked bones, the ragge
clothing fluttering on corpses like pennons to call the scav
engers. These wanted to bury the corpses, but they wer
convinced after long arguing that they had neither the tim
nor the tools for this. The same had been said of the dead i
the glen. It seemed to Dalamar that the forest must be strew
north and south with corpses. The Wildrunners did the con
vincing, but they were not unmoved. One said to another, "
don't care if Phair Caron doubles her army. I don't care if sh
triples it! I am going back to fight, I swear it, and no one wi
stop me."

"Will she double her army?" Dalamar asked as the
crossed the road and went into the forest again. They woul
not follow this weary path, for the refugees now clogged th
broad highway. He looked back over his shoulder at th
ruin, the dead, and the ravens.

The Wildrunner—she who had called him out of th
glen—shrugged. "That's what we heard on the way dow
from the battle. Lord Garan doesn't care. He's asking fo
more soldiers from the Speaker. He's sent word by Wind
rider."

All agreed, almost with one voice, that Lorac would giv

the Lord of House Protector all the help he needed. How not?

Once more Dalamar looked back at the dead. They were all old, none of fighting age. Phair Caron had seen to it that the war-worthy were killed in their villages and towns. Where would Lorac find more men and women to fight? From the sparsely settled southern part of the kingdom? From the east where they were sailors but not fighters?

A light mist of rain began to fall, chilling the skin. Dalamar hunched his shoulders against the cold and pulled up the hood of his filthy white robe. The trees all around seemed to fade, even the bright gold of the aspen leaves did not shine. It was, Dalamar thought, as though the forest were fading around them, vanishing before their eyes.

A day later, when they crossed the Thon-Thalas on the ferry and entered Silvanost in the first hour of the morning, nothing seemed more substantial to him. The scent of baking drifted through the broad streets, dogs barked, children ran chasing each other through the gardens. Sun shone on the towers. Dew glittered in the grass. The temples gathered round the Garden of Astarin rang with prayer-chants, and the air hung with the smoke of incense. Dalamar saw it all, he smelled the city, he heard it, and it all felt like a dream of a place he used to know.

The home of the best beloved of the gods . . . It was a lie, and he saw that lie in every shining tower, in the face of everyone he passed, elves still certain—though a dark and terrible goddess pounded at their very door!—that E'li would save them, E'li still loved them. Dalamar recognized the lie each time he remembered the final words of a cleric who had died with his last prayer on his lips, with no god to intervene.

Chapter 9

The world is lost!

The words whispered in the darkest corner of Lorac Caladon's heart, as they had since the night he'd been awakened from his dream of Istar.

The world is lost unless you heed!

So said the dragon orb. The crystal sphere lay shrouded in heavy white velvet upon its transformed stand. So said this artifact of his Tests in the Tower of High Sorcery, taken by him from a place where he'd been bidden to take nothing. Not taken, he reminded himself. Rescued! *I rescued this orb, and it must have been right that I did, for did I not come out of my Tests whole and strong?*

Rescued . . . but soon to be lost again, for the world is lost!

Lorac heard the voice in his heart, in his bones. He heard it in his very soul, and sometimes it seemed that voice counseled despair, while at other times it seemed to offer hope. *That's where we stand*, he thought as he looked out from his throne to the small conclave he'd gathered in the Tower of the Stars. *We stand between despair and hope.*

The light of the noontide poured in through the spiraling windows and down into the audience hall. Bitterly bright, that noon sun shed a cruel glare on the marble floor and the bejeweled walls. It made the gems and gold worn by those gathered look like brittle paste, lending them no beauty. Their faces seemed winter-pale and drawn in lines so hard and stark that these might have been the faces of starving people.

Only see these people to know the truth of hopelessness, said his heart.

Or was that the dragon orb speaking? One and all, his people protested that they had hope enough to keep the kingdom alive, hope enough to commit their sons and daughters to the cause of beating back the Dragon Queen's minions. And yet, and yet . . .

So well do they love you, said the voice of the orb, *so well, and thus do they show it, pretending to hope as though pretense might one day change into truth.*

He looked at those gathered, his daughter, the Lords of House Protector and House Metalline, the Lady of House Cleric. Each cast secret glances at the white-shrouded object beside the throne. What is that? said the eyes of those who had not long before wondered at the ivory sculpture.

None of the other House Holders were present. This was no gathering of the Sinthal-Elish, no formal seeking of advice from the Houses and the priests of the seven temples. This was a secret council swiftly summoned, each member chosen at the king's will, for the king's purpose.

Lord Garan had come on his griffin, still wearing the grime and the filth of battle—blood, mud, tears, and sweat. The Lord of House Protector hadn't understood the message he'd received from the king last night, the sudden word to come home and to come swiftly. It showed on him, the puzzlement.

Near Garan stood Elaran and Keilar. One spent all her days in prayer, the other spent all his in the making of weapons and armor. "Prayer and weapons, they will be all we need," Elaran had said in the summer when news had come of the first forays of Phair Caron's armies. Keilar had agreed with all his heart and all his faith in the sword-smiths of his House. Now it did seem to each—Lorac saw it in their eyes, was sure he read it in their hearts—that both prayer and sword were failing.

Sunlight moved across the floor in increments so small that only an ancient eye could mark them. Lorac's eye marked each moving of the light, as he marked the changes, war-wrought and cruel, that had come to his people. His heart ached for them all. Garan, who had lost so many of his

Wildrunners in this wretched summer, seemed to have aged years in only months. Garan loved his soldiers, every one as though they were his own sons and daughters. Upon scrolls in the libraries of House Protector, their names had been written, made immortal in the annals of the kingdom. If all those scrolls perished, burned by war, it would be Lord Garan who could speak those names still. They lived in his heart.

The world is lost. The land is lost!

As lives the land, so live the elves. Silvanos himself had spoken these words. A prayer, a chant, the sound of one's blood beating in the heart—those simple words were all that and more. They were how an elf understood the world and his place in it. In his heart, King Lorac repeated them reverently. Ah, but who would speak those words otherwise?

And the orb beneath his hand—Lorac started, withdrawing his hand from the thick white velvet shroud. When had he reached to touch the orb? With artful carelessness, he placed his hand on the arm of his throne.

Recalled to his purpose, Lorac said, "My lords and ladies. Will you do me the kindness of paying your attention?"

A form of speaking. Of course they would. All eyes turned to him as he breathed the words of an imaging spell, ancient words, soft and silken, learned in Istar in the years before anyone imagined Takhisis would call dragons back to Krynn.

The Speaker of the Stars lifted his hand, gnarled and old. He gestured with one finger as though it were an artist's brush. He drew images upon the air, a map broad and tall. It showed the world of the Silvanesti, a world of beloved forests, of beauty and grace, of people whose lives moved in quiet, well-ordered rounds of peaceful watches, for long generations untroubled and untouched by the clamor of the folk who lived outside. Here was the Silvanesti Nation, shown from its northern border, now burning, to the southern tip where stood the port of Phalinost. Even now the broad bay was filling with a fleet of tall ships. White sails shining in the sun, filling with the wind, those swan-breasted ships tugged restlessly at their moorings, eager for the sea.

"Now, heed," said the elf-king.

Alhana's hand tightened on his shoulder, then loosed. He felt it trembling, slightly. Lord Garan held still, but Elaran and Keilar looked up, their eyes narrowing.

"Lord Garan, tell me: How did you leave the borderland?"

Garan drew himself up tall, the Lord of the Wildrunners. He took a step forward. "My lord king, Phair Caron has harried us all the summer long. She fights us now in autumn, but she hasn't claimed any land for herself. It all lies still in our hands."

A sigh whispered around the chamber, echoing hollowly. What Lord Garan said was truth, and yet it was not. Towns and cities in the north stood empty now, their towers the halls of ghosts. The dragonarmy had done nothing but drive out the people, whipping them down to the south, down to Silvanost, the capital of the Silvanesti. The first of a sea of them had entered the city only this morning, ragged, weeping, some—it must be said—half-mad with grief and rage. These were the first. It was said by Wildrunners who had seen them that more would follow. Silvanost would choke on the ever-swelling river of refugees, for the Highlord would not abandon the tactics that had served her well till now. Phair Caron would move swiftly and strongly, in hatred sweeping down through the emptied land to camp outside the walls of the city until towered Silvanost starved in winter and begged for surrender terms before spring.

"Tell me this, Lord Garan: Can you beat her back?"

The old warrior lifted his head proudly, standing eye to

eye with his king. "We will die to the last man and woman trying."

Lorac nodded. It was the reply he had expected. "If you don't die to the last man and woman, if you spend the rest of the season till winter fighting Phair Caron and her dark goddess, can you win?"

Lord Garan did not drop his gaze, and he did not stand any less proudly. "My lord king, we will not know until we try."

Robes rustled. From outside the hall came the quiet murmurings of servants in their goings and comings, a voice lifted in question, another laughing to answer. In the hall, silence sat upon all. Elaran glanced at Keilar. The weaponsmith kept still, his hands quiet. Only his eyes moved, darting from one to another, then to the king.

"Tell me this, Lord Garan, and speak truly: If you spend the rest of the season till winter and through to spring fighting Phair Caron, *can you win?*"

Lord Garan's face flushed. His long eyes glittered. "My lord king—"

"Can you win, my old friend? Or will you stand beside me all winter long, each time I must turn away another refugee driven down from the northlands, from the midlands, from outside our very city? Will you stand and say, 'Forgive us, but we are choking on refugees now and we cannot feed ourselves. You may not enter here, but you may go out into the forest and die knowing how sorry we all feel about that.' Will you stand with me and say that?"

A silence settled in the great audience hall. Only breathing was heard.

The world is lost! Unless you heed!

The elf-king almost shouted those very words, the dictum of the orb. They beat in him like the rhythm of his own heart. He'd heard them over and again, waking and sleeping, and he found in them, curiously, not despair but hope. *Unless you heed . . .* The orb spoke of hope, and it spoke of power. It spoke of promise, and it spoke of a way to defeat the Highlord Phair Caron.

Not only her defeat did it promise. It promised the defeat of the Dark Queen herself, the ruin of Takhisis. O you sweet gods of Goodness and Light! How to measure that boon if it were granted?

The world is lost, unless you heed me! Come and take what I have for you. If you do otherwise, the world is lost!

Lorac rose from the Emerald Throne. Though the orb remained hidden beneath the white velvet shroud, in his heart, in his veins, in his very blood, he felt its light pulsing, a drumbeat calling him to action. He looked at his daughter, Alhana, white as marble, her eyes glittering as with fever. What he would say would not surprise her. He had formed his plan alone, but he had spoken of it to her, for Alhana would play a heavy part in it. A burden unasked for would fall upon her slender shoulders. She did not smile to encourage; she had been all the night protesting. No matter, no matter, he knew what must be done.

"Now hear me," he said to Lord Garan. "Listen," he said to Elaran and Keilar. "I will not play at gambling with the lives of my people. Plans have been laid against this day, and this is what will happen: You, my Lord Garan, will sent out your scouts and you will bid them go to every village and town and city where people yet live, and into the woods where the refugees wander. They will proclaim this message: 'Gather up your families and go down to the sea. Go to Phalinost where every person will find a place made and waiting for him. Prepare for a sea journey, and know that you will return.' "

"Exile," Garan whispered, the terrible word like sentence of death. "Speaker, will you do that? Will you lead us all out of the land into exile while the foul armies of Takhisis flow into the kingdom and hold it forever against us?" In his eyes Lorac saw such pain as war-gotten wounds had never given him. "Tell me, Lorac Caladon: Have I failed you, then?"

Like an ache in the heart of the king, those words from the proud warrior.

"You have not failed me, my old friend." The Speaker of the Stars came down from the dais. He took Garan's hands in his, unconsciously shadowing the ritual blessing a king gives a new-made Wildrunner. So had these two stood, many years before, offering and accepting fealty. "No king has had better service than I have had from you, but I must ask you this one more time to serve me again in this cause of shepherding our people to safety. You will not be long gone from the kingdom, and when you and our people return, you will see that all has been done for the best."

"*I* will not be gone long. My lord king—what about you?"

Lorac turned from him, releasing his hands, and went back to his throne. It seemed to him that the steps to the dais had grown steeper in the moments since he'd descended, steeper and longer. When he reached the throne, his daughter took his hand. He looked into her eyes, the deep amethyst pools that so reminded him of her mother. There he saw fear, reckoning, and, above all other things, courage. He turned, and he looked down at the four gathered.

"I will remain," he said.

He let them gasp and murmur, and when his silence enjoined theirs, he said, "I will remain. 'As lives the land, so live the elves.' If you imagine that I am prepared to give up my kingdom—our Sylvan Lands!—to the darkness, you imagine wrongly.

"I have a magic to work," said the elf-king. With one swift twitch of long fingers, he whipped the white shroud from the orb, revealing the crystal globe grasped in the clawed talon. "Here is a dragon orb, and I don't expect that any of you will know what that is. . . ." He let the words trail, waiting to see whether any would contradict him. None did. "No matter. I do know what it is, and I believe the magic I work in company with this orb will be strong enough to save us all. But I will not risk the lives of my people while my belief is tested. Thus, only I will stay, with a guard of Wildrunners to ward and watch. My daughter will lead the people out from the kingdom, just as it will be she who will lead you back."

Now he heard her breathe, his Alhana Starbreeze. He turned to look at her and saw that all the color had drained from her face. A marble princess, she stood with her hand upon her breast, her eyes widening. He thought for a moment—only a moment!—that she would refuse him, that she would demand to stay. She did neither thing. She was the daughter of kings, the child of queens. She would accept and discharge whatever duty he laid upon her, for his sake and, more importantly, for the sake of their embattled kingdom. She took a step toward him and she bowed her head, not a daughter to her father, but a subject to her king.

"With the help of Lord Garan, with the prayers of Lady Elaran, with the iron goodwill of Lord Keilar and each of the House Holders, I will do as you wish, my lord king."

So close did she stand to him that Lorac saw the first tear shining in her eyes. None other saw what he did, the pearl of her grief. They saw only a princess whose courage matched her beauty, Alhana Starbreeze whom they would follow anywhere, even into exile.

* * * * *

On the last day of the month of Autumn Twilight, the day elves named Gateway, the sky stretched out over the Cooshee Gulf, hard and bright and blue as ice. Winter prowled near, the wolfish season whose teeth were cruel, whose claws knew nothing about mercy. Gulls creaked in the sky, and wind hummed along the ratlines already skimming over with a thin coating of ice.

The deck beneath Dalamar's boots groaned, an aching sound as though the ship could not bear the thought of leaving the shore and must moan for the loss of sweet Silvanesti. Such moaning as this was heard all through the close-packed hold of *King's Swan*, the cries of the seasick and the weary and those who felt the strings of their hearts stretched tight to breaking. All around the ship other vessels bobbed, rising and falling with the sea, as one after another, captains set sail and left the bay to follow *Wings of E'li*, Lord Garan's flagship. *King's Swan* would have her turn soon.

Dalamar leaned his arms on the rail and looked out across the bay to Phalinost, gleaming in the last light of day. Gulls sailed around the tall towers, gray ghosts haunting the empty city. Dalamar imagined that no one lived there now but the rats and the gulls. What he thought was very nearly the truth.

We are all exiles.

How spectacularly the gods of Good had failed the elves, who had in all ways professed their abiding love for these deities! They did all for these gods, the children of Silvanos. They permitted no other worship, no other magic, no other gods within the borders of their kingdom.

Dalamar shook his head, eyes on the restless waters of the bay. So much the elves had lost in that trust, so much. E'li and his clan had not been worthy of that love. He thought of Lord Tellin, one among many who'd died for faithless gods. He thought of all the others, the Wildrunners and Windriders, the refugees on the road, all turned into corpses and exiles. Where, then, were the gods they trusted? Nowhere, nowhere to be found.

In the north, upriver beyond Silvanost, lay four spellbooks, three small and one large. He had never had a chance to take them out from the cave, and now they lay hidden, perhaps until some soldier of Phair Caron's stumbled upon them.

But the king will save the city. He will save the land. No minion of the Highlord will dare set foot in the heart of the kingdom. . . . So said everyone aboard this ship, and everyone aboard the others.

Everyone but Dalamar. You leave a thing, you lose a thing. And so the books were lost to him, but he didn't rage and he didn't sorrow. They were but a few of many things lost in the abandoned kingdom. Perhaps it was that he'd gotten from them all he needed—more magic than the mages of House Mystic would give him. A glimpse, said a dangerous thought, of a darker god than elves liked to see. What promises did he make, Nuitari, who was the son of Takhisis and the god of vengeance? How well did he keep them? Dalamar didn't know, but he wondered.

A woman's voice shouted "Look!"

Dalamar saw a sailor point to the sky. High above, where stars had just waked to wonder what great voyage of elves was about to challenge the sea, the sky had changed from deepest blue to the sickish throbbing green of a wound too long unattended, of flesh rotting.

"In Zeboim's name," the sailor whispered. Her cheeks, sun-burnished and brown, drained to ashen. "In her sea-blessed name, what's happened to the sky?"

She swore by an unchancy goddess, the tempestuous daughter of Takhisis, but Dalamar noted that no one of the E'li-worshiping elves had anything to say in response. What should any landsman have to say about the niceties of worship to a sailor who plied Zeboim's realm? Nothing. At the rails dark figures gathered, sailors and Wildrunners and some passengers. All looked up, their faces shining ovals in the darkness. Some pointed to the sky, some kept still, and those, Dalamar was certain, were praying.

The waters of the bay woke, rough and restless, shoving against the shores of Phalinost. Upon the waters the waves ran, like horses galloping to the shore. Dalamar shuddered. The proud arched necks of the waves, Zeboim's Steeds the sailors named them, wore a green tint, and he thought of corpses washed up on the shore, the wreckage of a ruined ship, men and women with seaweed tangled in their hair.

His heart racing, Dalamar gripped the rail. The waters of the bay grew stronger, the waves heavier, and the deck rolled beneath his feet. In the sky, the green glow deepened.

"Some ploy of the Highlord's," an elderly elf-woman murmured. Her husband hushed her, but she went on. "Some new evil of hers to bring against the kingdom!"

Someone's prayer rose up above the frightened voices. "Into your hands, O E'li, we put ourselves. In perfect trust and with perfect faith. We are yours, O Shining One! O Champion Against the Dark, remember us, for we are yours!"

All around the deck people calmed, their voices weaving together in comforting prayer. Trusting, they offered themselves to the god who had not shown himself since first Phair Caron's army savaged Nordmaar, whose own dragons had not come to do battle against the evil dragons of Takhisis. "But he is near," they said. "He will come," they assured themselves, "and he will defend us." Even as the sky above the forest throbbed with eerie green light, even as the best beloved lifted sail and fled, they prayed and they hoped.

Only Dalamar was silent, only he did not pray. In the gods of his fathers he had no trust, for he had seen it broken, time and again. Blasphemy! He knew it. Elves have been cast out for such thoughts, banished from the company of the Children of Light, left to die in the outworld.

Yet, strangely, as he stood shivering in the cold winds off the water, watching the shore fall away, the strange green sky grow distant, Dalamar Argent did not fear his thoughts. He looked around to be sure that no one guessed his blasphemy, but the thoughts themselves—why, they held no fear for him.

* * * * *

All the voices of his past swirled around the ancient king. The voices of childhood, his playmates, his fellow students in the Academy of House Mystic, the young girls in the meadows plucking the flowers of spring and braiding them into their long shimmering hair. Hair like the pelts of foxes; hair the color of a deer's dark eye; tresses like honey poured from the jar. Among them was one who shone like a jewel , golden-haired, her eyes keen and gleaming as brightly as the north star, a light for hearts to steer by. Lorac Caladon had steered by that light all his days.

By the light of Iranialathlethsala's eyes he steered yet, for he saw those eyes in the crystal globe that was his dragon orb.

Your orb, yes, sighed the artifact of Istar. *I am yours, and in me you will find all that you need. Look! Look deeper, come closer, find in me what you must have.* The voice sighed, soft as the wash of the Thon-Thalas against its banks, soft as a breeze, and it seemed to the elf-king that the voice changed a little. He would not have that it sounded like the voice of his dear Iraniala, yet it did recall her voice, perhaps in the cadence.

My love, he sighed, in his heart, without words. Countless years of joy he recalled, and these were not embittered by the years death had denied him. My love!

Your land, said the orb. *Your kingdom, your people. The Dark Queen lurks at your borders, king.*

Lorac shuddered, and upon the marble walls of his great audience hall that shuddering was seen in shadow as curtains of darkness flowing down from the heights of the great tower, as light from the moons and the stars did flow.

Takhisis will tear down your kingdom. She will lift up the pieces as her warriors lift the bodies of your slain—spitted upon spears running with blood!

To hear those words spoken in rhythms so like those of Iraniala's, in a voice gone suddenly soft as hers had been, was to hear a terrible doom proclaimed with all the weight and authority of Iraniala's own magic. She had been a Seer. . . .

And she had foreseen her own death. O gods! My Iraniala! I am doomed, she had said on the day she knew the name of her illness and the day of her death. I am lost!

The world is lost!

So said the voice that was not hers and yet seemed so like to hers. The voice of the dragon orb turned mocking suddenly, as the wind shifting over the sea, it turned hard and cold as sleet.

What do you quest after, elf-king? Your queen so long dead? How can you think of her when a darker queen, a Warrior Queen, stands upon your doorstep, ready to tear apart your kingdom and make of your people her most wretched and despised slaves, your men for her armies, your women for their whores, your children for the meat on the boards of her minions so dark and terrible that even she has not granted them names?

Shuddering turned to shivering. Lorac returned his gaze to the orb.

She stood in the crystal silence of the dragon orb, a woman tall and slender, she whose eyes were his guiding light, whose heart held his love, whose body had held and delivered forth a daughter of such rare beauty that poets must shape new forms with which to tell of her grace and charm.

And now he saw his daughter, shown to him in the glass, his Alhana Starbreeze, standing at the prow of *Wings of E'li*, his flagship, his pride. The salt winds blew back her hair, a dark pennon sailing against a leaden sky. She lifted her hand to shade her eyes against the limitless horizons.

Lost! She is lost!

His heart twisted, wrenching in his breast, and he saw all the fleet behind his flagship, straggling out and losing their way, some turning east and some north. The wind in the sails roared, and it moaned down the ratlines, humming in the ropes like mourners at a funeral.

The world is lost! So said the wind, so said the voice of the orb.

"No!" cried the king, sitting back from the orb but never taking his hands from it. "Show me no dark visions! Make good your promises, the ones you tempt and tease with."

The green light pulsed, a heart beating in stone, a mind roaming and questing always, touching his and dropping back, then touching again.

Very well. You have been a long time admitting your wish, Elf-king, but I am here to grant it. Now heed, and heed me well! What you want can be, and I will be the agency of its birth. You need only dream.

Only dream. Lorac sat closer to the crystal globe again, letting himself touch the green glow with his mind. Only dream. He closed his eyes, and yet he saw the beating light.

Now you must trust me, isn't it so, Elf-king? You must trust me as once I trusted you.

A shiver of memory rippled across Lorac's mind, across the green glow and the mind of whatever being touched him through the crystal.

Dream, Lorac Caladon. Dream of the world you will save, dream of the people who will go all their days touched by your vision. Ah, dream, Elf-king.

"Who are you?" Lorac whispered.

In his mind, in his heart, he felt as though someone had smiled upon him. Warmth filled him, bone and blood, and it seemed to him then that he sat in a garden on the first day of spring when breezes are perfumed with the waking of the world. He heard his heart beating, and the green light pulsed in perfect rhythm to match.

I am he who will save your lost kingdom, Elf-king!

Until now Lorac Caladon had been very careful not to engage the mind he sensed living in the orb, very careful not to extend his own magic to touch the magic within the crystal sphere. This was, after all, an artifact out of Istar, and it was a thing that had lived in older days than even those of the Kingpriest. Still, he dared now what he had never dared before, what all his training and all the wisdom of his many long years had cautioned: Do not engage the magic of such a thing as this dragon orb. Do not, unless you are certain you can control it.

He touched the magic, and as his hands grasped the orb, he felt it running in him, eager and swift.

I am yours, said the orb, like a woman sighing in her lover's bed, like the shore to the sea.

"You are mine," whispered the elf-king, his face hollowed by shadows, made unwholesome in the green light.

Unwholesome, green, and sickly . . . but when he saw his reflection in the orb, he saw himself not as unwholesome, not as one whose shadow-sculpted face most resembled a skull. When he saw himself in the orb, King Lorac Caladon saw a young warrior with a shining sword girded on, a king to save the land, a father to rescue his children from the dark terrors of the night. A soldier of E'li, of Paladine the Eternal Champion!

In the globe, in his mind, the elf-king lifted up his sword and all the light of stars, the light of the red moon and the silver, chased down the steel, running like water and blood.

Beneath his hands, the orb shifted size, growing, swelling, so that he must extend his arms now to keep his hands on it, wide as though to embrace it. In the crystal he dreamed himself a golden warrior in the heart of his kingdom. All around him in vision he saw the forests and glades, each tree gently shaped and coaxed, grown by the devoted elves of House Woodshaper, those whose blood knew the blood of the sprits of nature. He saw the mighty Thon-Thalas running down to the sea, surging past the cities and the towns, running past the towers of his people. In Silvanost, the precious jewel upon the breast of the Sylvan Lands, the temples to the gods shone pearly white in the streaming sunlight, clustered round the Garden of Astarin. His heart swelling with love, Lorac Caladon cried:

"We are the children of the gods! We are their firstborn, their best beloved! We are what gods meant all the mortals of the world to be, and we are most deserving of their love!"

He shouted it, that shining warrior, and he never blushed to wonder whether he was wrong. How could he be? Centuries of lore had taught him this creed, and when he looked around him, in waking and in vision, he saw the proofs of lore everywhere.

"For the Sylvan Lands!" cried the warrior, his yellow hair blowing back, his eyes shining.

Behind him where he did not see, in the tiniest corner of his vision, his saving-dream, a small corruption throbbed, a darkness on the land like the first small spot of disease upon the lung of a fair young queen. Unseen, unfelt yet, still it was there and quietly killing.

In the Tower of the Stars, the elf-king howled high to the heavens, shrieking to the gods. So loudly did he scream that the echoes of his agony rolled 'round and 'round his circular walls, like thunder never-ending. So long did he scream that his throat began to bleed, and he would have choked on the blood, but that was not to be permitted.

Out from the orb leaped a dragon, wings wide, fangs gleaming, he who had been prisoned there since before the days of Istar's glory, who had watched as a kingpriest thought he might like to become a god, who had found a way out of the destruction to come by whispering his dire warnings and false promises to a young mage flushed with his first glory, to Lorac Caladon. He had heard Takhisis call her dragons and wake them. Like fire in him, the sound of the goddess's call, like flames running all through his mind and his soul. *Awake! Awake! My dragons, awake!* But, enspelled and unable to find a way out from his crystal prison, Viper had remained trapped—until now.

The touch of a reptilian mind, cold and dry and with no other feeling than death-lust, froze the mind of Lorac

Caladon, making motionless his hands. He could not scream. He could not breathe. He felt that mind twine around his like a snake around the limbs of a helpless child. His heart had no prayer. Fear felled faith. His soul turned chill, and the magic in him writhed like something dying.

And then—in an instant!—that dragon-mind was gone from his, the grip broken. Lorac breathed, but only once. Then came another mind, a stronger one, and this one seized him heart and soul in a taloned grip the like of which Viper could not hope to achieve. Too late, too late, he knew he had opened the magic of the orb and that was like opening a door. Another dragon, this one stronger, this one crueler, came rushing in. Viper roared, but the sound of his fury was already distant, the beast banished. In the soul of Lorac Caladon, a voice whispered words, like fire rushing, like wild wind in the winter-bare forest, the voice of another dragon.

Now you may scream, my little mageling-king!

Lorac did scream, so long and so hard that at last he became voiceless. Yet, unvoiced, still he screamed, and all his dreams of the golden warrior come to save his kingdom turned into nightmares, dreams grown so hideous as to sow the seeds of madness into a mind once celebrated for wit and wisdom and cunning.

He did not scream wordlessly, and he did not howl as beasts howl in the wilderlands. He screamed the words he had learned at his mother's knee.

"We are the land, the land is us!"

And so—it must be, it must be, for the mightiest mage of the Silvanesti spoke in the fullness of his magic—the insanity of the king fell upon his land and every living thing became warped, twisted in body, twisted in soul, imprisoned within the nightmare of the king as Lorac Caladon fell spiraling into despair.

* * * * *

The Nightmare King went out from his palace, his Tower of the Stars, and before him his guard of Wildrunners ran screaming, their faces etched in horror, their eyes the eyes of those who stand at the brink of the Abyss, the dread of damnation opening before them, the bone-white hands of the Dark Queen reaching to snatch them. In prayers one hears of that place—*Save us from the Abyss, O E'li! Turn our step from there, O Guardian of Light!*—in the darkest hours of night one imagines it. These, the flower of Lorac's army, the ones who would not leave their king no matter the danger, these saw the Abyss, that place in which dwells the darkest of goddesses and all the torments she can devise, torments for the body, the flaying of flesh, the shattering of bones, the blinding, the mutilations, the rivers of blood and fountains of tears. He showed this to them, with his merest glance he shaped it like their worst fears, their most secret dread. Wailing like demented children, they fled him, the Nightmare King. He laughed to see them flee, laughed to feel their madness running in him as though it were the blood running in his veins.

As the first winds of winter blew around him, cold and clawing, he turned to look at the Tower of the Stars, the shining beauty of masonry and magic, made in the days of Silvanos and raised up as a seat of power from which the line of that storied king had ruled in majesty for centuries. His glance made the marble run as the wax of a candle melts. The turrets tumbled, and the tower bent and twisted as though it were an old man writhing in grief.

The Nightmare King laughed, and he turned his back on the place of power. Howling as banshees howl, as the mad howl, he strode through the Garden of Astarin, and everywhere he went harm followed. Birds fell dead, small bundles of bone and feathers. He trod upon them and they woke, savage creatures dragon-shaped, with needle teeth and a lust for blood, their feathers changed to scales, their hearts to malignance. He touched the plants as he walked, moonvine and winter jasmine, the thorny rose and the winding wisteria. In this first hour of winter, they bloomed, their flowers the color of bruises and blood, their fragrance vileness and pestilence. The Nightmare King's shadow fell upon the boxwood, and the hedges collapsed, taken by disease; blighted, they fell into piles of brown bubbling slime.

Singing a madman's song, he went into each of the temples and made the marble walls melt. The altars collapsed under his merest glance. Wands of incense turned putrid. Scrolls burst into flame, and the smoke of those burnings rose up to a sky the color of bile. The houses of the lords and ladies collapsed. The homes of the humble ran like molten lava. All this because the Nightmare King cast his glance upon them.

He went walking through his kingdom, the golden warrior debased. No more the straight-backed king, the wisdom-bearer. No more the lover of the land. His thoughts were poison. The sky above his kingdom turned to roiling green, and when the rains came, they fell as acid, hissing and burning. Each stream he passed turned to blood, running into the mighty Thon-Thalas until that river itself became a red-running artery. He went in despair, in hatred, his mind ruled by the will of a venomous green dragon. The flesh rotted from his limbs, the hair fell from his head so that shining patches of skull gleamed in the green light.

As fell the king, so fell the land. In every part of the Silvanesti Forest, the trees that had been so lovingly tended by the elves of House Woodshaper bent and bled, sap running from them, leaves falling, bark peeling as though they languished in disease. In the forest the deer fell dead. In the river the fish became monsters, fanged things, growing legs and arms and crawling up onto the land.

The Nightmare King strode wide across his kingdom, turning everything to dying. A long, slow dying it was, for this nightmare that rode Lorac Caladon came from a dragon who knew the devices of the Dark Queen well.

Cyan Bloodbane was his name, and he had spent time in the Abyss, learning his trade.

Each, dragon and Nightmare King, heard the howling of the land, the screaming of the trees, the shrieking of the birds and animals as Lorac's nightmare caught them and broke them, making from the ruin creatures more horrible than any outside of dementia. They reveled in it, drunken with their own rage. And they heard the wailing of the mortal folk, caught in the terror. Some of them were elves, others were not.

It must not be said, though, that in his madness the elf-king failed of his promise to rid the kingdom of the dragon-army of Takhisis. Lorac Caladon, who had ruled the Silvanesti for six times as long as the span of the longest-lived human, kept his promise.

Phair Caron rampaged through his land, burning and killing, seeking the fair city of Silvanost. She had endured losses in her battle against Lord Garan's army, not the least the mage who was her finest captain. He was gone, his avatar killed and changed to dust, his mind returned to the prison of his ruined body somewhere far away. She cursed the loss and cursed the mage, but she eased her rage in killing. And so, it was in a small town on the Thon-Thalas that the hand of Lorac Caladon found her. She paused in the slaughter of children and felt herself fall, fast and hard, into a dark and terrible place.

Falling, she had not the wit to wonder whether her mind was whole. When the fall ended, she had no wit at all. She stood, not in a ruined elven village, but in Tarsis, the city of her childhood. She stood outside the doors of the brothel in which she had, at need, earned the money it would take to keep her little sister alive, fed and clothed—and out of this very place. Not far from here, some streets over, across the boulevard that marked the territory of whore from that of the finer folk, she had scrambled in a gutter for an elven coin.

All around her she heard laughter and rough music. She heard men growling and roaring like animals. The voices of women rose up in shrieking laughter and fell low in sobbing, and still the men came in and out of those rough wooden doors, entering eager, returning sated. She knew the place. She went a step forward and then another, like a child tiptoeing to the door she'd been forbidden to enter. She knew who ruled beyond that door. She knew—

The door opened wide. A woman stood upon the threshold, dressed in black silks thin as gossamer and artfully torn to look like the rags of a gutter-girl. Her golden hair spilled down her shoulders, her face the canvas of some demented hand that had painted upon it with rouges and kohl to make her white cheeks red and her pale eyes dark.

"Phair!" cried the woman in drunken laughter. She opened her arms to welcome in yet another man to the brothel and grabbed him before he got past her, giggling and then howling laughter as he kissed and fondled her. Over his shoulder, she cried, "Sister, come in! I have kept your pallet ready for you!"

'Twas then the Highlord of Takhisis fell to screaming, 'twas then she saw all she'd tried lifelong to prevent, her sister grasping greedily the coin offered for use of her body.

Phair Caron ran among her army, hair streaming, mouth gaped wide in shrieking as she tore at her eyes, finally plucking them from the sockets so that she might cease to see the living nightmare into which she'd been plunged. It mattered not at all that she went running now with bleeding holes where her blue eyes once were. Still she saw the horror. Still she saw the nightmare that ruled her mind, and that nightmare did not end until at last, thinking her a foeman charging, screaming in their own nightmares, three of her warriors fell upon her and hacked her, shrieking, to death.

The dragonarmy did not again ravage the Kingdom of Silvanesti. Some got out, but most did not. All, those who fled and those who stayed, died raving, screaming and shrieking, in nightmare defeated.

And in the audience chamber of the Tower of the Stars, the body of the Speaker sat in perfect stillness, eyes starting wide, mouth open in a wrenching, soundless scream.

Chapter 10

Though the moons over Krynn were the usual ones, red Lunitari and his brother white Solinari, though the stars took their regular shapes and traveled their accustomed routes across the sky, though the sun was the same, the light in an exile's eye glares bitterly bright. By that light the exile fleet watched as the ship *Aspengold*, that lovely ship upon which traveled Alhana Starbreeze, separated from the others and sailed away from those who fled, taking a southerly route. It was her decision to leave the exiles in the hands of Lord Belthanos, her cousin, and go out among the cities of Krynn to seek help for her beleaguered land. Seeing her go was like seeing the shadow of one's own soul passing over the ocean.

"Ah, gods!" cried the elves. "She is going among outlanders! Our dear princess! What has become of us? What will she face out there where the people are but savage barbarians?" In the bitterly bright light of exile, they watched her leave. They prayed her away, wishing her well in her journey through the gutter they considered the rest of the world.

Yet soon it was seen by some among the Silvanesti that the Sylvan Land was not, after all, the center of the world. Fleeing from a dragonarmy and the disaster of a king's magic, some among the elves began to recognize that a wider world lay outside their wooded borders. The winds of winter drove the refugee fleet north around the Blood Sea of Istar, past Kothas and Mithas and the ravening minotaur pirates who had thrown in their lot with the forces of Takhisis.

Cold winds buffeted them, the winds off foreign lands around the Cape of Nordmaar. These winds took them past the shores of Solamnia, the home of the ancient knighthood, which, by all accounts, found itself reviled on all sides and torn from within. Old feuds died hard, as knights will testify. The people of Krynn had not forgiven them their part in the ancient tragedy of Istar, as though the sons must still account for the folly of their distant fathers who did not ride at once to defend that city from the arrogance of a king-priest determined to flout the gods. And, as though the enmity of the world around were not enough, the knights fought each other; within their own ranks, they bickered for position and power.

"You can hear them fighting," said one elf to another, one night as *King's Swan* plied the seas off the shores of that land, "like quarrelsome children." One could not, of course, hear them, but it wasn't hard to imagine.

In their exodus, the elves tasted the salt spray of seas unimagined in the straits between the land of Solamnia and the isle of Northern Ergoth. Wherever they went, they gathered news. Some few of them, the venturesome, went into the port cities among the taverns and the shops to learn what they could. In this way, they discovered the fate of their king, Lorac, trapped in magic. Bitterly, they learned that Silvanesti was now being called the Nightmare Kingdom. They heard, too, news of their princess—none of it was the stuff of hope, for Alhana Starbreeze wandered the ports of the world, their lily princess going in and out of the cities, looking for help and finding none. She did not falter. Even as green dragons came to nest in the tormented forests, to claim the haunted land, she went to the houses of the high in every city she could, searching for a way to rescue her homeland from the grip of an evil magic.

"And to save her father," said an elf who had heard this in a port not far from the ruin of the City of Lost Names, there at the topmost part of Solamnia, "for she believes he is not dead." Shuddering, he said, "Our Alhana believes the Speaker of the Stars yet lives."

And so the venturesome ventured, and the news they brought to the fleet made wider the world. One such gatherer of news was Dalamar Argent, for while others sought always after word of Silvanesti, his ears were keen for word of the world around. Each time the fleet put into a port, he went down to the docks and walked among the people in the taverns, seeking to learn all he could. It was no easy thing, this going among outlanders—for he thought of all others than elves that way—but he did it. How wide the word of which Silvanesti was not the center! How strange the languages—lovely some and ugly others. He spoke with humans in the wild ports near Kalaman, in Palanthas, and in the bazaars of Caergoth. All around him, the sights of humans and dwarves and kender enchanted him—the smells of cooking in the stalls, of spices in the marketplaces, the weaves of foreign fabrics. The flashing eyes of strangers were intoxicating, rich and deep and wonderfully strange.

They came, at last, to Southern Ergoth, the elves who fled, and they made a home for themselves. In exile, Lord Belthanos, he of blood kinship to the Speaker of the Stars, shaped a council from the Heads of the Houses. This council-in-exile was made of much the same folk as Speaker Lorac's had been, with two exceptions. Lady Ylle Savath was gone from its ranks, dead in the Silvanesti Forest, and Lord Garan of House Protector had not survived the sea. He had died in the first month of the journey. The old warrior's heart had simply stopped beating in his breast. It broke, said some, because he believed that he could not survive being gone from the kingdom he had so long defended. And so House Mystic gave Lord Feleran to the new council, and House Protector gave Lord Konnal, who had served with Lord Garan in the war.

The council-in-exile convened and began at once the task of establishing the Silvanesti claim to this land of sea-breeze and sweet pine forests, of rich hunting grounds and coastal waters thick with fish. It didn't much matter to them that the wild Kagonesti lived there, those proud hunters whom Silvanos had tried to change into servitors in ancient days. The Silvanesti came with weapons; they came armed with the certainty that they were, among all races, the best beloved of the gods, thus deserving of the best of everything. This, no matter what events suggested, was not a belief the Children of Silvanos were ready to lay down. And so they forced servitude upon the Kagonesti and built upon their land a city they named Silvamori, their home in exile. This was, by honest account, a harder thing for the Kagonesti than for their aristocratic cousins, though most of the moaning and sighing came winding out from the houses of the Silvanesti, the lorn exiles.

Dalamar Argent didn't complain much, and for a time this surprised him. He did ache for his homeland, the aspenwood, the orderliness of the city, the scent of the gardens, and the deep tolling of bells in the harbors. Sometimes he took out the embroidered scroll case that held the Dawn Hymn to E'li, and he looked at it, smudged with dirt from the day of Lord Tellin's death. He had tried to return it to Lady Lynntha, but she would not have it. She'd looked at him long, her eyes filled with sorrow and with an unvoiced plea: Don't make me take it, don't make me think of that which could never have been. And so Dalamar kept it, an artifact of another time, another place, and gods whose names rang through the pine forest of Silvamori but not in his heart.

He found himself free of service, with so many others to take his place, and he found himself a lover among the Wilder Elves, a woman with hair the color of Solinari's moon, eyes green as the sea, and long sun-gilded limbs. K'gathala was a woman wise in the ways of Kagonesti magic, and one who believed strongly in the meaning of names. She said his was a strange name for one of the Light Elves, for if "argent" meant "silver" in the language of the Silvanesti, it meant "night's son" in the speech of the

Kagonesti. "And that," she said one night as she lay in his arms, twining her long fingers in his dark hair, "that is a strange name for one of your kind, but perhaps not so strange for you."

She was full of these sayings, these takings and givings, and Dalamar enjoyed that, the mystery and the magic. He did not go to her openly. It wasn't a thing encouraged by Lord Belthanos or his council-in-exile. The possibility of dilution of Silvanesti blood through a line of half-Kagonesti, half-Silvanesti children was a thing to make them shudder. Nonetheless, Dalamar went, and he continued his habit of learning magic. In secret nights and stolen days, he learned such things as he had never dreamed—how the Kagonesti did not whisper their spells or even declaim them, but sang them. And the spells of the Wilder Elves were not made up of words. Rather, they were made up of weavings of notes so complex that the mortal voice must struggle for months to learn them. He had the months, he had the will, and within the first year of the exile, he'd advanced so far in his studies that he began to think again that he might find a way to travel to the Tower of High Sorcery at Wayreth and be tested in his skill and knowledge. How? He did not know, and he didn't even know whether that tower would survive the war that raged in the world outside of Silvamori.

For war did rage. He knew this. He had friends among the sailors who went out to the port cities, and they brought back news. As the first year of exile passed and the new years progressed, he learned that the world beyond Silvamori was being taught to hate the coming of spring. It was, ever, the return of spring that brought the renewal of war.

After the disaster in Silvanesti, the armies of Takhisis took stock and found their strength again. They left behind the Nightmare Kingdom and turned west. Phair Caron's had been a force of red dragons. This new one was a force of blues, and so all knew and feared it as the Blue Army. It swept through the Plains of Solamnia like wildfire, merciless and hungry for conquest. It rolled over Kalaman and rampaged down the Vingaard River valleys, burning and looting and killing. Everywhere it went, the dragonarmy conquered. People wailed to the gods of Good, cried out to E'li—Paladine, as outlanders named him—but no god answered. The sky over the land grew dark with dragons. The land itself ran red with blood, and corpses clogged the great Vingaard River. The army surged through Vingaard Keep and left behind the dead and the broken in Solanthus.

Armies of white dragons took Icewall in the south. Highlords on black dragons held Goodlund and Kendermore while the Red Army regrouped, kicking off the dust of Phair Caron's failure, and ripped into Abanasinia, slaughtering Plainsmen and running right up to the borders of Qualinesti. And out came the elves of that land, and the sundered kindred—Silvanesti and Qualinesti—met again in Southern Ergoth. A new city was built under the auspices of the Qualinesti king, he who styled himself Speaker of the Sun. The two factions of the best beloved of the gods glared at each other across Thunder Bay, and for a time the story amused Silvamori that the son of the Qualinesti king, Porthios, decided that he must take part in the fighting and do battle against the forces of Takhisis. Madman! What are the affairs of outlanders to elves? They must have lost their minds, those Qualinesti. No sooner had the folk of Silvamori tired of that story than did a delicious bit of gossip whisper that if the son of the Qualinesti king was mad, his daughter was worse. Laurana, it was said, had fallen so far below herself as to run off with her half-elven lover, disgracing her family to the point where her poor old father took to his bed, and decided she too must become a soldier in the fight against the forces of Takhisis.

It was at this time that word came to Silvamori about the fate of their own wandering princess and the state of their nightmare-ridden homeland. People argued about it for months, some saying, "Well, it must be true," others declaring the news an outright lie. "After all," muttered the naysayers, "who in the world would believe that Alhana Starbreeze had found help in Tarsis—of all benighted places!—and that help at the hands of a scruffy band made up of a half-elf, some humans, an elf-maid, a kender, and a dwarf? Insanity!"

"Aye, but it's so," said the fisherman who sat talking with Dalamar late one night while the red moon and the silver shone down on the beach and the sea ran in to the shore and out. "It's so, I know it, because I had word with one who saw the princess's guard escorting her through the city. It was the very night the dragonarmy attacked Tarsis, burning everything they could. Must've been awful. And you know who that elf-maid was? Laurana of Qualinesti, pity her poor father. All those strange folk did meet—a princess, her Wildrunners, and that ragged band of questers. Gone 'round the place looking for a dragon orb." The fisherman laughed, for it was a fine joke to him that the questers should meet with the very woman who sought help in freeing her homeland and her father from the magic of one of those very things. "Wanted one for the same reason your king did, I suppose—wanted to control the dragons, and so some of 'em went with her back to the Sylvan Land."

"And freed the king?"

"And freed the king. But, sorry to say, he found his freedom in death, and things aren't so good in the Nightmare Kingdom these days."

"But how was the king freed? How was the spell undone? How did people manage to enter the land and come out alive?" All this Dalamar wanted to know.

The fisherman shrugged, said some mage or another did it, one of the questers, and he didn't remember much more about it except that the fellow wore red robes and part of his name was the name of a god. "Majere . . ." he said. "Something, somebody Majere."

When Dalamar asked to know more of this mage, the fisherman shook his head. He'd told all he knew, and there wasn't more to say. No more news of the mysterious mage came to Silvamori that year, or any year after, though often Dalamar listened to see if more would. Magic and power, these things were as gold and silver to him. Tales of them were nearly as good.

Still, if one servitor among them was unsatisfied with the amount of news he gathered, most of Silvamori had more news than they knew what to do with. A red mage undoing evil magic in a land where no magic was honored but white, the Speaker of the Stars dead, the children of the Speaker of the Suns running around wild . . . By the end of the second year of the war, the people of Silvamori and Qualimori decided that all the world beyond their own homes in exile was doomed to damnation.

"Ah, but things are finally changing," said the Kagonesti fisherman, one day in the spring of the third year of the war. The Blue Army, filled up with humans, ogres, and the foul traitors from Lemish who'd thrown in their lot with the minions of Takhisis, prepared to fling itself against the High Clerist's Tower, that bastion of the Knights of Solamnia that stands at the head of a high mountain pass to ward the way to Palanthas. A rich prize, that city of Palanthas, with access to Coastlund in the west and the Bay of Branchala in the north. That whole sector of Solamnia would be squeezed and starved and find itself pleading for mercy if this ploy worked. "But it won't," said the fisherman, laughing. "Those knights have finally got themselves sorted out and are ready to fight."

Indeed, they had, and they'd found themselves a general as well. Laurana of Qualinesti went for a soldier, and she aimed for high rank. Well she was, after all, the daughter of a king. They called her the Golden General, and under her leadership the Knights of Solamnia became a force worth counting on. For the first time in all the war, a dragonarmy fled the field of battle, bloody and beaten. "Because they had something called dragonlances," the fisherman said. "Old weapons from old times. Made the difference, it did."

Soon—gods be praised—dragons of brass and silver and gold and copper were seen in the skies, come at last to defend the people of Krynn against the evil of Takhisis and her servants. At Whitestone Glade, dwarves and humans and elves were making treaties of alliance left and right, swearing to defend each other one and all.

"And so," said Dalamar Argent, who secretly liked the name Dalamar Nightson, "for whatever reason, the gods of Good have roused at last."

The fisherman, eyes wide at this near-blasphemy, made a sign against ill luck. "They have their reasons, Dalamar Argent. It's being said near and far that they have been working in the world all along, through the hearts and hands of people of good faith. Look you, aren't the races coming together now, putting aside their differences to work for a common good? Why, I heard it said that last winter the dwarves took human refugees into Thorbardin!" He laughed, as at a good joke. "Who'd ever have imagined that, eh? Enough to rouse any god and make him take notice. And the knights are united again, E'li's dragons come to save us at last . . . It's been a time of wonders. Which goes to show it was, after all, not just a war on the ground, but a war in the heavens as well."

So it was, Dalamar thought. He didn't speak his bitterness aloud. He took it with him, though, the question no one dared ask: How many have died praying for this moment so long delayed while gods played their games with each other, moving the people of Krynn around as though they were gaming pieces on a board? He thought of Lord Tellin Windglimmer, the cleric who died with E'li's name on his lips, his prayer unanswered.

Dalamar thanked the fisherman for his news and, as though in ritual long planned, he went to his house—his own small home, not that of his lover—and took off his white mage's robe, that mark of one who has been dedicated to Solinari. Instead, he dressed in the dun garb of a servant. Earthen brown boots, trews the color of mahogany, a shirt dyed walnut, these were the darkest clothes he could find. So changed, he walked down to the sea to the place where exiles had landed years before, from where exiles would soon again sail. He took with him the embroidered scroll case, that artifact of another time.

For a long moment he stood in the sun, a tall dark figure on the shining strand, an elf whose black hair blew around his pale face in the wind off the sea. Waves foamed around his feet and gulls cried in the sky. He turned the case over in his hands again and then again, looking at the silken hummingbirds hovering over ruby roses, those roses faded to brown as though the petals had withered.

With a cry like a curse, Dalamar hurled that artifact of another time into the sea, the scroll case and the Dawn Hymn to E'li consigned to the streams and the tides and the fishes.

* * * * *

Two days later, the watch in the crow's nest of the elven ship *Bright Sun* saw that scroll case bobbing in the waters. He wondered, briefly, what it could be, but then he didn't think more about it, for he was far up among the gulls in the bright blue sky, and it was just then sinking into the sea. *Bright Sun* was a Qualinesti ship, not one out of Qualimori but one coming into Qualimori from the Nightmare Kingdom. Aboard was an elven prince, Porthios himself, whose sister commanded the Knights of Solamnia, whose father had nearly died of the grief of that. He had with him messages for the two elf kindreds, greetings for his father, and a message to Lord Belthanos and his council-in-exile from their princess.

"Come home," she had written, Alhana Starbreeze in her far tower in ruined Silvanost. "Prepare ships and come home. Bring clerics to cleanse the temples, mages to unwork the vestiges of evil magic, and Wildrunners to ward all."

She gave the missive to Porthios, and gave to him the care of those who would return. They had been, over the last months of the war, often in correspondence, a prince and a princess of sundered kindred. No light of love shone in the eyes of one, nothing like that gleamed in the heart of the other. They were, always, the children of their fathers, and when their hearts burned, they burned for their people. And so, at the end of the war when all of Krynn looked around to see what must be put back together, these children of kings wondered whether something long ago broken might again be made whole. Could it be, they said each to the other secretly and in whispers, could it be that we two can make the sundered elven nations whole?

Chapter 11

~

Dalamar stood at the rail of the ship *Bright Solinari*. At the end of the day, with the sun setting behind, sinking in red glory into the white-maned sea, he stood looking east as the ship rounded the Cape of Nordmaar. Stiff winds filled the sails, and they bellied out proud as a swan's white breast. Beside *Bright Solinari*, the golden sails of *Bright Sun*, Porthios's ship, filled and rounded. Six other ships came behind, but these two, *Solinari* and *Sun*, kept abreast as though neither would let the other range even a little ahead.

It was not, Dalamar thought, much of a thing for pride that the elves of Silvanesti must be led home by their estranged cousins.

Though the world turned toward summer and the winds off the cape carried the quickening scent of green and growing things, here on the sea all winds were hard winds. They sapped the moisture from a man's skin, peeled the flesh from his face where the sun did not, and moaned incessantly in the ear until the sound rode him day and night, waking and sleeping. The Silvanesti, some of whom were seamen but many of whom were not, had no love for the wind, the constant droning. Dalamar didn't mind it. He had become attuned to song in his years with K'gathala; he knew how to hear what the wind sang, what the sea chanted. "Elves are sailing home," they cried, each to the other. "Elves are sailing home."

He almost turned to look back to the setting sun, to the places he'd been, to K'gathala, who had not wept to see him leave and had not cursed him for a deserter. She had kissed him, wished him well, and whispered, "Come back when you can," though neither thought he would, even if he could. Almost he turned, and then he didn't. That was finished, that was done. He was going home now, and in his belly excitement ran like threads of fire.

He didn't know what would remain of Silvanost, what of the towers and the temples and the houses of the high folk and low. He had heard tales, dark and grim and filled with sorrow. He had listened, and he had asked questions, and it seemed that no one, no matter how hard he tried, could say what the Sylvan Land truly looked like these days. No matter, no matter. He was going to see for himself, and for that privilege he paid in rough and long work. A loader of supplies in every port, a swabber of decks, repairer of ropes—with the hemp-torn flesh to prove that— he did not mind the fee.

He did not wonder, looking out at the leaping sea, why he did not mind, though he had for so much of his life resented his servitor status. Then, he had been chained by tradition and law as strongly as though by forged steel links. Now, he wore no chain. He had the kind of freedom no other elf aboard this ship or any of the others possessed. He had made a choice no elf here would dare to make, and he'd made it with all his heart.

Gold spilled across the sea, the last of the day. In the west, the moons were rising, pale ghosts of themselves in this light. The Cape of Nordmaar slipped past, that land where dragons still lived, the remnants of dragonarmies yet lurked. Those, claimed Porthios, would be hard to root out. "As hard as the green dragons who made their home in the Silvanesti Forest." His sun-gold face had gone a little pale when he'd said that. Whose did not when thinking on the greens who had made claim to the land that one of their own had ravaged? The aftermath of war came not only in ruined trade, broken cities, the legions of dead whose bones yet bleached in the sun on the Plains of Dust, rotted in the Khalkist Mountains, and lay frozen into Icewall Glacier. It was found in the scattered forces of the broken dragon-armies, mortal folk, and dragons who held with deathgrips to their dark corners, who fought among themselves, terrorized the civilian population, and waited only for another leader to pull them together and make of them what they had been: the terror of Krynn.

Dalamar leaned a little over the rail, watching porpoises leaping, the shining curve of their backs glittering. Some said there were creatures who lived in the sea who looked like porpoises but were other—sea-elves, the sailors called them, people of elf-kind who had found their own way to survive the Cataclysm.

Well, Dalamar thought, we all find ways.

Him, he must find a way, too. He was sailing home, returning to a land that had once loved its people, but one that the Children of Silvanos wouldn't find so welcoming now. To the land of E'li he sailed, to the land where the gods of Good had once ruled, where they would be set up again. Not by his hand would that happen, though, and not in answer to any prayer of his heart. Dalamar Nightson his lover had named him, saying it was a strange name for a Light Elf, yet a fitting one—almost fitting. In the cave north of Silvanost, that secret place from years gone, it might well be that his hidden spellbooks yet remained. It might well be. If they were, if even one was, he would lay his hand upon it, and he would do a thing his heart now clearly called him to do.

To the Dark Son, from a dark son . . .

Those words had dedicated four spellbooks to god-Nuitari, that dark god who was the son of Takhisis and Sargonnas, the god of Vengeance. A better god, this one, for though he walked in darkness, he made no game of what he loved and what he treasured. Nuitari loved only magic, only secrets, only those. A better god for one who had spent his life chained by tradition and kept from the magic he so loved, the magic that fueled his heart with passion.

To the Dark Son, from a dark son . . .

Those words would as fittingly dedicate the heart of

Dalamar Nightson, for he had not done with gods, only with those of Good who had made promises they had not remembered to keep until the world lay broken, their game board in ruin.

* * * * *

"Who was he?" asked the Wildrunner, Elisaad Windsweep. Off to the west, the first thin line of Silvanesti's coast stretched dark as an ink-line. So far out, the coves were straightened by distance, the sweet curves but a sketch. Nonetheless, the winds of home blew off those shores. Home! Every heart on *Bright Solinari* yearned westward, longing to see the forested shores, the shining towers. . . . Beyond reason, they longed for what they'd left and had only the smallest idea of what actually remained. In cabins, on decks, and in the hold where the cargomen tended their loads, tales of Silvanesti sang on the air, stories of the homeland so long left, so deeply missed.

Elisaad stepped across the deck and came a little closer to the soldier who sat perched on the pile of rope. "Raistlin Majere," she said, "the mage who ended the Nightmare. Who was he?"

Dalamar, kneeling near and winding another pile of rope, picked up his head to listen.

"Not *was*," said the soldier. "Is. He's not dead, just gone from our story." He was an elder, this soldier, Arath Wingwild his name, and he had a way of smiling that made everyone near seem no older than a child at his father's knee. Elisaad appeared to like that; Dalamar didn't. Still, he wanted the story as much as Elisaad, and so he kept quiet. Though the hemp scraped his palms raw, he kept working, and he listened.

"Raistlin Majere is a human," said Arath, his nose wrinkling a little, as elves' noses tended to do when outlanders were under discussion. "A mage, and it's said he went to

Wayreth and took his Tests of High Sorcery earlier than most do." His expression darkened. He didn't actually shudder, but he came close. "They didn't deal kindly with him—"

"The wizards there?"

"No, girl. The Tests." The west wind freshened. Arath picked up his head, wondering whether he scented the forest yet. He did not, only the salt sea. "The wizards, they don't come down in favor of a mage or against. They administer the Tests, that's all. What comes of them, well, the mage determines. He passes or he fails on the merit of his knowledge of magic, his ability, and his strength. I've heard it said the Tests always take something from a mage, leaving him marked in some way. This one, this Raistlin Majere, he passed his Tests, but he paid a high fee. Ruined his health, it's said. Frail as a lamb in winter. If you saw him"—now the teller shuddered—"well, you'd know. His skin is a terrible golden color, not sun-gold, not that. Like the metal itself, that kind of gold. And his eyes—"

"His eyes are gold?"

"No. They are black, and the irises . . . they're shaped like an hourglass."

Elisaad snorted, plainly unbelieving. "It's a fantastic enough story. You don't have to add your own touches."

Arath shook his head. "None of these things are my making, girl. What I tell you is true. I saw him in Tarsis with his companions. I was part of Lady Alhana's guard when she went wandering. I saw him when he and his companions met her."

Winding the hemp, leaving small spots of bright blood on the rope, Dalamar remembered the fisherman's story. Some humans, a half-elf, an elf-maid, a kender, and a dwarf—those were the folk who'd given aid to Alhana Starbreeze, the princess wandering in foreign ports. These, the searchers who wanted a dragon orb, went into the Nightmare Kingdom to break the spell of Cyan Bloodbane.

The mage, Raistlin Majere, was one of the humans.

Gulls cried overhead, gray against the blue sky. Dalamar looked westward to the coastline coming nearer . . . to home.

"He has a great power, that mage," Arath said. "It's said all over the ports—in the darker quarters—that if he isn't one to be reckoned with right now, he will be soon."

"A hero?" asked Elisaad.

The old warrior snorted. "Depends on what you mean by that."

"Well, he saved the kingdom, didn't he?"

"He did, but as I hear it, he wanted the dragon orb more than he cared about the kingdom." Arath shrugged. "Ice water in his veins would warm things up for him. He looked at me once, just once, only glancing, and it was like falling into some dark place where the best thing you'll find is terror." Arath pushed away from the rail, away from the memory. "He's gone from the Red magic to the Black, that's what I hear. And so it's just as well he's gone from our story, and since he is, there no need to worry about him more."

"Well, I wasn't worrying about him," Elisaad muttered, not to Arath but to his back as he walked away. "I was just curious."

She walked away, but Dalamar stayed where he was, winding rope and listening to the sea and the cries of the sailors as they worked in the rigging. Home, he thought. Home. But the story of the mage with the hourglass eyes, he who had gone from Red magic to Black, lingered with him, winding like a whisper through all his other thoughts. Who was he? And, more insistent: How did he come to such power that he could lift a green dragon's enchantment from a whole land? Like as not he wouldn't learn the answers to those questions, soon or ever. The mage Raistlin, as Arath had said, was gone from the story of Silvanesti.

* * * * *

By slow, aching degrees, the first skiff made its way up the Thon-Thalas River. It was filled with temple-gear, for the returning elves deemed proper that before anything be set in order, the Temple of E'li must be reconsecrated. The altars must be cleansed, new candles set, and new wands of incense lighted. A lot had been taken out of E'li's Temple for the flight to Silvamori—altar stones, statues of the god, all of the scrolls from the scriptorium. Tapestries sat in long rolls in water-proofed crates, as did jeweled candelabra of silver and gold—all the accoutrements of worship. Dalamar, whose credentials as a servant and who had once worked in the Temple, stood in the back of the skiff. Who better to begin the task of cleaning out the debris?

Weeping over the ruin of the river, the ravaged Thon-Thalas, the wind felt like nothing out of summer. With its cold clammy fingers, it felt like a winter wind. The reeds along the banks drooped, faintly green at the base, pasty brown along the shaft, black and slimy where the feathery seed pods should now be starting to form. It was as though they tried to grow, managed to stagger, and then fell to die. Fish lay rotting in the coves, silvery sheen turned to the blue of a corpse's lips as the scales rotted. Some of these, it seemed, were whole when they'd died. Others bore the marks of mutation, some with thin, twisted limbs, others with three eyes. One or two had wings, and these, trying to fly, had died; for they had wings, but they did not have lungs that liked air better than water.

Above the misery, the sky hung a pall of ragged clouds. In the air, thin mist stank of death, the tatters that dressed the decay and decorated the corruption seen on all sides.

"By the gods," whispered Lord Konnal, his hand upon the hilt of his sword. It was a warrior's gesture, and useless here. "By the gods, I had heard what the place looked like, but I never imagined . . ."

"It is a bitter sight," agreed Porthios.

In this, the elf-prince and the Silvanesti House Holder stood in perfect and rare agreement.

Along the banks of the Thon-Thalas, trees stood like blackened skeletons; in summer's season they were winter's ghosts. Writhen by foul magic, they staggered in terrible twisted shapes. Once-proud aspens bowed low, their slender shapes brutalized by the dragon Cyan Blood-bane's nightmarish spells. Some of those trees bled, not sap but red blood as mortals bleed. Some wept, silver tears running down their trunks as rain runs down.

No one dared touch the trunks or anything else, not even the water in the river. Yet, some yearned to do that, aching to reach out with healing touches, aching to comfort the ravaged land. One of these was a cleric, Caylain, a young woman whose cheeks shone white as a ghost's. She reached, now and then, only to remember that she dared not reach too far.

"Dearest E'li," she whispered, her voice barely heard beneath the muffling of the sleeve she pressed against her mouth and nose. Dalamar heard her, though, for they stood near one another. And he saw the tears streaming down her cheeks as those from the aspens—ever dying, never healing.

Dearest E'li, Dalamar thought, watching the ruin of their homeland slide by. Well, dearest E'li hasn't walked here in a long time.

Dragons did, though. He saw marks of their passage everywhere—snapped branches, the slithering trail of long scaly tails in the mud at the river's edge, and broad flat footprints with the pegged marks of talons. Once, when the skiff came close to the bank, he saw in a nest of mud the jagged shells of leathery eggs, freshly burst. Those eggs had been as large as his torso, and they had held a clutch of dragon young. Soon after, he spotted the sullen gleam of green scales and an eye the size of his hand, evil gold in a midnight iris. These were green dragons, the kind who seldom grew longer than thirty feet—small in comparison to the beasts who had descended from the iron sky over the northern border five years before. Small, but not less dangerous. These greens had great cunning in magic; to them fang and talon were but the crude tools of the lesser of their race. And so, all round the little skiff like a silken cloak, lay spells of protection, magic made and maintained by the two mages who sat, still and silent, in the center of the craft. Eyes closed, lips moving always at the silent weaving of their spell, the mages worked with sweat rolling down their faces, hands clasped so tightly that their knuckles gleamed white. By their strength, those who kept within the skiff were warded from the enticements of the green dragons, safe from the magic that would otherwise lure them into the ravaged forest and to their deaths.

Dragons lived here in the ruined kingdom, yet so did a princess. No, not that. Alhana Starbreeze was more than princess now. She was Speaker of the Stars, for her father was dead. She waited in Silvanost in the Tower of the Stars, anxious for the coming of Porthios and his little fleet. She waited in safety, warded by a full troop of Porthios's own household guard. That troop was a thing Lord Konnal deeply resented, and no one could fail to know it. His face was drawn in lines of indignation; his steely eyes shone with it. Even as he understood it would have been insanity to ask Alhana to wait for protection until he could sail home, he hated the fact that a Qualinesti prince would deploy his own men to protect the Lady of the Silvanesti. Still, he had done that, and none must complain—at least not aloud. Alhana had been at the work of healing each day since Raistlin had freed her realm from the nightmare, a lone woman using only the small skills of earth-heal that most elves have, the tender touch, the loving glance, the dreams in the night in which health and growth first take place. She must be protected in that work; she must be kept safe. None could doubt her gratitude for the help Porthios extended.

The river groaned, and on board the little skiff one of the rowers swore he had to work twice as hard for half the distance as he and his crew forced the vessel to creep against the tide.

"Aye, well," growled Lord Konnal, "then don't waste breath complaining. Row!"

Porthios heard that, but he did not comment, keeping diplomatically out of the lord's way. He stood in the prow of the skiff, looking northward as though it were his only task.

"He is a fine and handsome fellow, this Porthios," said the rower to Dalamar.

Dalamar shrugged. Fair enough for a barbarian Qualinesti, he thought. Aloud, he said, "It's the cut of his weapons I like better than anything else about him."

Behind him, a curse. An oar hit something. "Damn," the Wildrunner growled, tugging at the oar, trying to free it. Curious, Dalamar left the side of flat-bottomed boat and stepped around the mages in the center to peer over the other side.

Lord Konnal turned at the sound of the curse. His glance lighted on Dalamar, dark and baleful. "Lend a hand, you," he snapped.

Dalamar twisted a sour smile, one the lord could not see as he stepped in front of the rower and bent his back to the task of pulling out the oar from whatever snare had caught it. He pulled hard, then again, moving in concert with the Wildrunner. Something had the broad paddle of the oar and held it hard. He shifted his stance and peered out over the edge. The river water slid against the sides of the skiff, oily and brown and thick with silt.

"What is it?" Porthios called, coming back to see. He balanced easily in the shifting skiff, then put his hand on Dalamar's shoulder to move him aside. "Ach, branches—"

The water slapped against the sides of the boat, and the oar slipped suddenly in Dalamar's hands. Startled, he gripped harder, pulling back against what pulled forward. Something *did* pull at the oar; something with intent worked beneath the waters. Clacking and clattering sounded from under the water, then a high keening shrieked up.

The brown water broke, a hand reached up—one of whitened bone, fingers grasping the oar.

"By all the gods!" Porthios stepped back to give himself sword-room.

A hand grabbed Dalamar's arm—Caylain's—and yanked him away from the side of the boat. Porthios's sword came singing from its sheath, the blade gleaming dully in the gray daylight. In one swift arcing motion, the prince swung and brought his sword down, shattering the grip of the bony hand. But it was only one hand, and there were others now, reaching with clattering fingers to grab the sides of the skiff. Once more, hands yanked at the oars, but now the rowers were prepared and held hard.

More swords sang in the air as Wildrunners leaped to defend their charges against the mute and gaping creatures who clawed up from the water. Some, Dalamar saw, were the skeletons of elves, others were of ogres, goblins, and humans. Here were the dead of the last battle for Lorac Caladon's doomed kingdom, and a few yet wore bucklers and swords of their own, hoary weapons whose finest decorations were rust.

A Wildrunner shouted in pain, then in sudden terror. "E'li!" she cried, as though the name of her god must be the last thing she spent breath on. Dalamar knew her by her voice: Elisaad Windsweep, who had wondered about the mage who'd waked the land from Lorac Caladon's nightmare. "O E'li—!"

A bony arm thrust up from the water and grabbed the woman by the hair, yanking her down. Dalamar leaped across the bowed back of a rower still struggling for his oar against another of the bone-warriors. Dragged overboard, Elisaad screamed, her cry heard even above the crash of swords and the rattle of bones as the water claimed her. In the next moment, her hand broke the surface of the brown river, but her face—eyes wide and full of panic, mouth stubbornly shut against the river—showed only hazily through the turmoil of muddy water. Dalamar leaned far over the side of the skiff. Someone grabbed him by the belt and he leaned farther, reaching into the water for the drowning Wildrunner.

"There she is!" Caylain cried, holding onto Dalamar's belt with two hands now. "There!"

"Fight!" Dalamar shouted to her. "Reach for me! Give me your hand!"

Three faces looked up at him, one full of terror, two with empty eye-sockets that nonetheless left the feeling that they were filled with malice.

Swiftly, Dalamar called out a word of magic, one he hadn't used in many long years. It was not the first he'd learned—the call for light, *Shirak*, is ever the first a mage learns—but it was the next. It was, in itself, also a call for light, for it was a call for focus and clarity.

"*Azral!*" he shouted, and Elisaad's eyes went wide to hear magic from this servant, wider still to feel terror fall away from her and purpose flow in after. She surged upward, reaching for his hand, unhampered now by fear.

Skeletal jaws opened and closed in some kind of frantic speech, the brittle clattering heard even above the water's surface. It was the sound of old leaves scrabbling on midnight paths. Elisaad's hand closed tight around Dalamar's wrist, her eyes met his, bright and clear and filled with trust. Someone cursed; someone else sobbed in pain or terror.

Lord Konnal shouted, "Behind! There are more behind!"

Dalamar dared not look to see behind *where*. He could only hope they were not behind Caylain, for two of the undead grabbed Elisaad, one to hold her shoulders, another her legs.

Elisaad screamed.

The attackers held, and they had the same strength they might have had in life. Some elves, others old foes, all of them had a consuming hatred of the living. Dalamar pulled again, and now Elisaad's head was above water.

"Caylain!" he shouted, hanging on to Elisaad.

Caylain, pull! Caylain, don't let go! All these things he meant when he shouted, all these things the cleric understood at once. With one mighty surge, Caylain threw herself backward, dragging Dalamar, dragging Elisaad with him. The Wildrunner came up, head and shoulders, and she had a hand free to grasp the side of the wildly rocking boat. The release of resistance sent Caylain tumbling. Dalamar staggered, then reached for Elisaad again.

"Take my hand!"

She dragged herself higher out of the water, reaching. Someone came between Dalamar and her—Porthios in pursuit of a rattling, clattering foe—and her eyes went wide in horror again.

"No!" she screamed. "No-o-o-o!"

She vanished and disappeared, screaming beneath the water. Cursing, Dalamar leaped for the side of the boat. But he was too late. He reached the water's edge only in time to see the last of Elisaad, the pale oval of her face, the terror in her eyes as her lungs filled with brackish river water and the undead dragged her to her death.

Raging, Dalamar turned, and he snatched up the nearest thing he could find for a weapon—a rusted sword, the blade pitted and scarred. One, two, and three of the skeletal beings came clattering after him, jaws working but no sound issuing, their eye-sockets empty as dry wells. He swung about as though he were a warrior trained, instinctively holding the sword in a two-handed grip, not flailing but finding the same rhythm he saw Porthios using—arc and swing, for thrusting did a man no good in this kind of fight. He must swipe heads from neck and chop bony limbs from their sockets. He must dismantle in order to kill. This he did in rage, the wail of the woman stolen from his grasp like a spur to his fury.

Not until a hard hand grabbed his arm and held his swing did he stop. Not until Porthios pried the rusted sword from his grip did he look up to see that the fighting was finished, the battle won. In the fallen stillness, Dalamar heard the slap of water against the skiff, the hiss of a quickening wind in the dying reeds. Someone coughed. Someone else groaned, and he smelled blood. He looked around him and saw that two of the Wildrunners had deep wounds. The mages sat in the center of the skiff, still bowed over, still white-faced and weaving their spells.

In the moment Dalamar's glance alighted on them, Konnal's gaze touched him. Cool and narrow, that glance, glittering with suspicion as he eyed him from brown boots to dun shirt.

"Servitor," he said, "you dress strangely for a mage."

Dalamar's tongue leaped nimbly for the lie. "I haven't practiced magic since the war, my lord. I was the servant of Lord Tellin Windglimmer and served him in the Temple of E'li. He was pleased to have me learn the ways of magic. He's dead now, and no one seems to have taken as much interest." His history neatly amended, he shrugged. "No matter. I'm pleased to have remembered some little of what I learned." He glanced at the river and the calming surface of the water. Now he didn't have to feign his feeling. "I wish I had been able to do more for the Wildrunner."

"Indeed," Konnal said, eyes no less narrow, no less cold. "I've never approved of teaching a servitor the arts of magic. They get above themselves and find their heads filled with ideas they can't properly understand. Nothing but trouble comes of that."

He seemed to expect a reply, and Dalamar had none that would please him. After a moment, eyes properly lowered, he murmured, "If you have no other question, my lord, I'll return to minding the crates."

Konnal gestured curtly and sent Dalamar to his work. Somewhere upriver, a long moaning howl wound through the thickness of green mist. A dragon called, and another answered. In the water around the skiff, one small line of bubbles sailed up to break the brackish surface. Then all was still and remained so for the rest of the journey.

Chapter 12

~

The pain of the land moaned in Dalamar's very bones. He felt it most keenly as the little skiff put in at the docks on the north side of the city. He stepped gingerly from the vessel to creaking wood, hoping the rotting posts would hold. It was not easier when he walked into the city. In the Arts District the towers had tumbled, and the fair buildings of marble and quartz were fallen to ruin.

"It might have been a thousand years since we last walked here," whispered the cleric Caylain to one of her fellows. Her face was as pale as Solinari's moon, her long eyes wide and dark with sorrow.

The rose marble walls of the museums and theaters and libraries bore the wounds of cracks, and smaller buildings had fallen in on themselves, roofs shattered, walls collapsed. The statuary lining the streets were unrecognizable. Where the generals on their wide-winged griffins? Where the Wildrunner, bow nocked, fierce eyes glaring? Where the gods, Kiri-Jolith with his Sword of Justice, E'li, the dragon rampant? Where, Quenesti-Pah, her arms outstretched, and the Blue Phoenix, and Astarin with his harp? Gone, all gone, their images melted, shattered, fallen to dust and blown away. Not even ravens clung to the ruined aspen branches.

Down the long boulevard from the Arts District to the Garden of Astarin, on shattered pavers, the cracks oozing slime as green as the mist hanging in the air, the first elves to return from Silvamori went like a funeral. All walked in silence, each in grief, until at last they came to the Garden of Astarin. Then did they cry out, the lords and the Wildrunners and the clerics. They cried to see the garden, the boxwood that framed it into a star only naked sticks, brown and lifeless. They wept for the silence of the place and sobbed to see the Tower of the Stars. This, of all the structures in the city, had fared worst. Turrets lay in piles of rubble on the ground, and the walls bore cracks that went right through to the heart of the stone. The gems that once studded the walls lay scattered about the lifeless grounds, fallen years before.

And the elves wept, they wept, to see their princess, Alhana Starbreeze, come out from that ruin to greet them, for in her amethyst eyes lay all her pain, her grief for her father's folly and death, her sorrow for the land. None could look into those eyes and not think her aged beyond the count of her years. None could look and not weep, for she was now—as once her father had been—the embodiment of the land.

Only Dalamar kept still, only he didn't weep or cry out, and that was because had he shouted, he'd have shouted in rage against those very gods whose statues now lay fallen, those gods who played out their bids for power in the hearts of mortals, jockeying for position as though Krynn were only a khasboard and Silvanesti simply a quarter of the field.

And so, in the ruin of high places, the high met. In aching gardens, among trees only weakly healing and others simply dying, among the skeletons of boxwood and hydrangea and peonies, Porthios of the Qualinesti greeted Alhana of the Silvanesti. The two exchanged dry kisses of state while Qualinesti Wildrunners warded the Tower of the Stars and the Head of House Protector, Lord Konnal, stood by. His unhappiness was not veiled, and all who saw him knew he had no love for Porthios, to whom he had stood subservient on the voyage home. Anyone with eyes knew he disliked the idea that Alhana seemed so willing to welcome this Qualinesti so warmly.

Dalamar saw no more of that meeting. "Go," said Lord Konnal, even as the rest went to greet their princess. "You are not wanted here. Start your work in the Temple of E'li.

Dalamar went, wandered the temple grounds, and walked in the broken building. In sanctuaries and meditation rooms, the wind echoed mournfully. In the scriptorium where he had, for a while, been the one who sharpened the quills and scraped the parchments clean for new use, was only dust. Beyond the window the garden lay dead; not even weeds grew. Where had he stood on the morning he'd taken the little embroidered scroll case from the hand of Lady Lynntha for Lord Tellin Windglimmer? There, by that broken wall? So changed was everything, every place, that nothing woke the ghosts of memory.

Dalamar walked once down the chill corridor that ended in a room still sealed after five years. This was the place, the secret place, where a Circle of Darkness would be set if ever there was reason to do so. Here murderers and traitors were condemned to the worst punishment the Silvanesti could devise: exile. Here worshipers of the gods of Neutrality or those of Evil, mages found in magic other than white magic had been judged and cast out from the people. Upon the walls of that sealed chamber, the platinum mirrors were fixed. The Chain of Truth lay within, a wide circle of platinum links spread around the room where the accused would stand, waiting for gods to bid the chain to bind him or be still to keep him safe. He did not stay long there, for it was a cold place. When he left that place he saw, just a glimpse, a shadow on the broken earth outside. Someone else walked these grounds.

Aye, well, he thought, good luck finding comfort here.

So thinking, Dalamar went through the rest of the ruined Temple, walking through the debris of years and listening to the dry wind moaning, the skitter and scrabble of old leaves on cracked marble floors. He walked into the garden windblown, wild as any heathen forest. Who could recognize this place now?

Dalamar stood among the ruin of the Temple and looked

orth to the place where, all that summer before the war, he ad kept hidden his most precious secret, his found spellooks, his dark tutors. They tugged, a little, memories of nose books. What pulled harder, what called in a stronger oice, was a resolution he had made, far away on the shores f Silvamori. Dalamar Nightson must tell a god that he had new name.

Who will know? he wondered, looking out over the wall the Tower of the Stars. Who will know if I am here taking iin's inventory, or if I am not? No one.

He went quickly through the city, through desolate garens whose borders would not now be discerned by any ho had not known them before war and nightmare. bove, the aspens reached aching branches to the sky, like lack claws and rotting bones. The sun shone harshly, glarg at him as he went. The ferry was gone, the enspelled irtles who used to pull it fled or killed, but he found a lace where the river ran thinly, speaking of damming pstream. Someone had erected a bridge, perhaps the Quanesti guard, and this he took to the other side. There, he n into the darker shadows of the forest. Running, he soon ime to a place where once two paths had forked. He saw nly barest sketches of them on the land now. He swerved ito the darker forest, leaping blowdowns easily. Running, e shouted aloud, the sound like thunder in the silence of a rest emptied of all life but malignant life, secret, sullen, rooding life. He felt what he always used to feel when he ft the tended paths, the designated ways. All the strictures f his life, all the ridiculous rules, all the choking ties that ound him to the intractable pattern of life among the Silanesti fell away.

Running, Dalamar was free. But, running, he was not lone. Swift behind him, silent behind him, ran others, like nadow-hounds coursing his trail.

* * * * *

Dalamar stood still on the edge of the path down to th[e] ravine, extending his senses as far as he could, both natur[al] and arcane. His magic had long ago fallen; the wards he s[et] years before were dead. Below the mouth of the cave gape[d] dark and wide. Would the wards on the books themselve[s] have held? He didn't know, though they were Nuitari's, [a] work dedicated to him. Perhaps they would have survive[d]

And if they hadn't?

Then they hadn't. They were treasures, and they wer[e] artifacts, but they were not more than physical manifest[a]tions of what he loved. They were not the magic, only on[e] mage's shaping of it.

All around lay silence. His ears ached for the sound [of] birds in the trees, water in the stream, but the land lay de[s]olate, exhausted. Birds had long ago flown away. Those th[at] had not were long dead. Somewhere, deep in the fores[t] green dragons roamed, and creatures worse than they. B[ut] not here. Here nothing lived. The wind stirred above th[e] ravine, high in the rattling branches of despoiled aspen[.] The miasma that befouled all of the air in the kingdo[m] swirled a little, like steam over a stinking pot. Dalam[a] lifted his arm to cover his nose and mouth with his sleev[e] and went down into the ravine, down to his cave and th[e] promise he longed to keep.

* * * * *

The pulse of magic no longer ran in the cave, not even [a] whisper of what had been breathed in the darkness. It w[as] a dead place, not but stone and dust and air long unbreathe[d]

Softly, Dalamar whispered, "*Shirak!*" and light leape[d] into this hand, a clear cool globe. He hung it in the darkne[ss] and looked around. The dust of years lay upon the flo[or] marked by the tiny tracks of mice and voles. His work tab[le] of wild green marble was broken, cracked in the middle an[d] fallen in two. The pots of herbs and oils and other spe[ll] components he had so secretly gathered in summer, a long time ago, were but shards in the dust, fallen from the niches in the stone wall, their colors dimmed, their contents dried and gone.

His light leading, Dalamar walked through the cave, dust puffing away from his boots, all the way to the back where he'd hidden his books. The wards were gone, too small to stand before the magic that had warped cities. The mice had found a treasure between the covers, nesting material for the generations. In the five years since last he'd seen the books, nothing remained but gnawed leather covers and a few scraps. He bent to touch one, yellow and brittle. A few letters marked the edge of the scrap, vestiges of some spell. Gone, all that work, all that crafting, gone.

Dalamar looked around at the cave, the ragged shadows, the ruin. Somewhere, beyond Krynn, beyond the battles of the rest of their godly kin, Nuitari and Solinari and red Lunitari did abide, the three gods of magic. To one, bright Solinari, Dalamar had allowed himself to be consecrated. He did not speak to that one now, but to the darkest god.

"Nuitari," he whispered, the name on his lips a prayer. "O Dark Son, in your shadows I have found comfort, in your darkness I have plied secrets. In your night, O Nuitari, I have hidden my heart."

The words came, unframed, unconsidered. Dalamar dropped to his knees. This gesture he made with the whole of his heart, he who had been bending the knee in one way or another all his life, knelt now because he wanted to do that.

"O child of dark gods, O keeper of secrets deep and terrifying, hear me."

In the ruin of his secret place, he lifted his hands and motes of dust made silver by the sphere of cool light danced around his fingers.

"Hear me, Dark Son! I have come to make a pledge to you, and I have come to consecrate myself truly."

On the floor, like a shard of darkness separated from shadows, a jagged piece of pottery lay. Dalamar took it up finding the sharpest edge with his thumb. He smiled and looked deeply into the shadows far back in the cave. All around him lay the broken remains of his small secret studies, the little trove of spellbooks shredded, his work table broken, the spell components he'd so carefully gathered dried and gone to dust. Before him lay shadows, darkness stretching far back to regions he had never gone. He listened to the cave breathe, the airs of distant places running around in darkness, and he breathed in rhythm with it. Breathing, he found magic, felt it sparkling in his blood firing his heart.

"Yours," he said to the god who was not there, yet who was ever near, "yours is the realm of magic and secrets." He lifted his heart and his hands, the potshard still held in his right, gleaming. "Yours is the dark path where power exist for its own sake, unbounded, unbridled. O Nuitari, yours is the path my feet will walk, and yours is the path my heart will follow."

He clenched his right hand, suddenly, convulsively grinding the jagged shard of pottery into the flesh of his palm. Blood, black in the cool mage-light, ran in one thin line from between his fingers. He moved his hand over the small scrap of parchment, the last of a wondrous page. The first drop of his blood fell on the scrap, hissing. In the moment he heard the sound, Dalamar felt his heart fill with dark and howling power. The hair on the back of his neck raised, and sudden sweat ran down his cheeks. The second drop of his blood fell, the parchment smoked, and the scrap rolled and tumbled, leaping into flame as though it were, in fact, the whole of all the pages of four books, not this little shred.

Shadows leaped up the walls. Flames as red as blood ran in sudden circle around the mage kneeling on the stony floor. Winds howled, though no wind stirred. Storm sounded hough no rain fell and outside the sky was bitterly bright. Heatless fire, dancing flames, light like the light in a dragon's eye . . .

Dalamar lifted his fists, the bleeding and the clean, and s he did, such fires of magic ran in him as would rival the flames he saw now. His blood burned, his heart soared, and his soul sang darkly, hymns to a god whose name elves never mentioned, whose image no elf made, whose prayer o elf chanted. In that moment, Dalamar knew the god of his heart, the god who makes no promise and so breaks no promise. He knew the god to whom magic is all.

"Nuitari!" he shouted, with all the strength of his heart, all the breath in his lungs. He cried, "Nuitari! Once I was Dalamar Argent. I have come to tell you that Dalamar Argent is dead! I am Dalamar Nightson, and I am yours, O Dark Son. I am yours in the hidden night, yours in the glaring day. I am yours in magic, yours in prayer. I am yours—"

Outside the cave, voices whispered, voices raised in question and then lowered in cursing. A twig snapped. Dalamar's heart leaped hard in his chest, thundering. The shadows on the walls retreated, scurrying down the stone s the blood-red fire fell and died. The magic gone, ripped from him, Dalamar turned toward the cave's entrance.

The opening shone like one malevolent eye, white and bright. Tall shapes stood there, dark as nightmare against the glare. He tried to gain his feet but could not. With the magic gone, so was all the strength he'd used to support it. He staggered, fell, and a woman's voice shouted, "Take him!"

Six Wildrunners ran into the cave. They circled him, as magic's fire had done, wary and glaring at him over drawn blades. Then one, the woman who had first cried out, laughed, a brittle, edgy sound.

"So this is what servants do when they ignore the orders of their betters. You'd have done better, servitor, to obey Lord Konnal's orders and kept to temple grounds."

He said nothing, for he knew no word of his would ava
now.

"He's weak," the Wildrunner sneered. "He has none o
that foul black magic to use. Take him to Lord Konnal!"

They fell on Dalamar. Roughly they tore him from th
floor and bound his hands tightly behind his back. Thei
faces were ugly, wrenched by fear and loathing. One,
stocky young man, spat at him, and the trail of his spittle o
Dalamar's cheek felt like acid etching into his flesl
Another put a noose round his neck to lead him by, an
thus he was taken from his secret place and dragged bac
through the forest to Silvanost and the Temple of E'li. Ther
they bound him, and they flung him into a small, lightles
cell in the Temple. They did not feed him; they gave him n
water to drink. They left him alone, and outside the cell
watch of Wildrunners stood constant guard.

In the night, owls mourned, and mice scurried. In th
night came pain so deep it was like a toothed thing gnaw
ing at his organs. Through the long watches, Dalamar la
on the hard cold floor, refusing to groan, refusing to tur
from the agony. Savaged by a green dragon's magic, broke
and filthy, still there were artifacts of E'li's magic in th
Temple, and these did not love a mage who had turne
from the Light, an elf whose heart now beat in the dar
rhythms of Nuitari's magic. No matter, no matter. He lay i
pain, and he didn't groan. He lay in pain, and he embrace
it. What else could he do? Wail and cry out?

Never.

* * * * *

The gray sky hung low. Wind rattled the naked branche
of ravaged aspens and made the green miasma writhe. Th
pale ruined towers of Silvanost loomed high over the cit
like wretched ghosts gathered to watch a terrible undertal
ing, the convening of the Ceremony of Darkness. With h

hands bound behind him, exhausted by pain and barely able to keep on his feet, Dalamar Argent, Dalamar Nightson stood in the garden of the Temple of E'li, still and silent. Wildrunners ranged all around him in a circle, weaponed and glaring as though they feared that the dark mage they'd found among them would suddenly rise up and destroy everyone in his sight. Smiling coldly, Dalamar lifted his head. They looked away, one by one, unwilling to meet the eye of a dark mage.

Upon a broken roof tile of the Temple, a dove dropped mournful notes into the silence, sounds like weeping. Though he did not turn to look, Dalamar knew the dove sat above the little room where the Ceremony of Darkness would soon take place. The ranks of the Wildrunners parted. Into the circle stepped Alhana Starbreeze, with Porthios on one side and Lord Konnal of House Protector on the other. The one, the Qualinesti, looked sober and solemn, his face pale, his eyes guarded. In the eyes of the other, the Lord of the Wildrunners, something glittered that reminded Dalamar of snakes. A little behind them came the clerics, the leader of them Caylain, who had once leaned over the edge of the skiff and longed to touch the wounded river. Her pale hair was bound upon her head in a crown of braids. Upon her breast lay her medallion of faith—E'li as the platinum dragon rampant. In her eyes, loathing like poison swirled. She, the lords Konnal and Porthios, and Alhana herself would be his judges, his Council of Truth. There should have been a host of clerics to accompany them, as well as a clutch of lords from House Mystic and enough Wildrunners to line every avenue to the Temple. There should have been drums, deep-voiced and solemn, and brittle bells ringing. There should have been incense burning, and someone, somewhere, should have been weeping—a friend, a lover, a sorrowful mother. None of these graced the ceremony, for here Dalamar had no friend or lover, no kin to grieve his fall from the Light, and the accoutrements of power and pomp were fallen to ruin. This was to be a casting out, but a casting out from a ravaged land.

Alhana lifted her head, her lovely eyes unreadable. "My lords," she said, her voice cold as winter night. "We are gathered here in reckoning and judgment. First, we reckon."

She gestured, a small motion of her white hand. Caylain stepped forward. Head high, plainly forcing herself to look into the eyes of the sinner, she said, "Dalamar Argent, you are brought here for judgment, taken in shameful acts of false worship, taken in the very act of dark magic. What have you to say?"

Dalamar stood in unyielding silence.

Caylain looked uneasily around, for tradition decreed that the accused must speak or that someone must speak for him. No one stepped forward. No one even moved. Faces like marble, pale and hard, eyes like diamonds glittering, the guard of Wildrunners barely breathed. The lords Konnal and Porthios didn't even swallow. Wind sighed; white robes rustled. Far away, deep in the forest, dragons roared. Behind Caylain one of the clerics moistened dry lips, his eyes darting right and left, afraid. Dalamar did not move.

Her voice unsteady, Caylain went on, "You have no champion, and you will not champion yourself. You will go into the Temple, into the Circle of Darkness. In that place a man who protests his innocence is judged. It is the place, where the man who is guilty is given a glimpse of the road he has chosen. Dalamar Argent, look into your heart, heed your soul, and prepare yourself for the Circle of Darkness."

Dalamar looked nowhere. He needed nothing. In his belly, fear turned sour and cold.

"Take him," Alhana said, her voice low and quiet as the dove. Ah, but a stone dove, a dove whose resolve could never be bent or reshaped. She nodded to Konnal, who directed two of his warriors to come forward.

"Aleaha," he said, snapping the name like a command. "Rilanth. Take him to the temple."

They came forward with jaws stubbornly set, the elf-woman Aleaha Takmarin and Rilanth her cousin. They came as though they'd been asked to take a dragon into the Temple. Determined, they seized him, one by each arm. Seeing him bound did not make things easier for them. Their fear communicated itself to Dalamar; he smelled it as a wolf would. He smiled, and he didn't care who saw it. Their fear acted on him like a tonic. It is said in all the houses of the powerful: *In the fear of others lies power for the man who can recognize it and use it.* Though Dalamar knew no use for the fear of these two, still it energized him and lent him strength.

Groaning, the wind grew stronger. Alhana's hair whipped about her face now, darkly foaming around her cheeks and shoulders. Again, a dragon cried, one loud long shriek of rage and joy drifting eerily on the air. Another answered, and one of the Wildrunners cursed under his breath. Out in the ravaged aspenwood, dragons were breeding and living as though they owned the kingdom.

The sun climbed limping up the sky, a sickly dull ball seen only dimly through the ever-shifting green mist, the last breath of Lorac's Nightmare hanging over the land as the two Wildrunners marched Dalamar out from the circle, through the garden, and into the Temple of E'li.

* * * * *

Praying ritual prayers, three clerics unwound a length of chain, thick and heavy. They made a circle around the whole of the little chamber, stitching the floor and creating a magical space from which Dalamar could not move.

"From darkness, O E'li," they whispered, "from darkness preserve us. From evil, O E'li, from evil defend us. From darkness, O E'li . . ." Thus did they pray to the very god who had not thought to shield them from darkness, who had not lifted even a hand to defend them from the evil that yet ravaged their city and tormented their land. The chain set, they lit wands of pungent incense and, trailing smoke and prayers, walked around the outside of the circle, sunwise three times. Low and stern, their voices demanded that evil not be allowed to enter into this chamber.

Dalamar watched them, narrow-eyed. They prayed, and yet, here evil was, standing ready to learn its fate, evil in the shape of an elf who was not blinded by the light.

At Caylain's command, Dalamar went and stood in the exact center of the circle, finding the place more easily than did she who directed him to go there. She was afraid of the circle, the ceremony, and the little room itself. He, too, was afraid, but he had the strength to keep his fear to himself, unwilling to lend weapons to enemies. He stood proudly defiant in the center of the circle, a servitor in dun clothing, a dark mage uncovered, bringing all his will to bear and forcing his weary muscles to keep still.

Burnished platinum mirrors hung upon the walls and even upon the door. These shone dully in the dim light that sifted down from the ceiling. By this light he saw himself in hazy reflection: a tall young elf, straight-backed, shoulders braced, head high. Not the least suggestion of dismay marked his face or dimmed his clear eyes as the Council of Truth—Alhana Starbreeze, Porthios of the Qualinesti, Lord Konnal, and the cleric Caylain—came to stand outside the circle. It fell to the cleric to speak.

"Dalamar Argent," she said, her voice dry as the rattle of naked branches, "hear the judgment that has been passed."

Alhana's hands clenched and unclenched; the pulse at the base of her neck jumped. Dalamar saw this in the mirrors. She looked like a woman standing in the halls of an ancient crypt where the souls of the dead do not rest easily. Porthios took a small step toward her, a side-step no one saw except Dalamar.

"This is what will be," Caylain said, and if her voice did not tremble, her hand certainly did as it absently smoothed creases from her white robe. "You will stand within this circle for the space of twelve hours. You will stand alone, and things will be shown to you, things of which I cannot warn you, for they are things I do not know."

These were the words of ritual now, not Caylain's own.

"As the images emerge, a thing will happen," said Caylain, "or a thing will not happen. In accordance with your guilt or innocence, the chain will move to bind you, or it will lie still and leave you free."

There was no doubt in the eyes of any how the platinum chain would behave. But forms must be honored, so it is among elves. Forms must be honored, even when they made no sense to the moment.

"May the gods preserve you," Caylain murmured.

Yet another form. No one in the chamber believed for an instant that any god they prayed to would preserve him. Caylain turned and walked out from the room, the hem of her robe whispering to the floor, her pale hands folded tightly. Lord Konnal followed, and Alhana after him with Porthios at her side, matching her step for step. Only the Qualinesti looked at Dalamar, his swift glance seen in reflection, perhaps thought secret. It was the glance of a warrior who wonders how well the courage of a man will stand him in his steepest test.

Well enough, said Dalamar's wry smile. Well enough, and you need not wonder.

Porthios's eyes flashed suddenly, the prince unhappy to have his thoughts so easily read, so ironically answered. Then he, too, no longer looked at the prisoner within the platinum circle. He walked from the chamber, his hand at the small of Alhana's back, guiding her as men politely guide women, in courtesy.

Alone, alone, Dalamar stood. In his belly fear sat, hard and cold and leeching poison. What road had he chosen, what road in the darkness would he walk?

Then came the ghosts, each reflected in mirrors, first hazily, then more clearly, marching to the sound of a platinum chain creeping ever closer, scraping upon the floor. Each phantom had his face. All the ghosts were him.

* * * * *

Ghost-Dalamar walked in wilderness, in foreign lands where the people did not know his name. He wandered the streets of fabled cities, and he was shunned. He walked in darkness, alone as only an elf can understand, and it seemed to him that his heart had broken long ago. Only lifeless shards rattled around in his breast now. He saw his name vanish from all the records of the Silvanesti. He saw himself un-made, and he heard his name in the mouths of humans, dwarves, kender, and others. *Lord Dalamar!* "Lord," they said, the title spoken in awe, sometimes with respect. In the mouths of many of them his name was the same as another word for fear.

He smiled to see that. Even as he did, the ghostly images swayed, sliding on the platinum, shifting in the mirrors, unforming and forming again.

Dalamar saw three mages, three with their heads together, talking or arguing. One was an old man in white robes, another a beautiful silver-haired woman in dark. The third was a limping man in his middle years, and he wore red. They turned from their talking and looked at him, their faces on all sides of him and behind, their eyes glittering with fierce knowledge, with slashing ambition, with stern commitment. Even in this vision Dalamar felt the weight of their regard, knowing that weight had crushed some, but not knowing whether or not it would crush him. He did not flinch, though he knew many others had, and in his heart rang these words, this greeting to the three: "I have nothing to lose." The three looked at one another, and the wizardess

n the dark robes said to her companions that these were the
words of the truly free.

Again the vision shifted, and now Dalamar saw himself
standing upon a threshold. Before him was a door beyond
which only darkness lay, a maelstrom of ambition, a storm
of hatred and longing and power so deep and strong that
the foundations of the world did shake to support it. He put
his hand upon the skull-shaped doorknob and pushed.

The images in the mirrors flowed again, slowly now, like
thick blood running. Dalamar saw himself standing with
two other mages, a man in white robes and a woman wearing red.

"Are you ready?" asked the red-robed woman. She
looked at him with a lover's eyes, and he read desperation
and a hopeless fear in there.

The vision flowed faster now, running like a river in
spate, racing, whirling, swirling all around him. If he could
have moved, Dalamar would have turned from it. Yet had
he done that, the vision would have followed.

Fire rose up out of the ocean. A hole gaped wide in the
sea that he somehow knew for the Turbidus Ocean. Darkness, bred of rage, flowed out from that fiery rift and all
around the clash of battle thundered, the screams of the
dying, the rage of dragons, illuminated by fire and the
battle-light flashing from swords. Someone screamed. It
was he! And all the blood was running out of him even as
eyes so terrible he dared not meet their glance raked him,
tearing flesh from his bones, clawing to find something in
him—his soul. Takhisis, he thought, for her name is the
name of terror. A voice like the howling in a madman's
mind shrieked in laughter.

Not she! The faithless whore! Not she!

And still the terrible eyes tore at him, peeling him layer
by layer, skin from muscle, muscle from bone, soul from
body. Ah, Nuitari! Shield me—

Never he! The serpent-son! Never he!

All the world fell away, even as the body fell from his soul. He saw now only insanity, destruction, no light, no darkness, nothing but ravening and annihilation, madness feeding on madness and rage upon rage like wolves turning upon each other. Towers tumbled and cities burned around him. Pledges came undone. Oaths unraveled. In all lands, among all kindred, brothers turned upon brothers, sons murdered their fathers, mothers their daughters. Children cut their teeth on the sword's blade and played with daggers in the cradle, while disease ran like fire, and fire ate stone. Stone rained down like stars falling out of the sky and gods ran screaming, wailing in midnight places. There was no evil now, no good. There was not that slender path between the poles upon which red-robed mages so carefully trod. There was only the maw of destruction that understood nothing of the balance of life and death, the eternal struggle between light and dark.

All this Dalamar saw in those terrible, devouring eyes, all this and more . . . and worse.

He saw his soul, and it lay in the clawed hand of that father of emptiness. About him fluttered something small and dully gleaming, something light as parchment and empty, empty with no magic in it or anything to love. It was the soul of a man whose touch made no mark in the world, the soul of a useless man, a helpless man. Emptiness drained the life out of this effectless soul as it drained out the life of the world.

Emptiness. Never to be filled, and even the weeping of gods did cease. . . .

And he stood again upon the threshold of the chamber whose door presented a knob like a grinning silver skull. He saw a mage standing in the shadows, dark-robed, his face hidden, his eyes not even two gleams of light in that darkness.

"Come," said the mage, his voice a strange, dry whisper.

"*Shalafi,*" whispered Dalamar, the image in the mirrors

194

the man in the circle. "Master," he said, as a student to his teacher. But what teacher, where? And in the mirrors five small marks, spaced as though they were the prints of all the fingers of a man's spread hand, appeared upon the breast of each image of Dalamar. Dark they were, then they were red, and the red ran slowly, like blood dripping down.

A man screamed, and then no one screamed. Then there was only darkness, and the touch of cold platinum round his ankles, the chain come so close now that it did begin to bind him, circling him around and around, the links piling up and climbing to his knees as a line of light opened in the darkness behind.

"And so you see," whispered a voice, that of Caylain the cleric. "And so you see what road you will travel, Dalamar Argent. A road of blood and darkness."

So he had seen, and though it seemed only an instant in passing, these visions had flowed over him, around him, and through him for twelve hours. His leaden limbs knew that, his knees shaking with exhaustion, his belly growling with hunger. His throat, dry as a desert, knew that.

Dalamar lifted his head, and his eyes still filled with visions of emptiness, of blood and wounding and the mage whose face was lost in darkness. "I have seen," he said, his voice thick and ragged.

They shuddered to hear him, the simplicity of his words, the starkness of his thirst-ravaged voice. They shuddered, and they looked to each other, taking his pain as confirmation of his guilt.

Aye, well. There was surely pain—all the pain of standing within this temple, this hall of white gods, flowing into him from the tiles. It rose up from the floor through his feet. It ran into his arms, and from the ceiling it rained down like fire.

"I am yours," he said to the pain and the darkness yet to befall. For there would be more, and soon. This Ceremony of Darkness was not nearly done. "I am yours," he said to the god no one here dared name. He smiled, not with joy and certainly not for mirth. He smiled, though, and he did so because he had chosen his path. He who had been allowed to choose nothing in all his life, whose days were ordered by custom and traditions forged by a king long dead, he chose his path. "Nuitari . . ."

Caylain shuddered, and in that moment others came into the chamber, their faces white in the shadowed hoods of their cloaks. Porthios came, and Alhana whose eyes were cold as stone, whose face was set in an unyielding expression of disdain. A chill struck Dalamar, hard to the heart. She was, this princess, the embodiment of the land. She looked upon him now as though she did not see him, as though he were not standing before her. As Lord Konnal led a small troop of Wildrunners into the chamber, Alhana Starbreeze turned her face from Dalamar, from the dark elf, and walked away. The land forsook him.

It was the first moment of his exile.

Chapter 13

~

"Dark elf," they called him, the name of an exile, the name of one who has fallen from the light and the kindred of Silvanos. *Dark elf.* The name sat on Dalamar's heart like ice, cold and creeping, dragging numbness through his very blood.

Through gray, raining woodlands they took him, until they came to the banks of the Thon-Thalas, the river that would run swiftly to the sea and bring him out of Silvanesti, out of the company of elves. They would rather have marched him through the forest, hands bound, feet hobbled, face hidden behind a dark cowl. In other times, in better times, they would have done that, crying his crime to all they passed, farmers and villagers, boatmen and potters and princes. "Here is a dark mage! Here is a criminal of the worst order! Look away from Dalamar Argent! Never speak his name again! Forbid him the forest if ever you see him! He is dead to us! Here is a dark mage! Here is a criminal . . . !"

But they could not parade him through the aspenwood, not here in the ruined kingdom. They could only shout to the green dragons out in the wilderness. What did the dragons care? Still, they shouted. Ritual demanded it. Form must be filled. They made the best of their Ceremony of Darkness that they could without the traditional accoutrements.

On the barren grounds of the Tower of the Stars, Lord Konnal read from a newly inscribed parchment, detailing Dalamar's crime in a voice that echoed and re-echoed from the empty stone towers of the city. "He has worshiped falsely, cleaving to evil gods! He has made dark magics and done evil deeds! He has turned from the Light!"

That done, he passed the scroll to Caylain. This record would be entered into the libraries of House Cleric, where his name would be stricken from all documents that held it. Any mention made of him in the houses where he'd served would vanish. All record that he had studied in House Mystic would be erased. Only his birth record would remain, and it would be copied over to the secret tomes kept in the Temple of E'li where the names of dark elves were kept. Then, even his birth record would vanish. He would not exist in the annals of his people. His homeland would never hear his name spoken, or ever feel the tread of his feet upon its soil.

While the rain dripped down and mist moved in sickly green waves, Alhana Starbreeze judged Dalamar guilty of crimes of magic, and she declaimed his sentence of exile to all gathered.

"He has turned from the Light," she cried in a firm, clear voice, "and the Light will turn from him." Her eyes cold as ice, she lifted her head and looked him full in the face. "Be gone from us, Dalamar Argent. Never come here again, and never seek to hear your name upon the lips of any of the Children of Silvanos."

In the eyes of Porthios, of Alhana and Konnal, upon the faces of all present, Dalamar saw this: He was dead to them, less than a ghost. And it felt as if he were, for it seemed no blood ran in him to warm. It seemed his heart had stopped its beating.

In the ruined land, they had no cleric but Caylain to bless the Dark Escort in the name of E'li, those charged with removing the dark elf from the precincts of Light, from Silvanesti. And even that escort was not so thick with Wildrunners as tradition wished it could be. Of mages there were some, those who had warded the little skiff from the spells of green dragons on the trip up the Thon-Thalas to Silvanost. This work they would do again, for the journey downriver would be just as dangerous.

No one looked at Dalamar as he was loaded into the skiff. Loaded, yes, for he could hardly walk, and his hands were not free to help him balance. He hit the hard bottom of the boat on his knees, then fell over onto his side. Rain, falling heavier now, slid down his face, almost like tears, but he did not weep. Instead he lay in silence, cold and shivering, his body wracked with pain that came from no physical wounds. Nothing he endured in the Temple of E'li as he'd waited his Ceremony of Darkness felt like this. Nothing he'd seen in the Circle of Darkness had given him to know he would feel pain like this.

Something is being cut out from me, he thought. I am being cut out from something. And this, he knew, was not like leaving Silvanesti for Silvamori. This was different. Here, at the start of this journey, lay no hope for return.

Ah gods. Ah, gods . . .

Had the risk been worth the fee? He did not know. Now, here, he did not know.

The skiff rocked on the water, moving swiftly downriver as the Wildrunners took long and powerful strokes on the oars. It was as though they could not wait to cast out the dark elf from their company. No one touched him. No one stood near. And the river flowed down to the sea, running, while fore and aft of the skiff Wildrunners shouted his crime to dragons, calling his name and bidding all who heard to never speak it again.

* * * * *

They put him ashore on the far western side of the southernmost tip of the kingdom. The fleet of eight ships had watched the Dark Escort, men and women at the rails, standing in grim silence, watching, then turning away one after another, putting their backs to him. In the sky, gray clouds hung down in rain; no gulls cried. The water rose and fell, heaving and choppy with white manes curling on the wave-tops. Zeboim's Steeds, even these seemed to turn and run from the abomination of the dark elf.

At the end of the day, they set him ashore on the dock near a tavern roaring with laughter and cursing and song. The stink of sweat and ale and greasy food flowed out the doors, turning Dalamar's stomach each time he had to breathe it. This was still Silvanesti, but the little port town had more a feel of other lands about it than elven lands. His escort paid for his passage aboard an outbound merchant ship, a three-master whose white sails shone impossibly bright against the lowering sky.

"Take him safely, Captain," said Lord Porthios, handing over the fee and never looking at Dalamar. "Put him ashore wherever he wills."

"Ar, he's a dark 'un," the minotaur said, eyeing Dalamar narrowly. "An exile, eh? Ay, well, as long as he's paid for it makes no matter to me." He offered to close the deal with a drink, but Porthios thanked him with chill politeness and refused. What elf would drink with an outlander, and one whose ship would soon hold a despised exile? None, and certainly not this prince of the Qualinesti.

All this happened around Dalamar, above him where he sat huddled in his dark cloak, shivering in the rain. It hardly seemed to him that it was happening to him at all. He could not but shake and shiver, as though with fever. He could not feel more than that, for icy numbness held him in merciless grip. My heart must be beating, he thought. Otherwise I'd have fallen over dead. But he could not feel the pulse.

"He is dead to us," they had said. It seemed he was, indeed. This is shock, he told himself, and this is not going to last. Then, no matter if it lasts forever. I don't care.

He had no gear to stow, no mage-fare, no packs and parcels of fragrant spell components and precious spellbooks. The dark elf owned nothing, only the dun trews and shirt, his boots and the black hooded cloak that signaled his status. He rose and went up the gangplank when ordered to do so. Once on board, he turned to look back. In the rigging, sailors scrambled to unfurl the sails. On deck, the captain shouted orders, bidding his rowers to bend their backs and pull. The ship caught the wind, moving quickly under oar and under sail.

Dalamar did not look to the shore or to the forest beyond. Instead, he looked at the sea, at the wide gulf growing between him and his homeland. He felt something stir in him then, something sharp and painful as fangs. Before he could acknowledge it, he turned from the rail and set his eyes upon the vast and boundless sea. A shaft of sunlight shot through the clouds, illuminating the tossing waves. He looked away from that, too, from the light and the brightness of water.

"I have nothing to do with light," he said. Saying, hearing the words and his own voice, he felt the stirring of pain again. This time he let it come, the long aching flood. He was getting good at embracing pain.

Thus did the dark elf begin his wandering.

Chapter 14

~

In the first year of his wandering, Dalamar had little use for the company of anyone—elf, dwarf, human, goblin, or ogre. He lived wild in the reaches outside the cities and towns, wintering under roof when the season blew cold and finding the port cities the most hospitable and the most interesting. He took no lover, for no elfwoman would have him, and in Silvanost the hearts of young men are not filled with longings for outlander women. The fee for his lodging and meals he paid with the steel he earned charming rats from warehouses—inglorious work that he hated.

However, despite his misery, Dalamar was still a reaper of news, and there where the water meets the land he found much to reap. In taverns where seamen gathered, he learned of the rehabilitation of lands long ravaged by war. He heard how after making treaties, the soldiers of the Whitestone Army left the field of battle and returned to their farms, crafts, and shops. In little shops where magic-users traded in spellbooks, herbs, oils, and strange and powerful artifacts, he heard from mages of all the three Orders that the armies of the Dark Queen had no such peaceful intent. The alliance between the armies of red and black and white and blue collapsed at the end of the war, though the armies themselves still maintained control of vast territories. The fallen Highlords ruled their fiefdoms roughly, brandishing their iron fists over the heads of their subjects and quarreling among themselves. In the taverns the drinkers were happy to consider the war over, the matter between gods settled, and they passed winter nights comfortably planning for a springtime that would, at last, not signal the start of another blood-drenched campaign of war. In the mage shops the folk were not so sure that the matter between the gods had all been said and done.

Through the winter, brooding, Dalamar did not think so broadly as this. He considered himself, his choices, and his chances. By night he dreamed of home, aching dreams of loss, and by day he wondered what place he could make for himself in the world outside Silvanesti. He thought of the cities to which he might travel—Palanthas, Tarsis, Caergoth, and North Keep. He thought of the libraries, the opportunities for study . . .

But he didn't think about journeying to the Tower of High Sorcery at Wayreth. That old dream lay quiet in him.

Come spring, Dalamar felt dark winds at his back, restless winds, and these seemed always to push him from the places where people congregated, away from the taverns and the bars, from the brothels and the temples and the mage-ware shops. These winds pushed him to the old places where mortals no longer walked. He, who had seen the ruin of his homeland, the ruin of his own place in that kingdom, was surprised to discover a taste for ruins, the skeletons of old cities, old places whose names were only half-remembered, whose stories had long before flown to the winds.

Dalamar walked among the ghosts who haunted Bloodwatch, the fallen tower that used to stand within sight of the Sea of Istar, and was now only a pile of stone. He found ways into the hidden parts of the ruins, went down deep into the earth and discovered vaults filled up with debris— rolls of parchments detailing supplies and requisitions, old chests filled with rusting weapons, and in the farthest corner of the deepest chamber, a golden coffer no larger than his two hands outspread. Though it had lain in dust and the moist cellar air for years unknown, this coffer was clean as though newly made. It sang to him, through his hands, through his bones and his blood, for it held something of magic in it, and he knew by the thrill he felt that here was a dark magic.

With great care, he examined the coffer, detected magical wards, and released them. Within lay a ring of silver, etched with runes and set with a perfectly cut ruby, dark as spilled blood. What power lay in the ring, he did not know, but he took it out from that place. Sitting on the shore, watching the tossing sea, he listened to the wind moaning around the ruins of Bloodwatch for two days and three long nights. He remembered what he had learned in Silvamori, that all things are voiced and all things may sing, and so he learned the language of the wind, the song of the sea, and he spoke with the ghosts wandering by. One told him, at last, what power the ring had. It would dry the blood in the veins of any foe.

Fate directing, in the hour before dawn, a small boat landed on the stony shore below the ruin of Bloodwatch. A goblin slipped out, prowling. In silence, Dalamar sat while the intruder scouted the ruins, waited to hear footsteps coming near, almost hoping . . .

The last light of the fading stars cast a shadow, a slim dark mark on the ground. He smelled the reek of goblin's breath and sat stony still, pretending to notice nothing. A steel blade hissed free of its sheath. Dalamar turned, all his will pouring into the ruby ring, directing the magic. The goblin's eyes went wide, its jaw dropped as it pulled one rattling gasp of air into its lungs, then fell over, dead. Using the goblin's own knife, Dalamar saw that the blood had indeed dried in its veins. He found nothing but brownish dust wherever he cut.

In the summer of the year, Dalamar Nightson went north to the ruins of the City of Lost Names and roamed through the wailing streets, searching for what artifacts of magic he might find. He found none, and it seemed to him that someone had been there recently before him. He did unearth a chest filled with a great richness of jewels, necklaces, brooches, rings, and tiaras. None had any magical value, but he took some of the pieces. Most he left hidden beneath his own warding spell.

He went into the Kharolis Mountains in the autumn, walking 'round and 'round the terrible ruins of Zhaman, which the dwarves of Thorbardin now named Skullcap, that fortress which, so legend says, the great mage Fistandantilus caused to be built. What treasure of magic must lie in there! Dalamar listened to the wind and the wailing, but he found no ghosts except for those of dwarves. They had nothing to say to him that did not have to do with the great wars of days gone when fabulous Zhaman was destroyed in the turmoil that ravaged Krynn after the fall of Istar. He would gladly have entered in to see what wonders lay hidden, but the towers had melted and run down the side of the hill upon which it stood, making the shape of the skull for which it was named. All entrances were sealed.

From there Dalamar went to winter in Tarsis, tired of smelling the sea and eating fish in the port cities. Walking upon the ancient seawall of a city that had not stood in sight of the sea in the three hundred and more years since the Cataclysm had reshaped the world, he looked out over the dry plain that had once been a harbor, at the hulls of sea-abandoned ships now serving as hovels for the poor folk of the city who lived cheek by jowl with the outlawed, the bandits, and all those who preyed upon the weak. Five hundred years later, one hardly saw the outlines of hulls, for work had been done to expand each hulk and repair age's damage. Ramshackle rooms had been added on, taken off, added again—all in haphazard fashion.

Outside the breakwater that now broke no water lay the Plains of Dust and, beyond, the foothills of the Kharolis Mountains, nearly a hundred miles distant. Dry wind blew off the plains, gritty with dust and stinking of piles of the garbage Tarsians had long been in the habit of pitching over their walls as though there were still swift currents of water to carry it all out to sea.

Dalamar turned from the hulks and left the wall, walking down into the city. He went through the marketplace, past booths where dark-eyed girls sold flowers and stalls where old women hawked brightly painted pottery. All around the smell of food hung—roasting meats, simmering soups, and fat loaves of bread haloed in steam.

In the darker corners, up against the wall beyond the central plaza, he found the quiet shops where mages gathered, Nuitari's Night, The Three Children, Wings of Magic, all the places where mages in Red robes, Black, and White came to trade magical artifacts for spell components, spell components for spellbooks, and gossip for news. He went into the Old City where he found ruins not unlike those he'd seen in other lands, only these lay within the walls of Tarsis itself. There he found the Library of Khrystann, that underground chamber filled with books and scrolls, very little of it in reasonable order.

Tarsis the Beautiful, Tarsis the Ruin . . . Dalamar found the place to his liking. He rented chambers above a mageware shop in the marketplace, near the iron gate in the wall where one passes through to the street behind the library. He recalled tales of the war, stories told of how Alhana Starbreeze had met with a disparate band of travelers questing after a dragon orb. There had been a mage among them, that one whose eyes were like hourglasses, whose skin was like gold, but not the gold of sun—the gold of metal. He remembered what had been said aboard *Bright Solinari* on the way from Silvamori: tales of a mage who made a Silvanesti Wildrunner shudder. Remembering this, Dalamar listened in the marketplace, he haunted the mage-ware shops, curious and hoping to learn about this mage who had broken a green dragon's spell. He heard nothing, and he wondered if Raistlin Majere was gone from the story of Krynn as the Wildrunner had sworn him gone from the story of Silvanesti.

This year Dalamar had no need to make his living charming rats from warehouses. The baubles out of the City of Lost Names sold handsomely in the marketplace. He settled into winter, spending much of his time in the library in the Old City, among old books and ancient scrolls. He made a further study of herbs, and he expanded his studies to include knowledge of magical runes of all kinds. In a city where half the land is ruin, where outlaws and bandits roam freely outside the walls and in, this last was a good study to make. In short time he knew how to speak the two runes of ancient Istarian—in exact cadence, with perfect focus—that would kill a man standing. He knew the three runes first etched by dark dwarf mages in the bowels of Thorbardin that would find an enemy in his bed and kill him there. He tried that out on a man who lived out in the hulks, a petty thief who'd had the mad idea of picking his pocket one day when he was walking in the market. The man died screaming. No one knew what had befallen but Dalamar, watching the death in a scrying bowl.

In a city where mages congregated, his name became familiar and respected. A rune-master they named him, and his reputation spoke of one who had gathered as many secrets as runes are said to keep. In midwinter he took a lover, and she was no elf but a human woman whose shining black hair fell all the way to her heels, whose eyes were the color of an aspen's bark, gray and sweet. He did not shy from the outlander, as he had done in the past. He was tired of the celibate bed, and he found her swift to laugh and slow to complain of a mage who walked in shadows and kept more secrets than she did hairpins.

He decorated his bedchamber with a tapestry woven in Silvanesti, a lovely weaving of the forest in spring, and he bought a half-case of Silvanesti wine, the kind that tastes of autumn. He drank the wine as one drinks the memories of all that is lost to him, bitterly and sweetly. When spring came again, Dalamar parted with his lover, unwilling to be chained by her expectation of the resumption of their affair upon his return. She didn't weep. She only laughed, and she did not look back when she walked out the door. He stood for a while, breathing the last wisps of her perfume, the musky odor of some golden oil imported from Northern Ergoth, then he sealed his chambers with invisible locks, with warding spells and secret traps. That done, he took up his pack and went down the stairs to pay his landlord rent for the next full year before he left the city. He had, at last, a home.

Into Valkinord he went. He found no magical scrolls, no secret artifacts, and again he saw that someone had been before him. He did find a small shrine to Nuitari, hung with shadows and the thin gray lace of spider webs. He cleaned it and stopped to worship, alone in the dust with the wind and the ghosts, the wanderer among the ruins. He found himself thinking about the Tower of High Sorcery and the hidden forest of Wayreth. Some sources told him that the forest lay at the edge of Icewall Glacier, others declared it would be found in the north part of Abanasinia. Still others took oaths that Wayreth Forest stood near Qualimori—no!—just beyond Tarsis. The forest found, one still had to locate the Tower which, all stories agreed, moved within the forest as easily as fish move in water. In there, no mage would find his way unless he was invited or unless he had so clear a focus on his goal, so unwavering a will to gain it, that nothing of the forest's magic could confuse or deter him. At night he dreamed about the Tower, but in the morning when he woke, he remembered only the barest threads of the dream, the faintest whisper.

That summer, Dalamar traveled as far as Neraka where he learned that the Highlords of Takhisis now often gathered to plot and make ready to launch another campaign against the people of Krynn. He spent a long time sitting in the hills outside the broken city, listening to rumors and feeling the power emanating from the place, a strength of magic and armed force. What power would he gain if he went into Neraka, presented himself to a Highlord, and offered his service? None, he decided, and only another master to serve.

He got up and walked away from Neraka, from the brooding armies of Takhisis, and went down to Southern Ergoth.

Forbidden all elven lands, still Dalamar slipped into Silvamori and went into the tower of Daltigoth, that pile which was, once and a long time ago, one of the five Towers of High Sorcery. This one had been the haunt of mages who'd dedicated themselves to the dark gods. The studies conducted there were grim and terrible, perfections in the arts of torment and woe. Another of the five towers had stood in Goodlund, but even the foundation of that was lost. A third tower was raised up in doomed Istar; there Lorac Caladon had taken his Tests of High Sorcery. That, like all of Istar, lay now beneath the sea, fallen in the Cataclysm. Two towers yet stood—one in Palanthas and one in the secret Forest of Wayreth. Only Wayreth's tower now functioned, kept and warded by its present master, Par-Salian of the Order of the White Robe, and only there could a mage take his Tests of High Sorcery. The tower in Palanthas, well, that one was cursed, and Dalamar had never heard of anyone going in there.

Thinking of towers, of the dream he had lately had, the one he had long held, he went through the Tower of High Sorcery at Daltigoth. Water dripped ceaselessly down the walls, outside and in. Winds sighed through broken stone. In the dungeons, piles of bones lay, brown and gnawed. In the upper chambers, nothing remained of the people who'd lived and worked there, not even the sob of a ghost. He went up and down crumbling stone stairs and brushed the dust of ages from musty tapestries. In libraries, he found nothing, not the least scroll, the smallest book. Here he didn't wonder whether some treasure hunter had been before him. The vast chambers and the deep vaults all had the look of places that had been systematically emptied a long time ago. Libraries, studies, scriptoria, laboratories . . . through all these Dalamar wandered listlessly and with little interest in what he saw. He had something else on his mind.

"It's time," Dalamar said, standing in the wide space that might once have been a vast reception hall. He did not speak loudly, but the echo of his words ran 'round and 'round the tower, bounding from the stone walls, leaping down the stairs, and falling into the well. The time had come to search and see if he could find the Tower of High Sorcery at Wayreth, to see whether the Master of the Tower would grant him the chance to take his Tests. He looked around and saw the hem of his black robe grayed with dust, his own footsteps marked behind him and before.

Shouldering his pack, Dalamar walked out the door, past the crumbling gargoyles, and down the shattered stone stairs. The courtyard tumbled with weeds. A wind blew stiffly off the waters of the Straits of Algoni, cold and smelling of the sea. Gulls cried in the hard blue sky, their voices like wounds on the silence. Something dark darted, swiftly caught out the corner of his eye. Dalamar looked up, and looking, he took a step into the courtyard.

Pain shot through him, lancing from his back and leaping through to his chest. He choked, he tried to turn to defend himself, and a flying weight hit him, driving him down to the broken pavement. Laughter rang out, leaping from the high walls of the ruined tower, shrieking in the sky, and burning in his mind like fire. He struggled, trying to throw off the weight that pinned and held him hard to the ground. Heart hammering, he kicked, twisting his shoulders. He never moved the weight, never stopped the shrieking laughter, but he got a breath, a short staggered gasp of air, and—

* * * * *

They were not cracked paving stones beneath Dalamar's cheek, tearing the flesh. Blood from his cut cheek seeped into the earth of a forest floor. A thin breeze drifted, smelling of oak and faintly of distant pine. Dalamar, groaning, finished taking his breath. He got his hands under him and found no weight held him. Carefully, he pushed to his knees, and he heard a soft chuckle.

"Gently, mage," said a low voice, the speaker clearly amused. "Gently."

He looked up, slowly, and saw a woman perched upon a tall boulder, smiling as she tapped the shining blade of a dagger against her knee. Two sapphires gleamed in the grip of the blade, the eyes of a dragon etched into the ivory grip. Dalamar noted the weapon, and he saw no threat in the eyes of the woman tapping rhythms against her knee with the blade. Though she sat, he knew she was tall as he, her long legs said so. Dressed in hunting leathers and a red shirt, she wore her night-black hair bound back from her face by a white scarf. A human, he noted, and tall as a barbarian Plainswoman, though she hadn't the look of one of those. Too pale of cheek, and too dark of hair, and not many Plainswomen had eyes the exact color of sapphires.

"Who are you?" he asked, climbing to his feet. One swift glance showed him he'd lost his pack. The little pouch of steel coins, his spare boots, the last leather flask of his autumn wine . . . all were gone. "Who are you?" he repeated coldly, and though the look he bent on her had chilled the blood of strong folk, this woman never moved but to smile.

"Best to ask, Dalamar Nightson, *where* am I? Or, more to the point, where are *you?*"

Wind sighed high in the treetops, and it didn't smell of the sea. It dropped low, and it carried the scent of the woman, her leathers, the faint tang of sweat, and the sweetness of the herbs with which she washed her hair. A stream gurgled, water talking to stone on its way by. He stood in an upland forest, so said the boulders strewn about, great chunks of stone of the kind found in the Kharolis Mountains. God-flung stone, the dwarves said, debris from the Cataclysm.

"Where are you?" asked the woman, tapping the dagger's blade against her knee. The rhythm quickened, suddenly impatient. "Where are you, Dalamar Nightson?"

"In the Forest of Wayreth," he said, his heart thudding in his chest.

Out the corner of his eye, he saw something black racing, low on the ground like a hound running. He braced and turned. He saw nothing but forest, trees running upslope, mighty oaks, broad of girth and rough-barked. Sunlight shone through the leaves. So tall were the trees that to stand looking up gave him the feeling of being far down, perhaps beneath the sea where the sky, when seen at all, was but a round disk. As water ripples, so did the light ripple, running with shadow. As water speaks, so did the forest, wind sighing through the oaks.

"What was that?" he asked, turning to the woman.

But she was gone.

Only sun-dappled moss sat on the boulder, thick and golden green. Not even the least scratch marred the softness. All around the stone the moss grew undisturbed. He touched it—springy and cool. He lifted his head and breathed the air. Nothing lingered of the dark-haired woman's scent, not even the faintest trace of leather.

"Very well," he said. Excitement ran in his belly. His heart beat, and the rhythm of it was the same as the beat of the tapping blade. "I am in Wayreth Forest."

And the forest does not, he thought even as he looked around, lie just east of Qualimori after all. It didn't lie north of Tarsis or south of Abanasinia. Apparently, the Forest of Wayreth stood wherever it pleased to stand. Be that as it was, he did not stand in sight of his true goal, the Tower of High Sorcery. If the moving forest had caught him, Dalamar had yet to catch the Tower.

Trees marched, streams gurgled, and in the sky, high white clouds ran before the north faring wind. The path northward through the oaks was a slender one, winding and climbing. All the light in the forest seemed to be behind him. There, glades stretched out, islands of meadows starred by flowers. A stag leaped, sun glinting off the six points of its tall crown of antlers. Dalamar would have taken his oath that he heard a bluebird singing, though no bluebird prefers forests to fields. Out the corner of his eye—Dalamar nodded, understanding—out the corner of his eye, he saw something dark, flying this time, a shadow streaking through the trees, ranging northward.

Dalamar Nightson turned his back on the glades, on the stag and the bluebird's song, and followed the shadow.

* * * * *

Dalamar climbed up rock-strewn paths, around washed-out paths, and broad oak trees, and over boulders that surely giants had wedged between the fat oaks. The stout boots he wore, those that had served him well in rough ruins, might as well have been a lord's velvet slippers. His ankles turned on small rocks in the path; he slipped on scree and slid backward, cursing the distance lost. He bled from cuts, and he ached from bruises. Always, he got up again.

The birds who flitted in this northern wood—crows and rooks mostly—had raucous voices, and they followed him like a mocking mob as he climbed. He looked around, trying to see the leading shadow, that swift streak of darkness. Nothing. He looked straight ahead, attending only a little to his peripheral vision, hoping to catch the glimpse. He did not, but he refused to let himself consider turning back. He had never walked an easy path and had never chosen the straight road, the even ground. It made no sense to do that now. The wind dropped, falling away as though it had no mind to lead him farther. Sweat rolled ceaselessly down his face and itched between his shoulders.

He went on, muscles aching, heart thudding hard in his chest, and the pulse in his neck hammering. For a time he went to the rhythm of a prayer, one that began as a request for strength from the Dark Son, from Nuitari of the Night. Soon he had no strength or mind to frame his prayer in words. Soon he let only the hammering of his heart act as his plea. Climbing, slipping back, climbing again, he went on until at last he fell and lay still. His heart beat into the earth. His sweat stained the stones as he lay still on the hard road up.

When at last he stood, he saw a gentling of the path, a leveling of the way. He saw it as a man sees vindication. He put his back into the climb, shouldering forward against the rise, and he walked onto level ground. There he stood, panting and sweating before a large mossy-shouldered boulder upon which sat the dark haired woman, tapping her sapphire-eyed dagger against her knee.

Smiling, she said, "Where are you, Dalamar Nightson?"

He didn't answer. He could not. His throat closed up with sudden thirst, and his knees turned weak.

"Ah," she said, brushing a lock of raven hair from her forehead. She reached behind the boulder and lifted his pack. Rummaging through it as familiarly as though the contents were her own, she pulled out a leather flask and handed it to him. "You look like you need this."

He drank the wine, glaring at her. He drank, and all the smoky sweetness of the Silvanesti Forest in autumn drifted around him and through him as the first mists of the season drift through the aspenwood. The ache he felt then was not an ache of muscle, not a weariness of bone. What he felt was like the melting of ice, the cracking, the groaning. He closed his eyes, tears stung, and grief held tight to his throat. Tighter to his heart did he hold, and he forbade tears, forbade himself to show any sign of sorrow or weakness before this prankster, this sapphire-eyed woman.

"Yes," she said. "It's really all about control, Dalamar Nightson."

"What is?" he asked, wearily opening his eyes.

"Well, all of it." She pulled up her legs tight to her chest, wrapped her arms round her shins and rested her chin on her knees. "Control of yourself. You do that well, don't you? Control of your life—not a concept with which most elves have intimate understanding, I dare say—and, of course, control of the magic each time you embrace it."

Ah, magic, the forest and the paths that led to nowhere. "So, it has all been illusion," he said.

Her blue eyes shone suddenly bright. "The hill and the road up? Not at all. Do your legs feel like you've been walking through an illusion?"

They did not.

She sat up, sweeping her arms wide, embracing all the woodland around, the Forest of Wayreth. "All this is real, and all this is magic. The Master of the Tower is in control of this magic, but that doesn't mean you've lost control—which might be part of the problem."

And then she was gone, vanished, her mossy boulder showing no sign she'd ever been there. Gone, too, was the wine-flask from Dalamar's hand and his pack from the ground.

* * * * *

South into the glades went the wanderer, through meadows where butterflies danced on daises and ruby hummingbirds floated over the sweet soft throats of honeysuckle. South into the sunlight, Dalamar walked beside streams where fish shone like bright silver and dragonflies the color of blue steel darted. When he walked through all the wonders of springtime, he came back to the boulder and the blue-eyed woman. He turned from her before she could speak, and he went away west into an endless purpling twilight. Stars hung low over the trees, and the three moons graced the darkling sky but never moved, not even a hand's width across the night. Owls woke in the oaks and bats

flitted. A fox barked, another answered. A shadow darte
across his path. He looked, and he again saw her, the trick
ster, the blue-eyed woman, smiling at him and sitting on he
gray craggy boulder.

Magic and control. Someone else controlled the forest h
wandered in; someone else knew where all the paths led to
and where they all led away from. Magic and control. Dala
mar smiled a little.

She looked around, found his pack, and took out th
leather wine-flask. He refused when she offered, bu
politely.

"I've had enough of Silvanesti, of any place outside here
For now." He did not smile, though he wanted to, and h
chose his next words with care. "I am here, where I need t
be."

"What makes you think that?" asked the dark-haire
woman.

He sketched a bow, not so deep but respectful. "All th
reports of my senses seem to lie, and yet my feet lead m
always here, to this place. You said it yourself: the magic i
this forest isn't mine to control; the way and the road belon
to someone else. But if I cannot control the magic, I can con
trol my response to it."

She looked at him, a long sapphire stare, and then sh
threw back her head, her laughter sailing up through th
trees. In the next breath, the trees and the tall gray oak
receded all around, drawing back from Dalamar and th
woman. Moving, they made no sound, and whatever bird
or squirrels inhabited bough or nest made not the leas
protest. Withdrawing, the trees left a wide clear space—no
a glade of waving grasses but a close-cropped swar
through which a broad road passed. Six knights ridin
abreast might have passed comfortably on that roac
though they would have had to pass round the boulder, th
moss-cloaked stone. Above, the sky shone deeply blu
shading toward the end of the day.

His belly clenching with excitement, his skin tingling as it does when magic is being done, Dalamar looked around, trying to catch a glimpse of the Tower of High Sorcery. He saw nothing, not rising stone, not gated walls . . . nothing.

"Remember," said the woman, her voice soft as with distance.

Quickly, he turned back to her. In the act of slipping from the stone, the woman vanished. As though mist had risen from the ground, the boulder shimmered behind a gray veil, and the air around it shivered. A man must blink; the eye does it, not the will. In the instant that he did, Dalamar felt all the world change around him, as though the forest folded itself in upon itself, collapsing and then suddenly springing whole and straight again.

The boulder was gone. No mark of it remained on the firmly packed earth of the road. In its place—and in the place of many trees!—rose great high walls of shining stone. Dalamar's heart leaped, and the blood raced through his veins, singing. He saw not one tower, a solitary monolith such as that at Daltigoth. He saw seven towers.

Chapter 15

~

True time settled over the forest, or what Dalamar reck
oned must be true time. He had walked under skies when
the sun showed only a time and season the maker of th
magic wished it to show. Now shadows shifted on the hig
stone walls, moving by subtle degrees the patient eye knew
how to detect. Light changed on the ground, deepening a
the day aged, and this, too, the patient eye understood. Th
time was nearing toward sunset. As in the world he'd left t
come here, the season was summer.

The patient eye, the patient soul, Dalamar stood outsid
the gate that was the only breach in the high black wall sur
rounding seven towers—nor was it much of a breach, for
was locked and shut tight. He wondered how he would g
within.

All around him the Forest of Wayreth rustled. Dove
murmured in the eaves of the towers. Wind sighed in th
oaks outside the walls. Faintly, the musky scent of ligustrun
drifted on the air, though where that hedge-climbing vin
grew with its frothing flowers, he could not imagine. Some
thing darted past on the ground. He turned to look, expect
ing to see that leading shadow, but he saw only a gray rabb
leaping into the brush. He returned to contemplation.

Seven towers loomed above the three high walls, on
each at the point of the triangle made by the meeting c
those walls, and four within the compound rising above al
The three at each corner where the walls met were obv
ously secondary towers. Two tall towers, one on the nort
side of the compound, one on the south, were separated b
two smaller ones, fore and behind. A gate breached th
wall, but it seemed to have no mechanisms for opening i
at least not on this side.

Dalamar went boldly to the wall, and the great age of the stone made itself known to him, the knowledge seeping into his bones. This was not common stone. Poets named stone "the bones of the earth," but Dalamar knew, standing there, that the stuff the wall was made of was truly that— part of the fabric, the essence of Krynn itself. Upon the walls he found many inscriptions. He went close to see them. Some he could read—magical inscriptions to make the wall strong, warnings to intruders, spells to keep out the prying eyes of any diviner using methods of Seeing—others he could not, though he had mastered three ancient scripts and knew somewhat of four more.

He touched the gate, and, as his fingertips brushed the wood and steel, the air around him changed again, as it had when the towers revealed themselves. This time he did not blink but watched to see what would happen.

The world did not fold, the air did not shimmer, nothing happened at all.

And then he found himself at once on the other side of the wall within the compound. He stood in a courtyard paved with gleaming gray stone, and before him rose the four towers.

"Welcome," said a voice, a woman's, low and laughing.

Dalamar turned swiftly and found himself looking into the eyes of a human woman, a mage in white robes whose hair lay in two thick black braids upon her shoulders. He knew her, but not by her robes. Here was his guide in the forest, betrayed by her sapphire eyes.

"Which," she said, "is *the* Tower of High Sorcery? You're wondering, aren't you?"

Dalamar said he wasn't wondering that at all. He said he'd reckoned that already. "They are all the Tower. It is as with runes—the name of a rune stands for more than the shape of it. It seems the name 'Tower of High Sorcery' stands for more than the shape of one structure."

"Impressive," she said, but her expression, faintly

amused, said something else. Precocious would have been the polite word. Cocky was the word she was thinking. "Come with me."

Dalamar followed her closely, not willing to let her lose him in here as she had done in the forest. With each step he took it seemed that the compound became more and more crowded, filling up with mages of all Orders. Some went in groups, dwarves and humans and elves, all talking. Most of the elves he saw were white robed, and none who passed him seemed to care that he wore the dark robe of exile. Other mages walked singly, head down and focused on some inner conversation. One, a dwarf whose robes were as dark as Dalamar's own, looked up when he passed. Dalamar felt his glance like two burning points of fire, and yet he saw no eyes at all within the shadow of the dwarf's hood.

"Oh, him," said the woman with the sapphire eyes, "don't mind him."

She said it, but Dalamar heard a kind of lean chuckle in her voice, as though she meant exactly the opposite. Be careful of him? Pay attention to him? That he could not determine.

The sound of the mages' voices was the hum of a hive, the colors of their robes like a swirl of pennons. What seemed most remarkable to him was that White Robes and Red, even Black, seemed to have no trouble being in each other's company. In Tarsis and most of the world without, White Robes stayed together, mixing rarely with Red and never with those of his own Order.

"It isn't like that here," she said. "Here, we leave all the baggage on the front stoop, as it were. Here, we don't care which of the three magical children one or the other of us honors. A White robed elf will speak to you as graciously as though you wore snowy samite. Outside, another matter. In here, peace. You come in here, you come to study, to reflect, to breathe the air with mages and speak the arcane language people don't understand who do not hear magic singing in their blood. Or," she said as she stopped before the Foretower, "or you come here to Test." She cocked her head. "That's a thing you'll soon know about, isn't it, Dalamar Argent? The rigors of the Tests?"

In the warm air of summer, a chill touched him, not because she knew he'd come here seeking to take the Tests of High Sorcery. It was a fair guess and an accurate one. It was the use of his old name that chilled him, sending him suddenly, painfully to the last day he'd seen Silvanesti. Not even the smoky autumn wine could do that.

"I am," he said, "not Dalamar Argent. If you send to Silvanost and ask them there, you will learn that Dalamar Argent does not exist. And they should know. They keep meticulous records."

She shook her head as if to say, "But of course Dalamar Argent exists." Aloud, though, she said, "Forgive my mistake. Let us introduce ourselves, then—and properly. I am Regene of Schallsea, and sometimes I'm not what you think I am. You are . . .?"

"I am Dalamar Nightson," he said, "and, yes, I have come here to take the Tests."

"Deadly things, those Tests," she said, as one would say, "Pesky things, those bees." She led him across the compound and past the knots of mages talking. "There is much you will want to see of our Tower of High Sorcery, but little you will have access to just now. You are a visitor, a guest. We will see if that changes after your Tests. Come inside, if you are well and truly ready."

It was on the tip of his tongue to ask her what she knew about testing, but he did not. She turned to see if he was following, and he caught a glimpse of her sapphire eyes. Then, in that moment at the end of the long summer day, they reminded him not of the young woman laughing on the boulder, but of the dragon, cold and fierce, carved in the ivory handle of the knife she'd been tapping on her knee. "I am dangerous," said those eyes, "and don't mistake me."

He gestured as a man does to usher a lady forth, and he followed her into the foretower.

The bright light of day's end vanished, leaving him blinking and blind, waiting for his eyes to adjust to the cool darkness within. In moments they did, and he saw the place was but a windowless room, round, with one entrance behind and two doors to the right and left. A Red-robed mage, stooped with age, his white hair thin on his scalp, stood in the exact center of the room.

Dalamar glanced at Regene to take his cue from her. She was, of course, gone.

"Yes, yes, yes," said the mage, his eyes narrowed as though the torches on the walls did not lend the light he needed. "She's gone. Comes and goes, that one. Here and there. Flittering. Sparrow-girl, that's what I call her, and she's no girl at all really, is she?"

"I would not lay a wager, one way or the other," Dalamar said, testing to see if this would elicit more information.

The mage snorted. "Then you've more sense than you look to have. There, there, go there! Go on!" He pointed to a bench, one that had not been there only a moment before. Plump green pillows lay on the seat and against the oaken back. Only to see them bought all of Dalamar's muscles awake with reminders that he had been walking long in the magical Forest of Wayreth—up hill and down, through glades and into twilight. He had not been walking in illusion. Above the bench a book floated, a fat tome. "Go sit, and go see. Go on now, go on."

Dalamar went, and he paused by the book to see his name appearing just as his glance lighted on the page. *Dalamar Argent.* He looked around at the old man and saw him laughing silently.

"Yes, yes, I know. You're not Dalamar Argent. So you say. Well, sit down, boy," said the man who, aged as he was, did not have as many years as Dalamar. "Sit, Dalamar Whoever You Are, and wait. Keep yourself in patience." He looked right and left. He looked up, and he looked down. "They know you're here."

"Who knows?" Dalamar asked, sitting.

"*They* know. Now hush, and wait."

He hushed, he sat, and he waited. The mage left the room, slipping quietly into the corridor leading into south tower. Once, a swift shadow passing, Dalamar saw the Black-robed dwarf—he of the burning glance, the hidden eyes—passing by the doorway in the corridor that led out from the foretower and into the north tower. The dwarf didn't pause. He never turned his head, yet Dalamar had the feeling that his presence was again noted.

* * * * *

Quiet as a cloud drifting, Ladonna, the Mistress of the Order of the Black Robes, went out from her chambers on the thirteenth level of the north tower and went down the stairs, the winding granite way, trailing the hem of her silk robe and the scents of magic behind. She liked to sweep grandly down the stairs, to hear the sigh of her hem on the steps, the respectful murmur of the mages in the corridors as she passed.

"My lady, the gods grant you health, my lady. . . . Good-even, my lady. . . ."

She liked that and counted it worth the walk to see the students with their arms full of scrolls turn and stare, the elders with their heads full of spells and schemes step aside to let her pass. She went past the guest rooms where visitors rested, past the solaria and the chambers where students sat poring over old scrolls and freshly penned books. She knew by name each of the Black-robed mages she encountered, and she recognized most of the others. Smiling and greeting, Ladonna had an eye out for one of the dark robes, the dwarf who spent all his days in the libraries and all his nights in his chamber studying. She'd known him long and not liked him even a little. It had been a great frustration to her when he hadn't died in the war. He should have, for what mischief he'd worked then, he had learned how to double now. As she went, she watched out for him, and she saw him neither in corridor or solarium or on his way to his chamber. Sitting late in the south tower, no doubt, haunting the libraries like some wretched ghost. Well, he wasn't exactly that, and he wasn't exactly not.

That one, Ladonna thought, should never have survived his Tests.

Down and down she went, greeting and receiving greeting, until she came at last to the study where the Master of the Tower waited. On the threshold of his study, she smiled. He did, indeed, wait. For though she had not announced her visit, he knew of it nonetheless. It was that way between them, Ladonna and Par-Salian. They had not been lovers in many long years; still the connection remained, the bond unbroken.

"Good evening, my old dear," said Ladonna, coming quietly into the Master's study.

Par-Salian smiled with a mixture of affection and impatience. He disliked that expression, and yet her impulse to speak it pleased him. He looked up from the book spread open upon the polished oak desk and tugged a little at his thin white beard.

"Is he here?" he asked. "Your dark elf, is he here?"

"*My* dark elf?" She shrugged at the designation, then nodded. She supposed he was her dark elf, at least by virtue of the fact that she had brought him to the Master's attention. "He's here. He'd have been a while wandering in the wood, but Regene found him." Her eyes sparkled with sudden amusement. "She didn't make it too easy for him, but she got him here in better time than he'd have made for himself. Time, after all, is our dearest coin these days."

It was, and it was in short supply. Par-Salian closed the book and settled against the back of his chair with a sigh.

He supposed he should have felt brighter, more eager at the start of what work this dark elf might do, but he hadn't felt bright or eager in some time—not since the end of the war. He looked around at the silk wall-hangings woven by an elf-woman in Silvanesti a long time ago. They shimmered to life, the delicate silken threads, the pictures they made as Ladonna went around the room, kindling candles with the touch of her finger. Light glinted on the jewels decorating the elaborate fantasy of braids she'd made of her silver tresses. It gleamed from brass fittings and silver candle holders and slid down the silver chasing of the mirror upon the wall. The book-lined walls seemed to sigh in the shadows, leather spines shimmering. All the air hung with the scents of herbs and spices and some things not so pleasingly perfumed. Spell components were sometimes lovely and sometimes not. Here was the study of the Master of the Tower of High Sorcery.

At Wayreth, he reminded himself carefully, the Tower of High Sorcery at Wayreth. There had been a time when only this tower functioned, the last of five original towers. That was not so now. Now another, darker tower was opened.

Candlelight on silver tresses, the gleam caught Par-Salian's eye, and he smiled. White mage, dark wizardess, they had been each other's strength during the hard times of the War of the Lance when it seemed that the gods would rend the world between them. In seasons of doubt, she had been beside him. She would, he thought, stand by him in the harder times to come. He gazed at her fondly. She had been the one who taught him that each pole on the plane of life—Good and Evil—had its place and had its complement. Without one, there would not be the other, and there would be no balance.

Par-Salian sighed, a weary sound, for gods strove one against the other again—Paladine against Takhisis. He tried to imagine what strength the world would find to withstand another round of that. The same strength it always had, he supposed: the strong-hearted people of Krynn. And the striving was necessary, he knew it. Ladonna had taught him that. In the godly striving is tension, and tension keeps the balance. She was right, and the striving was eternal, never to be settled. No matter what treaties mortals made among themselves, still Takhisis plotted, and still Paladine planned against those plots. Already one of the Dark Queen's Highlords, Kitiara Majere, was growing strong and restless in Sanction, eager and ready to strike in the name of the Dark Queen, sundering the peace of Whitestone. The Blue Lady she named herself, for blue as steel was her armor, and blue was the dragon she rode. Like a wolf scenting weakness, she knew the races and nations who had forged the Whitestone Treaty were not ready for a resurgence of Takhisis's forces, that few believed such a thing was possible. She could, if allowed to grow strong enough, fight a war whose outcome would be far different than the first.

As if she weren't enough, lately there had risen another who conspired in spite of both gods, a mage whose power had grown strong in the few years of his young life. Raistlin Majere. If the Silvanesti elves had found reason to thank and praise him for lifting Lorac's Nightmare from their land, Par-Salian knew that no one had reason to be grateful for him now. He was the Blue Lady's brother, though not her ally. His sister had ambitions to rule nations. Raistlin's ambition was deeper and more terrible. What form it took, the Conclave of Wizards did not know. They did know that he had the strength to break the curse that, ever since the Cataclysm, had sealed the Tower of High Sorcery at Palanthas and take that stronghold for himself.

"Your dark elf," he said, stretching his arms high, working shoulders weary with bending over books. "Will he be worthy, Ladonna?"

She walked past the banks of candles to the window Outside, the twilight glowed, warm and fragrant with the scent of the forest, a magical forest, a Guardian Forest such as those that once stood to ward all five Towers of High Sorcery. The one that had warded Daltigoth had caused intruders to fall into dreamless sleep. That around Goodlund's tower inflamed the uninvited with uncontrollable passions. When Istar had reigned, the forest guarding the tower there induced a simple forgetfulness so that intruders failed to remember why they'd come that way. Not so gentle the forest around the Tower at Palanthas. Shoikan Grove was home to spectres and monsters and dread, so deep madness was the only way out. And yet, though five towers were built, only two remained. It was not impossible to imagine that Wayreth's tower, too, could fall one day.

Turning from the window, Ladonna said, "I think—I *think*, mind you—that this one, this Dalamar, might well be a man with enough courage to help us do what must be done about that most dangerous of mages in Palanthas."

That most dangerous of mages . . . She did not speak his name. She never did unless the speaking was unavoidable. Ladonna hated Raistlin Majere, and she feared him. Par-Salian knew how much it pained her to admit, even to herself, that she, the Mistress of her Order, must be wary of the dark-robed mage who had so precipitously taken over the Tower of Palanthas. He also knew that were she and Raistlin Majere to meet in ritual contest, his magic would best hers, and then there would be a new head of the Order of Black Robes, one who would rule from his own Tower, and with whom Par-Salian would have less than cordial relations.

"Your dark elf—"

"Dalamar Argent."

"Dalamar Argent, then. I haven't heard it said he's had much formal training. How much could he have, really? Ylle Savath of House Mystic would have put out her own eyes before teaching him dark magic, yet here he is in black robes, calling himself a mage."

Ladonna's eyes flashed. "Lady Ylle never taught him Nuitari's magic. He is—or he was—a servitor. You've heard how that is—all the food and clothing and work you could want. Nothing more than that, though. She hardly permitted him any instruction at all, and only grudged him the little she did to keep him from turning to wild magic"—she smiled sourly—"or to dark magic. No, he has little formal training, something of the magic of the Wilder Elves, something of White magic, and everything else he's picked up along the way. But it is also true that Dalamar has been three years in his exile, and you know this as well as I do: If that doesn't kill one of his kind, it makes him strong and canny beyond his years." She tilted her head to smile at him, that smile slow as a drawl. "He is that, strong and canny. And he is—or could be—our man."

Wind sighed through the forest. An owl cried in one of the towers on the warding wall. Far away in Palanthas, ghosts groaned in Shoikan Grove, doubtless music to the ears of the renegade mage who would make ghosts of the plans of gods and men.

"And what must be done with your dark elf?" Par-Salian asked.

Ladonna shrugged. That careless gesture didn't hide the gleam in her eyes, her sudden satisfaction. "He must take his Tests. It is only when he comes out of those alive that I'll know if he's the one. If he fails . . . well, if he fails, we'll clean up the mess and find another, for something must be done about Palanthas."

On that matter, they agreed.

"Very well," said Par-Salian, "you may leave the matter to me. Where is he?"

"Still waiting in the reception area in the foretower."

Par-Salian shrugged. "As good a place as any, then."

She smiled and praised his sagacity, then she settled comfortably into a corner of the large chair near the window, listening to the night and the owls while the Master of the

Tower returned to his reading. The discussion of her dark elf ended, she still had that dwarf to consider. If she could have him banished from the Tower, she would do that in the instant, but he'd done nothing to earn that, at least not yet. This trip to the Tower he'd come bearing gifts, magical artifacts he'd found in his travels.

"And books for the library," he'd told her, sweeping a bow to mimic the respect he did not feel. "I spend so much time there, it seemed only right to offer something in return." He'd smiled, a pale skinning of his teeth. His eyes had not lighted with it, but then she seldom saw them light with any emotion.

By Nuitari's night, she thought, how much longer can that pile of rotting flesh and bone live? She shivered a little. The carcass of him didn't have to live long at all, did it? Only the mind to slip in and out of the avatars he made for himself.

The breeze drifting in from the forest brushed chill on her skin. An owl cried suddenly, sharp and piercing; a rabbit screamed, caught. Ladonna watched the light of the red moon and the silver glinting from the gems on her beringed fingers. She felt the dark moon surging in her heart, as though a god spoke warning. She had heeded this warning before, and she did not forget it now. Raistlin Majere was a problem, she did not deny, and his sister the Blue Lady was another. No mage herself, the Blue Lady employed mages of the strongest magic. The best of these, the canniest and most vicious, sat late in the library tonight, the dwarf reading and studying that he might craft stronger, fiercer magics for his lady. They were in the thrall of Takhisis, those two, the Blue Lady and the dwarf.

Tramd o' the Dark, he called himself. Tramd Heading For the Abyss, Ladonna named him. She would rather send him there sooner than later.

Outside the window, the three moons rode the sky, each the sign of one of the three magical children, Solinari,

Lunitari, Nuitari. They went on balanced paths, in unbroken rhythm swinging across the sky. They were always the image of the balance that kept the world turning, the seasons passing, the magic running. Without that balance, the world would fall apart in chaos. The Blue Lady threatened that balance, she and her dark dwarf mage.

We are beset, she thought. On one side by a Dragon Highlord who would rip the world apart and deliver the bleeding corpse into the hands of the Queen of Darkness, on the other by a mage who has taken possession of a Tower of High Sorcery and thought it might be a good idea to challenge the gods themselves, those of Good, those of Neutrality, those of Evil.

A book thumped closed.

The Master of the Tower of High Sorcery rose from his desk and dropped a chaste kiss upon her cheek as he passed. Gone to see to the dark elf, she thought. Then, smiling, she settled back against the pillows to watch the moons travel.

The dark elf and the dwarf . . . perhaps there was a way to settle all things at once.

Chapter 16

Murmured greetings drifted after him as the Master of the Tower drew near the reception area, the voices of mages of all Orders bidding him good even. By these Dalamar knew him as Par-Salian. A tall human, thin with age, the Master did not quite come into the chamber. He stood upon the threshold of the passage leading out from the foretower and into the south tower. At sight of him, Dalamar rose, hands folded within the sleeves of his own dark robe. He had known humans of greater age than he, elders among their kind who were old at fifty years and nearly dead at eighty. His own ninety-eight years, the count of a young man among elves, astounded them, and in turn, their fleeting years appalled him. He did not feel this way in the presence of Par-Salian. He was old by human standards, but he had a strength of will that made strength of body seem like nothing but crude brawn. To this strength Dalamar responded, his heart, seldom moved to respect, warmed.

"Good evening, my lord," he said. He inclined his head to bow.

Par-Salian made no such gesture. He stood still a long moment, his blue eyes glinting with keen intelligence, his wrinkled face stony, betraying nothing of his assessment of this young dark elf standing before him. On the walls, the torches burned smokeless flames of magic. Shadows spun webs on the floor and the scent of sorcery hung on the air.

At last, "You've come to be tested."

Dalamar's belly clenched, fear and excitement both. "I have, my lord."

"With whom have you studied?"

Not even the least flush of shame would Dalamar

permit. He held the Master's gaze and said, "For a little while, with the mages of Ylle Savath of Silvanost. For the rest of the time, I have been my own tutor."

Par-Salian raised a brow. "Indeed. And you know that not all mages come out from these Tests whole, few come out unmarked. Some are consumed by the magic they can't control, and those don't return from this Tower alive."

He said so coldly, with no glimmer of emotion in his eye. Firmly, head high, Dalamar answered in kind. "I know this, my lord, and I am here."

A soft breeze sighed through the chamber, drifting out from the south tower, scented of magic, of age and the beeswax of countless candles burned over countless years. Dalamar lifted his head to that scent, as though to the sound of a voice calling.

Par-Salian nodded as one who considers something. "I know some things about you, Dalamar Argent."

Dalamar stood in silence, forbearing to correct the Master of the Tower on the matter of his name.

"I know you had some part in the defense of Silvanesti." The White Robe smiled now, leanly. "It might have worked, your scheme of illusion."

"It did work, my lord," Dalamar said. "It worked for a time, and the Highlord was damaged."

"Damaged, and soon to have all the reinforcements she needed. But, you're right. It was not your magic that failed the kingdom. Something more did." Into Dalamar's questioning silence, he said, "The heart of your king did. He did not trust his people, and he did not trust his gods." His voice grew chill. "And you lost faith along with the king."

"No, my lord. In those gods of his"—again he inclined his head respectfully—"in those gods of yours, I never had much faith. I have found a god who guides me now, and in Nuitari I have placed all my faith."

In the silence stretching out between them, Dalamar knew himself weighed, knew himself considered, and felt all the corners of his heart scrutinized. He trembled—who could not under that gaze?—and he forced himself to stand, though his knees wanted to buckle. That he would never permit, not here, not now, never before this mage who held in his hand his chance to take the Tests of High Sorcery.

"Well enough, then." The Master of the Tower made a small, welcoming gesture, the kind meant to usher a guest into the hall. He stepped back, indicating that Dalamar should precede him into the south tower.

Hands clenched tightly, that clenching hidden in the wide sleeves of his robe, Dalamar took a step forward—one, one only—and all the world filled up with shouting, all that shouting pouring out from one throat: His own. A wild wind roared in his head, thundering and shrieking. He struggled, and then he stopped, willing himself to be still. In that moment he framed his will in words, the roaring in his head stopped, and the blackness engulfing him felt as normal and friendly as sleep.

To that blackness he gave himself, surrendering his will because that surrender *was* his will, trusting that he would find himself where he needed to be. Quietly, he fell . . . and then things were not so quiet.

* * * * *

Fire ran in Dalamar, coursing through his veins like lust and rage. Fire became his very blood, burning in rampage, the flames roaring in him with the sound of his own voice. This was the fire of magic, the fierce running power of Nuitari's sorcery tearing into him, out of him, a fire no one commanded but he.

See how the power flashes through him! Like lightning charging the sky! He will not be able to hold it. . . . He will not be able to—

Dalamar stood on a foggy plain howling with glee, and his voice was the song of the wind wailing wild in the tree-tops, the high canopy of the Forest of Wayreth. His soul soared on that howling, magic running in him, leaping, laughing. He tamed the howling, brought it back inside himself, and let it out again, sending his voice out powerfully as though it were a thing that lived independently of him. On his voice flew all the chants he had learned in Silvamori, words of achingly beautiful simplicity, words that were useless without the music to carry them, a weaving of notes so complex no one could map it for another to follow.

He sings. He sings. He must have learned this from the Kagonesti in Silvamori. . . .

Dalamar thought he would say, *Yes, I have learned this from a Kagonesti, from a wizardess there whose power lay in the music of her untamed soul, and this magic is so like to the Wild Magic you all fear that the difference is hard to see. I see it, though! I do, for I have learned well this magic others have scorned. . . .* He thought he would say that, but he didn't have words for other than speaking the shape of his magic and all the spells he loved as though they were his own heart and his own soul.

He flung forth fireballs, and he caught them and quenched them in his hands. Every spell he knew, he cast—those learned in Silvanost of House Mystic, in Silvamori, gleaned from the dusty tomes in the library at Tarsis, and those precious spells stolen in secret from the tutors hidden in his little cave. He cast them, and he gave no thought to whether the casting would drain him of strength, even of life. How, when the casting of spells and the weaving of magic was all he'd ever wanted to do. In all his life he wanted nothing more than this. If he died of this, what better way to die? He laughed, and he wept, and both these things were expressions of his joy, of his power and the utter certainty that he could go on and on, spending himself in magic until the world was woven up in his spells.

With word and song and gesture, Dalamar drew wonders from the earth, and he pulled down terrors from the sky. He conjured a misty world where there was no sky and no earth existed. There, he walked among shadow-beings and ghosts. He stood beside dryads in their glens and spoke with centaurs from the darkest part of Darken Wood. Demons came to stand before him, creatures with two heads or nine eyes, beings whose breath was a fume of acid, whose breast held no heart but only the empty place where a heart should have beat; horned beings, fanged beings, creatures with wings as leathery as any dragon's. They called him lord and came bowing and pleading for a chance to serve him. These creatures he brought to him, summoning them with magic and the force of his unbending will, and he sent them away again, but not before he gained from each the promise to return at his command. Thus he bound creatures to himself that would have terrified others to see.

In rapture, he summoned the ghost of a Dragon Highlord, and that one he laughed at, for she was Phair Caron and she wept and wailed at his feet, blood pouring from the empty sockets where her eyes should have been, her fingers wet with that blood. He turned from her, still laughing, and now he saw that he was not standing upon the foggy plain but in a street with tall buildings rising up all around him, with smooth pavement beneath his feet and the sweet scent of gardens in the air—

* * * * *

"I am in Silvanost!" Dalamar took a long slow breath. His head ached with memories of conflicting dreams, some sweet, others nightmares. "I am in Silvanost. Or—or am I in Tarsis? No, no, not there. I am at the Tower."

"Tarsis?" The tall human woman beside him smiled, though that smile at best was never more than a sneer. Her dark robe glittered in the shining day, sewn with diamonds and hemmed in rubies. Her black hair, piled high in a crown of braids, shimmered with ropes of pearls.

"Regene," he said, thinking he stood again with the White Robe who liked so well to change her shape.

"Who?" said the woman, frowning. "Don't you recognize me, Dalamar Argent? Or have you been too long in the taverns, sitting in shadows and drinking your pale elven wine?"

He did recognize her, even as she asked the question, he did recognize her. "My lady," he said, to Kesela of the Black Robes.

She laughed, a low, throaty sound. "Well, now that you've got me straight, look around and get yourself straight. You're not in *Tarsis*, of all places! And we're certainly not at the Tower yet, but we're close. It's yonder, far into the woods. Look, you can see the trees of the Guardian Forest." She snorted her disdain. "Though it looks more like a Warding Woodland to me. I suppose the city has grown so big around it that it seems diminished."

Dalamar looked around him. Behind, he caught a glimpse of shining houses. Roofs supported domes of glass so that the inhabitants need not suffer without their gardens in winter but could tend them in warmth all year round. He was in Istar! And, after all, where else would he be? He was in Istar with Lady Kesela, she whose name turned the blood of brave men to water, whose reputation for ruthlessness was the shame of her father, a Solamnic Knight, and the delight of the dark gods she worshiped. They had come here on the wings of magic, bearing scrolls of ancient work and beauty to give to the Master of the Tower of High Sorcery, this wizardess of fearsome repute and he, her apprentice. This gift they brought with little fanfare, for if it was not a secret, still it was not something they would trumpet through the city. The Kingpriest had already declared the worship of the dark gods unwelcome in his city. Talk ran all around Krynn that he would soon declare it outlawed and then turn his eye toward those who worshiped the gods of Neutrality.

Voices rose and fell, singing and chattering, laughing and shouting, Istar talking to itself. All around them the city streets flowed with people—darting kender, dwarves out of Thorbardin, elves from Silvanesti, humans from the Solamnic Plain, from Khur and Nordmaar. Mages went among them, and clerics of all kinds, though it wasn't but a moment before Dalamar's eye picked out the truth of what rumor had been saying. There were more clerics and mages wearing white robes than red, and hardly any black robes at all. The more precious this gift they bore, for the Master of Tower had no mind to purge his libraries of texts because some king who thought himself the arbiter of Krynn's religion had no sense of balance and proportion. And, it would not be doubted, in exchange for this scroll, Lady Kesela would come away with something of value, a charm, a talisman, the favor of the Master of the Tower. She did not give from graciousness.

"Come," Lady Kesela said, not looking at him, not imagining he wouldn't follow. "Attend me."

He did, resenting her tone but showing no sign of that. He had borne more and worse in exchange for her teaching and judged it a good bargain. Sunlight shone, glinting from Kesela's midnight hair as they set out through the city.

The scent of herbs and flowers perfumed the air. Stone arches of magnificent craft swept over the boulevard, and from their crowns flowering plants cascaded, decorating the stone that decorated the street. Incense drifted out from minor temples, and always the song of worship drifted through the streets in voices so pure they rang like bells. Istar, the jewel of Krynn, swirled all around them in sight and scent and sound. A choir of voices rose up as though upon wings, soaring out from a temple as the two dark-robed mages passed by.

"Elven voices," Dalamar said, moving aside to let a silken lady pass where, otherwise, she'd have to have had to step into the gutter. She smelled of exotic perfumes, complex notes of scent mingled like the woven notes of song. "My lady, I heard it in the taproom at the inn that they are gathering a choir at the Great Temple of Paladine made all of elves, for the purity of their voices. The Kingpriest, they say, will have no others than elves in all the choirs of all the temples."

"You mean," she said drily, "of all the temples dedicated to the gods of Good. What elf would serve in the temples where they worshiped the gods of Neutrality or those of Evil?"

Dalamar smiled into her narrow-eyed jibe. No elf would but those who made the hard choice, the aching choice to walk the shadowed paths outside of Silvanesti. *You are dead to us!* The cry was the same, heard by every elf who wore the red robes or the black. *You are dead to us!* Dead to them, but wakened to gods no elf of Silvanesti dared hear.

Through the swirling city they went, past the markets and across the wide, sunny verandas where pretty girls sold flowers from their carts, while jugglers tossed balls and pins for the laughter of children. Lords and ladies rode by in gilded carriages, and thin-cheeked urchins dashed in and out between the horses of the guards trotting beside, shouting for boon. Now and then a hand reached out from a carriage window, gloved and spilling coins. The children shrieked and laughed and praised the generosity of the one who had not deigned to even glance out the window.

By the time they left the city proper and came within sight of the Tower's Guardian Forest, fresh breezes filled the air, smelling of loam and leaves. The shadow of the wood stretched out, reaching like long fingers. Kesela hung back a proper distance to allow her apprentice to go before her. Dalamar leading, they stepped into the shadow and took the first path, a narrow ribbon winding away into the trees. Sunlight spilled down through the branches, dappling the shade, and all the while they walked in and out of light and shadow, through bright patches and dark, until they came to a tall iron fence whose highly wrought gates stood open, as in invitation. No Tower of High Sorcery stood beyond the fence, no building of any kind, only woodland stretching as far as they could see.

Dalamar stepped ahead of his teacher, shifting the scroll-case from beneath his arm to his hand as he passed through the gateway. They did not take three steps past the gate before they found themselves in a wide, cobbled courtyard with a tall tower rising up in the center, its turrets soaring beyond the treetops. People went back and forth in that courtyard, men and women in robes of red and robes of white who had not appeared to be there before. Singly, in pairs, in small groups, they went about their business, talking or in silence. None seemed to notice the visitors, but even as Dalamar thought so, a Red-robed mage appeared at Kesela's elbow, a dwarf who bowed and said, "My lady, you are expected."

The dwarf touched her arm, lightly to guide. "Come with me, you and your apprentice. Quarters have been prepared where you can refresh yourselves while the Master of the Tower is advised of your coming."

No more than that did he say or do, for in the instant, Kesela and Dalamar no longer stood in the courtyard outside the Tower of High Sorcery.

Kesela staggered, dizzied by the sudden change of venue. White in the face, cold-sweating, she gripped the back of a large, cushioned chair for balance. "Wretched dwarf! If he were a mage of mine, I'd break all his fingers for that miscast spell—" She stopped, swallowing hard, sick at her stomach.

Quickly Dalamar poured a glass of water from the crystal carafe on the table beside that plush chair. "Easy, my lady. Take a breath, then sip this."

With trembling hand, she took the glass and raised it to her lips, water slopping over the edge. She swallowed once and then again. Color began to return to her cheeks, reluctantly. "Watch me turn that dwarf into a cockroach next time I see him," she muttered.

Dalamar took the glass and filled it again. Scowling, she accepted it and sank into the chair, breathing deeply, her stomach settling from the wrench of the poorly cast transport spell. She looked around at the chair and the table and the crystal, at the chamber itself, well-appointed and spacious. Tapestries hung on the walls, silks dressed the stone casements of the three windows. In the windowless wall, a fire crackled in a wide hearth. Her expression softened, her anger abated. If they did not transport very well here, they did keep comfortable chambers in which to await the Master of the Tower.

"Someday," she said, idly, as though speaking of a thing that held little consequence, "someday, Dalamar, you might come here again, alone to take your Tests of High Sorcery."

Someday, perhaps, maybe. Those were the words she always attached to any talk of his Tests. She believed him held to her, enthralled by the chance of gaining more knowledge the longer he stayed. She believed so, but he did not. He would leave when he knew himself ready. Made suddenly restless by her suggestion, Dalamar walked around the room, looking out of windows to the courtyard below and the forest in the distance. Voices drifted past the oaken door, mages coming and going. He listened, but he could not make out what was being said, though some of those voices sounded so close he was sure the speakers stood not a foot away outside the room.

"What do you hear?" Kesela asked. She didn't rise, but she leaned forward, curious.

Dalamar shook his head. "I hear voices, but no words."

A door opened, perhaps across the corridor. Someone bade another to enter and, in a clear tone, said, "Touch nothing. Take nothing, and leave all as you see it. I will return."

A tingle of excitement skittered along Dalamar's neck. No one had warned him or Lady Kesela in this way. The guest chamber and all in it seemed to be utterly at their disposal. What lay in that room across the corridor that required such a warning? Breath held, he listened for more and heard only the sound of retreating footfalls, soft and shuffling as though the walker were very old.

Kesela gestured. When Dalamar was sure no one stood in the corridor, he opened the door, just a crack. Golden light spilled in from bracketed torches flaring outside each of the dozen doors on the corridor. Tapestries hung upon the walls, brightly woven scenes of Krynn's history. Here, the building of Thorbardin, there the raising of the Tower of the Stars in Silvanost, farther along the corridor the broadest, tallest of the hangings depicted the anointing of the Kingpriest of Istar. The scent of magic drifted on the air—dried rose petals, bitter valerian root, woodsy oils, and the unpleasantness of things long dead. The Tower was, no doubt, suffused with such perfume, but this drifting felt fresh, as though someone whose hands are ever filled with the tools of magic had only a moment before walked by. Across the hall, the door of the chamber exactly opposite theirs stood open, just a crack. A thin light showed at the space between the door and the threshold—not firelight, not ruddy at all, but pale and swirling, as though it wanted to change to another color.

"Ah," said Lady Kesela, suddenly at his elbow. "Now that's curious."

Soft, a piteous sound, a voice moaned, "Save me."

The voice came from the room across the corridor, and now Dalamar sensed a thing he had not before—an aura hung on the air, and all around that room opposite, a shimmering, tingling charge of magic. Someone in that room had recently spent himself in mage-craft. Dalamar's heart skipped a beat. Someone had lately taken his Test!

"Save me! Oh, disaster is near!"

With no other word, Kesela pushed past Dalamar, who tried to stop her. "No!" he whispered. "My lady, don't!"

Kesela shook him off, and the voice moaned louder now pleading for help, begging for aid and warning of disaster.

"My lady!" Greatly daring, Dalamar leaped, taking hold of her sleeve. "Listen to me," he whispered harshly. The green light flared, sending shadows swirling across the flagged stone floor in frantic patterns. "Whoever is in there is reeking of magic, and I think he's just taken his Test—or perhaps he is still taking it. You don't know what's going on in there, what magic is in play. You could cost a mage his life if you interfere with his Test."

She looked at him, staring coldly. The jewels sewn into her robe ran in the torchlight, and her face seemed made of marble. "There is no Test going on, Dalamar. What makes you think so? There is only magic, something in play, some artifact engaged. I would see."

"Oh, have pity! Do not leave me here! *Save me!*"

She would see, and if that voice were the voice of a mage who had overreached in magic, engaged some artifact or spell, she would not hesitate to pluck the book from his table, the talisman from his hand.

But this was a Test. Dalamar knew it. In his bones, he knew. In his blood where magic sang, he knew. Within that chamber someone was taking his Tests of High Sorcery and to mages, there was no more sacred rite.

"*Save me!*" Like a ghost's moan, that cry wound through the corridor. The light leaking from beneath the door changed to softest green now, like sunlight shining through aspen leaves. "Do not leave me here!"

Kesela grasped the doorknob, and Dalamar reached to grab her. She turned, her eyes cold with rage of a kind he had never seen on her. Fear ran icy in his belly. She saw it and she laughed. The wizardess shouted a word of magic and into her hand sprang a ball of fire, pulsing, glowing. Dalamar felt the heat of it, and he heard a roaring like the forgeman's furnace as Kesela flung the fire, cursing.

Heart racing, he ducked, and he fell hard to his knees, the fire roaring overhead. Mad! The woman must have gone mad! Only a word was needed to shape his own magic, and in the breathing of it he had in hand, like a shining spear, a bolt of lightning so powerful it might have been plucked from the storm. Coldly, permitting himself no anger, allowing her all her own, he struck out, flinging that bolt. Kesela screamed as the bolt struck her full in the chest. Burning flesh sizzled, the stench of burning hair filled the corridor. Kesela slumped to the floor, her eyes wide, her mouth twitching around words she could not manage. She choked, and blood poured out from her mouth, spilling down her chin, her neck, dimming the diamonds sewn into her black robe.

"Save me! Oh, save me!"

The light beneath the door pulsed now, deeply green. Its energy clawed at Dalamar, raising up the hair on his neck, on his arms. Above him, the door that had been a little ajar opened fully.

"Save me! Disaster is near! Don't leave me!"

Green light poured out from the chamber, then went suddenly still and dark. Footfalls sounded softly, and a young elf dressed in white robes came out of the room, a chamber so small it might have been a closet. He had a thing in his hand, something small and round. Torchlight glinted from it as from crystal. One beam of that light struck Dalamar in the eye, and he did not flinch. With great clarity he saw a vision of whirlwind madness, a nightmare of screaming and killing, of trees dying, of woodlands withering. He saw Silvanesti crumble, the towers of Silvanost—even the Tower of the Stars itself!—melt like wax, while a green miasma replaced the air and poisoned all that breathed it. Beasts ran mad, elves died screaming, each man and woman and child of them flung into the pit of his own worst nightmare. All this he saw before the light winked out and the elf-mage slipped silently down the corridor like a thief cloaked in shadows. Once the thief turned, a furtive glance over his shoulder, and every nerve in Dalamar's body screamed as he recognized him—Lorac Caladon of Silvanesti.

What plague did Lorac carry out of the Tower of High Sorcery? What devastation did he bring now to the Sylvan Land? These things Dalamar wondered, but not so painfully as he wondered one other thing.

"Ah, gods," Dalamar groaned, *"why* did I let him go?"

For the same reason, whispered a dark and true voice deep in his heart, *for the same reason you stopped Lady Kesela from intruding upon a Test. For the magic you love more than anything else.*

A dark shape, huddled and bleeding, Kesela moved, but only a little. Her breath a groaning, she moved again, wrenching herself over onto her back. Her eyes glared, two hard stones. Her mouth was a red gash like a wound in her white, white face.

"Apprentice," she groaned. Hatred filled the corridor, stinking on the air. Her hand twitched a little.

She's dying, Dalamar thought, but he didn't trouble himself long or hard about it. She deserved that, a wizardess who sought to interfere with a Test. He groaned, though, as she did, and not for her death or for any pain he himself felt. Dalamar groaned, the sound echoing along the corridor, winding up to the high stone ceiling, for a truth he hated and must acknowledge. He had sent Lorac Caladon out into the world, back from his Test and into Silvanesti, with an artifact of magic that would tear the Sylvan Land to ruin. And he would not have done otherwise.

He could not have.

"So much would I give up for magic," he whispered. "Even this chance to stop a plague from overtaking my homeland."

Kesela's hand twitched again, her eyes shone with dire

lee. "More than that, Dalamar Argent," she groaned.
More than that . . ."

Hissing filled the corridor, like steam escaping a lidded
kettle, like snakes. Down from the ceiling, out from the corners and the shadows lurking, came a red tide running, red
as fire, red as blood. The leading edge of it touched them
both at the same time, and the corridor filled with screaming. Her screaming. His screaming as the flesh melted from
his bones; his bones burst and spilled out their marrow.

Screaming, he died in agony and in fire. Screaming, he
died.

Chapter 17

Dalamar lay in silence, still and barely breathing. He fe
as though he'd lain that way for days, sleeping withou
waking, never dreaming. Beneath his cheek was a thic
pillow of down; a blue blanket of soft combed wool covere
his nakedness. Somewhere a bird sang, a wren by the soun
of the intricate weaving of notes. Incense drifted lik
memory through the air, hanging low, a gray ghost come t
seek him. It smelled of lavender. It smelled of the Temple o
E'li, of Silvanost, sun, and soft breezes.

Perhaps I am not dead, he thought.

A hand touched him lightly on the brow, brushing hi
hair from his cheek, inviting him to wake fully. "You ar
not," a woman's voice said. It was not a gentle voic
though he thought it could be if she wanted that. "Thoug
I don't blame you if you feel as if you are."

Dalamar opened his eyes and turned onto his back. H
was in a small room with only a bed and a table near t
hand, a chest at the foot, and a desk for writing. A woma
stood beside the bed, tall and lovely. She was, by the look o
her, human. Her hair, the color of pure polished silver an
arranged in an intricate fantasy of braids, gleamed in th
sunlight. She wore black robes of velvet, diamonds an
rubies sewn into the seams, and her fingers sparkled wit
gemmed rings. Her face was lined, but lightly. He knew he
He had seen her in Istar, only she had been younger, an
her name, her name was Kesela. He had killed her. She ha
killed him. In Istar . . .

He closed his eyes again, swallowing dryly.

No one, it seemed, had killed anyone, and certainly n
in fallen Istar.

"My lady," he said, "how long have I been ill?"

"You have not been ill," said the woman. "Illusions are ll you suffer from, young mage—illusions and illusions ithin illusions. I am"—she smiled a little—"not Kesela. I t the illusion borrow my face, my younger face. I am adonna. Can you sit and take some of this wine I've ought?"

Ladonna! Dalamar thought he would have to struggle to t, but to his surprise the feeling of weighty lassitude fell om him as he pushed himself onto his elbow, then sat up. Ie gathered the blue blanket around his waist. The woman niled at his modesty.

"I've seen more of you than you imagine, Dalamar rgent, and other things than the body you wear." She atched him sip the wine, then said, "Congratulations. You ave been Tested."

He had been, he knew that now, and he remembered very detail of that Test, the casting of spells, the journey rough Istar. Ah, the theft of the dragon orb that would ndo a king and ravage his kingdom! He had permitted at theft when he might have stopped it. This, in the eamscape, he'd done for magic, and he knew, even as tter regret yet clung to the memories, that he would do as uch or more in the waking world to defend the integrity f a Test, the integrity of High Sorcery itself, should he be lled upon.

"Yes," he said, putting aside the goblet. "I have been ested. I remember. And I did not fare well."

"Do you think so? Interesting."

The scent of lavender incense drifted around them, the cent of fair Silvanost in the days before a king's nightmare avaged her. "Then I did not fail?"

"You are hard on your teachers but no, you did not fail. here were no tasks to accomplish, young mage. We only are about whether you are skilled, and your level of devo- on to magic. These things we now know. How do you el?"

Numb, weary, and confused. That's how he felt, and h would not say as much to her or to anyone. "I have heard my lady, that even those mages who survive the Tests com away with scars. I see none on me." He gestured down th length of his body. "I feel none."

Ladonna shrugged, a small, elegant gesture. "Do yo think, then, that you are the wonder of the age, the onl mage in Krynn to come away from his Tests with no mar on him at all?"

Like ravens circling, memories of the dreamscape cam cawing back to him, screeching in his mind. He was a ma who had set Lorac Caladon loose to wreak havoc upon th most beautiful kingdom in all of Krynn. No, he did no think he had come away unscarred. It was, after all, onl that his scars did not immediately show.

Ladonna let the matter go. "Now tell me this, Dalama Argent: Do you feel strong? Do you feel ready to wal abroad in the land, a wizard young in his power and grov ing stronger?"

Dalamar Argent. Twice she had named him so, and eac time the naming had stung. "My lady," he said with all th considerable dignity an elf can summon, "my name used be Dalamar Argent. It has not been since—" Since it wa struck from the records in Silvanesti, making him a no person. "It has not been since I went to live in Tarsis. M name is Dalamar Nightson."

As though the matter of his name were no concern hers, she turned from him and crossed the room to the doc Before she opened it, she looked over her shoulder and sai "A servant has come and taken your clothing to be cleane You will find replacements in the chest, and your boots a beneath the bed. Rest a while now, but come into the Hall Mages at the first hour after noon, Dalamar Nightson. Yc will be expected."

She said no more, and she did not actually trouble wit the door. In the space between one breath and anothe

adonna vanished from the chamber, leaving behind only
e scent of her perfume and the after-image of bejeweled
ngers twinkling.

* * * * *

They met, only three, in the vast Hall of Mages; the
eads of the Orders convened in conference. Their voices
hoed thinly, their every breath rustled around the walls
o to the very ceiling. They met in perfect confidence that
e secret matter they had come to discuss would remain
st that, as secret in this room as though it remained unspo-
n, a secret in their breasts. Their secret, however, did not
o unheard by others, though never would it be betrayed.
eneath the marble floor, far below in catacombs deep, lay
e crypts, the last, longest home of mages who had, for
ears uncounted, come here to die or commanded their
odies be brought for entombment. In this hall, the dead
bserved what work the living did, and no one minded, for
e dead were the best keepers of secrets.

Cold, white light shone down from the ceiling, motion-
ss, allowing no shadow as it illuminated the vast hall. It
illed onto the twenty high-backed seats of polished
ood, seventeen of those arranged in a semi-circle, three in
escent within that semi-circle. One chair, hewn of mighty
ranite, the gray shot through with veins of black, sat facing
. Firelight might waken the heart of the twenty mahog-
y chairs, bringing out the red gleams of polished wood.
is light did not. Neither did it make the granite of the
llest, grandest chair in which would sit the Head of the
onclave of Wizards seem less cold than it was.

In this hall of chairs, the Heads of the Orders did not sit
t ranged around pacing. The pale light made Par-Salian's
be seem like the dead-white of a funeral shroud, the black
lvet of Ladonna's deep as moonless midnight, and like
ood lately spilled the robe of Justarius, he who ruled the

Order of the Red Robes. He went with a limping walk, fc
if some mages are not marked visibly by their Tests, othe
are.

"Ladonna, I've said it before, and I will again: You ask t
to take a great risk by delaying our plan. The mage Dalama
has taken his Tests. By all accounts he's done well. Wha
more do you want?"

Ladonna laughed, a low, throaty sound. Neither ma
mistook it for a sign of humor, this laughter like a grow
"Since when are you averse to risk, Justarius? Somethin
new in the last hour?" His eyes narrowed, glinting wit
anger. She smiled, and this time not so fiercely. "I don
mind a risk, either, but I like a well-chosen one. Before w
send the dark elf to Palanthas, I want him proven."

Justarius said nothing, still glaring. Into the silence, Pa
Salian spoke.

"My lady," he said, "my lord. We waste time. We kno
what danger is brooding in Palanthas, and we have agree
what measure we will take against that. I am sure yc
agree, Justarius, that we dare not act precipitously. We mu
know that the tool we use in the Palanthas matter is stror
and keen-edged. If we send the wrong man on our missio
we will not have a second chance to send another. Raistli
Majere grows stronger each day and, locked away in h
tower—"

His tower. They winced, the lady of the dark robes an
the lord of the red.

"Yes, *his* tower, though I like the sound of that no bett
than you do. What else to call it? He's shut himself up
there, no one who has tried to enter after him has gotten fa
ther than his doorstep before dying, and not many of tho
have gotten even so far. Shall we pretend otherwise? No, w
are all agreed that we must discover what he's up to, ar
we are agreed on the way we will do that, what tool w
should employ. I say let Ladonna try out our tool. Let h
use her dark elf in whatever cause she likes."

Justarius shook his head, his face clouded. He said nothing, not to disagree or agree.

Ladonna lowered her eyes, in courtesy veiling the gleam of triumph she knew must be shining there. Softly, she said, "Very well then, my lords. I thank you for your trust. I will do what I have planned, and I will let you know how well my plan turns out."

* * * * *

Regene of Schallsea stood in the doorway, her back to the jamb, her long legs crossed at the ankle. A studied pose, Dalamar thought as he looked up from the desk and the book he'd found lying there. A small book, this treatise on herb-craft was more of interest for the illustrations than for the outdated prescriptions in its text. Sunlight ran through her dark hair, spinning silver. She was the Regene of the forest, the hunting girl in leathers with her midnight hair bound back from her forehead by a white silk scarf. As he eyed her, so did Regene eye him. Neither found the other easy to read.

Dalamar flicked a faint mark of dust from the sleeve of his robe, smoothing the soft black wool, his fingers brushing the runes marked in silver embroidery on the hem. It was a finer robe than he'd ever worn, and the note he found folded upon the breast said it was a gift from Ladonna herself "to welcome you to the company of mages, Black Robe, Red Robe and White." Of softest wool, the robe sat comfortably on him, hanging from his shoulders as though the finest tailor in all Krynn had taken the measure of him in the night and swiftly sewn from moons rising to sun rising. The sleeve smoothed, he raised a brow, again eyeing his visitor.

"Aren't you concerned they might mistake you for a guest gone astray in that hunting gear?"

Blue eyes flashed, sharply bright. "No one mistakes me if I don't want them to, but you're right. Robes are the costume of the day here, and so robes I will wear." She raised her arms, graceful as a swan lifting in flight, and breathed a short phrase. The air around her sparkled, shimmering. Laughter rang in the chamber as she stood for the barest wink of time utterly disrobed—a glory of long alabaster limbs, rosy breasts and curving hips—then suddenly robed in flowing white, her hair again in two thick braids over her shoulders. She inclined her head. "Better?"

He looked at her, as though she were yet the alabaster woman, then shrugged. "As it pleases you."

"I've come," she said, "to show you the Tower, if you like. You are as welcome here now as the Master of the place himself. You might want to get to know it."

She'd come for more than that, he was certain. Her eyes were too keen, her expression too carefully guarded. She'd come to learn things about him. Whether she'd come in her own behalf or to satisfy the curiosity of others remained to be learned. Well enough. Let her look and watch. Let her try to see what she could uncover.

"I would like to tour the Tower with you, Regene of Schallsea." He picked up the book from his desk. "Perhaps we can start with the library?"

Regene shrugged, then she snapped her fingers. The book vanished out of Dalamar's hand, leaving only a warm tingling behind on his skin.

"No sense carrying it all that way. Now, come with me. We're quite proud of our Tower, and you'll enjoy seeing why."

His hand still warm from her magic, Dalamar followed Regene out of the guest chamber and into the wide reaches of a Tower of High Sorcery.

* * * * *

Magic moved all around, on the air, in the corridors, and in the chambers of the Tower. Its scent hung in every corner, clung to each tapestry on every wall, to the soft settles, to the pillows adorning the chairs, to the very stone, floor, and wall. Dalamar breathed it, filling his lungs with the fragrance. Mages, white and red and black, went and in and out of the vast records room where librarians worked to sort the ever-increasing piles of papers and books that seemed to breed in the Tower of High Sorcery—journals and diaries, old parchments penned two centuries earlier . . .

"We throw nothing away," Regene said, and she did not exaggerate. "Here in the Tower we keep every scrap that might one day be deemed important."

Row upon row of shelves and bookcases filled each of the records rooms on the first and second floor of the north tower. Mages went among them, some cataloging, some searching.

"What you see here on the first floor is only recently cataloqued, the flotsam of the years just before the war and till now. Across the hall are records of ages past. We shrink the storage crates." She held out her palm, her blue eyes laughing. "Make them as small as my hand and unshrink them if we need to find something."

She took him from the first-floor records room and into the rear tower, telling him that this place was only a back door. "Or sometimes a mage who has died will lie in state here until we entomb him in the crypts below the Hall of Mages. Still, after all, the back door, isn't it?"

Down into the crypts she took him, among the dead of the ages, sorcerers and wizards whose names had long been sung in legend, others whose quiet lives left not even a whisper to echo after them. Beyond and below lay the dungeons, dark, damp chambers where no chains hung from the walls and no doors barred the cells. And why should they? Could not the mages of the Tower command magic to hold those they wanted held? Out into the rear courtyard she took him, and when Dalamar saw the gardens there, filled with flowers, with fruit trees and vegetable patches and herb beds, she noted the look on him, the swift shadow of longing, as though he thought of fair Silvanost, that place to which he might never return.

"Come," she said, pointing to the three towers crowning each junction of the high black walls. "If I wagered that you thought those were guard towers, would I lose?"

He looked up, the touch of a fragrant herb still soft on his fingers. "Yes," he said, "you would. What use would this place have for guards and watch-walks?"

None, of course, but the Tower had every use for laboratories well removed from the central towers. Powerful magics were worked in those places, such experiments of sorcery that would turn white the hair of the downiest youth and wake the first, most terrible nightmare of the hoariest elder. "And do worse than that," Regene said. "I won't take you there now; they are all in use. But you'll have your chance at them later, when you find the need."

Last, Regene took him into the south tower by back stairs beyond the level of the Hall of Mages and into the libraries. In that place of wonders she let him roam, watching as he went from aisle to aisle, wandering in and out among shelves of books until, in the stacks far back in the shadowy corners where the oldest tomes were kept, he crossed the path of a dwarf. Silence stood between them, a moment when absent nods might have been exchanged before one moved on or the other did. Their eyes might never have met, and yet they did. In that moment of meeting Regene knew they recognized each other.

The dwarf laughed, a harsh, hard bark. His lips twisted in a sneering smile, with exaggerated care he stroked his beard, that gesture of insult clear to even those who were not born in Thorbardin. *You are no man, you are but a beardless boy and hardly worth my notice.*

Dalamar Nightson stood unmoving, a mage who might have been carved out of obsidian. Unmoving, he was not unmoved. Then his hand twitched, his right hand, his power hand, as though he were preparing to cast a killing spell. Just for an instant, Regene wondered if the charge of hospitality that lay on all who entered the Tower would be broken, breached for the first time in the memory of the oldest mage here. Dalamar lifted his head, his eyes cold, his expression stony. Some communication passed between them, a thing Regene could not sense, for they spoke mind to mind, mage to mage. The dark elf turned, and he walked away. When he returned to her side, Regene felt the anger in him not as fire but as ice. Her blood ran cold. She slipped her hands into the wide sleeves of her robe to hide their sudden shaking.

Still, she suspected that what she sought to hide, he recognized. He did not speak of it, however, or acknowledge it in any way. It was as though her reaction couldn't possibly matter to him, to laugh at, to soothe, to scorn. With careful politeness Dalamar said, "Thank you for the tour, Regene. I must leave now, for I have an appointment I'd rather not miss."

She glanced into the shadows to where the dwarf had been. He was gone now. Her eyes on those shadows, she told Dalamar she would gladly guide him to his destination.

"No," he said, "I can find my way." He bowed, as gallantly as any elf-lord in Silvanost, but his voice was chill. "I bid you good day."

Dismissed, she let him go. When he was gone, she went into the stacks where he had met the dwarf mage. She extended her senses, intuitive and magical, but read nothing there of what had passed between them more than the last rippling of scorn and rage. What, she wondered, would move the dark elf out from his cool silence into rage? She could not imagine, and she did not want to waste time doing that. She was known to the mages of the Tower as a clever young woman. "Long-headed," said Par-Salian of her, meaning she had a fine memory and a keen wit sometimes overlooked in the light of more charming talents of dressing and undressing in illusion. To the observant, those who knew how to look past all her pretty faces, Regene of Schallsea was also known for a young woman of ambition. She hoped—not unrealistically—that one day she would sit as a member of the Conclave of Wizards and have a place in the Hall of Mages among the twenty-one who steered the course of High Sorcery in Krynn.

Long-headed, keen-witted, she knew there was something about this dark elf, something that attracted the attention of the Master of the Tower. Par-Salian had sent her out into his Guardian Forest to lead Dalamar Nightson through the winding ways. "Don't make it too easy," he had said, "but get him here."

She had not asked why. No one would dare such a question, but she was curious. This one, this dark elf, a self-taught mage who had been nothing but a servant in Silvanost, seemed interesting to the Master of the Tower. It would serve ambition well to keep near him, to watch him, and to see what she might learn.

* * * * *

Through the wonders of the Tower, Dalamar walked insensible. He passed mages and he did not see them. All the scents of magic that had charmed him no longer touched him. He walked through the Tower, but in his mind, in his soul, he walked through the Silvanesti Forest, through the woods on the border where a dragon died screaming, where the cleric Tellin Windglimmer lay, writhing and choking on his last, futile prayer. All around him, the forest burned while he looked into the black depths of a red dragon helm and saw the burning eyes of a minion of Phair Caron, a mage who had come to kill the illusion crafters.

In his blood, fury ran. *Fire! Fire! Fire in the woods!* The cry rang in him, tolling like a bell. In bitter memory, Dalamar looked again upon the death-stilled corpse, the body of Lord Tellin, who had not been, after all, the hardest master he'd served. He had been, like so many other elves that season, a man who did not normally think of himself as a warrior. A cleric used to softer days and easier ways, he had taken his courage and gone north to fight in the hope of freeing the homeland from the terror that savaged their borders, in hope of realizing a dream he should not ever have entertained. . . .

And did Dalamar think his own dream killed, murdered on the border that day? Back then, he might have thought so. Now, he didn't. Now, he knew that the roads he walked, the paths of the world leading through wild places, through port cities and ruined towers, even around the rim of Neraka and into Tarsis, were roads fate had guided him to walk. He was, now and then, a child of the Dark Son, that god who best loved secrets and magic. He was Nuitari's. He would have learned that, one way or another. He would have paid for his devotion in the coin of exile, later if not sooner. His rage, the fury in his heart, was for the maiming of his homeland, that forest more precious to him now than it had been when he could freely run the tended paths. He raged for the city, fair Silvanost, more lovely in memory than when he could wake in the morning to the sound of birdsong, the scent of the Thon-Thalas running, the voices of the city, the lords and their ladies, the bakers, the carters, the butcher-boys and the seamstresses as they went in and out the houses of the high folk.

In the library of this mighty Tower, he had looked into the eyes of one who had taken part in the rape of Silvanesti. Eight years ago! It seemed like the merest breath of time since those fiery eyes had glared at him from a red dragon helm. Then the eyes had been those of a man tall as a barbarian Plainsman. Now they were the eyes of a mountain dwarf, a dark mage who, looking at him, had known him and dismissed him as one of no consequence.

Plainsman and dwarf, they were the same man.

Dalamar stopped, only then realizing that he trembled with rage. He stood a long, slow breath, and he saw that the door into the Hall of Mages stood slightly ajar. Inside, the Head of his Order waited, Ladonna who had bid him come here. She had a matter to take up with him. Whatever it was, he would not let her see him as he now stood, pale with rage. He took a breath, only one, and closed his eyes, focusing inward until his mind calmed and his heart no longer beat to the drums of his rage. When he was again still, he put his hand on the door to the Hall of Mages. His lightest touch caused it to shiver, just a little, and to swing slowly, silently inward.

Dalamar looked swiftly around the high dark chamber. He had a sense that it was a cavernous place, stretching wide and reaching high. Even as he did, he understood that it was not nearly so large as it seemed. The light made the illusion, the pale glow seeping down from the ceiling.

Dark as shadows, Ladonna stood before a tall wooden chair, one of three arranged in semi-circle, beyond which nineteen others formed an embracing crescent. One tall granite seat stood so that whoever sat there could look out upon all. To this one, Ladonna had her back, and her hand upon the arm of the mahogany chair seemed white as bone in the strange, unwavering light.

"My lady, I have come as you commanded."

She turned and looked at him through narrowed eyes. He felt her regard like the touch of a cold hand. He did not flinch, even when she said, "You have seen him."

Dalamar nodded, just once. "I have."

"Good. Now come in. There is a thing you and I must talk about."

You have seen him. Good. How, good? Why, good? Curiosity compelled him. Dalamar went deeper into the hall, and as he walked, it seemed to him that the very air was shivering, that the stone floor beneath his feet shifted. He kept his stride, looking neither up nor down.

"I'm making a map, Dalamar Nightson. Come in, and come closer."

She waved her hand again, a languid gesture that caught the pale light from above in the facets of her ringed fingers and trailed it through the air in colors of sapphire and ruby and emerald. Those light trails were like threads, and with these she wove her map upon the gray stone floor. Towers rose up in the middle of the floor, towers as tall as his shoulder, and these warded a dark castle that sat upon the highest peak of a mountain dominating an island. On the next peak, one only a little smaller, a dragon lay coiled in the warmth of the day, sunlight glinting like bright arrows from its talons and steel-blue scales. Ladonna waved her hand again, and now the light of diamonds depicted water shimmering on the floor, the Courrain Ocean and, just outside the embrace of the Isles of Karthay, Mithas and Kothas, a roiling of water like a wound forever unhealing.

"The Blood Sea of Istar," Ladonna said. She smiled a little, and darkly. "You have lately seen what used to stand in that place in the days before the Cataclysm."

In his Tests he had, in the dreamscape where he'd chosen to let Lorac Caladon take a dragon orb from the Tower of Istar. That orb plunged the fairest kingdom of the world into nightmare. He had weighed in the balance the fate of the beloved kingdom and the strictures of High Sorcery, which command that no one may interfere with a mage in his Tests. He had chosen, as he always had, for sorcery, and he would not show sign of regret or sorrow to this woman whose eyes watched him so coldly. Still, and he could not help it, Dalamar looked south and west from the Blood Sea, and without thinking his eye went to find Silvanesti. This magical map did not show it, and in his heart his most private voice whispered his deepest sorrow: No road leads home for you, not even those drawn on maps.

"My lady," he said, turning his eyes from the place he could not see or ever go, turning his mind from the pain to the moment. "Why are you showing me this castle in Karthay?"

And what does this have to do with your satisfaction that I have seen the dwarf mage and he me?

She looked at him long, her gaze keen with reckoning.

"Listen to me, Dalamar Nightson, and learn this well: You have lived through the War of the Lance, you know that gods work ever in the world with mortals as their instruments and weapons, and you know, for you are no fool, that they have not stopped striving, no matter what treaties mortals have inked among themselves."

Dalamar folded his hands inside the wide sleeves of his dark robe, waiting.

"There are gods, however, who forbear to play this game. You know them, too. They are the three magical children, the gods of High Sorcery. They cherish balance above all things, and we who practice their Art know that if the balance between the three spheres fails . . ."

Dalamar shuddered. "Then magic will fail."

She lifted a hand to tuck back a small wisp of her silver hair. Gems sparked on her fingers, dazzling. "Exactly. Let Paladine and Takhisis play at war, let Gilean watch and record all in sublime impartiality—no matter to them if balance fails. But we who walk on sorcery's way must always strive to keep the balance of light and dark so that our magic may survive. Did not Istar show us that?"

"My lady, no one knows how precious the balance better than a dark elf. You tell me what I already know."

She raised a brow, one cool brow, and he fell silent. In the silence nothing stirred, not even the image of the map on the floor; it was as though the oceans she'd drawn had frozen, as though the towers she'd raised hung in the very moment between the lash of the earthquake and the tumbling of stone.

"Well," she said in a voice that raised the hair on the back of his neck, "let me see, master mage, if I can tell you something you don't know. This balance we cherish has fallen into danger of tipping." Her eyes narrowed, glittering and dangerous. "The one who works to overweight the scales is that mage you met recently in the library"—her lips moved in a cruel smile—"a mage whom you know from other days."

Boldly he spoke, for there was only one other way to speak, and that was in fear. Not now, not ever. "The mage I knew in other days, my lady, was a tall Plainsman, a barbarian in red armor who rode upon a crimson dragon. The mage I saw today is a dwarf."

"Yes, and if you see him again outside this Tower, you might see not a Plainsman or a dwarf. You might not see a man, but a lovely woman or a child. His name, the one his parents gave to him in Thorbardin, is Tramd Stonestrike. He is known to most others as Tramd o' the Dark. We spoke, lately, you and I, about the marks a mage's Test can leave on him. This one's Test left him a rotting ruin, blind, incapable of leaving his bed, of feeding himself or keeping himself clean. All he has left to him is his mind and magic."

"A mind," Dalamar said, suddenly understanding, "that he sends abroad in avatars."

"Yes. He is a wanderer, one who seeks everywhere for the spell or the talisman or the artifact that will restore him to health. You met him in Silvanesti because he had come upon a way to facilitate his search—he attached himself to the army of the Highlord Phair Caron. He went through all the lands she conquered, searching for the magic he needs. After the war, he walked through the world he helped to wound, still searching. At times, he turns up here, checking the libraries and the records rooms."

"He has not, it seems, been successful wherever he searches."

"He hasn't. But he has found another Highlord to serve, and she most certainly has made promises to him, promises he has chosen to trust. She is the Blue Lady."

The Blue Lady, that one who sat even now in Sanction, waiting for her chance to begin the war anew for the Dark Queen, she whose forces filled Neraka. Her title rang like the clash of distant swords in the chamber, echoing. She was, he knew, the sister of the mage who had broken the Nightmare gripping Silvanesti.

"Is she so powerful, then, my lady, that you fear she will tip the balance in the battle between the gods?"

"She is powerful and growing stronger. She has the favor of Her Dark Majesty, and she has Tramd to make such magic for her as the world has not lately seen. He is stronger now than he was when Phair Caron was his Highlord. Some things he has learned in his wanderings, if not the one thing he seeks." She paused, a thoughtful silence in which she allowed him to see her considering. "And other things are happening, far away in Palanthas. Another force . . . well, we can talk about that in proper time. For now, we have gone far afield. Would you like to undertake a mission for me, Dalamar Nightson?"

Dalamar's pulse quickened. She had the look on her of one who is about to bestow a boon. He could guess what boon that was. "My lady, only name it. I will do it."

"Kill the dwarf. Not the avatar, that is but inspired clay. When it falls, the mind of the man flies homeward again back to Karthay and the ruin that is his body. Kill that ruin when there is no avatar for his mind to fly back to, and you kill the dwarf himself." She laughed then, for she saw his eyes shining, the eagerness leaping. "I thought you would find this mission to your liking. But understand: By undertaking my mission, you risk the ire of Her Dark Majesty. Tramd is part of her work."

Now Dalamar's pounding heart pumped blood as cold as snow melt. No matter, no matter. Revenge lay within his reach. Close at hand, too, lay a chance to stand high in Ladonna's favor. For these things Dalamar would risk his life and count the gamble a good one.

"My lady, I don't seek the Dark Queen's ire, but I will not be paralyzed by fear of it."

"It is my hope that you will not be," Ladonna murmured wryly. "And my hope that you will remember that dragon, who suns himself by day on the peaks and wards the mage in his helplessness by night."

He lifted his head then, looking her boldly in the eye. "I will not forget. Nor will I forget that it is your hope that I will not fail this test you set me."

Ladonna's expression showed surprise, only a flicker. "A test? Have you not had enough of tests?"

"It seems not."

"Well, well. You are a keen one, aren't you? Yes, this is another test. Are you eager to know what lies beyond the test, should you succeed?"

Dalamar shrugged.

She looked at him again, again to search. When she had done so, she said, "Palanthas lies beyond the test."

Palanthas, where the only other surviving Tower of High Sorcery lay, surrounded by Shoikan Grove and a host of undead and ghosts and worse to discourage trespassers. No one had been in Palanthas's Tower since the fall of Istar. Sealed with a curse, the curse itself bound by the blood of the Master of that tower, a mage who flung himself from the highest battlement and fell, impaled, upon the iron fence far below. Since that time, no one had entered the Tower of High Sorcery at Palanthas.

"And what is in Palanthas for me, my lady?"

"No," she said, "I will tell you none of that. There we stray into matters best discussed by the Master of this Tower. Go relieve the world of that dwarf, then we will deal in questions and answers."

"Very well," he said, his eyes still on hers. "I will do that, my lady."

She smiled then, and it was not a warm smile. In that instant, the interview was over. She turned on her heel and walked away. The dark sweep of the hem of her robe whispering to the floor was the only sound in the high wide chamber. Upon that floor her illusion still sat, the frozen sea and the towers of the citadel upon the mountains of Karthay, and the dragon like an image forged in blue steel.

*   *   *   *   *

In the hour of dawn, as the first rosy fingers of light spread out upon the sea, shining on whitecaps and gilding the wings of gulls as they sailed over the heights where the water met the cliffs of northmost Karthay, a dwarf mage roused from his tortured sleep in the castle all folk around knew as the Citadel of Night. The air in his chamber hung thick with incense, fragrances meant to cover the darkly sweet stench of death and rotting emanating from his body. He cared nothing for what smelled sweet or ill. These perfumes he allowed for the sake of those who tended him, the servants who fed and cleaned and clothed him.

He had only one care, only one purpose, and the stench of his long, long dying never diverted his mind from it. The mage did not move, for he could not. His limbs were useless to him, long ago withered, his muscles contracted and unavailing, the flesh shrunken and juiceless. None would think, looking at him, that here was a dwarf out of Thorbardin who had once been thick-chested and so strong of arm and leg that in all the contests of strength he entered, no other dared hope for honor and prize. Those arms and legs were gone from him, just as if they had been cut from his body with an axe. Neither had Tramd eyes to open upon waking. Those were long ago taken from him. Plucked out. Burned out. Perhaps they'd been squeezed out. Sometimes his memory said one thing, sometimes it said another. Many long years had passed since his Tests in the Tower of High Sorcery at Wayreth, many since he'd walked the winding paths through the unstill forest and found the gates to the Tower. In those days, Her Dark Majesty, Takhisis Queen of Night, had not roused the dragons from their long slumber. In those days, the mortal races of Krynn did not dream, even in the most terrible of their nightmares, that the Dark Queen would spread her wings wide over the world again, once more to set out upon her quest to rule the hearts and souls of all races, to feel the world tremble as every man and woman bent the knee to her.

Thus, this morning as every morning, Tramd woke blindly, yet not in blindness at all. Though the magic of his Test had taken his physical sight from him, that same magic had given a kind of sight back. With his mind, he reached out and lifted to life the avatar all those in the Tower of High Sorcery knew as Tramd. Most like his own body, when it was hale and whole, was this avatar. The dark beard, the barrel chest, the arms thick and strong. Sometimes he stood before mirrors, gazing at the avatar through the avatar's own eyes, and thought nothing had changed, nothing since the day he first walked into the Tower all those years before. Sometimes, fleetingly . . . and then the impression faded before the reality known only to the dwarf who lay rotting on his bed of silks and satin, ever-dying, never dying.

This morning he gazed in no mirror. He let the avatar do nothing but clothe itself and relieve the pressure of its swollen bladder. He did not let it feed itself, though so closely linked were the senses of the avatar and the mind of the mage that its hunger was as his own.

He sent it out into the corridors of the Tower, sent it walking in the first light of day into the garden in the rear courtyard. Past beds of herbs it went, speaking to no one. None of those who tended the plants seemed to notice. Tramd was not known for his congeniality, not known for his charm.

At the command of the mage, the avatar went to that outer tower that faced north, into the first-floor laboratory where he had been for the past week, laboring over experiments of a lifting nature, magics with a winged bent, and those which made as nothing the pull of gravity. He kept no record of his work there, made no note at all but in his own mind. These were the most secret magics, spells he worked for the Blue Lady, spells that had come to him in the ecstasy of prayer, the praise-words he used to glorify Takhisis. Those spell words he put together here, with knowledge gained from the ancient texts found in the Tower's library. He fitted them one to another as a poet fits together the words of his lays. Word to word, line to line, he sought to shape a spell that would make the Blue Lady, the Highlord Kitiara, into the flashing sword in the cruel right hand of the goddess of the Abyss. If at last he crafted the magic she desired, he would have—so promised the Highlord—that which he most longed for: A body whole and hearty, restored to him by the Dark Queen herself.

He worked long in the laboratory, the mage in the avatar's body. At noon he let the avatar go, sent it to the kitchens in the north tower where it prepared a meal for itself and then returned to work. When, at dusk, it left the laboratory again, the avatar paused on the way across the courtyard. A dark figure slipped out of the gate, a mage in a black robe. The last light glinted on silver runes stitched into the hems of the sleeves, runes of protection and warding. There went the dark elf, that one who had killed the dragon upon which Tramd had flown into battle. The mageling had tested here, or so rumor said, and he had obviously done well enough to find himself walking around alive. Most of the newly tested enjoyed the chance to leave the Tower by the speediest, and it cannot be denied, most theatrical manner, to flash forth in magic to their destination. This one, however, seemed to prefer a quieter exit. Tramd muttered a curse, not a real one meant to kill or maim, just a half-hearted, sour imprecation, but he did not finish it. Like a ghost, a white shadow drifting, another figure left the compound, but she did not walk out of the Tower grounds and into the Guardian Forest. She stood a moment, tall in her white robes, her dark hair drifting around her cheeks in the lazy breeze at day's end. She lifted her head and her arms, raising them as a swan lifts her wings. She left the compound in that magical flash, that theatrical burst of light, and the after-image was, indeed, one of a swan in sudden flight.

Regene of Schallsea, he thought. Well, well.

But he thought no more about it. Not then. The avatar was weary, the muscles and bones of it aching with the work it had done. He let it go back to its chambers. He let go the connection between his mind and its body, but not before the avatar had arranged itself in some comfortable semblance of sleep. No matter, though, if the thing slumped to the floor in a tangle of arms and legs like some puppet whose strings are broken. No one dared intrude upon Tramd o' the Dark, or this thing they thought was he. It would lie, undisturbed, until the mage himself woke, once again in blindness, once again in the tall towers of the Citadel of Night, to rouse the avatar and work another day upon his spells of lifting, the magics that flew in the face of gravity.

Chapter 18
~

Wind blew hot off the Plains of Dust, moaning around the hulks outside the seawall, scouring the ship hulls, and stripping off the paint slapped on in winter by the foolishly hopeful. Children ran in the byways between the hulls, shouting and laughing in the shadows of the ships left marooned when the Cataclysm had stolen the sea. The scent of rotting garbage drifted on those dusty winds, wandering through the winding ways of the marketplace, invading all of New City. A sweetness of baking fell before the stench. Even the thrill of scent from the quiet corners where the mage-ware shops sat did not prevail over years of garbage flung insensibly over the walls by those who lived in better quarters of New City. Gray-winged gulls, far-faring scavengers, creaked over the heaps of trash, over the bazaars, over all the city, and any would think Tarsis was, even still, a port city.

Any who walked its streets and byways felt Tarsis had the pulse of a port city—the drumbeat of voices in the marketplace, women shouting to children, potters at the whining wheel, dwarf forgemen shouting to be heard above their own anvils. Parrots screeched in gilded cages, leopards snarled in pens near the south side of the marketplace, exotic creatures caught and held for sale to the wealthy of this city or another. There had been a sudden fashion for tigers in the winter, great stalking beasts to prowl outside the doors of those who considered themselves so wealthy or famous or politically valuable as to fear kidnapping. All over Krynn, the beasts of jungles were seen in the palace courtyards, and some of the wealthy had moats into which insatiable piranhas were introduced. By the savagery of his protection was a man's status judged, and the marketplace in Tarsis did a good business in all such creatures except the fish.

The sights, the smells, the song of the thousand-voiced people in bright-colored robes, glittering shirts, and silken hose swirled around Dalamar like a dance as he went through the streets, making his way from the south side and up through the Street of Potters, the euphemistically named row of brothels all folk in the city knew as the Avenue of the Maidens, and down Iron Row. He went quickly down that street, not so much heading for a destination as fleeing a din, hurrying past the forges and the smithies, the armorers where so much of the Dwarvish language filled the air— shouts, laughter, songs, and cursing—that a blind man would think himself in Thorbardin.

In the Lane of Flowers where produce and herbs and, of course, flowers were sold from shops with garden plots out their back doors, a pretty girl leaned out a window, shouting to a young man on the cobbled street. Dalamar looked up at the sound of her voice, and he smiled just a little. He knew her, his lover of the seasons past. She waved, but only in passing. She had an eye for someone else now. He did not return the gesture. She was gone from his life and not likely to come back. Neither did he care about that but to feel relieved the matter was closed, the thing between them finished.

He went on his way with eager steps now, shouldering through the crowd and heading for that part of the city to which no colorful name was attached, the place known simply and always as Their Quarter, or Our Quarter, if the speaker were a mage. Here the streets narrowed to lanes. He walked past the Shop of the Dark Night, past the Red Moon Waxing, Solinari's Hand, and finally to the Three Children where his own apartments waited. He did not take the back stair up or go inside to the speak with the one-eyed Palanthian who ran the shop for a mage no one knew or had ever seen. Dalamar stopped outside the door, where the two halves of a sawn whiskey butt stood filled with herbs, thyme, mint, and bright orange flowers of nasturtium spilling over the sides.

"Good day," said a woman, her white robes shining in the shadowed doorway, her dark hair pulled back from her cheeks. Her sapphire eyes shone as Regene of Schallsea approached. "Welcome home, Dalamar Nightson."

* * * * *

Dalamar served her elven wine in gray earthenware cups patterned with red swirling lines, two of three he'd uncovered in the ruins of Valkinord. He showed Regene to a comfortable seat on the couch near the window. He drew the shades so that the bright light of Tarsian summer shone muted, and the foul breezes off the garbage heaps made only slight incursion—he lit incense against that, for his own sake. He longed for forest breezes and would find none here.

Regene accepted his hospitality, smiling serenely over the wine, and she behaved in all ways as though her visit was expected—as did he. She thought she had never met a man more incapable of ruffled feathers than this dark elf out of Silvanesti.

They sat in silence a while, for a time playing the game of seeing which of them would speak first. Small psychic probes rustled the magical plane, seeking, rebuffed, seeking. In the end, Dalamar spoke first. The mask of hospitality fell from his face, his eyes glittered, and she thought of keen-edged blades.

"Explain yourself," he said.

Regene shrugged. "I would think I am as transparent as a whore's veil." She folded her legs beneath her, tugging the hem of her robe modestly over her ankles. "I'm here because I thought you would be here." She gestured around her, pleased. "And you are. You left the Tower in some haste after only a quarter hour in conversation with Ladonna, and I don't think she called you to her to tell you how poorly you fared in your Tests. Rather, the opposite. Something is a-brew, Dalamar Nightson, some storm of events magical and political. I have a good ear. I know when the Heads of the Orders are stirring and what type of brew they like to mix. If you are not at the eye of the storm, you are certainly within eye-shot."

Bold, he thought as he reached for her cup and filled it again. She took it, her fingers warm against his. He settled into the chair opposite her. He had not been here since spring, yet it seemed the cushions had only that morning felt the weight of him, the impression of his back still comfortably molded from months of long sitting with books, with thinking, with the dangerous dreams of mages when he fell asleep in the light of the three moons.

"You are a fool," he said quietly. He wasn't certain of that, but he liked to test. "You come here as though you expect good greeting, as though you know me well and can count on civil treatment."

Regene shrugged. She held up the cup of wine, looked around at how comfortably she was situated, and said, "If this is rough greeting, I will likely survive."

Dalamar sipped his wine, the smoky vintage that whispered of Silvanesti in autumn. He closed his eyes and saw the golden forest, heard the shivering of aspen leaves before the first breath of winter. He thought of the forest as he had last seen it, savaged, ruined, the trees falling dead, the forest home to green dragons. Silvanesti had not changed so much in three years, so said all the rumors and news. The prince of the Qualinesti had wed Alhana Starbreeze, and nominally the two elven nations were one. No doubt it all looked promising when discussed in the parlors of the powerful, but the forest yet lay in torment, that torment begun because Lorac Caladon had not the faith in his gods to withstand the onslaught of Phair Caron's dragonarmy.

How good it would feel to wring the life from the one of her minions who had survived Lorac's Nightmare!

"I am going," he said, the taste of Silvanesti on his lips, "to take a bit of personal revenge. You need not concern yourself about it."

Regene arched a brow, settling back in the couch. She drew her legs up closer, and a bare ankle peeked out from beneath the hem of her robe. "So Ladonna called you to her and bade you go and find yourself some revenge? I didn't know the lady brokered vengeance."

"When it suits her."

"Your, ah, bit of personal revenge," Regene murmured, "would that have to do with the dwarf Tramd?"

"Yes."

She nodded, satisfied in her reckoning. "Then that's where the storm is." Swiftly, she leaned forward. The hem of her robe slipped up the calf of her leg, revealing white smooth skin. "Let me tell you something, Dalamar Nightson—I know you are bound on some mission for Ladonna. Perhaps for Par-Salian as well." When he shook his head as though to deny, she stopped him. "Don't bother to say I'm wrong. I'm right, and the more you deny, the more certain I am. I want to go with you, whatever it is you're planning, I want to be part of it. Listen! I don't want your glory, I don't want anything more than to be part of what you do. I am young in my craft, but I am strong."

Regene sat back a moment to think. He let her have it, intrigued.

"I am young," she said, "but I am well regarded. There is a thing I want, a goal I have, and I don't know how it will harm you, but I can imagine it would help you. If you take the long view."

"The long view of what?"

"Of your life, Dalamar. I hope—and I don't hope without reason—that one day I'll sit among the Conclave of Wizards. But there are deeds that need doing before that will happen, a reputation to build, a body of work to which I may point before I can think to put myself in nomination."

And a life to live, he thought. They are such headlong fools, these short-lived humans, burning their candles as fast as they might, flinging themselves into a future they imagine and so trust will be. This is the one, he thought, who lectures me about long views.

"You make a nice plan for yourself," he said, forbearing to smile. "Have you noted that they are all well and strong, those wizards of the White Robes who sit in the Conclave?"

Regene nodded. "They are, for which I am grateful." Her sapphire eyes sparked with silent laughter. "Their continued good health provides me with plenty of time to do what I must in order to be what I will."

Dalamar eyed the white robe over the rim of his cup, the mage like a swan sitting comfortably upon his couch. She had many skills beyond illusion-crafting. He knew that because he'd checked. She went high in the regard of the head of her Order, and that meant in the regard of the Master of the Tower himself. She was not his ward, and neither was she his student. Perhaps her standing was better, for Par-Salian used her for his little missions, such as her turn as a guide in the Forest of Wayreth. This, more than anything he knew about her, recommended her to him.

Outside, the breeze grew stronger. Beneath the ever-present smell of garbage a fresher, cleaner scent ran. In this late summer season, when none could be expected, the breeze spoke of rain. Dalamar rose and lifted the window shade. The freshening air sent streamers of smoke drifting out from his front room and into the bedroom.

"The weather looks to turn foul," he said. "Have you a place to stay in the city? I'd be pleased to show you to a good inn."

Regene's eyes followed the small gray thread of smoke, the incense drifting through the arched doorway and into the room where she saw, just in glimpsing, a bed hung with soft netting, the standard drapery of a Tarsian summer rife with black flies. He smiled, a lean humorless twitch of his lips, and he made his choice in that moment. He would take her offer and take her with him to Karthay. Why not? She had her ambitions, and he sensed they would not clash with his own. He rose, took their cups and the bottle of wine, and held it to the light to see how much remained. He then tucked it under his arm, walked toward the bedroom, and said, "Come along, then."

She followed, and in the mirror on the wall he saw her satisfied smile. Later that day, as the sun set in gold over Tarsis, he watched her sleeping and touched her cheek, once in magic. Only that light touch did he need to read what she dreamed, to know what she felt and how deep and strong was her ambition. She would do, he thought, as a companion on this journey. He thought there was some symmetry to the two of them, White Robe and Black, putting their hand to this task, which, when it succeeded, would prevent the Blue Lady from waging her war and tearing apart the fragile balance five years of blood and grief had established.

He lay back, drowsy, listening to the sound of the city growing still at day's end. He thought this task Ladonna had set him would not be so hard in the doing.

In the morning, they woke, the dregs of wine in their cups, the memories of love-making still on their bodies, and they went to find breakfast. Fed, they returned to his rooms, and he told her of Tramd and the avatars and of Ladonna's charge to eliminate him.

"A political assassination?" Regene professed herself surprised that the resources of the Tower would be put to such a use.

"It would surprise me, too," he said, "if that were what's happening. It isn't."

She listened in silence when he told her the fullness of his charge, the intent and the hoped-for outcome. He did not tell her what lay beyond the task accomplished. He made no mention of Palanthas. What, after all, could he say about it? He knew only one more thing about the Tower of High Sorcery at Palanthas than he'd known when he'd left Wayreth. On the Old King's Road, two days before he returned to Tarsis, he had learned in a tavern that the Tower at Palanthas was not shut up and sealed with a curse. It had been—no story lied about that—but it was not now. A mage had entered it, one who had worn red robes in his time and changed them for black after the War of the Lance. That mage had walked through the horrors of Shoikan Grove as a lord walks in his peaceful garden at dawn. As a lord into his palace, he had entered into the Tower. Once inside, he forbade entry to all who approached, and Dalamar did not doubt this made the Conclave of Wizards uneasy. The mage was Raistlin Majere, he of the hourglass eyes and the golden skin. He had not gone out of the story of Krynn as an old Wildrunner once had suggested. He was, it seemed, enlarging his place in the tale.

None of this did Dalamar say to Regene, for whatever she professed of the shape of her own ambition, his was to please Ladonna with the completion of her mission. He would not chance it that this would look to Regene like a good way to add to her body of work. He would use her as she offered, but he would do no more.

After that, the two mages spoke only of ways to get to Karthay, and they did not deliberate long. They chose the wings of magic over the white-winged sails of ships that would take them over the sea. They left on the morning of the next day, and each thought, Well, I know how far I'll trust this one, and that far should get me what I want.

Chapter 19
❧

Dalamar stood on the shore of a grim isle. The groaning of the sea and the weary sigh of waves against the rocky shore filled the gray dawn. He looked from the cheerless sky to where Regene walked toward a broad arm of stone thrust out from the land. All around lay bleached bones, shattered skulls, and the wretched shards of once proud keels. These were not the remains of one shipwreck but many. They were not friendly harbors, the stony shores of Karthay. Hardly anyone put into them on purpose. Few who found themselves flung here by storm or chased by the pirates who haunted Mithas and her sister isle Kothas lived to bemoan their fate. Here was Karthay, that isle where the dark dwarf lived.

Regene stopped in her walking and waved him down the beach. He went, picking his way over stones, kicking aside bones. When he rounded the promontory, he saw that a road met the beach perhaps a quarter-mile away. Broad and smooth, it led in winding stages up the mountainside to where a towered citadel crowned the high peak. No magic warded the road, no traps, no barriers were erected. But then, why should there be? Somewhere near, on one of the lesser peaks behind the citadel, a dragon the color of blue steel lurked. He had seen it in Ladonna's magic-wrought map, and he remembered her warning.

High in the sky, gulls creaked, their gray wings and white backs catching the first glimmer of the day. Regene looked up to the crags rising above the sea. Her cheeks, always known to him as rosy and plump, shone pale now.

"Do you feel it?" she whispered. He had to step closer to hear her. "Do you feel it, Dalamar?"

He stood still, extending his senses, reaching in magic all around the isle, up to the sky, down to the sea, around the stone and mountains.

"Feel what?"

She shuddered. "It's been a long time since I've been outside the Tower. We are all calm in there, a peaceful lot. We study, and we observe the courtesy of the Master's hospitality." She wrapped her arms around herself, shivering. "And—you may have noticed—though Black Robes and White Robes and Red practice their magic, spin their spells, work their charms and talismans, we don't much feel the . . . the *intrusion* of another Order's sorcery. I feel it here, though, Black magic like claws raking my skin."

"Interesting." Dalamar looked up the hill to the towered citadel. "Hadn't you considered that?"

"I did," she said. "I just didn't think one place could hold so much evil." She looked at him along the length of her shoulder, eyeing him. He saw her re-thinking him, looking back to two nights in his bed, to conversations in his rooms. He saw her recognize him. "I hadn't thought," she said, not marveling and not afraid, "that you were part of this."

Dalamar shrugged. "I am what I am, Regene. Part of the dark, as you are part of the light. One, I think, is no better or worse than the other."

Her sapphire eyes widened, just for an instant, as though she heard blasphemy. Then, swiftly she said, "Yes, of course. We know that, we mages."

Cold wind ran down the road, down the hill to the sea. "But outside the world of the Tower," Dalamar said, "where theory meets the hard bones of the world, what we know is not so pretty as it once seemed, is it?"

She didn't answer. He nodded, and he didn't waste time wondering whether he had been foolish to bring her on this journey. In the instant he determined that she showed a sign of failing him, he would cast her aside as a warrior the weapon whose blade was chipped, whose grip was cracked.

* * * * *

You have visitors, said the dragon, the blue whose name was Blade.

On a bed of silks and satin, in a chamber high above the sea, a dwarf groaned, his mouth a ruin of split lips and bleeding gums, his teeth rotted, his flesh scaled. His beard hung in white tatters. His skull shone gray through patches of stringy hair. In his mind, an image flashed, dragon-sent to this one who could see nothing outside his own window. A dark elf walked upon the shore, heading for a White-robed mage not far ahead. He knew them! He had felt the dark elf's hatred days before in the library, but he hadn't thought it would amount to more than the wrath of a pup who had no chance at him. The White Robe, he knew her too.

He did not rage; he did not fall into fear. Tramd o' the Dark was one who long knew how the stars were patterned and what those patterns meant. A diviner, he could read hearts and minds. He understood how mages thought, how power ran. Best of all, he understood how swiftly the winds of politics can drop into calms and deflate the sails of the powerful with no more warning than a simple announcement.

You have visitors.

These two were Tower-sent. He knew it because he knew they were not minions of the Blue Lady, and no one else hated him enough to dare his citadel. Well enough, he thought, let them come, and let them try their luck. The winds are not so calm yet, and we may be able to work up a storm here.

In the Tower of High Sorcery at Wayreth, the avatar walked out from the library, down the long stairs and through the rear tower to the courtyard. Past the beds of herbs and vegetables, he went into the outer tower and into the laboratory where people were used to seeing this wight they knew as Tramd. It closed the heavy oaken door and flung down the bar. It walked to a long table, to the wide expanse of black marble. There it stood, just for a moment, still as breathless night. Then it filled up its chest with air, spoke one word of command in the deep voice all the Tower folk had known as Tramd's. The word spoken, the breath expelled, and the avatar collapsed. It fell to dust, not more than the clothing it wore remained. In the morning, it would be said that the dwarf had killed himself with some carelessness at his work. Now, no one knew, no one missed him.

At the same time, in Karthay, where the breezes blew in chill from the sea and the first gray light of dawn leaked into the shadowed chamber, the dwarf mage came to himself, blind, rotting, and filled up with pain as his mind inhabited the ruin of his body. He forced his lungs to fill with air. He let that air go again, seeping, and on the breath one word drifted, a word of command. In the shadows behind his bed something lurched, stiff-legged and jerky. Like moonlight sparkling on a dark sea, the mind of the mage went into the clay of a new avatar. Again a dwarf, but this time his hair gleamed red as copper, his eyes blue as the sea. He had the broad shoulders of a forgeman, the scarred hands, the keen eye that knew how to look into the heart of fire and see how well his iron was faring.

Said the mage with the voice of the avatar, the dwarf to the dragon, "Where are they?"

On the road up.

"Get rid of them," he said, and he went to the window to watch the dragon lift off, the wide wings spread, sun running on blue scales. The red eye of the beast gleamed as he opened his jaws wide to roar. Light glinted off fangs as

long as Tramd's arm. A sense of bloodlusty anticipatio
filled his mind as Blade soared out over the island, th
sound of his eagerness rebounding from the peaks and a
the towers of the citadel.

* * * * *

The dragon came screaming out of the morning sk
like storm falling, wide leathery wings blotting out th
sun. Standing at the first bend of the road, Dalamar felt th
shadow of the wyrm cold as winter wind. Looking up, h
saw the beast's eyes glaring hatred. Dust eddied on th
road, small whirlwinds of the dragon's passing. H
pointed east and Regene took his meaning at once. Fac
white as her robe, she positioned herself so that the drago
coming in fast, was between two mages. Dalamar gesture
a swift dance of the hands that made the first movement i
a spell she would know. She did the same.

Dalamar turned his attention inward. The drago
roared, but he ignored it, reaching deep into himself whe
his magic lay, that sparkling well from which all wonde
can be lifted. He gathered his strength as the dragon circle
high above them, each pass bringing it lower.

"Use yourself carefully!" he called to Regene. "There's
mage waiting for us, and I doubt he's lying helpless in h
bed!"

She laughed, the sound wild and harsh as the voice
the sea. "Oh, a fine plan! Fight and kill a dragon, then g
on to the mage! What's the difference between madne
and courage, Dalamar Nightson?"

Dalamar flung back his head, laughing up to the sk
"Not much!"

"For Solinari, then!" she shouted, her dark hair whi
ping back, her sapphire eyes burning.

As she shouted, so did Dalamar's heart lift in prayer
the Dark Son, to Nuitari who was his trusted god. "Yo

wish is my will, O Dark Son! An it please you, I strike for the sake of the magic you so love!"

In silence, gods speak, and Dalamar knew the will of his god as he felt himself fill with strength, secure in the knowledge that whatever else he was, Nuitari was an honest god who made no promises and so failed no promises. Joy ran in him like fiery wine, burning and delighting all at once.

"Come down!" he shouted. "Come down, dragon! Try us!"

Lightning poured from between the dragon's jaws. With swift, powerful wing thrusts, Blade tore across the sky, so low over the heads of the mages that the wind of his passing rocked them backward. Sunlight flashed on fangs and talons, glinting off steely blue scales. The carrion stench of the beast's breath sickened him.

Dalamar plunged deeply down to the place within himself where his magic lay, and he thrust both fists up to the sky. Lightning leaped from each hand, and one bolt struck the beast full in the chest, pushing him hard, staggering his flight. Another struck from behind, Regene's flashing spear of light. The tang of ozone stung his nostrils. No scent of burned flesh filled the sky—the dragon's hide was tougher than that—but the roar of pain deafened Dalamar. Blade bellowed, raging as he shot away over the beach. As two dancers in perfect synchronous motion, Dalamar and Regene turned to track his flight.

Like a comet streaking across the dawn, the dragon arced down, and now it had a target. Regene knew she was the prey in the instant before Dalamar did.

"Hold!" he shouted. "Fight! Don't run—!"

But she ran, heedless of his advice, unable to hear or simply compelled by instinct. No speed saved her. None could have.

Shrieking, Blade yanked her from the ground and banked, turning sharply, heading once more toward Dalamar.

Regene's white robe blossomed in blood along the right sleeve. She was alive, that much Dalamar knew, for he saw her face, her sapphire eyes, even the prayer moving on her lips. Solinari, reach out your hand!

"What then?" Dalamar shouted. "Will you fling a corpse at me, dragon? Or will you hold her up to protect you? She's not much of a shield."

Blade laughed, the sound like the blast of fire in Dalamar's mind. He passed once over the mage and then again, his prey limp now in his grasp. Small, warm drops of blood splashed on Dalamar's upturned face, tasting like the sea, salt on his lips. Regene's own lips still moved to shape a prayer whose words the wind tore away.

Blade unclenched his talons and Regene fell, tumbling from the heights of the sky.

Was she worth the expenditure of strength to save? Between the space of one heartbeat and another, Dalamar decided. Deciding, he reacted on the instant, sending all his strength up through his shoulders and along his arms, pushing up against the sky, in magic thrusting against the pull of gravity. Regene's fall slowed, but only a little. She hit the stony ground hard, the breath blasting out of her lungs. Dalamar staggered, feeling the fall itself through the circuit of his magic, his own bones rattled by the impact. He shook himself and looked around.

Regene groaned warning, choking only a word, a name. "Dalamar!"

Dalamar turned in time to see Blade sweep down from the sky, screaming in baleful glee. Wide black wings blotted out the sun, casting cold shadow on the winding road and the two mages. Spurred by rage, Dalamar gathered the lightning one more time and sent it lancing up to the sky. One bolt after another he flung. Weakened as he was, his aim was not so true as he'd have wished. Four of the hissing lightning lances missed the dragon, and only one hit. That one, though, that was enough. It struck the blue dragon between the eyes, burning the thin scales there and the shattering the dragon's skull to splinters.

Blade fell lifeless from the sky, the impetus of his last wing thrust taking him down into the sea.

* * * * *

The dragon's death-scream echoed against the cliffs, bounding from peak to peak and all around the towers of the Citadel of Night. Tramd watched the beast fall with the eyes of his avatar. In the avatar's ears, in his own, that scream resounded. The death of the noble beast who had flown in the battles over the Plains of Solamnia, fought for and taken Dargaard Keep, and led an army in the bitter fight for the High Clerist's Tower had fallen, unmarked by any in the Blue Lady's army but him.

"Return to your Queen," whispered the dwarf to the dragon, once part of the proud wing best beloved of Takhisis. "One last time let your soul fly to hers."

He turned from the window and stood in perfect silence, listening to the voices in the corridor outside his bedchamber. Servants ran, shouting one to another. A clash of metal. The ring of mail and the stamp of boots. His guard, a troop of dwarves out of the darkest warrens of Thorbardin—the worst of the clans, the ruined sons, the benighted whom the thanes of their clans cast out from society of their kin—came to ward his door. They were his and the Blue Lady's. On the bed, his body lay, faintly twitching, always dying. This dying hulk his guard would defend to the last breath, theirs or his.

He had no fear of the two mages on the road. It had been a long, long time since Tramd knew fear. He was, though, curious. They would come here, these two, searching not for the avatar but for the body of the mage, and he would like to know—from one or the other of them—who had sent them. Where in the Tower of High Sorcery lay his enemy?

Who was this foe who thought a chance at the death of Tramd worth the life of these two mages? It would be useful to know. He would not again slip an avatar into the Tower; most of his work was finished there. But he would like to know who in that Tower he would drag out from there, who—after the Blue Lady launched her war—he would rip from the ruined halls of magic that he might practice the long slow arts of killing upon his enemy's quivering body.

"Come, then," he said to the two mages out upon the road. "And be, more or less, welcome."

So saying, he left the bedchamber, the ruin of himself on the bed, and went out into the corridor to receive the salutes of his guard. He went along the winding ways and down the stone stairs where, at each landing, more guards stood, and finally into his study to await his guests.

* * * * *

Regene groaned. She bent her head, her hair not moving from her neck, plastered there by blood from a cut just above the curve of her ear. That cut she'd got in the fall, but the worse wound was that to her left arm. She mopped blood from there with the hem of her robe, showing the wound was not as bad as the bleeding made it seem.

"Some shield," she said. Her bitter smile looked more like a grimace. "I thank you for not using it."

Dalamar nodded, but absently. He looked around, down the road to the sea and up again to the citadel. The air had a peculiar, wavering quality to it, not of light but of light's absence, as though something beyond the sky tried to break through the brightness of day.

"What is that?" Regene said, her voice hushed with fear.

"Trouble. I don't think there is a dwarf who calls himself Tramd o' the Dark in the Tower at Wayreth anymore."

"You think he's—what?—come back here?"

Dalamar nodded. "Don't you?"

Regene sopped more blood from her arm. "What about the avatar?"

Swift came the bitter memory of a forest on fire, the corpse of a good man at his feet, and the hulk of red armor in which nothing lay but dust. "Gone," Dalamar said. "Someone will sweep up a pile of dust somewhere in the Tower and never know it was him.

"Listen," he said, turning. "You don't have to go farther if you don't want to."

He looked at her long, and they both knew he didn't speak from any concern for a woman who had for two nights lain in his bed. He was not, Regene had learned, a sentimental lover. He was not a man who invested much in the sweet dances of the night. Neither did he act for the sake of one who had led him through a wandering wood to the Tower of High Sorcery. He wondered whether she were strong enough to go on, whether the nearness of such evil as filled that citadel would still her, stop her, render her afraid and useless to him. Dalamar Nightson, she knew, would act ever and always for his own sake.

And she would act for hers.

Chill wind blew in off the sea. Gulls cried. The waves rushed in and ran out again while Regene ripped the hem of her gown and wrapped it, one-handed, round her arm. Clenching one end with her teeth and the other with her good hand, she tugged the bandage tight, wincing only a little against the pain. Face pale, she climbed to her feet, wiping bloody hands down the sides of her robe.

"Now, how do we do this? Just go up to the gate and demand admittance?"

Dalamar smiled then, but not warmly. "I don't think it will take that much effort. Look." He pointed to the sky where the shivering air became like gathering darkness.

Regene took a swift sharp breath. The darkness deepened, and it spread like a bruise on the bright blue of the day, flowing down the sky. It seemed now that it was not a thing imposed upon the light, but that light itself leaked out of the sky, out of the world, and into the dark wound. The wound in the sky opened wide, sucking the breath right out of Dalamar's lungs. He felt only one thing before he fell into senselessness: Regene's hand on his arm, gripping hard as though her fingers were talons.

Chapter 20

Regene's fingers dug hard into Dalamar's arm. Sharp lines of pain shot up from his forearm to his shoulder. In the enveloping darkness, pain was all he felt, radiating out from that hard grip, and he did not disdain to feel it. Just then, it was the only sensation.

After long moments, hearing returned. Dalamar heard the whistle of his own breath forced from his lungs and a sudden bark of laughter in the very moment he knew that he could not draw in more air. He took a step to see if he could. Light burst upon him in wild leaping colors, like the auroras that waver over the northmost part of the world. The light did not blind him. It hit him hard, like a fist in the chest, staggering him. Still gasping, Dalamar fell to one knee, reeling away from the force. He felt stone beneath his hands, hard and cold, stone beneath his knee, and no air in his lungs.

Laughter resounded, hard and booming, and breath rushed into his lungs with gasping force.

"Get up," said a voice. "Get up now, mageling."

Anger shot through Dalamar, anger like fire and ice. He stood, he breathed, and breathing, he was able to see. Before him rose a wall of shimmering light, red and blue and green and yellow, all the colors restlessly moving and shifting so that no color stayed the same but blended with others in change. The light made a small chamber, bounded on three sides by the rainbow glow and on the fourth by a thick stone wall into which lines had been scored to suggest a door, though no means of opening the door was seen. Beyond the wall of light, within the chamber, Regene stood, looking around. She saw Dalamar and, face white as her bloody robe should have been, she took a step toward him.

"Don't move!" Dalamar snapped. "Don't touch the light, Regene."

She stood still, warned.

Softly, behind him, Dalamar heard a step, and then a swift in-taking of breath. He turned, his hand already moving to shape an enchantment. Mid-gesture, he stopped. Before him stood a dwarf mage, dark-robed, red of beard and hair. Among dwarves he would be considered handsome: thick-chested, broad in the shoulders, with strong features and fiery eyes.

"It is you," Dalamar said, keeping his voice low and steady despite the aching of his lungs. He would show this mage nothing but a calm, considered mien.

The dwarf inclined his head in acknowledgment. "It is I, Tramd of Thorbardin, who is sometimes known as—"

"Tramd o' the Dark. Yes, I have heard."

The morning sun shone in through the window behind the dwarf, laying gold on the stone floor. A study, Dalamar thought. Shelves of books lined the three walls beyond the rippling rainbow light, and blocky chairs that seemed hewn from whole slabs of stone stood near the window. Thick cushions and pillows eased the hard surfaces and edges of those chairs, and banks of candles sat on tables near to hand. This was the chamber of one who read and wrote long into the night. To the left of the dwarf stood an oaken desk, and on that were stacks of parchment, pots of ebony ink, and newly made pens. Amidst all of this, pages were carelessly scattered—plans of some kind, design schematics and sheaves of notes. From where he stood, Dalamar could not see what shape those plans took. He gained only the swift impression of a fortress or castle of some kind.

Dalamar took his glance from the plans. "Tramd o' the Dark," he said. "Yes, and I remember you."

Tramd moved out of the sunlight, away from the window. "I imagine you would." His eyes narrowed. "I had forgotten you, until lately."

The dwarf gestured to Regene as one who wishes to show a guest some interesting object. Dalamar turned, and he saw that the scoring in the stone wall had changed, grown deeper, as though it did, indeed, mark a passage of some kind—one that was being opened from the inside, beyond the stone. Regene stood very still, facing the door and barely breathing.

"It's a pretty wall, don't you think? Look how the colors shine all over her."

Spilling down her robe, running on her flesh, it was as though the light were water running.

"It has some interesting properties, that light." Tramd stepped closer to the shimmering wall. Regene saw him and glared at him, lifting a hand. "Oh, no," he said, his voice filled with false concern. "No, girl, don't think to charm your way out of there or to send any magic through. What you do will turn on you, each force you extend will rebound back. I'd stand still and keep my hands to myself, were I you."

Unsure, but unwillingly to test it, Regene stood still.

"There are," said Tramd, turning from her to Dalamar, "some interesting creatures living beneath the mountains of Karthay. Some say there is a lost race of dwarves." He shrugged. "But that is outlander foolishness. Hill dwarves, mountain dwarves, gully dwarves—we know all about each other, and if we chose not to congregate, well, that does not mean we are lost."

The stone door moved, scraping on the floor. Regene gasped a swift prayer as she backed away, hasty steps that took her right to the wall of light. She touched that light with the hem of her sleeve and staggered back. Shaking, the woman took no more steps, watching the door open a small push at a time.

Tramd smiled again, expansively. "As I say, some interesting creatures live beneath the mountains here. What stands beyond that door is no kin of mine. Shall we see what is there?"

Dalamar looked at the dwarf through narrowed eyes. "What is it you want that you think you will gain by threatening the White Robe?"

The door moved again, ever inward. Regene shifted from one foot to another, trapped. She looked over her shoulder at Dalamar, her sapphire eyes filling with fear. Her lips moved in prayer. *Solinari shield me . . .*

The god hadn't shielded her well when the dragon snatched her. It didn't look like he would now. The wall of light shivered and shifted, colors blending and changing. Sunlight moved on the floor, touching the far edge of the light wall. Rainbows splashed around the chamber, painting the walls and even the oaken desk.

"Ah," said Tramd, crossing to the desk. He ruffled a few of the pages there, turning one so Dalamar could see it. "Look you, mageling. Isn't this interesting?"

Dalamar stood where he was, narrow-eyed, wary.

"Oh, come closer. I'm not going to hurt you, elf. Look, for it's something worth seeing."

Curious, Dalamar did go closer, and Tramd spread out his design on the table. The page he saw bore a scribe's notation indicating this was not an original but a working copy. The drawing showed a fortress, many-towered, filled with all the corridors and chambers, armories and meeting halls one would expect to find in a place of defense. Oddly drawn, though, Dalamar thought, turning one page and then another. Most renderings of new structures are shown in some kind of context, the fortress in a natural setting—upon a cliff-top, in a forest, guarding a mountain pass. That way the size of it is shown to best effect. This rendering, however, simply showed the fortress sitting in empty space, a dark drawing on the creamy white page.

And that was interesting, but not so fascinating as the writing, the thick lines of columns running down the right-hand side of the page. They were runes, Dalamar knew that much, and very old. Eyes narrowed, he went closer. Dwarven runes, and not the kind one usually sees on the work of dwarf craftsmen.

"A magical script," Tramd said. He flipped a page, and then another. "I have heard you have some skill with runes. What do these tell you?"

Rainbow light ran and shivered. Stone scraped on stone.

"They tell me," Dalamar said, "that you know a rune script I do not."

Tramd laughed, a dry, hard sound like coughing. "They tell more than that. They are runes that will one day enspell a fortress of this design—more than one. And those fortresses," he said, tracing the outline of the structure, "they will be flying citadels. From one of these an army does not *defend*. From here an army attacks, and attacks wherever it wants to."

Fear ran cold in Dalamar's belly. Ladonna had been right to say that the Blue Lady would win the next war. And when she won, all the nations who had forged the White-stone Treaty and compelled the dragonarmies to sign would be hers to rule. There would be no light. No god but Takhisis would receive worship. She, the Dark Queen, the Mother of Dragons, would at last achieve what she had attempted in the War of the Lance. She would be the Dark Queen in the hearts of all who lived, and their souls would be hers to devour, to torment, to hoard as a miser hoards his treasure.

"You see," said the dwarf with the rainbow light shining on him. "You see what can be. What will be." He laughed. "It is inevitable."

He looked up from his pages, right into Dalamar's eyes. So clear those eyes, so bright with cunning, that Dalamar had to remind himself he was not, after all, looking into the eyes of the dwarf Tramd. The real eyes of the dwarf were other, elsewhere, as was his body, the decaying hulk he had come to kill.

"Listen," said the dwarf, the avatar smiling. "You can be

part of this, mageling. You can throw in your lot with the Dark Queen. Step to the side of power now, while you will be welcomed."

Step into the dark, away from the light. He had been doing that all his life. He had walked out from Silvanest into the darkness of the world without and wandered in lightless ruins. He had sat upon the hills around Neraka and considered this very choice.

No, he had said then. No. And yet, if what must come must come, would he be a fool to turn aside from the darkness he had already embraced?

Dalamar glanced away from the dwarf and the drawings. In her prison of light, Regene stood watching him. He did not weigh her in any choice or say to himself, No, I must choose and try to save her life in the bargain. He had already told himself he would abandon her at need. It was not Regene he weighed or considered. He did, however, consider his mission.

Do you know, Ladonna had asked, what life would be like without balance?

He knew, he who had lived under the strictures of a culture that allowed only one kind of worship, one kind of magic. He knew, as only a dark elf can know, what it is like to need what no one will allow him to have. And yet, if the triumph of Her Dark Majesty were, indeed, inevitable wouldn't he be a fool to turn from the winning side and embrace the side of those who would become her slaves?

"Listen well, dark elf," said Tramd, the voice of the avatar softening into the tones used between reasonable men in sensible discussion. "Join me and I will commend you to the Blue Lady herself. I will say to her, 'Here is a new Highlord for you,' and you will rule over whatever kingdom it pleases you to have."

Cold into his heart came the sudden memory of an image he'd seen in the platinum mirrors in the Chamber of Darkness. People bowed to him, and they named him Lord

Dalamar. He was feared, and he was respected, even honored. For this? For what Tramd now offered? Would he walk in a world that trembled to see him and receive the salutations of lesser men as though he were, indeed, the lord his own people would never have allowed him to be? He would, so said the prophecy of the mirrors, and in that moment his heart yearned toward it, rising to the idea of lordship, of temporal power to match his magical power. The title "Lord Dalamar" rang in his most secret soul.

Tramd sighed, a small sound of satisfaction. "So, you see what I see for you, what Takhisis herself sees. You will be a man of great effect, a man whose smallest whim will change the fates of nations. Paladine and all his puny kin will go down before Her Dark Majesty. Nothing will stand before her, and we who are hers will rule as no lord or king has ruled in all the history of Krynn.

"All this is yours, dark elf, if you only tell me this one thing: Who is your master? Who sent you to kill me?"

Only turn from the mission, turn from his word, his honor. Only turn from the magic, the High Sorcery that would die when the balance between light and dark, good and evil, Paladine and Takhisis, is fallen in ruin.

"Dwarf," Dalamar said, "go lick the boots of your mistress in Sanction."

Anger, like a storm, darkened Tramd's face. He whispered a word, softly he said, "Enter."

The scraping of stone on stone sounded louder now, longer, and out the corner of his eye Dalamar saw one gray-skinned hand curve around the door in the wall, grasping. It was a big hand, broad and long with nails like talons. The stink of filth and a long-unwashed body drifted on the air.

"In the name of all the gods of Good, in your own dear name, Bright Solinari . . ."

Regene's prayer lifted up from her prison. She had no magic, and she had no weapon, only her little belt knife and her trustful prayer.

"And what," said Tramd, head high, sun gleaming on his red beard, "what does yon White Robe imagine her prayers will do for her?"

Baited, Dalamar said nothing. A deep growling came out from the darkness behind the door, and the stench grew stronger. Dalamar knew it for the reek of carrion or that of a carrion-eater. Sweat rolled down the sides of Regene's face. Her prayer grew louder, and the flesh of her knuckles whitened, so hard did she grip her little knife. Tramd turned his back on the enclosure as though what happened there was no matter to him. Crossing the room to a small table near the door into the corridor, he murmured a few words. From out of the air appeared a silver flagon and two gleaming silver cups. He poured the cups full of a wine so deeply red that it seemed almost black. From one he sipped carefully, as though judging a vintage. Satisfied, he offered the other to Dalamar.

"Thank you," Dalamar said to the host from whose hand he would accept no gift, "but no."

Tramd shrugged and drank more deeply. "Your friend won't have to die, if you tell me what I want to know. Who sent you for me?"

Dalamar stood still as stone, watching Regene pray. He would not plead for her, and he would not bargain for her. She had made her choice to come here. In the cause of her own ambition, she had followed him from the Tower. In her cause she had come here, knowing he would serve only his cause.

Wild roaring filled the room as a beast-man, something with blind, cauled eyes, gray-scaled skin, and fangs for teeth burst out of the darkness beyond the stone door. Filthy black hair like a wild mane cascaded down the thing's back, and in its hands it held a broad-axe whose blade gleamed in the rainbow-light.

"It is a grimlock," Tramd said, "and a hungry one, too. It mostly eats rat flesh down in those caves, but it's always

294

happy for a bit of human meat when it can get that."

Regene leaped back, hit the wall of light, and fell to her knees. Scrambling, she rose, her knife still in hand. "In the names of the gods of Good—" She ducked as the grimlock swung the broad-axe, fell again, and rolled away. She was no fighter, but she was quick on her feet.

"Tell me what I want to know, mageling," said Tramd, his tone not so reasonable as it had been, "and I will call off the grimlock."

Again, Dalamar turned away. "She's a White Robe. Why do you imagine I would care if she fattens some grimlock's larder?"

Regene slashed at the grimlock, swift with her little knife. The beast-man sprang, swinging down the blade of its axe. Regene cried out in pain, and blood sprang bright on the shoulder of her robe. The grimlock roared, furious that the blow hadn't struck true and severed the woman's arm. The broad axe whistled in the air, and Regene flung herself aside. Sparks leaped from the stone where the iron struck. Regene staggered back, hit the light again, and this time used the repelling force to her advantage, letting it fling her out from under another axe blow. The grimlock roared, turned swiftly, then stumbled, falling into the barrier of light. Flung, it staggered forward, the axe falling from its grip.

Regene dashed for the axe, bleeding from the shoulder wound made by the savage claws of the blue dragon. She snatched the weapon, swinging wide with it. She had not the least technique, not the first idea how to fight. She knew, though, that she must keep the staggered grimlock from her, and the best way to do that was to keep the axe in motion.

Dalamar did not move or even shudder. He kept his eyes on Regene. Her eyes alight, her teeth bared in a warrior's grin, she advanced, one step and then another, bleeding and swinging the axe. The grimlock retreated, stunned by the contact with the light barrier and compelled back toward it. Tramd's breath sounded harshly in Dalamar's ears, then seemed to stagger.

"Kill her!" the dwarf shouted to the grimlock, who wanted nothing more than to do that. "Kill the mage!"

Enraged, the grimlock lunged for Regene with taloned hands. The axe caught it at the elbow, severing its right arm. Blood black as pitch spouted from the wound, and the beast-man shrieked. Screaming in a language whose every word sounded like curses, the grimlock twisted aside, staggering back. It hit the wall of light and was flung forward again. Regene dashed in, the axe high above her head like a headsman's blade. She let it fall, and the beast-man died, the shining blade buried between the grimlock's shoulders.

Regene turned, her sapphire eyes shining with her triumph—

—And the light-prison collapsed around her as she and the corpse of the grimlock vanished.

* * * * *

The carrion stench of the dead grimlock lingered on the air, not covered by the sticks of pungent incense Tramd lit. "Now," said Tramd, waving his hand to disperse the fragrant smoke. "Will you tell me what I want to know, Dalamar Nightson? Who sent you?"

Dalamar noted the change of address, and he did not indicate his satisfaction or curiosity in any way. Once again, the dwarf offered him wine. Again, he declined to take the cup. "I will tell you nothing, Tramd, and I don't see why it matters that you know."

"Do you not?" Tramd looked around the tower chamber. The only light in the room now was that of the sun, strong at mid-morning and growing stronger. "It matters to your friend. Do you doubt that?"

Dalamar did not. "What goes on between you and me

seems to matter a great deal to Regene. But what matters to her, as you have surely seen, doesn't so much matter to me."

A small, sea-scented breeze drifted through the window, carrying the sharp cries of gulls. Dalamar thought he heard the sea itself, but so high up, that was only his imagination. He wondered where Regene was, but not in words, for he did not doubt Tramd would be able to scan his thoughts. He buried the wondering in a deeper field of varying emotions.

"Ah," Tramd sighed. He pressed his lips together, shaking his head in disappointment. "Then it must be as you wish. I can do no more." He lifted his hand, a languid gesture, almost a weary one. But not weary, not really, for in his eyes a cold killing light shone, and glee.

Dalamar turned, his belly tightening. In the corner behind him, darkness gathered, shadows coalescing in despite of sunlight and spreading on the stone floor to become substantial, vaguely man-shaped, and tall. Pale eyes glared in the darkness—not points of light, but simply places where darkness was not. Cold flowed out from that darkness, wintry fingers determined to find warmth and kill it.

Swiftly, Dalamar lifted his hands in the dance of magical gesture, and his voice in a spell sung in Kagonesti words to charm the coalescing shadow.

"Heed," he sang, "hear and heed! In my words, find my need. Hear, heed and hear! My song commands, come not near!

The lightless being shivered, but not under the sway of magic, only with grim laughter.

"I hear," the Shadow hissed, its voice like wind in frozen leaves, "and I do not heed. I hear and care not for your need!"

Closer it came, cold running before it. The first edge of its darkness touched Dalamar, and weakness flowed through him, turning his knees watery. Trembling, he lifted his hands again, and he sang another spell, a charm to put the creature to sleep. But shadows don't sleep, they only hide, and this Shadow laughed as the magic ran through it, effectless.

Closer, closer, the darkness flowed closer, and now it seemed to Dalamar that his muscles were turning to tallow. Useless! He staggered and scrambled around in his mind for the catalog of his spellwork, the magic he knew, whatever he could grab and use before this Shadow sucked all the life from his body. But his wit was like numb hands, like fingers too cold and weak to pick up and use anything. Chants seemed like nonsense, filled with sounds that were not words. The Shadow came closer, reaching with its winter grasp.

Tramd laughed. From some safe place, the dwarf called, "You have made a poor choice, mageling! And I will enjoy watching you die of it!"

The taunt did not sting. It was so much noise swallowed into the incessant ringing in Dalamar's ears as his strength leeched out of him. A spell, a spell . . . something to chase away the darkness—

"*Shirak!*" he shouted and fell, coughing on the word, weak as a fevered man whose lungs were filling with fluid. Staggering, he stepped back before the light, the small wavering globe that was all his magic could manage. As he staggered, so did the Shadow, but not for long. The light shivered, his magic sighed, and the Shadow lunged.

Dalamar stumbled, he fell to one knee and rolled away from the advancing darkness. Magic! Where was it in him? Deep, he plunged deep into himself, into the heart of him, the soul, and he flung off fear and all dread of the weakness sapping his strength. Light, said his mind, light and fire and—

The Shadow reached for him with arms grown broad and long. Strength and life drained out from Dalamar, running from him as though it were his very blood. Fed upon his strength, the Shadow surged forward to grasp even more. Dalamar gathered his waning strength and his faltering wit. In his mind he put the image of his need, of fire and light and a weapon. He lurched to his feet, to the sound of Tramd's laughter, he rose and filled his right hand with a fiery lance. He had nothing of magic or wit to form protection for himself.

The Shadow reached. Dalamar's flesh blackened and peeled back from bone. Someone screamed—ah, gods!—it was he, the sound of his pain and that of Tramd's laughter weaving one around the other, becoming a single, terrible anthem. Howling in rage, rage dispelling pain, Dalamar drew back his arm to let fly the flame-lance, his eyes on the eyes of the Shadow. And so he saw what he had not before. He *knew* that Shadow, that reaching wight. In those pale eyes he saw consciousness, wit, soul and pleading urgency. He saw a sapphire glint! Regene! Too late he knew illusion, in the moment he let fly the lance.

The Shadow screamed, and Tramd's illusion fell away. Regene fell, struck by the fiery lance, her robe, her very flesh, burning. Dalamar flung himself forward and beat out flames with his good hand. Eyes wide with pain, choking, Regene tried to form some word, some warning. She need not have, Dalamar felt danger behind him in the itching between his shoulders, the crawling of his skin.

Raging, Dalamar turned, stumbling in weakness. Tramd backed away, groping behind him for a weapon. Dalamar smiled coldly to see that, for it told him the thing he needed to know—Tramd had spent himself deeply to support the light-cage, to call forth the grimlock, and to create this illusion that cloaked Regene. A fool would think he had nothing more to spend, but a wise man would see that he had not so much as he would like.

"Dwarf," Dalamar said, his voice rasping, his hand trembling even as he reached within for one last burst of strength, one last weapon. "You've been dying since the day of your Test. It is time for that to end."

Sweat glistened on Tramd's face and ran into his red beard. He took another step backward. Behind him, Dalamar heard groaning, Regene's breathing sounded like a death-rattle and like sobbing all at the same time. Rage rose up in Dalamar, and with it such strength as he did not think he could find. He lifted his burned hand, the flesh peeled from the bone, the bone glaring white at him, glistening with his own blood and the thin lines of blood vessels and muscle. He felt the pain, and he embraced it, changing it to strength. Fingers moved, his fingers, bones shining in the sunlight pouring in from the window. He created, from magic and from his own will, a lightning-lance, the kind that had killed a dragon.

Eyes wide with fear, Tramd dug down deep for his magic, and he came up wanting. Light shimmered before him, as though he'd been trying to magic a shield. The light turned dark, and the darkness collapsed upon itself. He tried again, and Dalamar let him, a cat toying with a mouse. The collapsing darkness before Tramd shifted, changed, magic still struggling. Fear and rage both battled in him, giving him a mad look.

Laughing, Dalamar let fly his bolt. It sizzled on the air, and the darkness before Tramd coalesced at last, turning to something black as obsidian, strong as steel. The bolt hit, exploding into a burst of blinding light.

The sting of ozone hung in the air. Dalamar filled up his lungs with the smell, and he filled up his hands again with power and magic. He hurled no bolt now but fistfuls of energy, the stuff of which lightning is born. He flung these bright weapons, one after another. Tramd's magic trembled and it wavered. The dwarf turned as his shield collapsed. Three more balls of energy Dalamar threw, and in the exact moment he did, Tramd lifted his hands in one last spell.

Nothing happened, and then all the killing power Dalamar had flung turned back on him in a wave of energy like an ocean's wave. Crested red as the sea-waves are crested white, it surged back, screaming on the air and not to be turned.

Strangely still and numb to pain or fear, Dalamar thought, There is my death.

A hand grabbed his ankle, tumbling him. He fell, hit stone, then something soft and yielding. Regene! He scrambled aside, dragging Regene with him, and rolled until he hit a stone wall. The wave passed over him, burning and clawing at his skin, bearing down on his chest.

Gray and sweating, the dwarf lifted a hand, that hand trembling, and it had no magic in it, but it did have a dagger. Sunlight gleamed on the blade, glinting as it swooped down, hungry for blood.

Regene coughed, and on the coughing, she rose, not swiftly, not strongly, but in time. Like silver streaking, like the silver hand of her own god descending, the shining blade cut the air, cut into the breast of Regene of Schallsea. Dalamar's hand shot up, clamping round the wrist of the dwarf mage. He snapped bone, and the avatar screamed. The knife fell from his hand and Dalamar snatched it up. In one swift motion, he lunged to his feet, knife grasped awkwardly in his left hand. He struck an upward blow, a heart-blow. Blood poured out from the breast of the avatar, spilling over Dalamar's hand onto Regene's ruined robes.

"Go!" she whispered, her sapphire eyes dimming, her face livid in the sunlight streaming in from the windows. Dying, she said, "Find the mage—"

* * * * *

Dalamar ran swiftly down long corridors until he found what he sought, the guarded door and clutch of dwarf soldiers outside. There were four, but he didn't care. He tore through them like a storm. Turning their weapons to slag, he killed one of them with only a glance. Two more rushed him, and these he reduced to ash as though their living flesh and bone were no more than the clay of which Tramd o' the Dark made his avatars. The fourth did not stay. He fled and got no farther than the stairwell before he met the fate of his fellows.

Servants cried out, but none on this floor. Dalamar heard them, men and women, and they shouted in several languages. Some were human, others dwarves, one or two were even elves. Servants and slaves, the staff of the Citadel of Night made up with the captives from Tramd's forays in war.

The door would not be locked; he knew it instinctively. What man lying on his sick bed manages that? What man so helpless forbids entry to the servants who will feed, clothe, and clean him? None.

Dalamar opened the door and entered into a bedchamber hung with satins and draped in silks. All around him he saw the booty of a man who had wandered far in war—silver-hinged chests from the North Keep in Nordmaar, tapestries from the halls of the wealthy in Palanthas. From Zhakar he'd stolen silver statuary and golden plate. From Kernen in Kern he had paintings. From Thelgaard Keep he had shields and lances, axes and swords. He didn't seem to have cared much about order. The stolen treasures lay all around, as though in a museum's vast storeroom.

Neither could Tramd see what treasure he had. He lay upon a bed of silk and satin, eyeless, his ruined body reeking, his limbs covered in scabrous flesh. His head tossed weakly, one side to another. Some time in the morning, servants must have lit incense and perfumed the air with oils. The incense was ash now, the oils not enough to cover the stench in the bedchamber of this mage who had fared so ruinously in his Tests of High Sorcery. Not even the breeze blowing in from the sea could do more than stir the stench.

"I see you, Tramd," Dalamar said, standing as near as he must and not minding the reek. "I see you."

The dwarf's head rolled from side to side, a blind man trying to place the speaker. His body quivered, but that was the trembling of his illness, not the will acting on muscle. Scabbed lips parted, and a line of spittle ran down this thin, patchy beard. He groaned, and the sound he made might have been a word. It might not have been. He had used his avatar's body in magic, but he had used his own strength as well.

Dalamar looked around and plucked a weapon from the wall, an axe with a fine, honed blade. He walked to the bed, his shadow on the dwarf.

"Do you feel me near, dwarf?"

The mage on the bed moaned. Silk coverings rustled. He could do no more.

"Now I think it a shame that you cannot see me. I think it a pity that you won't be able to look into my eyes when I kill you."

Outside in the corridor voices gathered, whispering. Servants had come, and soldiers, but no one ventured to cross the threshold. Softly, the hinges on the door creaked. Slowly, someone drew it closed. He had not been beloved, the master of this fortress. No one would interfere here. No one would challenge the mage who had come to kill their master.

Wind sighed across the window sill. The sea rushed to the shore far below and rushed out again. Somewhere a dragon's corpse floated, turning up, belly to the sky. Gulls would feed on that corpse, and sooner or later the sea would soften what even swords could not hurt. Then the gulls and fishes would pry the scales from the belly and pry the flesh from the bones.

"I will tell you," Dalamar said to the dying man on the bed, "what you have so dearly wanted to know. I have come to kill you, Tramd, and it will be my personal pleasure. You killed many good men and women in the battle for Silvanesti."

He stopped, watching the dwarf groan, watching his cracked lips bleed with his effort at speech. Standing there, Dalamar heard the forest burning. He heard the Wildrunners shouting. He heard a dragon dying, and the last prayer of a cleric who had put all his faith in gods who did not seem to know or care. Sunlight ran on the honed edge of the axe's blade, sliding down the curve as Dalamar shifted it from hand to hand.

"I have come in the name of Ladonna of the Tower of High Sorcery. I have come in the name of those who revere the High Art, the gift of the three magical children. I have come in my own name, Tramd Stonestrike, to remove you from the ranks of Her Dark Majesty's servants. There will be Light," he said, "and there will be Dark."

He lifted the axe higher, right over his head.

The dwarf heard the lifting, the sigh of air on the blade. He groaned and found a word. "No," he sobbed, "no."

"Yes," said Dalamar, very gently. "Yes."

He let fall the axe, a headsman, an executioner come to avenge early deaths and late.

"Yes," he said to the dead man. "There will be balance."

Dalamar put back the axe, the blood still running. He rolled the corpse to the floor and snatched up a sheet from the bed. With the silk he wrapped up the head, the eyes still staring, the ruined mouth still gaping.

"My lord," said one, a human woman, bowing to him as she spoke. "What is your will?"

He looked at her, and she cringed from his glare. "Go," he said, and he didn't care if she took the word to mean she must leave him alone or she must go out from the citadel and never come back. They made, servants and soldiers, the choice they had wanted to make for long years. They fled.

Dalamar didn't watch them. Their running footsteps meant nothing to him. He carried the head of Tramd o' the Dark, wrapped in bloody silk, back to the chamber where he had left Regene. She lay dead, her blue eyes wide, her lips a little parted. He knelt beside her, brushed her dark hair from her face, and he closed her eyes. He stayed that way for a time, listening to people flee the castle. Then he lifted her in his arms, took up the proof of the dwarf mage's death, and spoke a word of magic.

The floor fell away. The walls fell away. In the grip of the transport spell, Dalamar Nightson shouted, and this time he didn't cry a spell. This time he shouted a curse.

Out on the ocean, as far as the rim of the Blood Sea of Istar, sailors pointed north and they pointed east. A great fire burned on the Worldscap Mountains on Karthay. The flames of it reached as high as the tallest peak, then higher still. The smoke of the burning roiled out over the sea, darkening the day to dusk.

Epilogue

Dalamar walked through light and through darkness, up a winding stone staircase that seemed to have no end. Once he looked back over his shoulder, and he could not see the steps behind. They were lost in shadow and the fitful flaring of the torches upon the wall. He had no hand-light, for something had been done to dampen his magic. In the pit of his belly, fear fluttered.

The darkness of Shoikan Grove had not frightened him. He had walked beneath trees whose limbs were arms reaching down to grab him, through shadows where disembodied eyes glared at him. Beneath his feet, twigs had turned to skeletal hands, those hands plucking at the hem of his robe, but he had not faltered. Not even when ghosts came wandering out from the depths of that haunted wood did he allow himself fear. He had entered the precincts of the Tower of High Sorcery at Palanthas as boldly as though he were walking into his own home. The lightless court-yard, the great doors that opened of their own accord, even the soft, almost gentle voice, that bade him, "Enter, apprentice," did not disconcert him. But now, here, without his magic, Dalamar felt fear.

It is but an effect of *his* magic, he told himself as he went ever upward. *He* will not permit my magic, and so that is what must be. Here is the road I have chosen, and it has wound all the way from Silvanost to Palanthas. This is the road I will trust.

"*Shalafi*," he whispered, trying out the title, the Elvish word for "master." "It will be as you wish."

Up through the darkness and the light he went, never missing a step, though so many lay hidden in shadow and not all were of the same depth or breadth. No rail warded the unwary climber. A fall from this staircase would be a killing plunge, and yet it seemed to Dalamar that he'd found the rhythm of the uneven steps in the first moment he began his ascent. The higher he went the quicker his pulse—the old feeling he'd always known when he wandered from the safe ways, the quiet paths.

He came to a landing and passed it by. He did not know how or why, but he understood that he must keep climbing. Now as he went, a feeling of having been here before stirred in him, as though he had been to this place long ago. He had not been here in all his life, but still the feeling persisted.

His footfalls echoed from the walls, those echoes falling into the well below and whispering back up again, as though he were being followed. The hair raised up on the back of his neck; it prickled on his arms. Dalamar shivered, but he would not stop. He must go on, up and up and around the long spiral. He passed another landing, and when he glanced left, he saw a corridor brightly lit, the torches on the walls glimmering into the distance. Door after door he glimpsed, all shut tight, and yet he had the feeling that these rooms were occupied. By whom?

Fear whispered, By what?

When he thought his legs would carry him not another step, the staircase simply ended before a broad wooden door. Two torches stood in brackets on each side of that door, their flames like orange pennants waving in a breeze Dalamar did not feel. He did not look around to see why the fire flared. He did not look up or down or back. He could not, for he stood now in front of a door he had, indeed, seen before. The doorknob shone, polished silver in the torchlight. Shaped like a skull, the eye-sockets filled with the gleam of firelight, that knob invited his grip.

The quickening of his pulse became the drumbeat of his heart, a rhythm of excitement ran in him like magic itself. He'd stood here before, in a vision shown him by the

polished platinum mirrors in the Circle of Darkness. Whil
clerics and Wildrunners, a prince and a princess waited t
mete out to him the exile's fate, he had seen this door, thi
very handle shaped like a skull. A sound came from th
darkness, from behind, beside, before. The grating of chai
on stone, the quiet creeping of judgment and revelation. S
hard did his heart beat now that Dalamar wondere
whether the hammering could be heard throughout th
Tower.

He took a breath to steady himself.

Every moment he'd spent on the road away from th
White elven magic and into the darker realm of Nuitari'
magic had led him here, like inexorable steps upon a fore
ordained path. He reached for the silver skull. His han
closed round it, his thumb sought and found the smoot
round depression of an eye-socket. He composed himsel
By sheer force of will, he drove from his mind ever
thought, each trace of memory of the moment he accepte
his mission for the Conclave. It was worth his life, perhap
his soul, to hide that, and he had no magic to assist him. Ne
ther would he know if he succeeded until the moment h
failed.

And if he failed—!

He must not think of that. He must not permit even th
smallest thought of failure.

He gripped the silver skull, then pushed gently inwar
The door opened, as in his vision it had. Light poured ou
golden, flooding the corridor, and heat came with it a
though someone within could not feel the warmth of th
summer night but stood always in winter, shiverin
against cold. Dark against that light, a slight young ma
stood. He wore a robe of simple, unadorned black woo
The hood was thrown back, revealing a face Dalamar ha
never thought to see, even in nightmare. It was not th
golden skin that set his nerves to jangling, nor the whit
white hair. It was the eyes, the pupils dark as moonles

midnight, each shaped like an hourglass.

"He calls himself the Master of Past and Present," Par-Salian had said. In the name of all gods, Dalamar thought, it is no wonder that he does.

Dalamar's heart stopped. Between one beat and another, it stilled. In the stillness, in the silence, the voice of his soul whispered. *What will you do for magic, Dalamar Nightson? How far will you go to find it, to nurture it, to claim what is yours by right of talent?*

This far, he said, looking into the hourglass eyes of Raistlin Majere, feared by the three most powerful mages of Krynn. This far. If Nuitari wills, farther even than this, for I have no place but in magic, I have no heart but that which beats to magic's song. It was ever thus. It will ever be thus, and I have given up much, but that does not mean I will not give up more to grow even stronger in the art of sorcery.

"*Shalafi*," he said, inclining his head in a modest bow. "I am come, as you have agreed."

As though he could see with his hourglass eyes every moment of Dalamar's past, every thought he had now, each step he would take until whatever day would be his last, Raistlin Majere smiled, a cold, cunning smile. In the space between one beat of his heart and another, Dalamar felt himself weighed and judged. Raistlin stepped back from the threshold with a small, almost mocking bow.

Come in if you dare, said that gesture.

The sound of a chain dragging on stone yet rang in Dalamar's heart, the platinum chain that had wrapped round his ankles, his legs, his heart in the Circle of Darkness. By that close chain, others had judged him guilty of crimes of magic and crimes of worship. By that bitter embrace, he had judged himself strong enough to accept what pain he must in order to have the magic he could not live without. He heard the scraping of the chain as he stepped across the threshold, as he entered the chamber of the Master of Past and Present. Into the world of a dark mage, into a world no one knew and the wise feared, Dalamar Nightson walked with his heart singing, and it was though he had come home.

The Terror of Lord Soth

Once the greatest of all knights on Krynn, Lord Soth has been banished to the dark recesses of Ravenloft. In a land of shadows the undead knight struggles to escape his dark destiny.

Knight of the Black Rose
James Lowder

Lord Soth is transported to Barovia, where he must face the minions of Count Strahd von Zarovich, vampire lord of the nightmare land. With only a captive Vistani woman and an untrustworthy ghost for allies, Soth may have to join forces with the powerful vampire if he is ever to escape the realm of terror.

Spectre of the Black Rose
James Lowder and Voronica Whitney-Robinson

Factions vie for control of Sithicus as Lord Soth fights to keep his reign from crumbling. Even as he struggles to defeat his enemies, rumor reaches him that the White Rose haunts the land. Has Kitiara finally returned to Soth, or is this another spectre from the dead knight's past?

GREYHAWK

Novelizations of the best-selling game modules

Against the Giants
Ru Emerson

A village burns while its attackers flee into the
night. Enraged, the King of Keoland orders an
aging warrior to lead a band of adventurers on
a retaliatory strike. As they prepare to enter
the heart of the monsters' lair, each knows
only the bravest will survive. Against the odds.
Against the giants.

White Plume Mountain
Paul Kidd

Three companions find themselves trapped
in a city filled with warring priestly factions,
devious machinations, and an angry fiend.
To save the city they must find three weapons of power that lie in the most trap-laden,
monster-infested place this side of
Acererak's tomb: White Plume Mountain.

The Chaos War Series

This series of novels is set during the time of the bestselling *Dragons of Summer Flame* by Margaret Weis and Tracy Hickman.

The Doom Brigade
Margaret Weis and Don Perrin

An intrepid group of draconian engineers must unite with the dwarves, their despised enemies, when the Chaos War erupts.

The Last Thane
Douglas Niles

As the Chaos War rages across Ansalon, the dwarven kingdom of Thorbardin is gripped by treachery, anarchy, and bloodshed.

Tears of the Night Sky
Linda P. Baker and Nancy Varian Berberick

A quest of Paladine becomes a test of faith for Crysania, the blind cleric.

The Puppet King
Douglas Niles

A rebellion threatens Gilthas, ruler of the Silvanesti elves, as he deals with threats from green dragons and Knights of Takhisis.

Reavers of the Blood Sea
Richard A. Knaak

The minotaurs of the Blood Sea are forced to make an alliance with their deadliest enemies to stave off the forces of Chaos.

The Siege of Mt. Nevermind
Fergus Ryan

The gnomes of Mt. Nevermind battle the Knights of Takhisis with elbow grease and ingenuity (and a few accidental explosions).

Bridges of Time Series

This series of novels bridges the thirty-year span between the Chaos War and the Fifth Age DRAGONLANCE® novels.

Spirit of the Wind
Chris Pierson
Riverwind the Plainsman answers a call for help from the besieged kender in their struggle against the great red dragon Malystryx.

Legacy of Steel
Mary H. Herbert
Sara Dunstan, an outcast Knight of Takhisis, risks a perilous journey to Neraka to found a new order of knighthood in the land of Ansalon.

The Silver Stair
Jean Rabe
As the Fifth Age dawns, Goldmoon, Hero of the Lance, searches for a new magic and founds the great Citadel of Light, linked to the heavens by an endless stair.

The Rose and the Skull
Jeff Crook
When Lord Gunthar, head of the Solamnic Knights, dies mysteriously, the order must make an alliance with their deadliest enemy, as a troop of gully dwarves races across Krynn to unmask treachery.

Dezra's Quest
Chris Pierson
The daughter of Caramon Majere brings aid to the centaurs, as they try to escape a terrible pact made with Chaos.

Edited by Margaret Weis and Tracy Hickman

An anthology of short stories from prominent DRAGONLANCE authors, describing the terrible battles and brave exploits of heroes during the first decades of the Fifth Age.

Contributors include Margaret Weis and Don Perrin, Nancy Berberick, Richard A. Knaak, and Douglas Niles.